The MX Book of New Sherlock Holmes Stories

Part XI – Some Untold Cases
(1880-1891)

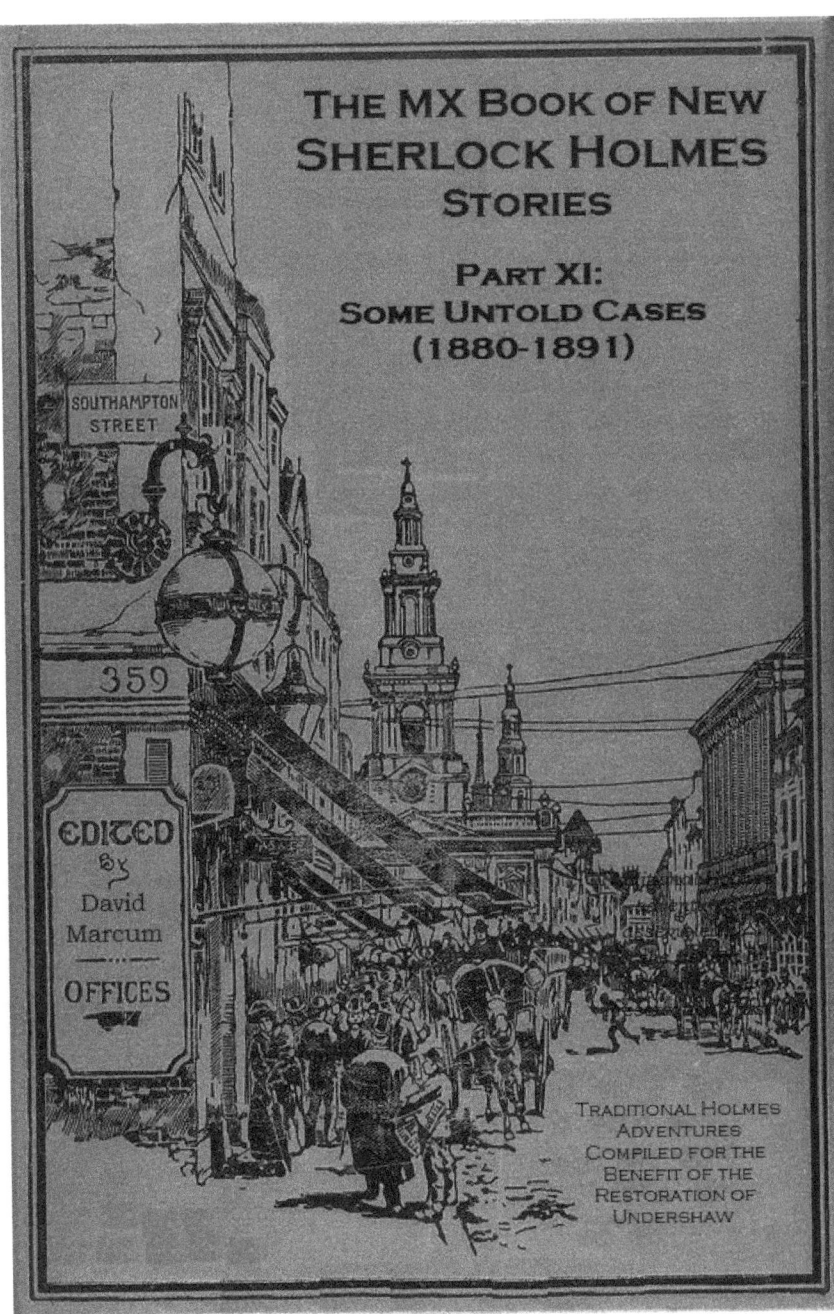

First edition published in 2018
© Copyright 2018

The right of the individuals listed on the Copyright Information page to be identified as the authors of this work has been asserted by them in accordance with the Copyright, Designs, and Patents Act 1998.

All rights reserved. No reproduction, copy, or transmission of this publication may be made without express prior written permission. No paragraph of this publication may be reproduced, copied, or transmitted except with express prior written permission or in accordance with the provisions of the Copyright Act 1956 (as amended). Any person who commits any unauthorised act in relation to this publication may be liable to criminal prosecution and civil claims for damage.

All characters appearing in this work are fictitious or used fictitiously. Except for certain historical personages, any resemblance to real persons, living or dead, is purely coincidental. The opinions expressed herein are those of the authors and not of MX Publishing.

ISBN Hardback 978-1-78705-373-1
ISBN Paperback 978-1-78705-374-8
AUK ePub ISBN 978-1-78705-375-5
AUK PDF ISBN 978-1-78705-379-3

Published in the UK by
MX Publishing
335 Princess Park Manor, Royal Drive,
London, N11 3GX
www.mxpublishing.co.uk

David Marcum can be reached at:
thepapersofsherlockholmes@gmail.com

Cover design by Brian Belanger
www.belangerbooks.com and *www.redbubble.com/people/zhahadun*

CONTENTS

Forewords

Editor's Introduction: Only Sixty? by David Marcum	1
Lose Yourself in New Pastiches by Lyndsay Faye	19
Known Unknowns by Roger Johnson	20
Strength to Strength by Steve Emecz	23
A Word from the Head Teacher of Stepping Stones by Melissa Grigsby	26
Unrecorded Holmes Cases (*A Sonnet*) by Arlene Mantin Levy and Mark Levy	37

Adventures

The Most Repellant Man by Jayantika Ganguly	39
The Singular Adventure of the Extinguished Wicks by Will Murray	53
Mrs. Forrester's Complication by Roger Riccard	74
The Adventure of Vittoria, the Circus Belle by Tracy Revels	100
The Adventure of the Silver Skull by Hugh Ashton	114

(Continued on the next page . . . .)

The Pimlico Poisoner 135
    By Matthew Simmonds

The Grosvenor Square Furniture Van 150
    by David Ruffle

The Adventure of the Paradol Chamber 157
    by Paul W. Nash

The Bishopgate Jewel Case 183
    by Mike Hogan

The Singular Tragedy of the Atkinson Brothers of Trincomalee 207
    by Craig Stephen Copland

Colonel Warburton's Madness 233
    by Gayle Lange Puhl

The Adventure at Bellingbeck Park 252
    by Deanna Baran

The Giant Rat of Sumatra 270
    by Leslie Charteris and Denis Green
    Introduction by Ian Dickerson

The Vatican Cameos 296
    by Kevin P. Thornton

The Case of the Gila Monster 312
    by Stephen Herczeg

The Bogus Laundry Affair 332
    by Robert Perret

Inspector Lestrade and the Molesey Mystery 353
    by M.A. Wilson and Richard Dean Starr

Appendix: *The Untold Cases* 379

About the Contributors 393

These additional adventures are contained in
The MX Book of New Sherlock Holmes Stories
Part XII: Some Untold Cases
(1894-1902)

It's Always Time (*A Poem*) – "Anon."
The Shanghaied Surgeon – C.H. Dye
The Trusted Advisor – David Marcum
A Shame Harder Than Death – Thomas Fortenberry
The Adventure of the Smith-Mortimer Succession – Daniel D. Victor
A Repulsive Story and a Terrible Death – Nik Morton
The Adventure of the Dishonourable Discharge – Craig Janacek
The Adventure of the Admirable Patriot – S. Subramanian
The Abernetty Transactions – Jim French
Dr. Agar and the Dinosaur – Robert Stapleton
The Giant Rat of Sumatra – Nick Cardillo
The Adventure of the Black Plague – Paul D. Gilbert
Vigor, the Hammersmith Wonder – Mike Hogan
A Correspondence Concerning Mr. James Phillimore – Derrick Belanger
The Curious Case of the Two Coptic Patriarchs – John Linwood Grant
The Conk-Singleton Forgery Case – Mark Mower
Another Case of Identity – Jane Rubino
The Adventure of the Exalted Victim – Arthur Hall

These additional Sherlock Holmes adventures
can be found in the previous volumes of
The MX Book of New Sherlock Holmes Stories

PART I: 1881-1889
Foreword – Leslie S. Klinger
Foreword – Roger Johnson
Sherlock Holmes of London (A Verse in Four Fits) – Michael Kurland
The Adventure of the Slipshod Charlady – John Hall
The Case of the Lichfield Murder – Hugh Ashton
The Kingdom of the Blind – Adrian Middleton
The Adventure of the Pawnbroker's Daughter – David Marcum
The Adventure of the Defenestrated Princess – Jayantika Ganguly
The Adventure of the Inn on the Marsh – Denis O. Smith
The Adventure of the Traveling Orchestra – Amy Thomas
The Haunting of Sherlock Holmes – Kevin David Barratt
Sherlock Holmes and the Allegro Mystery – Luke Benjamen Kuhns
The Deadly Soldier – Summer Perkins
The Case of the Vanishing Stars – Deanna Baran
The Song of the Mudlark – Shane Simmons
The Tale of the Forty Thieves – C.H. Dye
The Strange Missive of Germaine Wilkes – Mark Mower
The Case of the Vanished Killer – Derrick Belanger
The Adventure of the Aspen Papers – Daniel D. Victor
The Ululation of Wolves – Steve Mountain
The Case of the Vanishing Inn – Stephen Wade
The King of Diamonds – John Heywood
The Adventure of Urquhart Manse – Will Thomas
The Adventure of the Seventh Stain – Daniel McGachey
The Two Umbrellas – Martin Rosenstock
The Adventure of the Fateful Malady – Craig Janacek

PART II: 1890-1895
Foreword – Catherine Cooke
The Bachelor of Baker Street Muses on Irene Adler (A Poem) – Carole Nelson Douglas
The Affair of Miss Finney – Ann Margaret Lewis
The Adventure of the Bookshop Owner – Vincent W. Wright
The Case of the Unrepentant Husband – William Patrick Maynard
The Verse of Death – Matthew Booth
Lord Garnett's Skulls – J.R. Campbell
Larceny in the Sky with Diamonds – Robert V. Stapleton
The Glennon Falls – Sam Wiebe
The Adventure of *The Sleeping Cardinal* – Jeremy Branton Holstein

(Continued on the next page . . . .)

The Case of the Anarchist's Bomb – Bill Crider
The Riddle of the Rideau Rifles – Peter Calamai
The Adventure of the Willow Basket – Lyndsay Faye
The Onion Vendor's Secret – Marcia Wilson
The Adventure of the Murderous Numismatist – Jack Grochot
The Saviour of Cripplegate Square – Bert Coules
A Study in Abstruse Detail – Wendy C. Fries
The Adventure of the St. Nicholas the Elephant – Christopher Redmond
The Lady on the Bridge – Mike Hogan
The Adventure of the Poison Tea Epidemic – Carl L. Heifetz
The Man on Westminster Bridge – Dick Gillman

PART III: 1896-1929
Foreword – David Stuart Davies
Two Sonnets (Poems) – Bonnie MacBird
Harbinger of Death – Geri Schear
The Adventure of the Regular Passenger – Paul D. Gilbert
The Perfect Spy – Stuart Douglas
A Mistress – Missing – Lyn McConchie
Two Plus Two – Phil Growick
The Adventure of the Coptic Patriarch – Séamus Duffy
The Royal Arsenal Affair – Leslie F.E. Coombs
The Adventure of the Sunken Parsley – Mark Alberstat
The Strange Case of the Violin Savant – GC Rosenquist
The Hopkins Brothers Affair – Iain McLaughlin and Claire Bartlett
The Disembodied Assassin – Andrew Lane
The Adventure of the Dark Tower – Peter K. Andersson
The Adventure of the Reluctant Corpse – Matthew J. Elliott
The Inspector of Graves – Jim French
The Adventure of the Parson's Son – Bob Byrne
The Adventure of the Botanist's Glove – James Lovegrove
A Most Diabolical Plot – Tim Symonds
The Opera Thief – Larry Millett
Blood Brothers – Kim Krisco
The Adventure of *The White Bird* – C. Edward Davis
The Adventure of the Avaricious Bookkeeper – Joel and Carolyn Senter

PART IV – 2016 Annual
Foreword – Steven Rothman
Foreword – Richard Doyle
Foreword – Roger Johnson
Undershaw: An Ongoing Legacy – Foreword by Steve Emecz
A Word From the Head Teacher at Undershaw – Melissa Farnham
Toast to Mrs. Hudson (A Poem) – Arlene Mantin Levy
The Tale of the First Adventure – Derrick Belanger

(Continued on the next page . . . .)

The Adventure of the Turkish Cipher – Deanna Baran
The Adventure of the Missing Necklace – Daniel D. Victor
The Case of the Rondel Dagger – Mark Mower
The Adventure of the Double-Edged Hoard – Craig Janacek
The Adventure of the Impossible Murders – Jayantika Ganguly
The Watcher in the Woods – Denis O. Smith
The Wargrave Resurrection – Matthew Booth
Relating To One of My Old Cases – J.R. Campbell
The Adventure at the Beau Soleil – Bonnie MacBird
The Adventure of the Phantom Coachman – Arthur Hall
The Adventure of the Arsenic Dumplings – Bob Byrne
The Disappearing Anarchist Trick – Andrew Lane
The Adventure of the Grace Chalice – Roger Johnson
The Adventure of John Vincent Harden – Hugh Ashton
Murder at Tragere House – David Stuart Davies
The Adventure of *The Green Lady* – Vincent W. Wright
The Adventure of the Fellow Traveller – Daniel McGachey
The Adventure of the Highgate Financier – Nicholas Utechin
A Game of Illusion – Jeremy Holstein
The London Wheel – David Marcum
The Adventure of the Half-Melted Wolf – Marcia Wilson

PART V – Christmas Adventures
Foreword – Jonathan Kellerman
"This bids to be the merriest of Christmases." – Foreword by Roger Johnson
The Ballad of the Carbuncle (A Poem) – Ashley D. Polasek
The Case of the Ruby Necklace – Bob Byrne
The Jet Brooch – Denis O. Smith
The Adventure of the Missing Irregular – Amy Thomas
The Adventure of the Knighted Watchmaker – Derrick Belanger
The Stolen Relic – David Marcum
A Christmas Goose – C.H. Dye
The Adventure of the Long-Lost Enemy – Marcia Wilson
The Queen's Writing Table – Julie McKuras
The Blue Carbuncle – Sir Arthur Conan Doyle (Dramatised by Bert Coules)
The Case of the Christmas Cracker – John Hall
The Man Who Believed in Nothing – Jim French
The Case of the Christmas Star – S.F. Bennett
The Christmas Card Mystery – Narrelle M. Harris
The Question of the Death Bed Conversion – William Patrick Maynard
The Adventure of the Christmas Surprise – Vincent W. Wright
A Bauble in Scandinavia – James Lovegrove
The Adventure of Marcus Davery – Arthur Hall
The Adventure of the Purple Poet – Nicholas Utechin
The Adventure of the Vanishing Man – Mike Chinn

(Continued on the next page . . . .)

The Adventure of the Empty Manger – Tracy J. Revels
A Perpetrator in a Pear Tree – Roger Riccard
The Case of the Christmas Trifle – Wendy C. Fries
The Adventure of the Christmas Stocking – Paul D. Gilbert
The Adventure of the Golden Hunter – Jan Edwards
The Curious Case of the Well-Connected Criminal – Molly Carr
The Case of the Reformed Sinner – S. Subramanian
The Adventure of the Improbable Intruder – Peter K. Andersson
The Adventure of the Handsome Ogre – Matthew J. Elliott
The Adventure of the Deceased Doctor – Hugh Ashton
The Mile End Mynah Bird – Mark Mower

PART VI – 2017 Annual
Foreword – Colin Jeavons
Foreword – Nicholas Utechin
"The Universality of the Man's Interests" – Roger Johnson
Sweet Violin (A Poem) – Bonnie MacBird
The Adventure of the Murdered Spinster – Bob Byrne
The Irregular – Julie McKuras
The Coffee Trader's Dilemma – Derrick Belanger
The Two Patricks – Robert Perret
The Adventure at St. Catherine's – Deanna Baran
The Adventure of a Thousand Stings – GC Rosenquist
The Adventure of the Returned Captain – Hugh Ashton
The Adventure of the Wonderful Toy – David Timson
The Adventure of the Cat's Claws – Shane Simmons
The Grave Message – Stephen Wade
The Radicant Munificent Society – Mark Mower
The Adventure of the Apologetic Assassin – David Friend
The Adventure of the Traveling Corpse – Nick Cardillo
The Adventure of the Apothecary's Prescription – Roger Riccard
The Case of the Bereaved Author – S. Subramanian
The Tetanus Epidemic – Carl L. Heifetz
The Bubble Reputation – Geri Schear
The Case of the Vanishing Venus – S.F. Bennett
The Adventure of the Vanishing Apprentice – Jennifer Copping
The Adventure of the Apothecary Shop – Jim French
The Case of the Plummeting Painter – Carla Coupe
The Case of the Temperamental Terrier – Narrelle M. Harris
The Adventure of the Frightened Architect – Arthur Hall
The Adventure of the Sunken Indiaman – Craig Janacek
The Exorcism of the Haunted Stick – Marcia Wilson
The Adventure of the Queen's Teardrop – Tracy Revels
The Curious Case of the Charwoman's Brooch – Molly Carr
The Unwelcome Client – Keith Hann

(Continued on the next page . . . .)

The Tempest of Lyme – David Ruffle
The Problem of the Holy Oil – David Marcum
A Scandal in Serbia – Thomas A. Turley
The Curious Case of Mr. Marconi – Jan Edwards
Mr. Holmes and Dr. Watson Learn to Fly – C. Edward Davis
Die Weisse Frau – Tim Symonds
A Case of Mistaken Identity – Daniel D. Victor

PART VII – Eliminate the Impossible: 1880-1891
Foreword – Lee Child
Foreword – Rand B. Lee
Foreword – Michael Cox
Foreword – Roger Johnson
Foreword – Melissa Farnham
No Ghosts Need Apply (A Poem) – Jacquelynn Morris
The Melancholy Methodist – Mark Mower
The Curious Case of the Sweated Horse – Jan Edwards
The Adventure of the Second William Wilson – Daniel D. Victor
The Adventure of the Marchindale Stiletto – James Lovegrove
The Case of the Cursed Clock – Gayle Lange Puhl
The Tranquility of the Morning – Mike Hogan
A Ghost from Christmas Past – Thomas A. Turley
The Blank Photograph – James Moffett
The Adventure of A Rat. – Adrian Middleton
The Adventure of Vanaprastha – Hugh Ashton
The Ghost of Lincoln – Geri Schear
The Manor House Ghost – S. Subramanian
The Case of the Unquiet Grave – John Hall
The Adventure of the Mortal Combat – Jayantika Ganguly
The Last Encore of Quentin Carol – S.F. Bennett
The Case of the Petty Curses – Steven Philip Jones
The Tuttman Gallery – Jim French
The Second Life of Jabez Salt – John Linwood Grant
The Mystery of the Scarab Earrings – Thomas Fortenberry
The Adventure of the Haunted Room – Mike Chinn
The Pharaoh's Curse – Robert V. Stapleton
The Vampire of the Lyceum – Charles Veley and Anna Elliott
The Adventure of the Mind's Eye – Shane Simmons

PART VIII – Eliminate the Impossible: 1892-1905
Foreword – Lee Child
Foreword – Rand B. Lee
Foreword – Michael Cox
Foreword – Roger Johnson
Foreword – Melissa Farnham
Sherlock Holmes in the Lavender field (A Poem) – Christopher James

(Continued on the next page . . . .)

The Adventure of the Lama's Dream – Deanna Baran
The Ghost of Dorset House – Tim Symonds
The Peculiar Persecution of John Vincent Harden – Sandor Jay Sonnen
The Case of the Biblical Colours – Ben Cardall
The Inexplicable Death of Matthew Arnatt – Andrew Lane
The Adventure of the Highgate Spectre – Michael Mallory
The Case of the Corpse Flower – Wendy C. Fries
The Problem of the Five Razors – Aaron Smith
The Adventure of the Moonlit Shadow – Arthur Hall
The Ghost of Otis Maunder – David Friend
The Adventure of the Pharaoh's Tablet – Robert Perret
The Haunting of Hamilton Gardens – Nick Cardillo
The Adventure of the Risen Corpse – Paul D. Gilbert
The Mysterious Mourner – Cindy Dye
The Adventure of the Hungry Ghost – Tracy Revels
In the Realm of the Wretched King – Derrick Belanger
The Case of the Little Washerwoman – William Meikle
The Catacomb Saint Affair – Marcia Wilson
The Curious Case of Charlotte Musgrave – Roger Riccard
The Adventure of the Awakened Spirit – Craig Janacek
The Adventure of the Theatre Ghost – Jeremy Branton Holstein
The Adventure of the Glassy Ghost – Will Murray
The Affair of the Grange Haunting – David Ruffle
The Adventure of the Pallid Mask – Daniel McGachey
The Two Different Women – David Marcum

Part IX – 2018 Annual (1879-1895)
Forword – Nicholas Meyer
Foreword – Roger Johnson
Foreword – Melissa Farnham
Foreword – Steve Emecz
Violet Smith (A Poem) – Amy Thomas
The Adventure of the Temperance Society – Deanna Baran
The Adventure of the Fool and His Money – Roger Riccard
The Helverton Inheritance – David Marcum
The Adventure of the Faithful Servant – Tracy Revels
The Adventure of the Parisian Butcher – Nick Cardillo
The Missing Empress – Robert Stapleton
The Resplendent Plane Tree – Kevin P. Thornton
The Strange Adventure of the Doomed Sextette – Leslie Charteris and Denis Green
The Adventure of the Old Boys' Club – Shane Simmons
The Case of the Golden Trail – James Moffett
The Detective Who Cried Wolf – C.H. Dye
The Lambeth Poisoner Case – Stephen Gaspar

(Continued on the next page . . . .)

The Confession of Anna Jarrow – S. F. Bennett
The Adventure of the Disappearing Dictionary – Sonia Fetherston
The Fairy Hills Horror – Geri Schear
A Loathsome and Remarkable Adventure – Marcia Wilson
The Adventure of the Multiple Moriartys – David Friend
The Influence Machine – Mark Mower

Part X – 2018 Annual (1896-2016)
Forword – Nicholas Meyer
Foreword – Roger Johnson
Foreword – Melissa Farnham
Foreword – Steve Emecz
A Man of Twice Exceptions (A Poem) – Derrick Belanger
The Horned God – Kelvin Jones
The Coughing Man – by Jim French
The Adventure of Canal Reach – Arthur Hall
A Simple Case of Abduction – Mike Hogan
A Case of Embezzlement – Steven Ehrman
The Adventure of the Vanishing Diplomat – Greg Hatcher
The Adventure of the Perfidious Partner – Jayantika Ganguly
A Brush With Death – Dick Gillman
A Revenge Served Cold – Maurice Barkley
The Case of the Anonymous Client – Paul A. Freeman
Capitol Murder – Daniel D. Victor
The Case of the Dead Detective – Martin Rosenstock
The Musician Who Spoke From the Grave – Peter Coe Verbica
The Adventure of the Future Funeral – Hugh Ashton
The Problem of the Bruised Tongues – Will Murray
The Mystery of the Change of Art – Robert Perret
The Parsimonious Peacekeeper – Thaddeus Tuffentsamer
The Case of the Dirty Hand – G.L. Schulze
The Mystery of the Missing Artefacts – Tim Symonds

The following contributions appear in this volume:
**The MX Book of New Sherlock Holmes Stories
Part XI – Some Untold Cases (1880-1891)**

"A Poem" ©2018 by "Anon.". All Rights Reserved. First publication, original to this collection. Printed by permission of the author.

"The Adventure of the Silver Skull" ©2018 by Hugh Ashton and j-views Publishing. All Rights Reserved. Hugh Ashton appears by kind permission of j-views Publishing. First publication, original to this collection. Printed by permission of the author.

"The Adventure at Bellingbeck Park" ©2018 by Deanna Baran. All Rights Reserved. First publication, original to this collection. Printed by permission of the author.

"The Giant Rat of Sumatra" ©1944, 2017 by Leslie Charteris and Denis Green. First publication of text script in this collection. Originally broadcast on radio on July 31, 1944 as part of the *Sherlock Holmes* radio show, starring Basil Rathbone and Nigel Bruce. Printed by permission of the Leslie Charteris Estate. Introduction ©2018 by Ian Dickerson. First publication of this revised version, original to this collection. Printed by permission of the author.

"The Singular Tragedy of the Atkinson Brothers of Trincomalee" ©2018 by Craig Stephen Copland. All Rights Reserved. First publication, original to this collection. Printed by permission of the author.

"Strength to Strength" ©2018 by Steve Emecz. All Rights Reserved. First publication, original to this collection. Printed by permission of the author.

"Foreword" ©2018 by Lyndsay Faye. All Rights Reserved. First publication, original to this collection. Printed by permission of the author.

"The Most Repellant Man" ©2018 by Jayantika Ganguly. All Rights Reserved. First publication, original to this collection. Printed by permission of the author.

"A Word From the Head Teacher of Stepping Stones" ©2018 by Melissa Grisby. All Rights Reserved. First publication, original to this collection. Printed by permission of the author.

"The Case of the Gila Monster" ©2018 by Stephen Herczeg. All Rights Reserved. First publication, original to this collection. Printed by permission of the author.

"The Bishopgate Jewel Case" ©2018 by Mike Hogan. All Rights Reserved. First publication, original to this collection. Printed by permission of the author.

"Known Unknowns" ©2018 by Roger Johnson. All Rights Reserved. First publication, original to this collection. Printed by permission of the author.

"Unrecorded Holmes Cases: A Sonnet" ©2018 by Arlene Mantin Levy and Mark Levy. All Rights Reserved. First publication, original to this collection. Printed by permission of the author.

"Editor's Introduction: Only Sixty?" and "Appendix: The Untold Cases" ©2018 by David Marcum. All Rights Reserved. First publication, original to this collection. Printed by permission of the author.

"The Singular Adventure of the Extinguished Wicks" ©2017 by Will Murray. All Rights Reserved. First publication, original to this collection. Printed by permission of the author.

"The Adventure of the Paradol Chamber" ©2018 by Paul W. Nash. All Rights Reserved. First publication, original to this collection. Printed by permission of the author.

"The Bogus Laundry Affair" ©2018 by Robert Perret. All Rights Reserved. First publication, original to this collection. Printed by permission of the author.

"Colonel Warburton's Madness" ©2017 by Gayle Lange Puhl. All Rights Reserved. First publication, original to this collection. Printed by permission of the author.

"The Adventure of Vittoria, the Circus Belle" ©2017 by Tracy Revels. All Rights Reserved. First publication, original to this collection. Printed by permission of the author.

"Mrs. Forrester's Complication" ©2018 by Roger Riccard. All Rights Reserved. First publication, original to this collection. Printed by permission of the author.

"The Grosvenor Square Furniture Van" ©2018 by David Ruffle. All Rights Reserved. First publication, original to this collection. Printed by permission of the author.

"The Pimlico Poisoner" ©2018 by Matthew Simmonds. All Rights Reserved. First publication, original to this collection. Printed by permission of the author.

"The Vatican Cameos" ©2018 by Kevin P. Thornton. All Rights Reserved. First publication, original to this collection. Printed by permission of the author.

"Inspector Lestrade and the Molesey Mystery" ©2018 by M.A. Wilson and Richard Dean Starr. All Rights Reserved. First publication, original to this collection. Printed by permission of the authors.

*The following contributions appear
in the companion volume:*
The MX Book of New Sherlock Holmes Stories
Part XII – Some Untold Cases (1894-1902)

"It's Always Time" ©2018 by "Anon.". All Rights Reserved. First publication, original to this collection. Printed by permission of the author.

"A Correspondence Concerning Mr. James Phillimore" ©2018 by Derrick Belanger. All Rights Reserved. First publication, original to this collection. Printed by permission of the author.

"The Giant Rat of Sumatra" ©2018 by Nick Cardillo. All Rights Reserved. First publication, original to this collection. Printed by permission of the author.

"The Shanghaied Surgeon" ©2018 by C.H. Dye. All Rights Reserved. Originally published in a different and short version online as "Sink the *Friesland*", September 2009, and also as "The Adventure of the Shanghaied Surgeon", December 2014. First publication of this revised and expanded version, original to this collection. Printed by permission of the author.

"A Shame Harder Than Death" ©2018 by Thomas Fortenberry. All Rights Reserved. First publication, original to this collection. Printed by permission of the author.

"The Abernetty Transactions" ©2012, 2018 by Jim French. All Rights Reserved. First publication of text script in this collection. Originally broadcast on radio on September 23, 2012 as Episode No. 106 of *The Further Adventures of Sherlock Holmes*. Printed by permission Lawrence Albert for Jim Albert's Estate.

"The Adventure of the Black Plague" ©2018 by Paul D. Gilbert. All Rights Reserved. First publication, original to this collection. Printed by permission of the author.

"The Curious Case of the Coptic Patriarchs" ©2018 by John Linwood Grant. All Rights Reserved. First publication, original to this collection. Printed by permission of the author.'

"The Adventure of the Exalted Victim" ©2017 by Arthur Hall. All Rights Reserved. First publication, original to this collection. Printed by permission of the author.

"Vigor the Hammersmith Wonder" ©2018 by Mike Hogan. All Rights Reserved. First publication, original to this collection. Printed by permission of the author.

"The Adventure of the Dishonourable Discharge" ©2018 by Craig Janacek. All Rights Reserved. First publication, original to this collection. Printed by permission of the author.

"The Trusted Advisor" ©2018 by David Marcum. All Rights Reserved. First publication, original to this collection. Printed by permission of the author.

"A Repulsive Story and a Terrible Death" ©2018 by Nik Morton. All Rights Reserved. First publication, original to this collection. Printed by permission of the author.

"The Conk-Singleton Forgery Case" ©2017 by Mark Mower. All Rights Reserved. First publication, original to this collection. Printed by permission of the author.

"Another Case of Identity" ©2018 by Jane Rubino. All Rights Reserved. First publication, original to this collection. Printed by permission of the author.

"Dr. Agar and the Dinosaur" ©2018 by Robert Stapleton. All Rights Reserved. First publication, original to this collection. Printed by permission of the author.

"Some Untold Cases", *Parts XI and XII of*
The MX Book of New Sherlock Holmes Stories,
are dedicated to

Philip K. Jones

Phil passed away in June 2018.
As well as being a wonderful and very supportive
Holmesian collector and reviewer,
he was devoted to Sherlockian Pastiche
and an expert in the area of Untold Cases.
The theme for this collection grew from his suggestion,
and he will be missed.

Editor's Introduction:
Only Sixty?
by David Marcum

There are certain numbers that are triggers to deeply passionate Sherlockians. One of these is *221*. I've discussed this with other people of like mind. If you're one of us, you know that feeling – when you're going through your day and look up to see that it's *2:21* – hopefully in the afternoon, because you should be asleep for the other one. Seeing that it's 2:21 o'clock is a little thrill.

One can encounter *221* all over. Sometimes a lucky Sherlockian will be assigned 221 as a hotel room. (In her retirement home, my mother-in-law lived next door to someone in room 221, and I couldn't walk by that door without noticing it.) Maybe you have an office numbered *221*, or at least you might have an appointment in one. If you're very lucky, your house number is *221* – and I wonder how many non-London Baker Streets are there scattered throughout the world that have a 221 address?

I often notice when I reach page *221* in a book, and I know from asking that other Sherlockians do the same. (I was tickled a couple of years ago, while reading Lyndsay Faye's excellent collection of Holmes adventures, *The Whole Art of Detection*, to see that the story she'd written for the first MX collection, "The Adventure of the Willow Basket", began on page 221.)

Any American interstate that's long enough will have a marker for Mile *221*, and just east of Nashville, Tennessee, where I'm sometimes able to attend meetings of The Nashville Scholars of the Three Pipe Problem – a scion of which I'm a proudly invested member – there's a big sign for *Exit 221B* on the eastern side of Interstate-40. (My deerstalker and I have several photos in front of it.)

221 is a number that makes a Sherlockian look twice, but there's another – *1895*.

1895 is a year that falls squarely within Holmes's Baker Street practice – and I specify that location, because he had a Montague Street practice and unofficially a retirement-era Sussex practice as well, where he carried out the occasional investigation, while also spending a great amount of time first trying to prevent, and then trying to prepare for, the Great War of 1914-1918. But he was in Baker Street from 1881 to 1891 (when he was presumed to have died at the Reichenbach Falls,) and then again from 1894 (when he returned to London in April of that year) until autumn 1903, when his "retirement" began.

1895 isn't especially known as Holmes's busiest or most famous year. Make no mistake, there were some interesting cases then: "Wisteria Lodge", "The Three Students", "The Solitary Cyclist", "Black Peter", and "The Bruce-Partington Plans". But 1894 is when Watson specifically mentions, in "The Golden Pince-Nez", the three massive manuscript volumes which contain his and Holmes's work. And it was the 1880's, before The Great Hiatus, where all of those beloved adventures recorded in *The Adventures* and *The Memoirs* occurred. "The Speckled Band", possibly one of the most famous of them all, took place in 1883. All four of the long published adventures, *A Study in Scarlet*, *The Sign of Four*, *The Valley of Fear*, and perhaps the most famous of tales, *The Hound of the Baskervilles*, occur chronologically before 1895.

And yet, 1895 is still the representative year most mentioned by Sherlockians – *"where it is always 1895"* said Vincent Starrett at the conclusion of his famous poem *221B*, written in 1942, and so it is subsequently referenced in essays and gatherings and toasts as *the* year.

Written in the early days of U.S. involvement in World War II – but several years after much of the rest of the world had already tipped into the conflagration – the closing couplet of Starrett's poem reflects his likely despair at the terrible conflict:

> Here, though the world explode, these two survive,
> And it is always eighteen ninety-five.

I'm not a Starrett scholar, but I suspect that he was looking back to a more innocent time – or so it seemed when compared to the terrible war-torn world of 1942. (For many of the people actually in 1895, the world was a relatively terrible place for them too, for all kinds of different reasons.) But did Starrett simply mean to invoke the whole Holmesian era, a bygone past, or did he specifically want to focus on 1895? It's likely that the former is true, and that he simply used 1895 because *five* rhymes with *survive*. It could have just as easily have been a different number – although with less effect:

> Here, though the world explode, these two are fine,
> And it is always eighteen ninety-nine.

Imagine – but for a different word choice, we could have been finding ourselves misty-eyed when referring to *1899*. Or Starrett could have used *1885* and still made the original rhyme work. Still, it's *1895* that we have, and so that's what we'll be going on with as the year that we associate with Mr. Holmes and Dr. Watson – although I'm quick to point out that it's 1895, *along with several decades on either side of it*.

Sixty Stories

Having explored 221 and 1895, there's another Sherlockian number that might not immediately spring to mind, but that doesn't diminish it, because it holds a great deal of power for some Sherlockians. That number is *60* – as in, *sixty stories* in the original Sherlockian Canon. For some die-hard types out there, this is it. No more, forever, period, *The End*. There can only be sixty Holmes stories and anything beyond that is fraudulent abomination. (Except, of course, for those one or two stories on their lists that get a free pass because they're written by a friend, or a celebrity worthy of desperate cultivation, or by some deceased literary person.) It's amusing for me to read various scholarly works, such as Martin Dakin's *A Sherlock Holmes Commentary* (1972), that don't even really like all of the original sixty Canonical adventures, let alone anything post-Canonical, picking apart the originals and speculating that this or that later Canonical narrative is a forgery.

I don't buy into that philosophy. Early on, I ran out of Canonical stories to read and wanted more. And I found them – some admittedly of lesser quality, but some better than the originals. Even at a young age, I understood that some of the original tales weren't quite as good as others, but those first sixty stories, presented by the First Literary Agent and of whatever varying levels of quality, were about the *true* Sherlock Holmes, and they let me visit in his world, and I wanted more. Thankfully, before I'd even read all of The Canon, I'd discovered those post-Canonical adventures designated as *pastiches*, so even as I re-read the original adventures countless times, I also read and re-read all of those others that told of new cases, or filled in the spaces between the originals.

Luckily, even Watson never acted as if Holmes only solved sixty cases and that was it. No matter how intriguing a personality is Sherlock Holmes, or how vivid his adventures are that they make a visit to Baker Street sometimes more real than tedious daily life, how could we truly argue that he's the world's greatest detective based on a mere and pitifully few sixty stories?

In "The Problem of Thor Bridge", Watson tells us that:

> *Somewhere in the vaults of the bank of Cox and Co., at Charing Cross, there is a travel-worn and battered tin*

dispatch box with my name, John H. Watson, M.D., Late Indian Army, painted upon the lid. It is crammed with papers, nearly all of which are records of cases to illustrate the curious problems which Mr. Sherlock Holmes had at various times to examine. Some, and not the least interesting, were complete failures, and as such will hardly bear narrating, since no final explanation is forthcoming. A problem without a solution may interest the student, but can hardly fail to annoy the casual reader . . . Apart from these unfathomed cases, there are some which involve the secrets of private families to an extent which would mean consternation in many exalted quarters if it were thought possible that they might find their way into print. I need not say that such a breach of confidence is unthinkable, and that these records will be separated and destroyed now that my friend has time to turn his energies to the matter. There remain a considerable residue of cases of greater or less interest which I might have edited before had I not feared to give the public a surfeit which might react upon the reputation of the man whom above all others I revere. In some I was myself concerned and can speak as an eye-witness, while in others I was either not present or played so small a part that they could only be told as by a third person.

Thank goodness this incredible tin dispatch box has been accessed throughout the years by so many later Literary Agents to bring us all these other wonderful Holmes adventures. Many that have been revealed have been complete surprises, but sometimes we've discovered details about a special group of extra-Canonical adventures, those that fire the imagination to an even greater level: *The Untold Cases.*

Of course, they aren't called that in The Canon. The earliest references to *The Untold Cases* that I've heard of so far (with thanks to Beth Gallegos) are by Anthony Boucher in 1955, and by William S. Baring-Gould in his amazing *The Chronological Sherlock Holmes* (1955). Additionally, Charles Campbell located a reference to "stories yet untold" by Vincent Starrett in "In Praise of Sherlock Holmes" (in *Reedy's Mirror*, February 22, 1918). The *Untold Cases* are those intriguing references to Holmes's other cases that – for various reasons – were not chosen for publication. There were a lot of them – by some counts over one-hundred-and-forty – and in the years since Watson's passing in 1929, many of these narratives have been discovered and published.

For example, The Giant Rat of Sumatra . . . .

Since the mid-1990's, I've been chronologicizing both Canon and Pastiche, and as part of that, I note in my annotations when a particular narrative is an Untold Case. Glancing through my notes, I see that there are far too many narratives of The Untold Cases to list here. For example, just a quick glance through my own collection and Chronology reveals, in no particular order, these versions of perhaps the greatest and most intriguing Untold Case of them all, *The Giant Rat of Sumatra:*

- **The Giant Rat of Sumatra** – Rick Boyer (1976) *(Possibly the greatest pastiche of all time)*
- "*Matilda Briggs* and the Giant Rat of Sumatra", **The Elementary Cases of Sherlock Holmes** – Ian Charnock (1999)
- **Mrs Hudson and the Spirit's Curse** – Martin Davies (2004)
- **Sherlock Holmes' Lost Adventure: The True Story of the Giant Rats of Sumatra** – Laurel Steinhauer (2004)
- **The Giant Rat of Sumatra** – Paul D. Gilbert (2010)
- "The Giant Rat of Sumatra", **The Lost Stories of Sherlock Holmes** – Tony Reynolds (2010)
- **The Giant Rat of Sumatra** – Jake and Luke Thoene (1995)
- "The Adventure of the Giant Rat of Sumatra", **Mary Higgins Clark Mystery Magazine** – John Lescroart, (December 1988)
- "The Case of the Sumatran Rat", **The Secret Chronicles of Sherlock Holmes** – June Thomson (1992)
- "Sherlock Holmes and the Giant Rat of Sumatra", **More From the Deed Box of John H. Watson MD** – Hugh Ashton (2012)
- "The Case of the Giant Rat of Sumatra", **The Secret Notebooks of Sherlock Holmes** – Liz Hedgecock (2016)
- "The World is Now Prepared" – "slogging ruffian" (Fan Fiction) (Date unverified)
- "The Giant Rat of Sumatra", **Sherlock Holmes: The Lost Cases** – Alvin F. Rymsha (2006)
- "The Giant Rat of Sumatra", **The Oriental Casebook of Sherlock Holmes** – Ted Riccardi (2003)
- **Sherlock Holmes and the Limehouse Horror** – Phillip Pullman (1992, 2001)
- "No Rats Need Apply", **The Unexpected Adventures of Sherlock Holmes** – Amanda Knight (2004)
- **The Shadow of the Rat** – David Stuart Davies (1999)
- **The Giant Rat of Sumatra** – Daniel Gracely (2001)

- "The Giant Rat of Sumatra", **Resurrected Holmes** – Paula Volsky (1996)
- "The Mysterious Case of the Giant Rat of Sumatra", **The Mark of the Gunn** – Brian Gibson (2000)
- **Sherlock Holmes and the Giant Rat of Sumatra** – Alan Vanneman (2002)
- "The Giant Rat of Sumatra" – Paul Boler (2000)
- "The Case of the Missing Energy", **The Einstein Paradox** – Colin Bruce (1994)
- "All This and the Giant Rat of Sumatra", **Sherlock Holmes and The Baker Street Dozen** – Val Andrews (1997)

In addition to these that are available, there's also one that isn't – possibly the earliest telling of "The Giant Rat", the intriguing radio version by Edith Meiser, which was broadcast multiple times: With Richard Gordon as Holmes on April 20th (although some sources say June 9th), 1932, and again on July 18th, 1936; and then on March 1st, 1942 (with Basil Rathbone as Holmes). Sadly, these versions are apparently lost, although I'd dearly love to hear – and read – them!

Although Rathbone and Bruce performed Edith Meiser's version of "The Giant Rat" in 1942, they weren't limited to just that version. A completely different version, this time by Bruce Taylor (Leslie Charteris) and Denis Green, was broadcast on July 31st, 1944. Amazingly, Charteris's scripts have been located by Ian Dickerson, who is in the process of publishing them for modern audiences who would otherwise have never had the chance to enjoy these lost cases. And even more amazing, Mr. Dickerson has allowed the 1944 version of "The Giant Rat" to premiere here in these concurrent Untold Cases volumes.

What makes this twice as much fun is that also appearing in these books is Nick Cardillo's new 2018 version of "The Giant Rat", showing that there can be more than one version of an Untold Case without any of them being the definitive version.

More than one version . . . .

The list shown above is by no means a complete representation of all the Giant Rat narratives. These are simply the ones that I found when making a pass along the shelves of my Holmes Collection, and what jumped out during a quick search through my Chronology. The thing to remember is that *in spite of every one of these stories being about a Giant Rat, none of them contradict one another or cancel each other out to become the only true Giant Rat adventure.*

Something that I learned very early, far before I created my Chronology back in the mid-1990's, is that there are lots of sequels to the original Canonical tales, and there are also lots of different versions of the Untold Tales. Some readers, of course, don't like and will never accept any of them, since they didn't cross the First Literary Agent's desk. Others, however, only wish to seek out the sole and single account that satisfies them the most, therefore dismissing the others as *"fiction"* – a word that I find quite distasteful when directed toward Mr. Sherlock Holmes

My approach is that if the different versions of either sequels or Untold Cases are Canonical, and don't violate any of the same rules that define what types of tales appear in these anthologies – no parodies, no anachronisms, no actual supernatural encounters, no murderous sociopathic Holmes portrayals – then they are legitimate.

Perhaps it seems too unlikely for some that there were so many Giant Rats in London during Holmes's active years. Not at all. Each Giant Rat adventure mentioned above is very different, and in any case, Watson was a master at obfuscation. He changed names and dates to satisfy all sorts of needs. For instance, he often made it appear at times as if Holmes went for weeks in fits of settee-bound depression between cases, when in fact he was involved constantly in thousands upon thousands of cases, each intertwined like incredibly complex threads in The Great Holmes Tapestry.

Although not represented in this volume, there have been many stories about Holmes and Watson's encounter with Huret, the Boulevard Assassin, in 1894. Contradictory? Not at all. Holmes simply rooted out an entire nest of *Al Qaeda*-like assassins during that deadly summer. There are a lot of tales out there relating the peculiar persecution of John Vincent Harden in 1895. No problem – there were simply a lot of tobacco millionaires in London during that time, all peculiarly persecuted – but in very different ways – and Watson lumped them in his notes under the catch-all name of *John Vincent Harden.* Later Literary Agents, not quite knowing how to conquer Watson's personal codes and reverse-engineer who the real client was in these cases, simply left the name as written.

What Counts as an Untold Case?

As mentioned, there have been over one-hundred identified Untold Cases, although some arguments are made one way or another as to whether some should be included. Do Holmes's various stops during The Great Hiatus – such as Persia and Mecca and Khartoum – each count as an Untold Case? (To me they do.) What about certain entries in Holmes's good old index, like *"Viggo, the Hammersmith Wonder"* or *"Vittoria, the Circus Belle"*? Possibly they were just clippings about odd people from the newspaper, but I – and many other later Literary Agents – prefer to think of these as Holmes's past cases. Then there are the cases that involve someone else's triumph – or do they? – like Lestrade's "Molesley Mystery" (mentioned in "The Empty House", where the most well-known Scotland Yard inspector competently handled an investigation during Holmes's Hiatus absence), or "The Long Island Cave Mystery", as solved by Leverton of the Pinkertons, and referenced in "The Red Circle". (And as an aside, I have to castigate Owen Dudley Edwards, the editor of the Oxford annotated edition of The Canon [1993], who decided to change *the Long Island Cave* to *Cove* simply because *"there are no caves in Long Island, N.Y."* (p. 206) – thus derailing a long-standing point of Canonical speculation. Pfui!)

And then there's the matter of the Oxford Comma, sometimes known as the "Serial" or "Terminal" Comma. A quick search of the internet found this example of *incorrect* usage: *This book is dedicated to my parents, Ayn Rand and God.* Clearly this author either had some interesting parents, or more likely he or she needed to use a comma after *Rand* to differentiate that series of parents, Ayn, and Deity.

And that relates to Untold Cases in this way: There are two Untold Cases that might actually be four, depending on one's use (or not) of the Oxford Comma. In "The Adventure of the Golden Pince-Nez", Watson tells of some of the cases that occurred in 1894. As he states:

> As I turn over the pages I see my notes upon the repulsive story of the red leech and the terrible death of Crosby the banker. Here also I find an account of the Addleton tragedy and the singular contents of the ancient British barrow.

I have many adventures in my collection that present these as *two* cases: (1) *The repulsive story of the red leech and the terrible death of Crosby the banker* and (2) *The Addleton tragedy and the singular contents of the ancient British barrow.* All are very satisfying. But I also have others that split them up into *four* cases: (1) *The repulsive story of the red leech* and (2) *the terrible death of Crosby the banker* and (3) *the Addleton tragedy* and (4) *the singular contents of the ancient British barrow.* For this collection, Nik Morton and Thomas Fortenberry have chosen to assume that the comma was intentionally omitted, and that there are two cases here, and not four, to be related.

More about the Oxford Comma....

As an amateur editor, I honor the Oxford Comma. I've been aware of it for years, ever since reading – somewhere – that editor *extraordinaire* Frederic Dannay (of Ellery Queen-fame and founder and the founding editor of *Ellery Queen's Mystery Magazine* from 1941-1982,) was a strong supporter of it. When writing this foreword, I couldn't remember where I'd read that, so I asked his son, Richard Dannay, who replied:

> *I can say with certainty that my father believed in the serial, or Oxford, or terminal (pick your poison) comma. I have no doubt. But sitting here, I'm not sure where he said that in print. I'll need to think about that. But I will send you a secondary source, absolutely unimpeachable in accuracy, where his preference is described.*

And then he sent me a PDF excerpt from Eleanor Sullivan's *Whodunit: A Biblio-Bio-Anecdotal Memoir of Frederic Dannay* (Targ Editions, NY, 1984, pp. 17-18). Ms. Sullivan was Dannay's chief editorial assistant for *EQMM* for many years, and after he died, she became the *EQMM* editor as his successor for about ten years before her premature death. (As Richard pointed out, the current editor is Janet Hutchings, only the third *EQMM* editor in its now over seventy-five-year history.)

Ms. Sullivan wrote:

> *Fred's style in editing* EQMM *could be considered eccentric, but I soon became used to it because there was his special logic behind everything he did. I didn't know he was exasperated by my non-use of the terminal comma (that is, a comma between the second-to-last word in a series of words and the "and") until one day when we were discussing some copy I'd sent him, he sighed dramatically and said, "I wish you could learn to use the terminal comma." I've been scrupulous about using it ever since.*

Recalling Frederic Dannay's passion for the Oxford Comma, I try to notice and then to add one in every place that needs it in these books. Having hubristically stated that, I'm absolutely certain that sure you will find places where I've missed it, along with many other unfortunate typos. These books live and grow as a single ever-expanding Word document on my computer – I have no publishing software – until such time as I send the final version to amazing publisher Steve Emecz, and they aren't seen by anyone else before their publication. There are no other proof-readers or editors who have a crack at them, and I'm flying without a net here. (My incredible wife of thirty-plus years has a Bachelor's Degree in Journalism, and two Master's Degrees in English Literature and Library Science, and her first job years ago was as a copy editor, but these books are neither her passion nor her problem, so I can't ask her to proofread them.) I've had several offers from volunteers to proofread, but due to the fast turn-around involved in this new publishing paradigm, that simply isn't possible. Thus, the errors that you find that throw you out of the story are on my head. Mortifying things sometimes slip through, and I apologize. But I do try to catch and fix every Oxford Comma situation that I can.

Other Untold Cases

While editing and assembling this particular set of books, I was concurrently working on *Sherlock Holmes: Adventures Beyond the Canon* (2018) for Belanger books, a three-volume set of twenty-nine new adventures that are sequels to The Canon. (It was amazing fun reading and editing all of these stories – over fifty of them between these five books – fresh from the Tin Dispatch Box, while keeping straight which went with which book.) Like the Untold Cases, these sequels don't contradict any of the sequels that have come before. One can't have too many traditional tales about the true Sherlock Holmes, and thankfully there are many more still out there. (I'm already receiving stories for next year's *Part XIII: 2019 Annual* from MX, and sequels for the next Belanger collection.)

As mentioned, there are far too many Untold Cases to list or recommend. The first encounter that I recall with attempts to reveal the Untold Cases was in *The Exploits of Sherlock Holmes* (1954) by a son of the First Literary Agent, Adrian Conan Doyle, and famed locked-room author John Dickson Carr. At the end of each of those twelve stories, a quote from The Canon revealed which Untold Case that it was – since it wasn't always clear from the story's title – and how it was originally mentioned. I liked that, and have followed the same convention with this book.

Many later stories have related Untold Cases, such as some included in collections like *The Mammoth Book of New Sherlock Holmes Stories* (1997) and *The Further Adventures of Sherlock Holmes* (1985). Others have appeared in the new *Strand Magazine* edited by Andrew Gulli, Bert

Coules' amazing *The Further Adventures of Sherlock Holmes*, or on Jim French's famed *Imagination Theatre*, broadcast on radio for decades across the U.S.

Interestingly, Untold Cases have been presented in Holmes radio shows since the 1930's, but they are much more rare in television episodes and movies. Sadly, except for some Russian efforts and a few stand-alone films, there have been no Sherlock Holmes television shows whatsoever since the Jeremy Brett films from Granada in the 1980's and 1990's. Hopefully, a set of film scripts by Bert Coules featuring an age-appropriate Holmes and Watson, set in the early 1880's, will find a home soon. I've been wanting to see (or read) these for years, and I'm curious as to whether any other Untold Cases feature in them – especially since Bert covered some of them so well in his radio scripts.

Some authors have specialized in finding the Untold Cases, like June Thomson, and more recently Hugh Ashton. For the record, I tried to recruit June twice to these books, and she wrote me some nice letters declining due to age. From the beginning of this anthology series, Hugh has been extremely supportive, and I'm very glad that he's a part of these books.

Philip K. Jones and the Untold Cases

I first became aware of Phil Jones back in the mid-when I ran across his amazing and massive online Pastiche Database. I've been collecting pastiches since I first found Holmes at age ten, in 1975, and have thousands of them on my shelves. I've scoured libraries and copied them from magazines and journals – a dime a page at old Xerox machines – and I've printed and archived them from the internet. I've bought Holmes books and asked for books – with traditional pastiches having first priority – as birthday and Christmas presents. I think that I've acquired one of the best pastiche collections ever. But finding Phil's database made me realize that it was only a drop in the bucket – and it also gave me new directions in which to hunt.

Phil was born in Missouri in 1938 and raised in Michigan. He worked in Information Technology for many years, and upon retirement turned his attention to Sherlock Holmes Literature.

In 2011, I published my first Holmes story collection, *The Papers of Sherlock Holmes* (later reprinted by MX in 2013). I desperately wanted it to be included in Phil's database, because to me that felt like I was actually (and finally) a part of this amazing World of Holmes. Phil and I began emailing, and I learned that he also wrote very respected

Holmesian reviews. I was very thrilled when he took the time to review my book.

Later, when the first of the MX anthologies appeared, he was one of the most supportive fans. I still treasure his comment about the first volume, where he said: *This first volume, on its own, is the finest anthology of Sherlockian fiction I have ever read."* That means a lot coming from a man who has read so many Sherlockian adventures.

Over the years we continued to communicate. He sent me copies of his scholarly articles, and I learned that, not only did he list in his database when a story was an Untold Case, but he had also done a lot of research into defining all of them, as well as devising his own story-title code, rather like what Jay Finley Christ did for The Canonical stories. Back in November 2011, we traded emails where he lamented that that he had found a story for every one of the Untold Cases except for "The St. Pancras Case" (as mentioned in "Shoscombe Old Place"), where a cap was found beside the dead policeman, and Merivale of the Yard asked Holmes to look into it. I was able to point him toward a fan-fiction called "Merivale of the Yard" by the uniquely named "AdidasandPie", and he was able to cross it of his list.

Also in 2011, Phil wrote a book with Sherlockian Bob Burr, *The Punishment of Sherlock Holmes* (MX Publishing), demonstrating his great love of puns. A couple of times he offered to write a pun-filled story for the MX anthologies, but I had to turn him down, as the scope of the books was absolutely Canonical. Conversely, I never stopped trying to get him to write a traditional adventure, because I thought that he, who had done so much to support post-Canonical adventures, should be a part of these books. He didn't feel that he had one in him.

On January 31st, 2017, Phil wrote to Steve Emecz and me with an idea for a future anthology volume. He stated:

> *[M]y suggestion is that you produce an anthology in this series devoted to The Untold Tales . . . . One of the good features of this project is that authors would discover that there are more than the two- or three-dozen commonly told Untold tales, some quite obscure, but intriguing. Another is that authors could fit almost any story idea into the one-hundred-and-thirty available subjects.*

As you can see, Phil's idea stuck in my head, and on February 19th, 2017, I issued the first invitations for submissions to what became the volume that you hold in your hands.

I wanted Phil to write a foreword to this book, and on July 19th, 2018, I sent an email to follow up on that. Three days later, I received a reply from Phil's wife, Phyllis Jones, indicating that Phil had passed away in June 13th, 2018.

I was stunned, and when I related the information online to various Sherlockian groups, there was shock, as well as a great outpouring of what a great guy Phil was, and what a loss this was to the community.

Therefore, as you'll see, these two concurrent volumes, *Parts XI* and *XII: Some Untold Cases*, are dedicated to Phil Jones. He was the Untold Cases Scholar, and the theme for these books was his idea. If he wasn't able to write a foreword, at least he can be honored in this way.

> *"Of course, I could only stammer out my thanks."*
> – The unhappy John Hector McFarlane, "The Norwood Builder"

These last few years have been an amazing. I've been able to meet some incredible people, both in person and in the modern electronic way, and also I've been able to read several hundred new Holmes adventures, all to the benefit of the Stepping Stones School at Undershaw, one of Sir Arthur Conan Doyle's homes. The contributors to these MX anthologies donate their royalties to the school, and so far we've raised over $30,000.

First and foremost, as with every one of these projects that I attempt, I want to thank my amazing and incredibly wonderful wife (of thirty-plus years!) Rebecca, and our truly awesome son and my friend, Dan. I love you both, and you are everything to me!

I have all the gratitude in the world for the contributors who have used their time to create this project. I'm so glad to have gotten to know all of you through this process. It's an undeniable fact that Sherlock Holmes authors are the *best* people!

Next, I'd like to thank those who offer support, encouragement, and friendship, sometimes patiently waiting on me to reply as my time is directed in many other directions. Many many thanks to (in alphabetical order): Bob Byrne, Mark Mower, Denis Smith, Tom Turley, Dan Victor, and Marcia Wilson.

Additionally, I'd also like to especially thank:

- Steve Emecz – Always supportive of every idea that I pitch – and there are some forthcoming projects that aren't common knowledge yet. It's been my great good fortune to cross your path – it changed my life, and let me play in this Sherlockian Sandbox in a way that would have never happened otherwise. Thank you for every opportunity!

- Lyndsay Faye: I remember first reading her wonderful Holmes-versus-The Ripper novel *Dust and Shadow* (2009) while in a motel room in Asheville, NC, where my son and I had taken a weekend trip. (I see from the note on the front page where I wrote my name that it was a gift from my wife and son for my birthday that year.) By then, I'd been keeping my Holmes Chronology for over ten years, so I read it while making notes as to how it would fit into the Autumn of Terror, 1888 – since that's a very complex period, and certainly Holmes's finest hour.

    I recall seeing in several interviews that this book – her first – was written during a period of unemployment. Since it was published in 2009, possibly she was unemployed in 2008 – a year when I was also jobless, laid off from an engineering company at the start of The Great Recession and using my time to pull some stories from Watson's tin dispatch box.

    I continued to read her stories as they appeared in *The Strand* magazine, beginning with "The Case of the Beggar's Feast" – an Untold Case! – in issue No. 29, (October 2009). She clearly had hit a hot wire running into the Great Watsonian Oversoul.

    In January 2015, I had the idea for these anthologies and started writing to a few Sherlockian authors that I really admired, hoping that they might be convinced to join the party. On January 25th, 2015, 11:16 am, I wrote to Lyndsay, explaining the project, and hoping against hope that she would be interested. At 4:54 pm – the engineer in me had to go and check – she wrote back with: *Hi David, I'd be happy to – when do you need it by?*

    Later, when it became obvious that this would be a series instead of a one-time thing, I contacted everyone who had previously participated, including Lyndsay. However, her many commitments as a professional author prevented additional contributions – until now. On March 27th, 2018, I wrote to see if she would write a foreword. The next day, she replied, *Hey David, I would be absolutely delighted to write a foreword!*

Lyndsay is a true Sherlockian, and I'm very jealous that she's up there at Ground Zero of the U.S. Holmesian world, with Otto Penzler's Mysterious Bookshop and various Baker Street Irregular activities, while I'm looking on from out here the Delta Quadrant. Sometimes when I've pestered her too much for a story, or when she thinks that I've been too public with my views about certain television shows, she's made the effort to write and tell me how I've vexed her – and I'm glad to have her thoughts on these matters, even if she hasn't changed my mind. I'm very grateful for her time and the support that she's given to these books – and also personally to this Tennessee Sherlockian!

- Roger Johnson – From the first time I reached out to Roger, upon the occasion of my first published book, he has been amazingly supportive, and I'm glad that he's my friend. He and his wife Jean were incredible hosts when I stayed with them as part of Holmes Pilgrimage No. II in 2015, and I'll never forget the times that he has showed me Chelmsford, Colchester, and parts of London. He led me to the market where I purchased my black deerstalker – because even though I have two-dozen other deerstalkers, I absolutely needed a formal black one. And I'll also never forget when our late afternoon train to leave Colchester was delayed, and we were walking briskly through the crowds, back-and-forth, from one platform to another, trying to get the next train. I was having fun – after all, I was in England, and I was wearing my deerstalker on a British railway platform racing for a train. I told Roger that we were having an adventure, and he said indignantly, *"I don't have adventures!"*

  Roger has supported these and other books from the beginning, and I am incredibly thankful.

- Derrick Belanger – Even as I was putting these books together, I was editing stories for a three-volume set of stories from Belanger Books, *Sherlock Holmes: Adventures Beyond the Canon*, featuring twenty-nine sequels to the original tales. This is just one of many past and future projects that Derrick, his brother Brian, and I have going. But additionally, I've enjoyed getting to know Derrick over the last few years, ever since our first enthusiastic emails sharing all sorts of Sherlockian thoughts. Derrick: Thanks very much for your friendship, as well as the Sherlockian opportunities.

- Brian Belanger – Brian is incredibly talented graphic artist who grows from success to success. Additionally, he's a positive and gifted person. Brian: Thank you so much for all that you do – it's appreciated by many people besides me!

- Richard Dannay – I'm very grateful that I can write Richard every few months with a question, or just wanting to discuss some aspect of Ellery Queen, and he quickly replies with exactly what I need. It's a thrill being able to correspond with him.

- Ian Dickerson – In the previous MX anthology volume, *Part IX (1879-1895),* Ian explained how he came to be responsible for a number of long-lost scripts from the 1944 season of the Holmes radio show, starring Basil Rathbone and Nigel Bruce, and written by Denis Green and Leslie Charteris (under the name Bruce Taylor). When I was writing this foreword and researching various versions of "The Giant Rat", I came across mention of the Basil Rathbone version. It was simply going to be mentioned in passing, and then I thought to ask Ian about it.

    He's published one set of the scripts – *Sherlock Holmes: The Lost Radio Scripts* (2017), and more recently another set – *Sherlock Holmes: More Lost Radio Scripts* (2018). I either wanted to mention the Rathbone "Giant Rat" if it's going to be in the current volume, or possibly use it if it won't be published until a later collection. Ian informed me that "The Giant Rat" isn't in the current book, and that I could have it if I wished for this collection. Of course I wanted it.

    Ian then worked like a crazy man, transcribing the original script into a new Word document, and within a very few days of my request, I had it in hand, and ready for editing. It was an incredible effort.

I'm very grateful to Ian for allowing this one to appear in these volumes before it's reprinted in one of the other upcoming volumes. When I first discovered Holmes, I quickly found a number of Rathbone and Bruce broadcasts on records at the public library, and that was where I first "heard" Holmes. I can't express the thrill of getting to read these rediscovered lost treasures, having been tantalized by their titles for so long. Many thanks to Ian for making these available.

- Andrew Gulli – For resurrecting *The Strand* magazine, and then for (usually) including a Holmes story, I'm very thankful. Additionally, your support, especially in publishing some of my own Holmes adventures in *The Strand* – truly a bucket list item fulfilled! – and also for your kind words about me during your interview on *I Hear of Sherlock Everywhere* are very much appreciated.

- Joel Senter – While these volumes were being prepared, Sherlockian Joel Senter passed away. I'll write more about him in the next MX volumes (in Spring 2019), but I'm grateful for everything that he did to support me personally over the years, and also how he helped these books in so many ways, including writing (with his wife Carolyn) the final story in the original three-volume set, *Parts I, II,* and *III*. He will be missed.

- Melissa Grigsby – Thank you for the incredible work that you do at the Stepping Stones School in at Undershaw Hindhead. I was both amazed and thrilled to visit the school on opening day in 2016, and I hope to get back there again some time. You are doing amazing things, and it's my honor, as well that of all the contributors to this project, to be able to help.

In addition those mentioned above – Bob Byrne, Derrick Belanger, Roger Johnson, Mark Mower, Denis Smith, Tom Turley, Dan Victor, and Marcy Wilson – I'd also like to especially thank, in alphabetical order: Larry Albert, Hugh Ashton, Deanna Baran, Jayantika Ganguly,

Paul Gilbert, Dick Gillman, Arthur Hall, Mike Hogan, Craig Janacek, Tracy Revels, Roger Riccard, Geri Schear, and Tim Symonds. From the very beginning, these special contributors have stepped up and supported this and other projects over and over again with their contributions. They are the best and I can't explain how valued they are.

Finally, last but certainly *not* least, **Sir Arthur Conan Doyle**: Author, doctor, adventurer, and the Founder of the Sherlockian Feast. Present in spirit, and honored by all of us here.

As always, this collection, like those before it, has been a labor of love by both the participants and myself. As I've explained before, once again everyone did their sincerest best to produce an anthology that truly represents why Holmes and Watson have been so popular for so long. These are just more tiny threads woven into the ongoing Great Holmes Tapestry, continuing to grow and grow, for there can *never* be enough stories about the man whom Watson described as *"the best and wisest . . . whom I have ever known."*

David Marcum
August 7th, 2018
The 166th Birthday of Dr. John H. Watson

Questions, comments, and story submissions
may be addressed to David Marcum at
thepapersofsherlockholmes@gmail.com

Lose Yourself in New Pastiches
by Lyndsay Faye

When kindly folks ask me to write about Sherlock Holmes, my answer ought to be carved into a woodblock so I can stamp it on every occasion: I would love to. Yes, absolutely! But I do this for a living, weirdly – the writing, storytelling, etc. And it takes me about three weeks to craft a good short story, so I am careful about my *pro bono* projects. I always say, if you're not good enough for poetry, write short stories. And if you're not good enough for short stories, write novels.

I write mostly novels, by the way.

I can recall the exact moment when David asked me to contribute a Holmes pastiche for the first volume to benefit Undershaw. I remember it because I immediately said absolutely yes, turned it in, saw it in print, and then was relentlessly hounded for more pastiches until the point when I said (pretty much) never ever ask me this again.

So he asked me to write a forward.

I'm not telling this story in a negative light, in case anyone was wondering. In fact, David is responsible for a huge amount of new stories existing. He badgers, he cajoles, he solicits, he wheedles, and he cadges. It works. I value very few things more than I value new Sherlock Holmes stories, so I applaud these results.

Let this be a proclamation: David Marcum, and the authors featured herein, have brought more Sherlock Holmes stories into the world. The tales are fantastic. They are traditional, which is tricky. They are labors of love. And David Marcum loves Sherlock Holmes the way I do, never quite forgetting about him as we walk around grocery shopping or vegetable chopping or bar hopping.

Lose yourself in new pastiches. Nitpick them. Love them. Analyze them.

Whatever you do with them, I'm simply glad they exist in the world.

Lyndsay Faye
BSI, ASH
July 2018

Known Unknowns
by Roger Johnson

To borrow a phrase from a very different discipline, the cases that Dr. Watson mentions but doesn't actually relate are *known unknowns*. [1] We know that Sherlock Holmes did investigate the singular affair of the aluminium crutch, the Smith-Mortimer succession case, and the adventure of the old Russian woman, but the details are not recorded in the sixty Canonical accounts, and therefore remain unknown.

A recent meeting of *The Sherlock Holmes Society of London* was devoted to some of these unreported exploits. Eleven members were each invited to select the story that best deserved to be published and, within five minutes, to explain why. We were encouraged to avoid the likes of the giant rat of Sumatra and the whole story concerning the politician, the lighthouse, and the trained cormorant, but there were more than eighty others more to choose from.

I commended the case of the Second Stain.

"The Adventure of the Yellow Face" opens thus: *"In publishing these short sketches based upon the numerous cases in which my companion's singular gifts have made us the listeners to, and eventually the actors in, some strange drama, it is only natural that I should dwell rather upon his successes than upon his failures. And this not so much for the sake of his reputation – for, indeed, it was when he was at his wits' end that his energy and his versatility were most admirable – but because where he failed it happened too often that no one else succeeded, and that the tale was left forever without a conclusion. Now and again, however, it chanced that even when he erred, the truth was still discovered. I have noted of some half-dozen cases of the kind; the affair of the second stain and that which I am about to recount are the two which present the strongest features of interest."* [2]

Fascinating! But in "The Adventure of the Naval Treaty", we're told that the case of the Second Stain occurred in *"the July which immediately succeeded [Watson's] marriage"* and that it *"deals with interest of such importance and implicates so many of the first families in the kingdom that for many years it will be impossible to make it public. No case, however, in which Holmes was engaged has ever illustrated the value of his analytical methods so clearly or has impressed those who were associated with him so deeply. I still retain an almost verbatim report of the interview in which he demonstrated the true facts of the case to*

Monsieur Dubuque of the Paris police, and Fritz von Waldbaum, the well-known specialist of Dantzig, both of whom had wasted their energies upon what proved to be side-issues."

Clearly we have two different cases, each dependent upon a second stain! Even more extraordinary is that neither of them is the investigation eventually chronicled in *The Return of Sherlock Holmes*.

Having heard the outcome of each speaker's scholarly speculation – or inventive fiction – or outrageous parody – our listeners voted for the case that best merited actual publication. My preference was firmly for the case of the two Coptic Patriarchs, advocated by the Revd. Simon Smyth, who is himself a priest of the Coptic Orthodox Church. It was exciting to learn that there actually *were* two Coptic Patriarchs at the time, and their followers were not on friendly terms. (Imagine those tense years in Western Europe when there were rival Popes). However, the winner by several lengths was the Dundas Separation Case, of which Holmes said, *"as it happens, I was engaged in clearing up some small points in connection with it. The husband was a teetotaller, there was no other woman, and the conduct complained of was that he had drifted into the habit of winding up every meal by taking out his false teeth and hurling them at his wife . . . ."* According to Peter Horrocks, who claimed that an account of this investigation, more than any of the others, deserved to be published, the *"separation"* was not between husband and wife, but between Mr. Dundas and his dentures!

Fortunately – perhaps – you won't find anything of the sort in this book. David Marcum has ensured that the contributions are firmly in the tradition established by Sir Arthur Conan Doyle, and followed to their great credit by Adrian Conan Doyle and John Dickson Carr, William E. Dudley, Martin Edwards, M.J. Elliott, James C. Iraldi, Barrie Roberts, Denis O. Smith, Edgar W. Smith, June Thomson, Alan Wilson – and others who have written first-rate accounts of exploits that were merely hinted at by Dr. Watson. [3]

Enjoy!

Roger Johnson
BSI, ASH
July, 2018

NOTES

1. In 2002, speaking of the evidence, or lack of evidence, linking the Iraqi government to the supply of weapons to terrorist groups, Donald Rumsfeld used the expressions *"known knowns"*, *"known*

unknowns", and "*unknown unknowns*". This is not meaningless jargon: The terms are precise and entirely relevant.

2. At least, that's how it runs in the standard British text. The American text follows *The Strand Magazine* in classing "The Musgrave Ritual" as a case in which Holmes failed to discover the truth. Which is patently untrue.

3. I'll also recommend the adventures of Solar Pons, "The Sherlock Holmes of Praed Street", created by August Derleth and active between the wars. His cases included "The Adventure of Ricoletti of the Club Foot", "The Adventure of the Remarkable Worm", "The Adventure of the Grice-Paterson Curse", "The Adventure of the Trained Cormorant", and "The Adventure of the Aluminium Crutch". His authorised chronicler is now the amazingly industrious David Marcum.

An Ongoing Legacy for Sherlock Holmes
by Steve Emecz

Undershaw
Circa 1900

It is three years since the first volumes of this series, and it's wonderful that we've reached Volumes XI and XII. We have raised over $30,000 for Stepping Stones School – the majority of which from the generous donation of the royalties from all the authors, but also from some interesting licensing deals in Japan and India. With this money, the school has been able to fund projects that would be very difficult to organise otherwise – especially those to preserve the legacy of Sir Arthur Conan Doyle at Undershaw.

There are now over two-hundred-and-fifty stories and well over a hundred authors taking part. We have new writers, unknown authors, established names, and even a few *New York Times* bestselling authors (like Lee Child) taking part. With more stories on the way under the careful eye of our wonderful editor David Marcum, the collection goes from strength to strength.

The critics agree that not only is it the largest, but *The MX Book of New Sherlock Holmes Stories* is the highest quality collection of new Holmes stories ever compiled. The last five volumes have all had glowing reviews from Publishers Weekly – Here are a few sample quotes:

> *"The traditional pastiche is alive and well, as shown by the 35 Sherlock Holmes stories in Marcum's excellent sixth all-original anthology"*

> *"This is a must-have for all Sherlockians."*

> *"Marcum continues to impress with the quality of his selections, many from little-known authors, in his seventh anthology of traditional pastiches"*

> *"Sherlockians eager for faithful-to-the-canon plots and characters will be delighted."*

> *"The imagination of the contributors in coming up with variations on the volume's theme is matched by their ingenious resolutions."*

> *"Sherlockians will rejoice that more volumes are on the way."*

MX Publishing is a social enterprise – all the staff, including me, are volunteers with day jobs. In addition to Stepping Stones School, our main program that we support is the Happy Life Children's Home in Kenya. My wife Sharon and I have spent the last five Christmases at the baby rescue centre in Nairobi. We have written a book called *The Happy Life Story* which explains how this incredible project has saved the lives of over five-hundred abandoned babies in its first fifteen years, with many being adopted. During the time that we have been involved, we've seen the project expand to include a school and now an incredible hospital which is saving lives every week.

Our support of both of these projects is possible through the publishing of Sherlock Holmes books, which we have now been doing for a decade. Our very first book was called *Eliminate The Impossible*, and we now have over three-hundred titles in print.

You can find out more information about the Stepping Stones School at *www.steppingstones.org.uk*, and Happy Life at *www.happylifechildrenshomes.com*. You can obtain more books from MX, both fiction and non-fiction, at *www.sherlockholmesbooks.com*. If you would like to become involved with these projects or help out in any way, please reach out to me via LinkedIn.

Steve Emecz
July, 2018
Twitter: *@steveemecz*
LinkedIn: *https://www.linkedin.com/in/emecz/*

The Doyle Room at Stepping Stones, Undershaw
Partially funded through royalties from
The MX Book of New Sherlock Holmes Stories

A Word From the Head Teacher of Stepping Stones
by Melissa Grigsby

Undershaw
September 9, 2016
Grand Opening of the Stepping Stones School
(Photograph courtesy of Roger Johnson)

As Stepping Stones School sails into its third year at Undershaw, we reflect on the unfinished and unknown tales that Sir Arthur Conan Doyle never drew to a close or was unable to complete.

One such story was that of "The Giant Rat of Sumatra", a story that distorted one's imagination beyond the concepts of the days he sat to unfold and write his stories. Within his writings, Doyle has Sherlock Holmes declare, as an aside, to Dr. Watson:

> "Matilda Briggs *was not the name of a young woman, Watson . . . It was a ship which is associated with the giant rat of Sumatra, a story for which the world is not yet prepared.*"

The young people that have their educational journey hosted under the roof of Undershaw can at times be seen and labelled as the unknown, special, and – in our eyes – gifted with exotic rareness. People from the outside can be scared and unsure as they perceive that these young people do not fit the social norms of society. However, within the walls of Undershaw and under Doyle's watch, and with his wishes in mind, these young people participate in layered therapeutic interventions and differentiated education with the same outcomes as many young people of their age.

Like *Matilda Briggs*, they are the vessels of social mobility and changed mindset, preparing the world for the day that they dock and take their place in society.

Thank you for all your support and companionship on this voyage with the young people of Stepping Stones School.

Melissa Grigsby
Executive Head Teacher, *Stepping Stones,* Undershaw
July, 2018

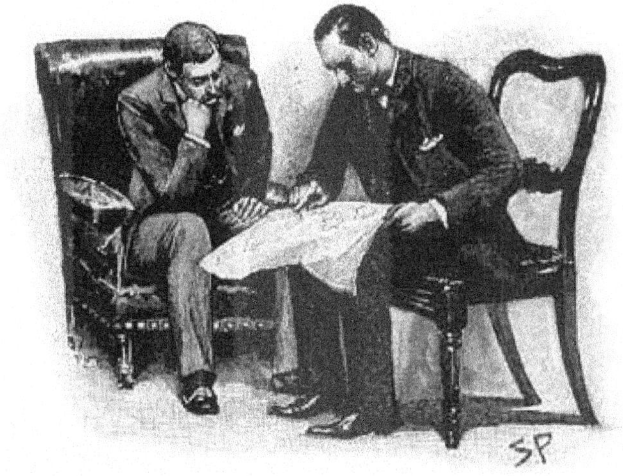
SP

Sherlock Holmes (1854-1957) was born in Yorkshire, England, on 6 January, 1854. In the mid-1870's, he moved to 24 Montague Street, London, where he established himself as the world's first Consulting Detective. After meeting Dr. John H. Watson in early 1881, he and Watson moved to rooms at 221b Baker Street, where his reputation as the world's greatest detective grew for several decades. He was presumed to have died battling noted criminal Professor James Moriarty on 4 May, 1891, but he returned to London on 5 April, 1894, resuming his consulting practice in Baker Street. Retiring to the Sussex coast near Beachy Head in October 1903, he continued to be associated in various private and government investigations while giving the impression of being a reclusive apiarist. He was very involved in the events encompassing World War I, and to a lesser degree those of World War II. He passed away peacefully upon the cliffs above his Sussex home on his 103rd birthday, 6 January, 1957.

Dr. John Hamish Watson (1852-1929) was born in Stranraer, Scotland on 7 August, 1852. In 1878, he took his Doctor of Medicine Degree from the University of London, and later joined the army as a surgeon. Wounded at the Battle of Maiwand in Afghanistan (27 July, 1880), he returned to London late that same year. On New Year's Day, 1881, he was introduced to Sherlock Holmes in the chemical laboratory at Barts. Agreeing to share rooms with Holmes in Baker Street, Watson became invaluable to Holmes's consulting detective practice. Watson was married and widowed three times, and from the late 1880's onward, in addition to his participation in Holmes's investigations and his medical practice, he chronicled Holmes's adventures, with the assistance of his literary agent, Sir Arthur Conan Doyle, in a series of popular narratives, most of which were first published in *The Strand* magazine. Watson's later years were spent preparing a vast number of his notes of Holmes's cases for future publication. Following a final important investigation with Holmes, Watson contracted pneumonia and passed away on 24 July, 1929.

Photos of Sherlock Holmes and Dr. John H. Watson courtesy of Roger Johnson

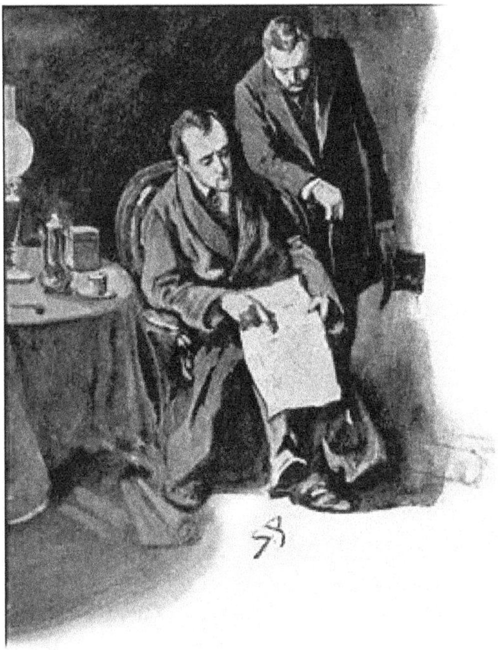

The MX Book Of New Sherlock Holmes Stories Part XI: Some Untold Cases (1880-1891)

Unrecorded Holmes Cases
A Sonnet
by Arlene Mantin Levy
and Mark Levy

The master Sherlock Holmes found many clues,
John Watson wrote them up and made them great;
His cases ranged from opal rings and shoes
And stains and smoke, to those of heavy weight;

But really those of most intrigue to us
Are unrecorded tales of quirky guys,
Like Ricoletti with his club foot plus
Abominable wife, or Upwood's lies;

Persano had a matchbox and big worm,
James Phillimore's umbrella disappeared;
A rat (Sumatran giant) took its turn
As did Vittoria, circus belle with beard;

So these and more add fun to Canon lore
We wish Doc Watson would have written more.

The Most Repellent Man
by Jayantika Ganguly

My visits to Baker Street were rather limited in the months following my marriage, and I didn't realise how much I had missed the company of my friend, Mr Sherlock Holmes, until one day when my annoyed wife all but pushed me out of our marital house with strict instructions to visit him.

"But Mary – " I protested.

She sighed, her beautiful face flushed. "John, darling," she said softly, in a voice I could never refuse. "I do believe that you owe Mr. Holmes a visit. Isn't he your dearest friend?"

"Yes, but – "

"And wouldn't it be preferable for you to accompany him on one of his cases, rather than investigating the mystery of the putrefying potato in our kitchen?" she continued as if I had not spoken.

"Yes, but – "

"You miss him, do you not?" she asked.

I couldn't deny that. Holmes and I had shared good times, and it was thanks to one of those adventures that I had met my wife. I smiled slightly as a wave of affection swept through my heart. My beloved Mary was perhaps the most understanding woman on earth.

She stepped forward and kissed my cheek. "Have yourself an adventure, my dear husband," she said, her eyes twinkling. "I shall wait for you to come home and regale me with your escapades."

And thus I found myself on the doorstep of 221b Baker Street once again, brimming with excitement. I chatted pleasantly with Mrs. Hudson for a few minutes. She seemed quite pleased to see me, and confessed that she would be relieved if I waited upstairs with the client she had just shown in, since Holmes had not yet returned, and the man's repugnant appearance had frightened her.

Curious, for the landlady was quite accustomed to bizarre and unusual figures thanks to her eccentric tenant, I made my way upstairs and entered the rooms in which I had recently resided. A middle-aged man sat quietly on one of the chairs, reading a thick book. He looked up as I entered and smiled slightly.

It was only my military training that allowed me to maintain a straight face. The man was just so . . . *wrong*. It is not that he was hideous or disfigured. His physical features, examined individually, were ordinary enough. However, there was something . . . not quite right . . . in the assembly. The overall impression was repugnant, as though the parts were arranged incorrectly – but there was no specific feature to isolate as incompatible.

"You must be Dr. Watson," the man said, standing up and extending a hand.

Even his voice was wrong, I thought to myself. I shook hands with him.

"You are the third man I have known not to initially recoil at my appearance," he said softly. To my horror, his eyes brimmed with tears. He pulled a pristine white handkerchief from his pockets and dabbed delicately at his eyes. The image was comical, but I was too astonished to react.

"My apologies," he wept. "No one other than Mr. Holmes and Albert, my son, has shown me such mercy at first sight. I have friends and acquaintances, of course, who have become used to my appearance, but everyone is disgusted when they see me for the first time. I cannot blame them, for my appearance is repellant to myself as well. I keep no mirrors or shiny surfaces that might reflect my abhorrent image."

What a pitiful man, I thought. I wondered if this was the philanthropist of whom Holmes had spoken at some point. I could only stare in shock as the man sobbed his heart out.

"Er . . . may I pour you a brandy to calm your nerves?" I enquired gently, afraid to upset him further.

"Thank you, Dr. Watson. You are indeed as kind as Mr. Holmes says," he said, hiccoughing. At least his tears had stopped. "I do not touch alcohol, though." He wiped his face and returned the now-soiled handkerchief to his pocket. "My apologies, again. I haven't introduced myself. My name is Xavier Brown."

"Are you a philanthropist?" I asked curiously.

His eyes widened. "Has Mr. Holmes spoken of me?"

"If you are the one that spent a quarter-of-a-million on the London poor, then yes."

Brown smiled, his face at once child-like and grotesque. I watched, fascinated. The man's repellant appearance was a mystery worthy of Holmes, I thought unkindly, and chastised myself for such uncharitable thoughts.

"I owe more to Mr. Holmes than I can ever thank him for," Brown said quietly. "Has he told you how we met?"

I shook my head.

"He really is rather modest," Brown muttered. "Though it has been quite a few years now."

Surprised, I asked, "Have you known Holmes for long?"

Brown nodded. "A young acquaintance of mine told me about him. Victor Trevor went to college with Mr. Holmes, you see. He moved to India a long time ago, and I was visiting some relatives there when I ran into him. Lovely country. Terribly hot, though. Have you been to India, Dr. Watson?"

I couldn't help my bitter smile. "Only as far as Bombay, before my military service took me elsewhere. I'm afraid that I don't remember much."

Brown was immediately contrite. "My apologies," he mumbled. "That was a very insensitive question. You mentioned your unfortunate injury in *A Study in Scarlet* – you write beautifully, I must say, and you depict Mr. Holmes's talents wonderfully. He is fortunate to have such a wonderful biographer! I hope you will continue to write about your adventures for a long time, Doctor."

I could not remain unaffected in face of his child-like glee. I thanked him, a little embarrassed.

"Do continue your story," I requested. "Holmes is rarely forthcoming."

Brown laughed. "You could say that. As I said, I first heard of Mr. Holmes in India, and I remembered Victor's words when I found myself in trouble here several years later. You see, I had found a young half-English boy in India who had been recently orphaned. His father had been a soldier, and his mother an Indian lady. His mother's family had disinherited her when she eloped with an English soldier, and she passed away soon after giving birth to the child. His father had taken to alcohol and gambling, and the boy had led a troubled life. The father died when the boy was young, leaving behind a huge gambling debt and no assets to cover it. The holders of the debt were determined to kill the boy in order to make an example. I really don't understand why our countrymen turn so savage in our colonies.

"The boy somehow managed to run away and hide himself in the inn where I was staying while waiting to board the ship back to England. The child was half-dead with hunger and quite injured when I found him, collapsed on the floor of my room. He had climbed up the pipes and entered through the window. I administered basic medical assistance and he told me his story when he awoke. I brought him back to England with me, adopted him, and sent him to school. Thankfully, he had already been well-schooled in India, and he was a bright child to begin with. He performed well, and was able to get into Cambridge after finishing his schooling. He is now a doctor and helps me with my work. I'm proud to call him my son." Brown smiled fondly, and pulled out a diary from his pocket. He flipped through the pages and handed me a photograph of a good-looking young fellow. "That is Albert," he said proudly.

"A fine young man," I told him, returning the picture. I did not see, however, what that had to do with Holmes.

As if reading my thoughts, Brown smiled slightly. "Ah, I am sure you're wondering why I'm rambling about my son when I said that I would tell you how Mr. Holmes saved us." He laughed and shrugged his shoulders. "Unlike you, I'm not a master storyteller, Doctor."

I could feel the heat rise up in cheeks at that comment. Brown, however, remained oblivious.

"You see," he continued. "A few years after our return to England, it appeared that the organisation that held Albert's father's debts discovered that he was in England and that I had adopted him. Two rogues approached Albert and demanded that he steal from me to pay his real father's debt. Darling child that he is, he refused immediately. They beat him half to death and left him at my doorstep. It was only after much persuasion that the boy divulged the details. I notified the police immediately, but they couldn't find anything. This shadow organisation was more discreet and powerful than anything I had previously imagined, for not even the police knew of them. In fact, they assured us that no such organisation existed," he paused for a moment. "Has Mr. Holmes ever spoken to you about . . . the Professor?"

"The Professor?" I repeated, being deliberately vague. I had no idea how much this man knew of Professor Moriarty, and it wasn't my place to share information. "We've had two or three cases where professors were involved, but I'm unsure of which one you refer."

Brown looked troubled for a moment. "My apologies. I digress too much," he said quietly. "Returning to the story . . . In light of the assault on Albert, the police appointed a constable to guard the house, but when nothing happened after a week and their investigations failed, the constable was recalled. However, I knew that the thugs wouldn't let go of Albert so easily. I'm not a poor man, Doctor, and the sum owed by Albert's real father, while significant, wouldn't have bankrupted me. I spent the week attempting to convince the boy to let me pay off the debt, but Albert was adamant. He told me that he would be killed regardless of whether I paid the debt or not, because that was how these villains operated. Moreover, he insisted that if I paid them once, they would keep threatening us over and over until I had exhausted all my funds.

"However, with the constable gone, danger appeared imminent. Our fears came to pass the very next day. A dead pigeon was pinned to the dining table with a knife, along with a letter that appeared to have been written in blood, demanding only one-thousand pounds, a fraction of the debt that was owed. Albert and I were immediately suspicious, for the thugs that had chased Albert in India had always demanded the full amount. It was then that I remembered Victor telling me about his friend Sherlock Holmes, who was supposed to be more skilled than the police. I enquired and was given his address – Mr. Holmes used to live in Montague Street near the Museum back then. I went to see him immediately. He was very kind and accompanied me back to my house.

"When we reached home, however, the place was in an uproar. While I was away, Albert had been abducted, and another dead pigeon was left on his bed with a note, this time asking for twice the amount demanded of Albert when he was beaten, but still not equal to the full amount owed. The note instructed me to bring the money in a bag to an abandoned neighbourhood church at midnight in exchange for Albert. Mr. Holmes gave the note a cursory glance and proceeded look around the room, while I sent my butler off to Scotland Yard to report the abduction.

"Finally, Mr. Holmes stood up and turned to the household staff assembled in the room. Other than the butler, we had a valet, a cook, a housekeeper, a gardener, two maids, and two footmen. I introduced each of them to Mr. Holmes. He greeted everyone politely, and then he asked, 'Who discovered that the boy was missing?'

"One the maids spoke up. 'It was me, sir. I went in to ask the young master what he would like for lunch and found him gone, with that ghastly bird left in his place . . . .' She burst into tears.

"Mr. Holmes was sympathetic. 'It must have been a shock,' he said gently. 'Could you tell us exactly what happened? Please start from the moment you came up the stairs. Your help would be invaluable in retrieving the boy.'

"The maid, Maria, nodded tearfully, eager to help. Everyone in the house adored Albert, you see. They still do. Maria did as Mr. Holmes said and began her narration. 'The young master was still recovering from last week's injury, so he was resting in his room. Mrs. Finn, the cook, told me to ask him what he would like for lunch, so I went upstairs. I was surprised to the see his door standing wide open, and when I entered, he was gone. The window was open, and there was a strange smell in the room. I looked out of the window, but there was no sign of anything. The blanket was missing and the sheets were dishevelled, as you can see now. I saw the bird and cried out in horror. Mr. Richards, the butler, heard me and came running. He told me not to touch anything and sent everyone else to look for the young master on the grounds until the master returned.'

"Mr. Holmes thanked her kindly and asked if anyone had visited the house after my departure, but before Albert was discovered to be missing. 'Only the doctor's assistant, Mr. Boone,' she replied. 'He's come to check up on the young master every day since the beating. Usually he comes with Dr. Saintsbury, but today he was alone. He was with the young master for nearly an hour today. As he left, he told us that the young master was recovering well and currently sleeping, and we shouldn't disturb him before lunch.'

"Mr. Holmes nodded absently and turned to the valet, Smith. 'Could you check the closet and tell me if any of his clothes are missing?'

"Smith obeyed wordlessly. He opened the closet and looked thoroughly before shaking his head. 'Everything is in its place. Not even a sock is gone,' he declared.

"Mr. Holmes faced the staff. "Can you tell me where you were this morning while Albert was sleeping?" Their answers confirmed that each had been busy with their usual tasks and, more importantly, the stairs and outside doors had never been unobserved during the entire time.

"Nodding absently, Mr. Holmes walked to the door. 'I shall return in a few moments. Please wait here.' Then we heard him go downstairs, and then out through the front door.

"No one spoke while he was gone, each wrapped in our own thoughts and fears. Before long, Mr. Holmes returned and began to examine the bedroom carefully, much to the shock of myself and my staff. You've described him as a bloodhound, Dr. Watson, crawling about on all fours, sniffing and picking at random. It was the first time that I had seen him in action, and I have to confess that I was afraid that I'd invited a lunatic into my house. He paused after examining the bedside table. 'Something is missing from here,' he said. 'Small and roughly round.'

"I stepped to the table and saw several circular marks in the delicate varnish. Even as I recognized what had caused them, Maria and Smith also glanced at the spot he indicated and both exclaimed, 'The Indian brooch!' It was the only memento Albert had of his late mother. It was a pretty thing, made of solid gold and exquisitely crafted in the shape of a dancing peacock, set with rubies for eyes, and emeralds, topazes, and sapphires for feathers.

"I explained this to Mr. Holmes quickly. 'Is the pin sharp?' he asked. I nodded, having stabbed myself accidentally the first time Albert had shown it to me. Mr. Holmes went through the bed clothes. He didn't find the brooch, but he curiously lifted the pillow to his nose and sniffed. Then, replacing it on the bed, he pulled out the table to look behind it. Finding nothing, he flattened himself on the floor and reached his arm under the bed. After a few moments, he stood and held out his palm. The gold brooch lay in his hand. "There was a chance that it had been taken, but fortunately not." He examined it carefully. 'It appears that Albert managed to stab his assailant with this. There are traces of blood at the tip of the pin. Clever boy.'

"Mr. Holmes looked up at us. 'Could you fetch Dr. Saintsbury and Mr. Boone?' he asked. We stared at him, shocked.

My valet was the first to recover. 'Certainly,' Smith replied and took his leave.

"Mr. Holmes walked to the window and inspected it again. 'Does the doctor use a carriage?' he asked. Maria nodded.

"'Did Mr. Boone use it today?'

"'Today it was a cab," Marie replied. She glanced at two of the men standing beside her. 'George and Nelson and Jarvis found the cabbie lurking about in the gardens, in fact.'

"The two footmen nodded anxiously. 'Mr. Boone had the cab deliver him right up to the door,' Jarvis said. 'I led the cabbie away after Mr. Boone alighted, but about half-an-hour later, George was tending to the garden as usual and saw the man wandering about where he had no business. He immediately informed Nelson. We caught him immediately and sent him back to his cab to wait for Mr. Boone. I stayed with him until Mr. Boone left.'

"Mr. Holmes nodded thoughtfully. He walked to the window. 'Where was he when you retrieved him?'

"Nelson stepped to the window. 'Down there, near the house but towards the right.'

"Mr. Holmes smiled slightly. 'As I thought,' he muttered. 'You foiled their plans.' Mr. Holmes turned to me. 'You sketch rather well, do you not?' he asked.

"Bewildered, I asked, 'How did you know?'

"He glanced at one of my drawings of Albert that my son had hung upon his bedroom wall, and then at my hands. 'Yours fingers told me,' he said enigmatically. 'There are traces of artist's charcoal residue under your fingernails, indicating that it's a regular pastime, and the position of that sketch on the wall shows how much your son treasures it. No matter where you sit in this room, that portrait is visible.'

"Tears spilled from my eyes and Mr. Holmes looked uncomfortable. 'Please save Albert,' I begged him. 'I shall have the money ready in a few minutes, Mr. Holmes. I just wish for my child to be back.'

"He shook his head. 'There is no need to raid your safe just yet, Mr. Brown.

"Mr. Holmes turned away. 'One last question, Mr. Brown. How long have you known Dr. Saintsbury and Mr. Boone?'

"I blinked, surprised. 'Surely you do not suspect them, Mr. Holmes? The doctor has been my G.P. since the day I was born.'

"Mr. Holmes ignored my protests and asked, 'Is the doctor aware of Albert's history?'

I nodded.

"Mr. Holmes's eyes were steady as he regarded me. 'And Mr. Boone?'

"Mrs. Hatcher replied. 'He's been visiting for about a year now,' she said, frowning. 'He used to be in America before that. He came to England to visit his aunt, but he found that she had passed away. He was out of funds, and fortunately he saw an advertisement by Dr. Saintsbury looking for a qualified assistant. He applied immediately. The doctor has never complained.'

"Mr. Holmes smiled. 'I see,' he said. 'Don't worry, Mr. Brown. Your son is safe. I do need a favour from you, though. Would you be so kind as to sketch a likeness of the errant cabbie that your footmen saw today?' The, without another word, he climbed out of the first-floor window and disappeared, nimble as an ape, while we stared open-mouthed.

"We rushed to the window and looked out to see that he was walking along the ledge easily, as if striding along a road. He stopped at a window about twenty feet away, just above where Nelson indicated that the cabbie had been located, and tugged it open. Next, he carefully examined the sturdy pipe next to it. Then he abruptly climbed down the pipe and stepped on to the grounds below. He looked up at us, waved, and climbed back up the pipe again. When he reached the window that he had opened, he slipped inside.

"We all watched, dumbfounded. Maria was the first to break the silence. "That's the window to the store-room!" she said. We left Albert's room and hurried down the hallway. Mrs. Hatcher withdrew the bunch of keys from her apron and unlocked the store-room door quickly.

"As it opened, we saw Mr. Holmes standing with Albert in his arms. A blanket and ropes lay on the floor. Mr. Holmes looked at me, his eyes gentle. 'He's fine,' he said softly. 'He'll wake up soon. They used chloroform. His pillow still had traces of it.'

"Jarvis was the one to ask the question that all of us wished to vocalise. 'How did you know where to find the young master?'

"Mr. Holmes smiled slightly as Nelson took Albert. 'My examination downstairs confirmed that there were no signs of a break-in. Nothing was carried out of the house – there are too many of you for that to have happened unseen – and I know of no organisations that use dead pigeons to leave messages. The assailant had to be someone who was allowed access into the house. Mr. Boone was the only outsider who visited Albert today, and he was also the last person to see him.

"'From the missing blanket, it was likely that the boy was wrapped in it and taken somewhere. If he hadn't been taken outside, as confirmed by the fact that no one could have passed unobserved through the staff downstairs, then it stood to reason that he was still in the house. There were some shoe marks on the window sill. I observed a nearby window next to a sturdy pipe, which seemed ideal, and sure enough, the latch was broken. I suspect that the cabbie, an accomplice and probably one of the two men who beat Albert last week, was supposed to climb up the pipe and retrieve Albert from the room where Boone had left him – but thanks to George, Nelson, and Jarvis, their plans were foiled. I must commend your staff, Mr. Brown.'

"Light-hearted with relief, we took Albert to my own room, and I drew the face of the cabbie, as requested by Mr. Holmes, based on the description provided by Nelson and Jarvis. Mrs. Finn and Maria left to prepare a light meal for Albert.

"When I finished the sketch, Nelson and Jarvis confirmed that it was a facsimile of the cabbie. Mr. Holmes wrote a note, handed it to Nelson, along with the sketch, and instructed, 'Please take it to Inspector Lestrade at Scotland Yard. In case he is already on his way here with your butler, give it to Inspector Gregson instead.'

"Soon, Mrs. Finn and Maria were back with hot cocoa and soup, and Albert was blinking sleepily as he regained consciousness. 'Papa?' he called groggily, catching sight of me.

"Tears of relief spilled down my cheeks as I hugged the child. 'How do you feel?' I asked him.

"He smiled blearily and muttered, 'Hungry.'

"Instantly, Maria placed the hot cocoa and soup before him. We watched fondly as he finished them off. 'I shall make your favourite dinner tonight,' Mrs. Finn promised him. Albert grinned up at us and spotted Mr. Holmes. "I don't know you," he said. He rubbed his temples as his memories returned. He looked up at me, his eyes full of fear, 'Papa, Mr. Boone, he . . . .'

"I gathered my son in my arms and rubbed his back to calm him down. 'It's all right now, child,' I murmured. 'We will catch them. Mr. Holmes is here to help.'

"Albert stopped trembling and I released him. He looked up at Mr. Holmes hopefully, who smiled gently and said, 'You have been very brave, Albert. You stabbed Boone with your mother's brooch, did you not?' Albert nodded and Mr. Holmes continued. 'Very well done. We need some more assistance from you, and I promise they will never bother you again. Could you identify this man?' He held up the sketch that I had made.

"Albert examined them carefully. 'This is one of the men that attacked me a week ago,' he said finally. 'Will the police arrest them?'

"Mr. Holmes nodded. 'I believe these men – the cabbie and the other – will be in gaol in a few hours. As for Boone – he will arrive shortly with the doctor.' He turned to me. 'These men have nothing to do with the collection of the Indian debt. This was simply an opportunity claimed by an opportunist.' He indicated the sketch. "This fellow is known to me – an associate of a certain Professor that I know." Then he glanced at the door. 'I believe that Scotland Yard has arrived.'

"He was right, of course. Richards walked in with an inspector and two constables. The inspector was introduced as Lestrade, and his eyes widened at the sight of Mr. Holmes. 'Why are you here?' he asked, clearly annoyed. Then he spotted Albert on the bed. 'Is this the boy that was supposedly abducted?'

"Albert sat up straighter. 'Mr. Holmes rescued me!' he declared. Everyone in the room agreed loyally.

"Mr. Holmes chuckled. 'Cheer up, Lestrade,' he said mirthfully. 'You, my friend, are about to make an arrest in a few minutes. Shall we head downstairs?'

"Leaving the ladies to watch over Albert, the rest of us followed Mr. Holmes to my office. He said a few quiet words to the policemen, who hid themselves in nearby rooms. Soon enough, Smith returned with Dr. Saintsbury and Mr. Boone. The doctor entered the office and rushed to me immediately. 'I heard from Smith about Albert's abduction. Have you notified the police yet?'

"Mr. Holmes stepped in and answered for me. 'It's usually better not to contact the police,' he said smoothly. 'Dr. Saintsbury, did you divulge Albert's history to anyone?'

"The doctor replied automatically, 'Only to my assistant, Mr. Boone here, a few weeks ago. Why do you ask?' He looked around the room, noticing the inspector standing quietly to one side, and then, taking a step toward Mr. Holmes, he asked, 'Who are you?'

"Mr. Holmes replied vaguely. 'A friend of the family." Then he turned to Boone, standing near the doorway. It had been all that I could do not to rush forward and strike the man when he entered my home. Seeing him there now, a fearful look in his eyes, I wondered that he'd been bold enough to attempt to kidnap my son.

"Mr. Holmes also seemed aware of this. 'Are you well, sir?' he asked with a smile. The inspector shifted slightly toward the doctor's assistant.

"'Of course,' replied Boone, swallowing nervously. 'Why not?'

"'It seems as if you're listening for something.'

"'Listening?' asked the doctor, looking back and forth between Holmes and his assistant. 'What for?'

"'Possibly,' replied Mr. Holmes, 'for the sound of young Albert being discovered in the upstairs store-room, where Mr. Boone left him just an hour or so ago after drugging him.' He turned squarely to face Boone. 'Knowing that the man driving the cab was prevented from climbing up and retrieving the boy must have stretched your nerves to the breaking point. At what point would he awaken and identify you as the man who must have locked him in the store-room? The decision to stay or flee must have been agonizing. You were really quite foolish to return here – and yet, you must have hoped to somehow repair the situation. Even now, you were considering how to slip upstairs, if only for a moment – to re-administer more chloroform to the boy . . . or perhaps worse. If we search you, Mr. Boone, will we find the skeleton key? Or other more questionable tools that let you lock the store-room after you'd hidden Albert there? Will we – *Catch him, Lestrade!*'

"With that, the man's courage broke, and he made a dash for the doorway. The inspector grabbed his arm as he passed, and the two constables suddenly appeared in the hallway, blocking his path. With a sob, the man gave up.

"Dr. Saintsbury was shocked to the core to learn the truth about Boone, or Reynolds, as he was known as in America. He turned out to be a wanted criminal who had fled to England to escape the gallows. He'd murdered at least three people there, and had robbed dozens. After his arrival in England, he'd found employment with the doctor, but his natural inclination was to make associations with the criminal element, including men who worked for this mysterious 'Professor'. Learning from the doctor some of Albert's past, and specifically the story of the old debt, he had conceived the idea of kidnapping him for ransom.

"He'd planned the crime with the two other men, both of whom were quickly caught. The man thought to be a cabbie was in nothing of the sort, and was quickly found using my sketch. He was a paroled thief, while the other was his brother. Both of them had initially beaten Albert on Boone's instructions, and then they had entered the house by night to leave the message on our dining table demanding money, simply as a way to prepare me for when Albert was kidnapped, so that I'd be more likely to pay the ransom without question.

"The amounts demanded, which didn't match the original debt, were yet another indicator to Mr. Holmes that this affair had nothing to do with the original debt owed by Albert's father. Inspector Lestrade was very pleased to have Boone and the others under arrest, and Mr. Holmes magnanimously diverted all credit to Scotland Yard.

"And that, Dr. Watson, is the story of how Mr. Holmes saved my family," Brown concluded, smiling beatifically. "Is he not a most impressive man?"

I returned his smile. "That he is," I replied.

Holmes chose that moment to enter. "Ah, Mr. Brown," he said, spotting his guest. "Forgive me, I've kept you waiting. I see you have met Watson already."

Brown greeted my friend enthusiastically, adulation shining in his eyes. "Not at all, Mr. Holmes. The fault lies with me for calling upon you so suddenly. Dr. Watson and I had a nice chat about old times. I apologise for the intrusion. It really is very gracious of you to accommodate my request at such short notice."

Holmes regarded the strange man with a slight smile. "How is your son?" he asked fondly.

Brown's eyes shone with pride. "Albert sends his regards. He's doing very well, thank you. He was quite eager to see you too, but an urgent patient called him away at the last minute."

Holmes's smile was affectionate as he nodded.

With a start, I realised that Holmes was genuinely fond of this person, which was quite unlike him. I knew my friend was a kind man despite his cold and reserved exterior, but it was unusual for him to display affection. I wondered what about this gentle person with such a repugnant exterior made Holmes uncharacteristically fond of him. Perhaps Holmes found the contrast between Brown's appearance and personality interesting. I certainly did. For such an unaffected, innocent soul to be trapped in such a repellant body . . . I felt a wave of pity for the poor man. Had he been comely, I am certain he would have no dearth of wooers.

Some of my thoughts must have shown on my face, for Holmes sent me a warning look surreptitiously. Brown, however, remained oblivious.

"I understand now why you hold Dr. Watson in such high regard, Mr. Holmes," he said enthusiastically. "He is so very kind. He treated me like an ordinary person at first sight!"

I felt a stab of guilt. "Surely you exaggerate, Mr. Brown. I have done nothing praiseworthy," I mumbled.

Holmes smiled fondly. "Watson is a most modest person, Mr. Brown," he said. "And I do wish you would cease demeaning yourself in such a morbid fashion. Believe me when I say that you are one of the best and kindest men I know, for I do not say these words lightly."

I stared at my friend in shock. So did Brown. Then his face crumpled as he wept again like a child. To my shock, Holmes stepped forward and lay a gentle hand on the man's shoulder.

"Come now, Mr. Brown," he said quietly. "Surely there is no need to get so emotional. I know Albert holds you in an even higher regard than I do."

"My apologies," Brown sobbed. "You have always been so kind, Mr. Holmes. Not only have you saved my life several times and looked out for Albert, you have even boosted my morale on more occasions than I can count."

Pale cheeks awash with colour, Holmes expertly guided the man back to his seat. I smiled.

Holmes caught my eye and chuckled, as if reading my thoughts. "Brown is an unusual person, Watson." His keen eyes fixed on my face. "I have almost as much faith in him as I have in you, my dear doctor," he added softly.

I could feel colour seep into my cheeks and I hastily looked away. Brown's excessive sentimentality had clearly affected us both.

Holmes turned to Brown. "How can I help you today?"

"There has been an attempt on my safe."

"The same one that you've always had?"

"Of course. It's served me well for nearly three decades without missing a single penny."

"As I recall, you keep large amounts of money in it, and it's opened by a simple key. May I see it?"

Brown handed it to him, and he examined it carefully. He sniffed at it – "Lavender," he muttered – and scraped a miniscule amount of residue from the key onto a piece of paper. He then handed it back to Brown with a serious expression. "Someone has made a copy of your key."

Brown stared at him in shock. "How? It is always on my person. Besides, my staff is entirely trustworthy. As you know, I've never had any reason to doubt them."

Holmes studied the residue with a frown. "This key is easy to replicate. One would merely need to press it into a bar of soap to make a cast – as someone has done. The design is quite simple." He looked up. "Does anyone in your house use lavender-scented soap?"

"I believe that Mrs. Hatcher put a new bar of lavender soap in the master's bath a few days ago. She indicated that the shopkeeper said it was a nice new product he'd obtained from France, and she thought that I would enjoy it. It was missing from the bath this morning."

Holmes cleared his throat and turned to me. "We have another case waiting for us, Watson, if you would care to join me."

"I shall be delighted to accompany you, my dear fellow," I replied earnestly.

Holmes's smile was proof that he had missed my company as much as I had missed his.

> ". . . the most repellant man of my acquaintance is a philanthropist who has spent nearly a quarter-of-a-million upon the London poor."
>
> Sherlock Holmes – *The Sign of Four*

The Singular Adventure of the Extinguished Wicks
by Will Murray

Among the myriad items at the bottom of my little tin dispatch box, to which I have referred so frequently, lies an oilskin packet containing the accounts of cases of Mr. Sherlock Holmes which, for various reasons, my esteemed friend has preferred to keep out of the public eye.

The reasons are many. Most have to do with strict confidences and the respect for privacy of notable persons, or like delicate matters. A few refer to individuals who, whilst they may have transgressed early in life, had redeemed themselves in later years.

There is one that I never believed Holmes would give me leave to write up for the edification of the general public. I do not mean to say that this was a case that was not brought to a successful conclusion. For it was.

Solving crimes is not the only kind of matter to which my friend's keen brain bent its energies, as I will relate.

I fear that the chief reason Sherlock Holmes has acquiesced to this revelation has more to do with his increasing age and the prospect of the nearing conclusion of an illustrious life.

Although I am glad to report on the matter now at hand, I am forced to conclude that Holmes is allowing me to offer it up, as it were, because he has concluded that a final resolution of the overarching problem is not within his power. At least, not insofar as his allotted span of life can be projected.

The matter opened, as nearly as I can recall, in the year 1881. It was the month of May. Of that, I am certain. I had not been living with Holmes for very long, and his recondite ways were still unfamiliar to me.

Returning home one evening, I was nearly knocked off my feet as I attempted to enter the door at 221b Baker Street. Sherlock Holmes abruptly flung the panel open and charged out.

"My dear Holmes!" I exclaimed. "Wherever are you bound in such an infernal hurry?"

"A woman has been found burnt to death in a most uncanny way," he replied urgently. "I would like to see her rooms before the corpse is carted off."

"What – Do you suspect murder?"

"Murder," replied Holmes cryptically, "is a commonplace compared to what had transpired. I am keen to see what remains. You may accompany me if you wish, Watson. Hallo! I spy a cab. Well, come along, if you are coming along."

Following him at great speed, I climbed into the hansom cab whilst Holmes gave an address in a neighborhood I did not hold in very high esteem.

"How did you hear of this?" I inquired.

"A fellow of my acquaintance in the fire brigade informed me. I have been awaiting such a case for several years. As you know, Watson, I make it my business to converse with tradesman of various types. A fire officer is, in his unique way, a tradesman. Much can be learned by conferring with people who do interesting work."

As the cab reeled around corner after corner, I asked, "Why would the prospect of so horrible a demise interest you?"

Holmes continued as if he had not heard the question, yet managed to answer it nevertheless.

"During the course of my conversation with the fellow, I was astonished to learn that such cases happen two and three times a year, but the fire officials go out of their way to cover them up with commonplace explanations."

"Death by fire is a distressing consequence of dwelling in these modern times in the metropolis the size of London," I offered.

"I am not referring to the consequences of failing to extinguish a candle, or of falling asleep whilst smoking a pipe or cigar," Holmes continued. "This type of mystery is much more impenetrable. Rarely do the facts get into the newspapers. And when they do, they are papered over with generalities and ambiguities."

"I confess that I cannot imagine what you are discoursing on, Holmes," I frankly admitted.

"You should see it with your own eyes," said my friend. "As will I. As a medical man, as well as a veteran of the British campaign in Afghanistan, you are no doubt inured to the horrible things that can befall a human being in the last ditch. But I must warn you: If I understand the situation correctly, we are about to witness the uncanny."

I cried out, "My dear fellow, you have piqued my interest! And rest assured, you need not fear for my nerve, or for that matter for my stomach."

A curl of a smile warped Holmes's austere profile.

"Consider this a test, Watson. For if you intend to accompany me on future excursions, you will need iron nerve and a stomach of steel."

His words evoked in me a nerve-chill I can still feel all these decades later. If I believed in supernatural presentiments, I would have regarded it then as a subconscious inkling of what I was about to experience.

Presently, the cab dropped us before a rather slatternly rooming house in congested Southwark, which only a few decades before, mature readers will recall, had been the site of the Great Fire of Tooley Street. The bitter odor of burnt timbers could yet be recognized on rainy days.

Brigadiers of the Metropolitan Fire Brigade stood about an idle scarlet parish steam engine, signifying that the blaze had been quenched. As we stepped to the ground, the grey-uniformed official in charge acknowledged Holmes with a rather grim wave.

"Hello!" Holmes responded, striding up to the man in his brisk, nervous way.

"It's a sad case, Mr. Holmes. A very sad case." He shook his helmeted head with a grave ponderousness.

"Has the body yet been removed, Mr. Clavering?"

"What remains awaits your pleasure. I would apply a handkerchief to my nostrils, were I you. Now come along."

Calling over my shoulder, Holmes said, "Watson!" I needed no more encouragement. I drew out a handkerchief as well, and applied its thick folds to my nose and mouth.

The room was on the second floor. No sooner had we ascended to the landing than I became aware of a faintly bluish haze in the air. A sweetish smell accompanied it. I did not care for the odor, despite its sweetness.

"Brace yourselves," said Clavering. Then he threw open the door. We entered.

We found ourselves in a parlor. It was neat and tidy. Possibly it could be called fastidious. It was clearly the apartment of a woman of conservative taste, if its appointments were any guide.

A maple rocking chair stood by one window. It bore scorch marks, and the unburnt wood showed an unusually thick coating of soot. As I looked around, I noticed the wallpaper was greyish with some oily deposit. A yellowish liquid clung to the solitary window. I recognized the color as similar to that of human fat, with which I was had been acquainted since my first dissection of a cadaver in medical school.

In my searching, I missed entirely the shoe that lay upon the hardwood floor. Or should I say the human foot, which was shod. It was only the one foot.

Giving forth a strange murmur of excitement, Sherlock Holmes went to it, knelt, and examined the member carefully, all without touching the grisly relic.

"This is all that remains of the poor woman?" he asked.

"There are fingers as well," Clavering added. He indicated three human digits from which the phalanges protruded. They made a loose pile on the floor, like gruesome kindling. One bore a ring of gold, set with a garnet. The scorched metal was deformed by the intense heat.

I examined them all. "Remarkable!" I exploded. "The finger bones appear to be calcined."

Holmes nodded shortly. "Exactly as was the case in previous occurrences of this sort."

"Of what sort?" I demanded curiously.

"The phenomenon of inexplicable human combustion. What you see on the floor here, Dr. Watson, is all that remains of the woman in question, Kathleen Wick."

"Unfortunate name," grumbled the fire officer through his handkerchief.

"What is this pile of ash in the chair?" I asked.

"The greater portion of Miss Wick," advised Holmes. "She was incinerated as she sat rocking."

Turning abruptly, Holmes swept about the room. He applied a finger to the wallpaper and the fingertip came away greasy and grey.

"She lived alone?"

Clavering nodded. "So I understand from the landlord. Would you like to speak with him?"

"Presently," said Holmes distractedly. I was astounded by the diffidence with which the fire official treated my friend. He was early in his long career in those days, but apparently had made a great impression upon certain persons in greater London.

A bottle of gin, three-quarters full, rested upon a taboret. A short glass stood beside it, its contents dirty and discolored.

"I am not surprised," murmured Holmes. "Spiritist liquor is typically found in such cases."

At that point, my mouth and nose protected by my handkerchief, and struggling with a compulsion to gag, I drew up to the rocking chair and studied the ashes. They lay moist and greasy upon the maple back and arms. Additional ash residue had formed a film on certain horizontal surfaces about the room, not quite so thickly as coated the rocker.

There was a fireplace, but it was cold, as this was not the season for keeping a fire.

As I studied the heap of ashes, I could not keep the incredulity out of my voice when I exclaimed, "My dear Holmes, the heat required to reduce a human body to mere ash can only be created in a proper crematorium. Even so, after the bones are incinerated, they must be pummeled with heavy tools in order to reduce them to an ashy state."

"I am well acquainted with mortuary practices," murmured Holmes. He was going about the room, looking at this item and that thing, taking in every detail with his piercing grey eyes. I knew him well enough in those days to understand that he was mentally cataloging every iota of datum, every detail, whether in place or out of place. Little, I was sure, would escape his notice. But what to make of it all? That was the question.

"If this woman died in this rocking chair, why is the wood not also incinerated?" I demanded.

"Why was the bed in which the late Mrs. Vanderlip was found burnt alive also untouched?" Holmes turned to the fire officer and asked, "Are you acquainted with that case?"

"I presided over the investigation," the man returned. "The poor woman was found in bed, reduced to a collection of disassociated arms and legs. There were some portions of her skull and jaw that survived, although they broke apart up on handling. Other than that, nothing but ashes, greasy fetid ashes."

"Yet the bed clothing, and her covering quilt, survived."

Claverling grunted, "The quilt was scorched, but the linen beneath the body bore only a blackening caused by close contact with the greasy ash remains."

Stupefied, I interjected, "Had she had not time to fling off her quilt and endeavor to escape the flames that consumed her?"

"That was not the conclusion I came to," admitted the fire official with evident reluctance.

"Impossible!" I blurted out.

"I would be inclined to agree with you, Watson," said Holmes flatly. "Except the literature is full of similar cases, going back many years. I consider myself to be fortunate to have been granted access to the death scene whilst it is still fresh."

I looked up from the ashes. "Do you propose to solve this enigma, Holmes?"

"I propose to investigate it thoroughly. Whether I solve it or not remains to be seen, for it most baffling. The circumstances seem to defy reason. Even if one could admit to the possibility that a human being could spontaneously burst into such ferocious fire that almost nothing remains, how to account for the surroundings remaining relatively untouched?"

"If I did not stand here as witness to the aftermath," I said somberly, "I would dismiss it as a figment of a drunken journalist's imagination. Poe could not have conjured up such a nightmarish scenario."

"May I," inquired Holmes of the fire official, "appropriate a sample of ash for scientific study?"

Claverling hesitated. "It is highly irregular, Mr. Holmes. But since you would like to speak to the landlord, I will go and fetch him now. What you do in the interim is your lookout." He gave the pile of ashes a regretful glance. "I daresay the poor woman will not miss any part of her mortal remains, such as they are."

"Thank you," said Holmes.

The fellow departed and Holmes removed from a pocket a stoppered vial. He employed it to scoop up some of the greasy matter that remained upon the scorched seat of the rocking chair. He availed himself of a liberal portion, then stoppered the receptacle, quickly pocketing it.

When the fire official returned, he poked his head in, saying, "Mr. Merridew prefers not to enter this room. Would you kindly step out to greet him?"

With a last wondering look at the flat, Sherlock Holmes exited, and I at his heels. I was glad to leave the death chamber. It was the most grisly charnel house I have ever imagined. Just being in it made me fear for my safety.

Merridew the landlord met us outside. He was a nervous chap, pale and quivering, and bathed in the perspiration of his agitation.

The fire official made formal introductions.

"This is Mr. Sherlock Holmes. He is a detective, but not officially with Scotland Yard. He would like to ask you several questions."

Merridew became flushed of face, and perspiration made his features shine oilily.

"I smelt that sickly sweetish order and I at once began going about the building, knocking on doors, endeavoring to locate the source of it. We have eight apartments let in this building, Mr. Holmes. As you can well imagine, a fire would be disastrous."

"An ordinary fire would, of course," said Holmes. "But this was no ordinary fire. I imagine you realize that by now."

Merridew patted his moist forehead with a sopping handkerchief. "I do not know how to take this event. It is beyond my ken. I forced the door when I realized the odor was coming from the room of poor Miss Wick. I was driven back by the smell, but then steeled myself. There was a candle burning. But nothing otherwise. I saw that ashy pile upon the chair but did not understand its significance until I came upon the shoe containing a dismembered foot. The surviving fingers I missed until I was told about them later. How this could have happened, I cannot conceive. Nor the why. What on God's green earth could have brought that woman to such destruction, yet spared the building?"

Sherlock Holmes studied the man and said, "These are the questions of the hour. As for answers, I do not have them, nor do I imagine they will be easy to come by. Tell me, how long was Miss Wick a resident here?"

"Five, almost six years. She was a widow. She had a younger sister who visited frequently, but very few friends. He spent a great deal of her time alone."

"Very well. Tell me of her drinking habits."

"I am not intimately acquainted with them. But I have noticed empty bottles of gin in her rubbish. I did not consider their number excessive, although they appeared with predictable regularity."

"Now, did you ever know Kathleen Wick to be drunk or disorderly?"

"Never!" the man said firmly. "She was a model tenant. Paid on time. Troubled no one. Was friendly enough, but kept to herself a great deal of the time. Her sister is a lovely woman, and I'm sure she will be heartbroken about the news."

"No doubt, no doubt," mused Holmes. "I noticed the ring on one of the surviving fingers. A garnet. Were you familiar with it?"

"Yes, I knew the ring well. She wore it from the first day until her very last hour."

"So you were certain that the remains, such as they are, belong to Miss Wick?" prodded Holmes.

The poor fellow nodded vigorously. "What damnable and ironic fate would so snuff out a healthy woman bearing such a name?" he raged. "It is enough to make one wonder about demons and the like. It smacks of some damned grisly jest."

"I would tend to agree with you, Mr. Merridew," said Holmes. "And if there was a jest, there is there must be a jester. Would you not agree?"

The distracted man tore at his hair and cried out, "If such a mad jester stalks London, what manner of monster could he be?"

"If it will ease your mind," said Holmes reasonably, "the fate of Miss Wick is not unique, even if it is extraordinary. But I feel confident in asserting that, once the remains are removed from this dwelling, and it is properly scoured of unpleasant residue, your present troubles will be entirely behind you."

Merridew took comfort in Holmes's reassuring words. "Oh thank you, oh thank you. This has been the most distressing and disagreeable day of my entire existence."

Returning to the fire official, Sherlock Holmes said, "I will take my leave now. I would like to express my gratitude for the opportunity to examine the scene of this inexplicable occurrence."

Claverling nodded deferentially. "Should your inquiry produce any illumining facts, Mr. Holmes, the superintendent would be gratified to hear them in full. Good day to you."

I was relieved to be departing the neighborhood, which we did on foot until coming across an idle hansom cab. We secured it.

"What do you think, Watson?" Holmes asked as we made our way back to Baker Street.

"I am staggered, Holmes. This is beyond my understanding. All of it. Have you any thoughts? Any inklings of what could have transpired in that chamber of hellish horrors?"

"I will offer this, Watson. There is a pattern to these occurrences. And what I observed today only confirms that pattern. Previous examples of spontaneous destruction of living persons by fire are alike in certain particulars. The victim is older, sedentary, often burdened with adipose tissue, and inclined towards consumption of spirits."

"Do you suspect that the regular consumption of alcohol lies at the heart of this enigma?"

"Only as a preliminary line of investigation. I rather doubt John Barleycorn will accept the full weight of responsibility. But it is a point from which to begin serious inquiry." He turned to me and asked, "Tell me, Watson, do you still have friends at the London Hospital Medical College?"

"Many," I replied. "Why?"

"I imagine I will need a human cadaver or two upon which to experiment," he returned dryly. "I wonder if you would be so kind as to make for me certain introductions toward that aim?"

I was so staggered by the casual request that I was unable to summon up an answer for some minutes.

"Well, it is highly irregular, Holmes. But I will endeavor to aid you to that end. What do you propose to do with these cadavers?"

"Why, I propose to burn them in various ways. Is that not self-evident?"

"Be good enough to do so outside of the confines of our shared quarters," I requested sincerely.

"That's a good fellow, Watson. It would not be fitting to have to dig up my own specimens, as it were."

The coachman was pulling up before 221b Baker Street when these words were uttered.

I distinctly recall staring at Holmes's enigmatic profile, aghast. I did not ask the question forming in my brain. Namely, if it came to it, would Sherlock Holmes resort to the dishonorable practice of grave robbing to achieve his scientific objectives? I could not convince myself that the detestable practice was beyond his imagination.

Over the next few weeks, Holmes experimented on the ashes of Miss Wick, and acquired a cadaver which he selected from several sad specimens known to have had a history of excessive consumption of alcohol.

I readily admit that I did not inquire often as to his progress. But his experiments occurred under the watchful eyes of certain medical authorities. I understand that he burned portions of the deceased using various chemical agents and accelerants – all to no avail.

I learned of this late one evening when I found him smoking his black clay pipe furiously. It was a sign that he was vexed.

"No progress, Holmes?" I inquired.

"None to speak of," he returned gruffly. "No matter how I try, I cannot duplicate the circumstances that brought Miss Wick to her fiery doom."

"You are not giving up?"

"Not giving up, no," he said somberly. "But when no progress is made, the mental machinery begins to clutch up and overheat. I may turn my attention to other problems and come back to this odious matter on a later occasion."

"What if, as you say, the spontaneous incinerations are a recurring event? Perhaps another will happen along to aid you in your inquiry."

Rather testily, Holmes dismissed the idea. "What I observed has been observed before. I think it unlikely another such death will add to the inventory of knowledge. But if such a case comes along, of course I will fling myself upon it. I merely doubt that another specimen will permit me to penetrate to the heart of the matter. The facts as they stand are both incontrovertible yet unsupportable by known science."

"You admit to the possibility of supernatural explanation?"

His reply was biting. "I admit no such thing. But I am forced to go outside of the normal channels of scientific thought. At the heart of this lies two mysteries: What would cause a human body to combust without outward sources of ignition, and how did the surroundings escape the fiery fate of the unfortunate victim?"

"It is devilishly baffling," I allowed. "But I agree that a respite is required. One cannot contend with the inexplicable for long, especially if progress is not being made. A change of mental scenery might allow you to look at the problem from a fresh perspective."

Yet even as I spoke those words, the expression on Sherlock Holmes's countenance suggested a dog chewing at the bone stronger than his teeth. I recognized that he was not ready to let go of this particular bone.

"Facts are stubborn, Watson. Very stubborn. Normally they are the building blocks for theory, the rungs of the logical ladder I must climb in order to achieve a solution. In this case, the facts fight one another like oil and water in solution. They refuse to combine. They will not cohere. Yet they cannot be separated, once mixed. If I could but uncover fresh facts to add to the potion, perhaps I could induce a reaction that would make all clear and simple. I fear that it is impossible in this case."

Holmes puffed away furiously, his expression a complicated knot of flesh and sinew.

"Had this occurrence been unique," he went on disconsolately, "I might have a better time of it. Perhaps I could drag in a culprit. Or possibly affix a motive. But Miss Wick was not the first victim of this phenomenon. Nor will she be the last, I imagine. The repeating pattern is what vexes me most. It can only mean that this is an old problem, possibly even an ancient one. I cannot look to the novelty of modern life for a solution. This may be a natural condition of the human body, and not anything external to it. But no substance can I find that will incinerate human flesh, reducing it to ash, yet not affect the surroundings appreciably."

"Alcohol is not the culprit, I gather."

"Dash it all!" snapped Holmes. "Alcohol is the most prominent feature in these damnable cases, yet I have immersed human muscle, bone, and every imaginable organ in it, but all organic matter refuses to burn in any meaningful way."

I felt for my friend. He was truly at a loss. His ways where those of logic and science, data and facts, and observations and inductions. None of these tools were helping him now. His natural skepticism, as sharply as it had been honed, had encountered a brick wall that could not be pierced by its probing keenness.

In an effort to be helpful, I said, "I imagine you have ruled out lightning."

"I can rule nothing out!" he said sharply. "Nothing! The fact that there were is no electrical disturbance on the night Miss Wick perished inclined me to rule it out. But alas, I dare not. It is abundantly clear that the victims in all cases I have reports on ignited suddenly and died at once. They did not have time to flee, only to combust and disintegrate. If I could ascribe such a feat to a bolt of lightning, I would happily do so. Regrettably, the literature provided me with no thunderstorms, no bolts from the blue, as it were. But if I could not admit lightning to my theories, neither can I exclude an electrical origin. Strive as I might, Watson, I cannot eliminate the impossible. I am at a loss. A dead loss."

So there of the matter stood for many months. Sherlock Holmes moved on to other cases, earned notable successes, and so his reputation grew.

Less than a year had elapsed when word was received of the second such horrible occurrence.

I half expected it, but not so swiftly. According to Holmes, these things happened at random intervals. There was no predicting when the next charred corpse would manifest.

Holmes came by where I was serving as a *locum* late one afternoon in a highly excitable state.

"Watson! Come quick if you have no patients. If you do, send them home. Another incinerated person has been discovered!"

"Where this time?" I asked, reaching for my coat and hat.

"In the very same room where Miss Wick perished!" Holmes said excitedly, all but dragging me out into open air.

"My word! Who is the victim this time?"

"Elizabeth Wick, the sister. She moved into the rooms shortly after they were made available. Apparently, she took some spiritual solace in doing so. Unfortunately, it led to her doom."

A cab was waiting and Holmes bundled me into it. His energy was astounding. I have known him to go through weeks of lethargy, and periods of high activity. Now he was a veritable dynamo.

The horses dashed through town and we came up before the dismal rooming house which looked outwardly as it had before.

Claverling the fire officer was there. He greeted Holmes somberly.

"I knew you would come, Mr. Holmes."

"And so I am here. I see Mr. Merridew is at hand."

"The poor beggar is shaken to his core. He is beside himself. Inconsolable. A second tragedy, and his thoughts are running wild."

"I will leave him to regather his wits. First I must see the room where the event transpired."

"It was by the fireplace this time," said Claverling. "Come, I will show it to you."

As we mounted the stairs, I noted a grayish haze, so different then the bluish one from before. As we approached the shut apartment door, the smell in the close air also differed from the previous incident.

For the place was redolent with the stench of burnt flesh. It was a very different, yet an equally disagreeable smell. Previously, I had considered the atmosphere to smell like cooked fat.

Of course, a burnt human being might emanate either or both odors. But I thought it so noteworthy that I called this to Sherlock Holmes his attention.

"Do you notice the odor?"

"Yes. It is very similar to that of roast pig. I am told the Polynesian cannibals who indulge in the consumption of their fellow human beings liken the taste of human flesh to that roast pork."

"Curious indeed."

Hesitating only slightly, we entered the death room.

The scene the greeted us was very different than the one before. The body of the victim lay sprawled across the hearth. It had been charred to a degree that was almost unbelievable. An arm was entirely missing, the right. Both legs were intact, and one appeared to have lost a shoe. I noticed it lying several feet away.

The rocking chair in which the previous Miss Wick had perished was not in evidence. Instead there was a comfortable overstuffed chair, quite new. Its brocaded covering showed no signs of scorching.

The body lay face down. Holmes stepped around it, studying the remains from every conceivable angle.

"It appears that the poor woman was struck down as she was about to light a fire," I ventured.

Holmes snapped, "I see no evidence of that. The logs are fresh, and there was no sign of a lucifer, or any other igniter."

"It may well have gone up with her."

"Conceivably," said Holmes. "But I would imagine that if a woman's clothing caught fire whilst she was attempting to start a blaze, the beginnings of the blaze would be evident."

The body was a horrid sight. There was not a portion of her that was untouched. There was a smudging of ash approximately where the missing arm would have rested. The head have been cooked thoroughly, but the features still yet survived, although the hair has been entirely burnt away, as was her clothing.

Kneeling, Holmes touched the body whilst I observed the surroundings. The walls were sooty. The window glass lacked the yellowish liqueur that Holmes had previously suggested was a precipitation created by the violent combustion of human flesh and fat. I did not doubt him – although such a thing had never seemed possible to me. I had attended to many burn victims, and Holmes had previously questioned me in depth on that subject. Fire tends to remove the outer layers of skin, but not penetrate very deeply into muscle or bone.

I threw off the preposterous possibility of a human body being incinerated to such a degree and found a portrait on the mantel that was grey with soot. The face was dimly visible – it was that of a youngish woman of perhaps forty. She was rather striking.

Pointing to the photograph in its frame, I asked the fire officer, "Is this the poor victim?"

Holmes's searching gaze snapped in my direction. He strolled over. Picking up the portrait, he announced, "Of course it is."

Using the fingers of a glove, Holmes lifted a line of soot off the glass covering the photograph and paid more attention to the residue than he did the image of the woman captured there.

He gave the deposit a great deal of scrutiny, rubbing his gloved fingers together and sniffing the black stuff.

"There was no question that this is a photograph of the victim. The shape of the head, the formation of the ears, and other particulars confirm it."

"Holmes," I cried out. "This woman has been cooked to a crisp! How can you be so certain?"

"The woman in the photograph lacks pendulous ear lobes, and although the configuration of the corpse's ears has been greatly deformed by fire, the fact that she lacked ear lobes in life is beyond dispute."

The patient fire officer offered a comment of his own. "Mr. Holmes, I have been studying the literature on spontaneous human ignition. It is a fact that many of the victims were found exactly in this position, sprawled up on their own hearths. In most cases, the fireplace was cold."

"But not in all," countered Holmes.

"If the act of lighting a fire is not the cause of death, one wonders if something demonic had come down the chimney to consume the poor victim," Claverling grunted.

"As outlandish as your theory sounds," Holmes admitted, "it is not to be dismissed out of hand."

"I admit gruesome spectacle rather makes one consider a supernatural agency at work. A woman burns in her own living room, and there are no scorch marks whatsoever."

"Perhaps not supernatural, but preternatural," suggested Holmes.

The fire officer looked strangely. "I fail to comprehend the difference."

"One is impossible, whilst the other is merely improbable."

"Beg pardon?"

"Consider the common humbug of a thunderbolt striking a human being and incinerating him. It is considered impossible. Lighting kills by electrical disruption of the nervous system, suppressing heart action and respiration, not through heat. The resulting electrical burns are incidental to the mortal result. Yet lightning often ignites trees it blasts, creating fires."

"I quite fail to follow your train of thought."

"That is because I am not finished. My thoughts hurl backward in time to reports of The Great Thunderstorm of October 21st, 1638. A sizable ball of fire intruded into St. Pancras Church in Widecombe-in-the-Moor, Dartmoor, smashing it to flinders before exiting in two discrete parts. Many were killed, and several badly burned, although not to the ultimate degree. Very mysterious. Reports of so-called ball lightning have persisted through the centuries, despite the skepticism of learned men."

"Do you imagine a freak of nature to be behind this phenomenon?" I demanded.

"I consider that theory to be improbable, but not demonstrably impossible," snapped Holmes. "Ball lightning has been rejected by science, yet sane persons continue to report encounters with luminous balls of light during thunderstorms. Hence, I cannot dismiss it."

He was back at the roasted corpse. This time he placed his unobstructed nostrils quite close to it. They quivered as he took in a terrible odor. He seemed to stand it well enough, but once he stood up, he resorted to his handkerchief.

Sherlock Holmes addressed the fire officer.

"If you will be good enough to summon Inspector Lestrade, I believe he will find this interesting."

"Do you suspect foul play?"

"No, I am certain of it."

I confess that I did not expect this turn of events.

After Claverling had left, I followed Holmes out onto the street.

"I beg you, Watson, to be silent as I make conversation with Mr. Merridew. I do not wish to alarm him in any way whilst we await Lestrade."

"The poor fellow," I remarked sympathetically.

"I imagine he is fated to become even poorer after the events of today," drawled Holmes.

"No doubt," said I, thinking of the reputation his little boarding house was destined to achieve. Soon the newspapers would christen it a "House of Horrors".

The landlord was beside himself, pacing madly. He did not describe circles, but rather eccentric parabolas in the trampled grass.

Holmes accosted him in his forthright manner.

"A word with you, Merridrew, if I could."

The landlord started violently, then turned. Before Holmes could pose a question, he began unburdening himself rapidly.

"It was an abominable sight, Mr. Holmes. Worse than the previous one. It happened just as before. The smell, that horrid, wretched stink alerted me. Knowing what it portended, I ran straight away to Miss Wick's room."

"I see," said Holmes. "What made you jump to such a conclusion?"

"The smell. I know it well. As for why I assumed it was emanating from Miss Wick's rooms – well you can imagine that as well as I. Where else would I first turn?"

"Your logic is impeccable," allowed Holmes. "Pray continue."

"Naturally, I used my key. When I went in, I received the full blast of smoke and I spied the remains. Although I only gave it a cursory glance, I deduced much."

"Ah! And what did you deduce in those few seconds, Mr. Merridew?"

"That Miss Wick had been in the act of lighting her fire when she was consumed. I noticed that she had thrown off a shoe, over behind the chair, as if she had attempted to flee before falling. It was uncanny. The hearth was stone cold, yet the floor beneath the body unscorched. What could produce such a baffling effect? Are there demons abroad in Southwark? Is Old Scratch himself claiming souls in his illimitable way?"

"I daresay no one could contradict your theory, inasmuch as all other theories are equally preposterous. Now tell me, by your own words you seemed more than commonly familiar with the uncanny phenomenon of inexplicable human combustion."

"Well, it was you who put me onto it in the first place, Mr. Holmes. Do you not remember? You declared that what happened to Miss Kathleen Wick was not so rare as one might suppose. Naturally, being the proprietor of a rooming house in the same parish as the Tooley Street fire, I would not want a repetition of such a tragedy. I sought out all accounts of the phenomenon I could lay hands on. They made distressing reading. Particularly, I was concerned that so many victims had fallen at their own hearths."

"Undeniably," said Holmes, "it is part of a pattern with no clear explanation. But this case differs from many."

Merridew eyes blinked rapidly. "In what way, sir?"

"It is common for the victim's trunk to be incinerated yet the extremities survive, at least in part. In this case, one arm alone seems to have been rendered into ash. I do not recall ever encountering that particular variation of the phenomenon in the literature."

"Well, my reading indicates that the state of the victims do vary considerably."

"Considerably, yes. But not with such a unique feature."

Merridew frowned. "Until such a time as the cause of these outrages can be determined scientifically, I do not see how any element can be dubbed unique. It sounds rather premature to me. But I am only a common man, with a common brain. I do not have the wits of a detective."

"How well did you know Miss Elizabeth Wick?" Holmes asked suddenly.

"She was a rare woman, a fine beauty. Such a tragedy that such a well-formed and handsome woman should be reduced to such a state. No doubt she had many years of healthy life ahead of her until this dark day."

"That is a fine compliment you have paid her, but that was not my question," returned Holmes flatly.

"Well, I did not know her intimately, if that is what you mean. She was a boarder. She had her own ways. Oh, she was friendly enough. But not excessively so. I could not tell you whether or not she was a widow. Only that she was not presently married."

Holmes pressed on. "Had she many visitors? Suitors? Relatives?"

"I would say that she had many admirers. She was popular in the neighborhood. I would not say that she had suitors so much as she had aroused the interest of the neighborhood men, regardless of their marital state, if you know what I mean."

"I take your meaning quite plainly," said Holmes. Without turning his head at the sound of familiar footfalls, he said, "Ah, I believe that Inspector Lestrade has gotten around to joining us."

Mr. Merridew turned about, spied Lestrade coming up the way, and said rather dismissively, "I cannot imagine what Scotland Yard will make of this awful tragedy."

"If you'll pardon me once more," said Holmes, stepping away and rushing to greet Lestrade.

The two men engaged in a rather animated exchange out of earshot. I made pleasantries with poor Merridew, hoping to keep his mind off his mounting troubles.

At length, Holmes returned with the inspector, and to my stark astonishment, he pointed at Mr. Merridew. "Inspector, let me suggest that you place Mr. Merridew in handcuffs whilst I explain the nature of his abominable crime."

Merridew started, and seemed at a loss for words. His natural pallor deepened astonishingly.

Inspector Lestrade produced handcuffs, but made no move to arrest the man, evidently lacking sound reason to do so.

"I should like to hear Mr. Holmes's accusations in full before I do anything official," said Lestrade.

"As I just explained to the inspector, there a certain irregularities in Mr. Merridew's account," stated Holmes.

Merridew stared wordlessly, eyes turning glassy. His forearms seemed to tremble.

"First, Merridew claimed to have been alerted to the tragedy as a result of a familiar odor. But as Dr. Watson will attest, we both noted that the smell surrounding the death of the second Miss Wick was not the odor of cooked fat, but rather roasted flesh. They are distinctly different. Smelling one might suggest the other, but only insofar the repulsiveness of the odors involved."

Merridew said suddenly, "When I smell a fire in my building, I do not question its origins. I leap into action."

"And happily land on the correct spot with the agility of a cat," said Holmes firmly. "The two odors were not identical. Yet you went to Miss Wick's room directly."

"Directly, and correctly as it turned out," snapped Merridew.

"Did you touch the body when you discovered it?"

"Absolutely not!" Merridew insisted. "I know better than to disturb a dead body before the authorities arrive. I touched nothing!"

"You touched nothing. You are certain?"

"I slammed the door and called the fire brigade. They were not long in arriving."

"If you did not touch anything, and how is it you are so confident in asserting as fact that there were no scorch marks on the floor beneath the body of the late Elizabeth Wick?"

"Why, it was plain to see that only the body was consumed. Your question, sir, seems beside the point."

"Perhaps. But the body has yet to be moved. Perhaps the time has come."

During this cold exchange, Lestrade said, "Let us look into this question."

We ascended to the second-floor flat, handkerchiefs protecting our noses once more. Lestrade went first, and so did not notice this precaution.

The inspector was taken aback by the stench once he entered the room, and he was obliged to pinch his nostrils shut and breathe through his mouth, which he guarded with the trailing portion of the linen.

His eyes were a little queer as he walked around the body. Taking a poker from the fireplace, he carefully nudged the black corpse at the shoulder. It appeared to be largely intact, for when he gave it a poke, it moved without crumbling.

The bare heath flags under the body bore no scorch marks.

Lestrade turned on Mr. Merridew and said, "It appears that you are correct, sir." He stood up and asked, "How is it you possess the knowledge, Mr. Merridew, when by your own admission you did not touch the body in any way?"

"Why – why," Merridew stammered. "I discerned no surrounding scorch marks and I suppose I drew a correct conclusion from what I witnessed." Glancing in Sherlock Holmes's direction, he added, "My understanding is that certain clever persons do the very same all the livelong day."

Ignoring the snide tone of the man's aside, Holmes asked, "How far did you advance into the room?"

"I stood upon the threshold and immediately closed the door."

"I see," said Holmes. "Let us recreate your actions by proxy. Lestrade, will you take a position on the threshold."

The man from Scotland Yard did so. Stopping at the far wall, he turned about and stood facing the interior of the room. "Please describe what you observe," requested Holmes. "Consider this a crime scene and take inventory of all that you notice."

Without hesitation. Inspector Lestrade commenced a crisp and clinical description of the body, the unpleasant soot on the walls and furniture, adding other details, leaving out nothing.

His final observation was, "The woman is wearing only one shoe. I do not see the other."

Holmes nodded with satisfaction. "You do not see the other. Because it is behind this rather substantial chair. Yet Mr. Merridew described the position of the shoe without hesitation. How is it that you were able to do perform such a feat, Mr. Merridew? Do you possess preternatural vision?"

"I did not say that I saw the shoe – only that it appeared to have been left behind with the woman attempted to flee her own combustion."

Holmes turned to me. "Dr. Watson, do you recall his exact words?"

"I do. He gave the distinct impression of having seen the shoe, for he described its position."

"From where you stand, Lestrade, do you see the location of the shod foot?"

"No, I do not."

"Come, come," said Holmes. "Put some effort into it. Strain your neck, twist your body. Surely you can perceive it if you put an effort into it. Mr. Merridew did so in with but a quick glance."

Inspector Lestrade did his best. In the end, he admitted, "I completely fail to discern the location of the shoe from this vantage point."

"Your story, Mr. Merridew," said Holmes stiffly, "appears not to be holding together very well. Let me add to the anomalies I have observed."

Holmes began pacing around the room. "First, the soot on the walls is different than the residue present on the previous tragic occasion. This soot appears to have been applied with a coal-oil lamp. It is not greasy at all. Nor is it the same color. It is also rather indifferently applied, whereas the other residue was uniform.

"I will also call your attention to the window sash. It appears to have been forced open, perhaps to let out smoke. There are fingermarks on the windowsill. I wonder whose they are?" His keen grey eyes went to the landlord's fidgety fingers.

At that, Mr. Merridew attempted to flee the room. The open door was of course blocked by Inspector Lestrade, so the frantic man turned towards the window and attempted to force it upwards.

"You'll not get me now!" he cried.

Holmes stepped in, and delivered a fist flow to the back of the man's head. It struck at the point at which the upper spine meets the lower skull. The blow rendered the fellow senseless. I had never seen such as expert work with the fist, although in the years that followed, Holmes performed similar feats.

After the man had fallen to the floor, Holmes said, "Inspector, I believe Mr. Merridew will not resist arrest if you consider his guilt clearly established."

"I do, Mr. Holmes. And I thank you most sincerely."

After Merridew was handcuffed, Lestrade strode up and asked, "What do you imagine is back of all this horror, Mr. Holmes?"

"This is supposition, but I imagine Mr. Merridew became infatuated with the Miss Wick, and she rebuffed his advances. Perhaps they were more forceful than prudent. But if you will look at the cranial remains of the poor woman, you will see an indentation suggesting a sharp blow from a heavy object. If my surmise is correct, having severely injured, if not slain Miss Wick, the abominable Mr. Merridew conjured up a novel way to cover for his crime. He surreptitiously bore the body to some other location and literally roasted it, at some point hacking off an arm and disposing of it.

"In his mind, he contrived to falsify an example of spontaneous human ignition. Although he had read deeply into the literature, he had not thought through his scheme quite so thoroughly. He failed to understand that in almost all cases, including that of the first Miss Wick, the trunk is typically incinerated, yet the extremities survive. The ashes that marked the spot of the missing limb, Inspector, you will find to be ordinary wood ash scooped out of the fireplace and arranged in the rough semblance of an arm. This would not fool an intelligent child, and it did not fool me. In the previous tragedy, particles of bone were found among the ashes. Although they were minute, they were still yet distinct from the ashes themselves. The ash I speak of is dry powder. Hardly a suitable substitute under the circumstances."

Lestrade nodded. "You will be expected to testify at the trial, Mr. Holmes."

"I look forward to it, inspector. But not as much as I look forward to the prospect of Mr. Merridew hanging for his abominations."

Merridew did hang. But not before he confessed, and revealed where the missing arm of Elizabeth Wick could be found. She was buried more or less intact beside her late sister.

As for the matter of the first Miss Wick, the inquest of 1881 returned no verdict. That mystery was never solved. Nor was Merridew implicated in that tragedy. It was an uncontested example of spontaneous human combustion and remains unsolved to this day.

In the intervening years, Holmes investigated several other such cases, including the remarkable one where two brothers, going about their business several miles apart, simultaneously ignited without a reason. They perished, alas.

In time, Holmes wrote a monograph on the subject of spontaneous human combustion. He put forth certain tentative theories, based on his observations and reading, and whilst the pamphlet was widely circulated, it came to no definite conclusion. Holmes himself confided to me that even his theories amounted to "educated rubbish".

I clearly recall him once lamenting, "It is as if I am faced with a mathematical equation to solve and some of the key integers are not numbers that I recognize, but alien symbols. The familiar numerals reassure me that I am facing a valid equation. Those that are not make it impossible for me to solve it. I've gone around and around on this matter. But I am stumped."

There the matter stands to this day. Holmes is quite certain that there is an explanation for the phenomenon. Yet every new example, every succeeding tragedy, merely adds fresh strands to the tangled web of mystery. The pattern fascinates him, but the solution continues to elude him.

Time and again, I have heard Sherlock Holmes lament, "If I could but eliminate the impossible, I would have something to go on. And yet, I cannot. I simply cannot."

I am forced to conclude that his willingness to release the singular matter of the two Wick sisters at this late date signifies that he is throwing in the towel, as it were. I cannot blame him. Perhaps future generations will unravel the riddle.

I am content to pen these words and note that whilst the problem of the two Wicks sisters was never satisfactorily concluded, Sherlock Holmes took great pride in the exposure of Mr. Merridew and his abominations.

> *"My collection of M's is a fine one," said [Holmes]. . . . [H]ere is . . . Merridew of abominable memory . . . ."*
>
> Sherlock Holmes, "The Adventure of the Empty House"

Mrs. Forrester's Complication
by Roger Riccard

Chapter I

The events of this case took place in the spring of 1881, shortly after I had taken up lodgings with the consulting detective, Sherlock Holmes, in our new Baker Street digs. I was not privy to the details at the time, as I was not sharing in many his adventures as of yet. However, it was this case that would be the catalyst for the happiest years of my life.

It was only years later that a celebratory dinner party for my engagement to Miss Mary Morstan brought Sherlock Holmes and his former client, Mrs. Cecil Forrester, into the same circle again. As we sat around the table at Simpson's in the Strand, the subject of that old case came up. Because it was this event that caused Mrs. Forrester to recommend Holmes to her young governess, now my fiancée, we implored him to tell us the details.

The detective attempted to demur, but with Mary seated on one side of him and Mrs. Forrester on the other, he was surrounded. Add in myself and Mrs. Hudson rounding out the table, and he was at quite the disadvantage, as four eager faces entreated, prodded, cajoled, and pleaded.

"Doctor, ladies," he objected. "Do you really expect me to recall the details of a case from seven years ago?"

"Yes!" came the simultaneous answer from Mrs. Hudson and myself, who had spent those seven years in his daily presence and knew exactly what his capabilities were as to memory of even the most trivial data when it concerned a case.

Taken aback by this immediate onslaught of denial of his excuse, he acquiesced and began to tell the story.

"If you remember, Doctor, my practice was not quite so lively then. Other than occasional tasks for my brother, Mycroft, in his government capacity, the majority of my work came from assistance offered to Lestrade and Bradstreet at the Yard. Fortunately, they would steer clients my way whose puzzles were inappropriate for police resources, and the rewards they offered allowed me enough to pay my share of the rent," he said, nodding to our landlady, Mrs. Hudson.

"It was in this way that my practice began to grow, as word of mouth spread my reputation," he continued, then looked at me pointedly.

"Unlike today, when I have to worry that any of my adventures might end up being published, as was the Jefferson Hope business last year."

I lifted my wineglass in his direction and merely replied, "You're welcome."

Not having gotten a rise out of me, he went on. "As I recall, Mrs. Forrester, you were referred by a cousin who lived here in London and was an acquaintance of Lestrade."

Mrs. Forrester, now in her mid-forties, with chestnut hair which curled down her cheeks and across her shoulders, nodded her winsome face. "Yes, Mr. Holmes. My cousin, Bruce McNab, was the one who thought you might be the man to solve the mystery of my missing husband."

We all started at that statement. We had only heard it referred to in the past as "a little domestic complication".

This immediately caused my Mary some concern and she looked apologetically at her employer and said, "Oh, Mrs. Forrester, I had no idea. If this is too painful for you, I insist we stop now."

Mrs. Forrester smiled and shook her head, "Not necessary, my dear. I have put the incident behind me long ago. I am just as anxious to hear how Mr. Holmes solved the case as any of you, since, when he did so, he only shared the results and not the methods."

She waved her dainty hand in Holmes's direction, bidding him to continue, and the detective did so.

"At the time of the incident, my client was living in Leith, on the north shore of Edinburgh. Her husband, Cecil, was a solicitor with a modest practice. When McNab came to me on her behalf, it was in regards to the fact that her husband had disappeared without a trace and the local police were stymied. This left her in a precarious position financially, as her brother-in-law was determined to have her husband declared dead and claim the inheritance, which included her assets under the old laws."

I spoke up and asked, "Wasn't 1881 the year the Married Women's Property Act went into effect in Scotland? Shouldn't that have protected her?"

Holmes shook his head at my interruption, like a schoolmaster correcting a pupil.

"This was late June, Doctor. The Act did not go into effect until mid-July."

I bowed my head, held my palms up from the table top in supplication, and he resumed.

"McNab came to me at the recommendation of Inspector Lestrade. I doubt you'd remember him, Watson, as he only visited Baker Street once and you merely passed through our sitting rooms at the time on your way to perform rounds at St. Barts. He was an ordinary looking fellow, whom I discerned as being a divinity student by the creases in his shoes, the wear pattern of his trouser knees, and the ink-stained fingers common to those who take copious notes.

"He told me of his cousin, Morna Forrester, her precarious position, and how the brother-in-law, Barclay Forrester, was attempting to use it to his advantage

"As I had no pressing matters in London at the time, I agreed to travel up to Edinburgh and conduct a private investigation. Thus, with a letter of introduction from Lestrade in hand, I made my way north and met with the Edinburgh police.

"I was pleased to find that an old schoolmate of mine, Ewan Gibson, [1] was working the case, and he took me through all the facts. Cecil Forrester was a hard-working solicitor of a sound legal mind with a fair reputation for success in the courts. He was a sole practitioner with no partners, though he did have a clerk who handled the more mundane tasks of the office, a fellow named Donald Duncan.

"The main facts were that Solicitor Forrester had left on a Friday afternoon to meet with a client in Eyemouth. As rail travel was not convenient, he took passage on a cutter bound for London which would drop him off at that coastal village, where he would meet his client the following morning. He was then planning to seek out a passing vessel to return home on Saturday afternoon or Sunday.

"The weekend came and went with no word. On Monday, a telegram arrived at his office from his client asking his whereabouts, stating he had not kept his appointment and the client wished to re-schedule.

"Duncan sought out Mrs. Forrester, who had not seen nor heard from her husband since lunchtime on Friday, and was concerned at the lack of communication. His disappearance was reported to the police and Her Majesty's Coast Guard.

"The cutter was a forty footer called *Harmonique,* owned by one Alick Lusk. Lusk was a young man who had taken over his father's small shipping business, ferrying goods and people back and forth between Edinburgh and London. Being a coastal vessel, he generally sailed alone, though occasionally he'd sign on a crewman or two if the weather called for rough seas, or if he had a heavy load. He had a reputation as a hard worker, but was also owing to a handful of creditors.

"The ship set sail on calm seas on Friday at one o'clock with just Lusk and Forrester on board and was expected to dock in Eyemouth that evening. According to the Harbor Master there, no vessel of that name or description arrived at any time on either Friday or Saturday. On Sunday morning, a life preserver with the name *Harmonique* was found by a fisherman just a few hundred yards off the coast. A search party was organized, and the waters around Eyemouth were searched all that day with no sign of the ship. Some few wooden planks that appeared to be from a ship's hull were retrieved from the sea about a mile out and a quarter-mile south from where the life preserver was found."

We all looked at Mrs. Forrester with sympathy at the obvious conclusion, which Holmes now stated in a most matter-of-fact tone.

"Until ports farther south could be contacted and searched, the *Harmonique* was presumed lost at sea with all hands."

"How horrible for you!" cried Mrs. Hudson, reaching out to place her hand on Mrs. Forrester's arm as it lay on the table, fingers loosely wrapped around the stem of her wineglass.

The employer of my fiancée patted my landlord's hand and replied.

"It's quite all right, dear. There's much more to the story, thanks to Mr. Holmes investigations."

Chapter II

I shall now endeavor to continue my friend's adventure in the manner to which my readers are accustomed.

Having read all the reports that Gibson had compiled, Holmes decided his next step would be a physical examination of evidence. Learning that the life preserver and hull planks were still in Eyemouth, it was decided that the first investigation would take place at Forrester's office. He and Constable Gibson arrived to find a harried Duncan with multiple papers and folders sorted into seemingly haphazard piles.

Duncan was a young man, still attending classes toward his final examinations to receive his law degree while he apprenticed with Forrester. His spare frame was just under six feet in height, and his youthful face sported a scraggly brown moustache of a military style, so common among young men of that era. His waistcoat was unbuttoned and sleeves rolled up to his elbows as he sat, feverishly attempting to bring about some order to the apparent chaos of the room.

Upon the entrance of Holmes and Gibson, he looked up in surprise, then resignation that he could not excuse the messy appearance of the office.

"Constable, I was not expecting anyone," he said, running his long thin fingers through his unkempt hair. Then he looked around and added, "Obviously."

The policeman waved his hand and replied in his Scots brogue, "Quite all right, Mr. Duncan. This is Sherlock Holmes from London. He has been engaged to look into the disappearance of yer employer."

The fellow stood up and came around the desk to shake the detective's hand, "Oh, thank you, sir! It would be a godsend if Mr. Forrester could be found alive."

Holmes took the proffered hand firmly and looked the young man over. His assessment complete, he expressed his opinion.

"I'm no miracle worker, Mr. Duncan. I shall investigate without prejudice to determine the true facts of the case, no matter where they lead. But your statement intrigues me. Do you have reason to believe that Forrester is still alive?"

The clerk went back behind the desk and sat before answering. "I suppose it's more wishful thinking. I know the evidence is against it, but Mr. Forrester was willing to take me on when a lot of law firms wouldn't because of my left-handedness."

Constable Gibson spoke up, "Why would that matter?"

Holmes replied for the young man, "Remember our old classmate, Colin Slattery? He always had to have a certain seat so he wouldn't be bumping his writing arm into his desk mate because of his left-handedness. His gyrations to avoid his hand smearing the words of what he had just written were painful to behold."

"Aye," replied the policeman. "I do recall that." Turning back to Duncan he continued, "I imagine, with all the documents ye must have to write, being left-handed would make for some difficulty."[2]

"A difficulty Mr. Forrester was willing to let me work around," replied the clerk. "Just tell me what you need, Mr. Holmes. I am at your disposal."

Holmes wanted to examine the room, and he asked some few questions of Duncan as he did so. After about twenty minutes of this, he gave the man a list of what he desired.

"If you can have those for me by four o'clock this afternoon, I should be grateful."

Duncan agreed that he would be ready upon Holmes's return, and the detective and constable went off to their next stop, the home of Mrs. Cecil Forrester.

At that time, Mrs. Forrester was a mother of two young children, both under the age of four. As such she had her hands full, keeping up the modest row house and looking after the little ones. When Holmes and Gibson arrived, she had just put them down for naps and was fixing herself a late lunch. Answering the door, she was accompanied by a black Labrador Retriever who stood warily on guard at the sight of two strangers. Emitting a low *woof,* he received a pat on the head from the plump young lady with the cherubic face. "It's all right, Pepper," she said in a soothing tone. "You remember Constable Gibson."

Gibson knelt down and scratched the dog behind the ears, speaking softly to it. He could see through to the kitchen and, noting the preparations, insisted that Mrs. Forrester not forestall her meal on their account. He then introduced Holmes as the detective that her cousin had sought on her behalf.

"I am so grateful that you have come, Mr. Holmes," she said, after inviting them to sit at her dining table. "Bruce said you were highly recommended by Inspector Lestrade as a very promising detective."

The young version of Holmes chuckled at that, "How kind of him. I have been able to steer the inspector in the right direction on some of his more puzzling cases. But your situation arouses my curiosity, Mrs. Forrester. The evidence, if you'll forgive me, seems fairly conclusive. What are your expectations of me?"

She set down the teacup, from which she had just taken a sip, and folded her hands above the table. "Something about the whole situation does not ring true. My brother–in-law's eagerness to claim the inheritance is highly suspicious. He has very heavy debts, and the timing of this incident appears too coincidental to my taste."

She paused, pulled a handkerchief from her sleeve, and held it at the ready against her cheek. "It would be no great surprise to me if Barclay had something to do with my husband's disappearance."

She reached out and placed her hand upon Holmes's forearm. "I need the truth, Mr. Holmes. Even if it means Cecil is . . . dead. The pain of not knowing is more than I can bear."

The detective looked into those pleading brown eyes and patted the hand that lay upon his sleeve. "I shall do what I can, Mrs. Forrester. I must ask some questions that may be painful, or even seem inconsequential to you, but please trust me that your truthful answers are essential to my investigation."

The beleaguered woman dabbed her eyes with her handkerchief, then refolded her hands, sat up straight, and bid Holmes to proceed.

The detective questioned her about her husband's clients, any cases that had proven difficult lately, or that he had lost. Also, about his recent behavior. Did he appear worried or secretive or distracted? How was their financial situation? Were there any overdue bills or significant payments coming due? Then, those of a more personal nature as to the state of their marriage, and how did he feel about fatherhood? Finally, he came around to Cecil's relationship with Barclay. Did they get along, were they close or estranged, etcetera.

Other than admitting that her husband seemed distracted recently, and ensuring Holmes that such was not unusual when his caseload was heavy, none of her answers caused any great concern to the detective.

At last, Holmes asked if he might examine two areas of the house: The bedroom, and the study or desk where her husband might have done work at home.

In the bedroom, he examined those sections of the closet and dresser drawers where clothes and jewelry were kept. The desk in the parlor where the solicitor sometimes did his work was bereft of any current case documents.

Gibson and Holmes bid Mrs. Forrester, "Good day," with a promise to keep her up to date on any new developments.

In the cab on the way back to Forrester's office, the constable questioned his old school mate.

"Did ye learn anything significant, Holmes?"

"Quite possibly, old friend. But it is all still in the realm of speculation. I need more data. If what I suspect comes to pass among the requests I made of Mr. Duncan, then I will have a working hypothesis to test."

"Can ye at least tell me if there's been foul play?" queried the concerned constable.

Holmes laid his elbow upon the cab window and looked out at the passing scenery, almost as if the answer would spring out from one of the shops they drove past. Finally he spoke, barely loud enough for his friend to hear. "Too soon. My mind still reels with possibilities."

Chapter III

It was just before four o'clock when the detective and the constable arrived back at Forrester's office. As they ascended the stairs, the sound of raised voices echoed down the stairwell. The high pitched tenor of young Duncan was easily discerned. The other voice was deeper, raspy, and certainly louder in its demands.

Upon their entrance, they found Duncan, standing behind his employer's desk, looking down upon a stout, middle-aged man of perhaps five feet and seven inches, with a receding brown hairline streaked with grey at the temples. The older fellow did not seem intimidated by Duncan's height and was, in fact, raising his walking stick in a threatening fashion, the lamplight flashing off a ruby ring on the hand that held it. Gibson rushed forward and yanked it from his grasp.

"There'll be none of that, Barclay Forrester!" ordered the constable who, at six-and-one-half feet and two-hundred-fifty pounds, was most intimidating. "What's yer business here?"

The older man turned with a huff. "That's the whole point, Officer. It is *my* business, and I need to see my brother's papers!"

"Ye know better than that!' declared Gibson. "The court hasn't declared your brother dead, and isn't likely to for some time. Until then, ye need to stay away from yer brother's property, both here *and* at his home. If ye bother Morna Forrester, I'll lock ye away for sure!"

"What more proof could you want?" cried the brother. "His ship was wrecked with no survivors! Bodies could float around out there for days without being found, or become waterlogged and sink."

"A fine way to talk of yer own brother! Have you no feelings at all?" denounced Gibson as he tossed the walking stick back at the smaller man, who attempted to snatch it out of the air but dropped it to the floor. He had to stoop to pick it up, much to his chagrin.

"My feelings are my own. But the police will hear them loud and clear if they keep dragging their feet on this!"

Holmes at last spoke up, "I assure you, sir, this matter could well be settled in just a few days. Interference on your part at this stage would serve no purpose, and could possibly even delay proceedings."

Forrester turned with a fury and voiced his displeasure. "Who the blazes are you to be telling me my business? What's this man doing here anyway, Gibson?"

Holmes, calm as could be, answered for himself, "My name is Sherlock Holmes. I am here from London on behalf of Mrs. Forrester to investigate her husband's disappearance."

Forrester looked at him sideways and asked, "What are you, some Scotland Yard Inspector?"

The detective smiled to himself and merely replied, "I have been known to work for the Yard, and I am currently here at the recommendation of Inspector Lestrade. I assure you that, once my investigation is complete, the courts will ensure that you will be receiving exactly what you are due."

Having swallowed the impression that Scotland Yard was now involved, the little man backed off slightly, but parted with a demand on his lips. "Then get on with it man and be quick about it!"

He pivoted on his heel and stormed out, slamming the door behind him.

"Thank you, gentlemen," piped up Duncan, now that all was quiet. As his fingers habitually found their way to run through his hair, he let out a breath he had not realized he was holding. "That man has been pestering and threatening both poor Mrs. Forrester and me with his demands. I'm glad you showed up before things got violent."

"I'll see that ye're not disturbed again," offered the big constable.

Holmes turned his attention to the young clerk and asked, "Were you able to assemble the documents I requested?"

"Aye, Mr. Holmes," he responded. "Everything you asked for is on that table." He pointed to a worktable on the opposite side of the room from the desk. There, in neat stacks, were the most recent cases of Cecil Forrester, as well as his account books. Holmes rubbed his hands together, removed his coat, and sat down, informing Gibson that he would likely be working well into the night and would report to him in the morning.

The constable left, Duncan stoked the heat stove, and the world's first consulting detective began sorting the puzzle pieces to solve his case.

Early the next morning, Holmes had Gibson meet him at the dockyards to catch the next steamer scheduled to stop at Eyemouth. En route, his old schoolmate enquired, "Did ye learn anything from those papers?"

The detective adjusted his scarf against the morning chill and replied, "Some of them were of moderate interest. The most telling fact lies in the ones that were missing. I've left a note for Duncan to make a further search and carry out certain enquiries on our behalf. Of course, it all may prove moot, based on what we discover regarding the apparent wreckage of the *Harmonique*."

Upon arrival at Eyemouth, the two investigators immediately sought out the Harbor Master, a heavy-set, older fellow named Angus Brodie, who showed them the evidence of the life preserver and hull planks.

Holmes used his lens to examine the items closely. As he studied the wooden planks, he asked Brodie, "Were these found by a fisherman or the Coast Guard?"

"A fisherman found the preserver. A Coast Guard Lieutenant Commander Niven and his crew on board the *HMS Darrow*, retrieved the planks."

"Hmm," answered the detective as he continued to examine both sides of the wooden boards. "I'd like to see the current charts and the location where these were found. Then I need to speak with Niven."

"Aye, Mr. Holmes," answered Brodie, his thick Scots burr filtered by a heavy grey beard and moustache and winding its way around the short stub of a pipe in his teeth. "I've charts marked out for ye. The *Darrow* is out on patrol, but should be coming in within the hour."

Gibson, unable to contain his curiosity, asked his old friend, "What do ye see, Holmes? Is there any evidence one way or the other?"

In response, Holmes handed the magnifying glass to the constable and said, "Look for yourself. Note especially the edges and what would have been the inner surface of the hull. Tell me what you observe."

Peering carefully through the powerful lens, Gibson worked his way along the edges and reverse side of the longest plank, which was about four feet in length. He spoke as he inspected the wood.

"One end is sawn clean and straight, obviously in its original condition. The other end is broken and jagged. The outer surface is painted yellow and the *Harmonique* was known to be yellow and white. The edges are smooth and straight, such as is common for hull planks."

Turning it over and peering along the inner surface, especially the jagged end, Gibson finished his examination and declared, "There doesn't seem to be anything remarkable along this side. Just plain unpainted wood."

Holmes, now seated in a chair across from Brodie's desk with his elbows propped on the arms, pointed at the constable with his long fingers steepled in front of his chest and spoke.

"You see what you expect to see, old friend. But you do not observe. Examining the edges, I note no less than seven places where the yellow paint has interceded. A watertight hull would not allow paint to drip through like that. You will also note that there are no holes for fastening screws. Finally, how did this piece, or any of them for that matter, break away from the boat? There is no damage to the outside from being struck by some external force and there are no signs of indentation, nor the charring of an explosion on the inside."

Chastened, Gibson handed the lens back to Holmes and asked, "So, what are ye saying? This is not from the *Harmonique*?"

"Certainly not from her hull, though I do believe the *Harmonique* left it behind, along with the life preserver, which you will note is quite old with faded letters and checked surface. Hardly in the condition one would keep for emergencies."

"So ye're thinkin' these were left on purpose?" enquired the constable.

"That is my belief," stated the detective.

Brodie spoke up and offered, "If ye be expecting some shenanigans or foul play, Mr. Holmes, ye may be on to something. Alick Lusk is suspected as a man who can be bought to run contraband or criminals to various ports o' call. He's never been caught, but circumstantial evidence has often pointed in his direction."

"Thank you, Mr. Brodie, that is helpful. May I see those charts now?"

The three men gathered round a chart table where Brodie explained the tides and currents of the day that Forrester should have been arriving.

Gibson asked a question, "I believe Holmes is on the right track, but if someone should ask, is there any possibility of an iceberg strike?"

Brodie stroked his beard in thought, then pulled the pipe from his mouth and pointed to the chart with its stem. "T'is certainly not unheard of, though they be more common to the North Atlantic rather than the North Sea. But if ye look at where they be calved and the various currents, t'is more likely they would flow closer to Europe than Scotland. It's also late in the year and water temperatures would be bound to melt anything afore it reached this far south."

Satisfied, the constable looked to his friend, "Well, Holmes, if Forrester is on the run, where do you think he would go? All English ports to the south have been notified to be on the lookout for the *Harmonique* or its wreckage, and we've heard nothing."

The detective peered at the charts for a long time and finally replied, "The possibilities narrow, Gibson. I should like to finish our business with Niven and return to Edinburgh on the next boat to review the missing man's papers one more time."

"The next boat north won't be 'til the morning tide, Mr. Holmes," offered the Harbor Master. "I can recommend a hotel for the night if ye wish."

Disappointed, but unable to overcome the reality of circumstance, Holmes agreed, and he and the constable set off to arrange rooms before proceeding to meet the *Darrow* when she came in.

Lt. Commander Niven proved to a young man, just slightly older than Holmes, and of a lean, sinewy build with light brown hair and clean-shaven face. His pea-coat was soaked with the mist of the day's patrol as he welcomed Gibson and Holmes aboard. Once in his cabin, he stoked the stove, shucked out of his coat, and sat behind his desk, while his visitors took the two guest chairs, merely unbuttoning their own overcoats in deference to the stove's heat.

The interview was short. Holmes ascertained the *Darrow's* search pattern and asked what Gibson took to be an odd question, but found himself surprised at the Coast Guard officer's reply.

"When the fisherman reported finding the life preserver, did he note if the boat's name was face up or down?"

Niven replied promptly, "Face up. He was familiar with the *Harmonique* and was surprised when he saw the name."

"And the planks your own crew found – were they yellow side up?"

"Why, yes, Mr. Holmes. I noted that in my log as it seemed unusual that all of them were face up like that."

Holmes smiled at this confirmation of his supposition, then enquired, "One final point, sir. What was the weather like off to the east on the day the *Harmonique* was due?"

Niven grabbed his logbook and flipped to the appropriate page, "Wind out of the northwest at twelve knots, waters calm, skies clear, temperature at fifty-seven degrees."

Holmes rose, thanked the officer, and led Gibson back to the hotel. As they walked, Gibson remarked, "So, the weather was perfect for sailing. There's no indication she was struck, or blown up by unstable cargo. What about pirates?"

Holmes shook his head as he continued his long strides, then suddenly turned into a telegraph office. As he wrote out a message, he answered his companion. "While modern day pirates still exist, preying on small, unescorted cargo ships, their presence is unlikely in this case. That scenario does not explain the planted life preserver and counterfeit planks. No, my friend. Forrester has either been abducted, or fled the country on his own."

Chapter IV

After the telegram was sent, Holmes and Gibson returned to their hotel. That evening, as they dined, a message arrived in response to Holmes's earlier enquiry. He tore open the form as Gibson tore into his halibut steak.

A brief glimpse of a smile crossed the detective's lips and the Edinburgh constable questioned his friend.

"Is it what ye expected, Holmes?"

Folding the paper and placing it in his inner breast pocket, Holmes proceeded to delve into his own meal as he answered, "It is a piece that fits nicely into the puzzle we face. I now have some direction which I can use to point to further enquiries."

He checked his watch, "I have a good half-an-hour before my next telegram can reach its recipient. I suggest we enjoy our meal, since there will be little time for breakfast before we sail on the morning tide."

Afterward, the two gentlemen proceeded once again to the post office to send Holmes's telegram.

"Who are ye sending these messages off to?" asked Holmes's old school chum as they left the telegrapher to walk back to their hotel.

"The earlier one was to friend Duncan who, in spite of appearances, is a well-organized fellow. Much more so than his employer. His answer has given me what I need to make a request of a contact I have in the government, who can make discreet enquiries in certain foreign countries."

"Ye suspect Forrester's on the Continent?"

Holmes stopped to light a cigarette before replying. "With near certainty. Whether by choice or by force, I have not yet ascertained. But an answer to my latest telegram should at least tell us where our search should continue, for I am convinced that the *Harmonique* did not sink as we were supposed to believe."

The next morning found a page knocking on Constable Gibson's hotel room door to deliver a telegram at a quarter-to-six. As he had already arisen and was dressing to catch the early boat north, he answered immediately. Upon reading the message, he stepped across to Holmes's door and found his knock immediately answered by the fully dressed detective.

"Look here, Holmes," he cried, holding the form out for his friend to read. "Someone broke into Forrester's home last night!"

Holmes quickly perused the telegram and declared, "The game is afoot, Gibson! I suggest you put the Forrester home and office under guard. I will telegraph Mrs. Forrester and request her to take leave to stay with her cousin in London until this case concludes."

Messages being sent, the two boarded ship and by late afternoon were again in Edinburgh. Holmes suggested that Gibson report in to his superiors while he made enquiries at various locations near the docks. They agreed to meet in one hour at the Forrester home.

At the scheduled time, they were at the place of the foiled burglary, sitting with Morna Forrester to learn the particulars.

"Mrs. Forrester," enquired Holmes, "we have the police report, but please tell us what happened in your own words and pray, be precise as to details."

The lady described how she was awakened by the dog barking just after three a.m. From her upstairs bedroom, she could hear a man's voice cry out in pain, and she rushed out to the landing with the thought of bolting herself into her children's room to protect them. She had snatched up her jewelry box and her husband's pistol case on the way. Seeing the dog with its teeth sunk into the intruder's arm, prone on the floor by the open front door, she took courage and kneeled to set down her jewelry box and retrieve the gun from its case. To her great surprise, it was empty, and she dropped it and ran with her jewels to her original destination. She told her children to hide in the closet while she kept a lookout through the crack in the door, which she held ajar. Though she could no longer see the entryway, the dog's growling and the intruder's cries of pain carried on for about a half-a-minute. Then she heard the dog yip in pain and a door slam.

"Pepper continued barking and was scratching at the door, trying to give chase," she recalled. "I called her off and she limped over to me and lay at my feet. I felt around her, looking for wounds and discovered a spot on her ribs that was sensitive. The brute must have kicked or kneed her hard enough to make her lose her grip so he could get away."

"Did you get a look at his face?" enquired the detective.

"No, sir. He was dressed all in black and was wearing one of those head masks. You know, like fishermen wear in the winter."

"A balaclava?" suggested Gibson.

"Yes, one of those."

"Could you judge his height or weight? Did he say anything that would let you describe his voice?" continued the detective.

"It was hard to tell his size in the dark, with him curled up on the floor fighting Pepper like that. Only a small wall lamp near the top of the stairs was still lit for the night. He wasn't tall and thin like you, Mr. Holmes. Just an averaged-size fellow. He didn't say anything other than his cries of pain. I would say they were more tenor than bass, if a musical reference would help."

"Does the dog usually stay in the house?" asked Holmes.

"This time of year she stays in her doghouse in the back yard at night. Unless my husband is out of town. Then she stays in here with us."

"A fact unlikely to be known by anyone outside the family," commented the detective.

"I should think so, Mr. Holmes. Who advertises the sleeping patterns of their pets?"

"What do ye think happened to yer husband's gun?" asked Gibson.

The beleaguered woman played with the handkerchief in her hands, trying unsuccessfully to stop them from shaking. Finally she replied, "I don't know. It's his old service revolver. He hasn't shot it in years. Not since he showed me how to use it shortly after we got married, in case of emergencies."

"Was he feeling threatened lately? Perhaps by a former client?" asked Holmes.

"He never said anything. He seemed perfectly normal up until the time he disappeared. Oh, Mr. Holmes, where could he be?"

Holmes tilted his head, then took the woman's shaking hands into his own.

"I've only theories at this point, madam. But I am hoping to have an answer soon. Did you make arrangements to stay with your cousin in London?"

"Yes. We go down on the morning train."

Gibson, chimed in, "The guards will remain posted outside until you leave and escort ye to the station. Have no fear, Mrs. Forrester."

"Thank you, Constable. But what if it was a burglar? If he finds us gone, he'll be back, won't he?"

"With your permission, I'll have Mr. Duncan spend his nights here while you're away. Does he get along with Pepper?" Holmes asked, as an afterthought.

"Oh, yes, yes, that's a fine idea. Pepper is quite used to Donald. He's been here often."

"Then the two of them, with police patrolling outside, should be quite sufficient to keep the house safe. I will send word as soon as I can to you at your cousin's."

The next stop for the detective and the constable was the office of Cecil Forrester, where Holmes explained his plan to Duncan. The young fellow was quite eager to be of service and readily agreed to the arrangement.

Then Holmes and the apprentice went over the information, about which the detective had telegraphed the day before. Reviewing the papers and receipts, Holmes suddenly stood and cried, "I have you!"

Donning his hat and coat, he swore Duncan to secrecy and bustled Gibson off to the nearest telegrapher and sent another wire to London.

"We've one more stop, old friend," declared Holmes. "Have you the address of Barclay Forrester?"

Arriving at the home of the solicitor's brother, the door was answered by the housekeeper, a dour old woman with her grey hair pulled back into a severe bun. It gave her a face a sour countenance, which was complemented by a raspy voice.

"The master's not home." she declared upon Gibson's inquiry. "Gone off to Glasgow on business."

She started to close the door, but Holmes's hand grabbed the handle and he stepped inside, his foot now braced against the bottom edge. "Excuse me, madam, but we are quite concerned for Mr. Forrester's safety. It is our belief he was the victim of an altercation last night and suffered injuries. We have the culprit in custody and should like him to make an identification for us."

The housekeeper's features softened slightly and she opened the door to allow the men to enter. "Now that you mention it, he didn't seem quite himself this morning. Had to use his left hand to carry his luggage and was walking with a bit of a limp."

"That sounds like the type of injuries our witness described," piped up Gibson, playing along with the detective's game.

Holmes eyes wandered about the room, taking in all the information he could glean about the man, and then asked, "Where does he stay when in Glasgow?"

"He's at the Mackintosh Station Hotel," replied the spinster.

"May we see his room? We'd like to see if his clothes of last evening have any evidence we can use against his attacker."

"Well, I suppose that'll be all right, if it'll help you convict the brute. Follow me."

She led the investigators upstairs to Forrester's bedroom where they found bloody bandages and a gentleman's shirt, torn at the forearm, stuffed into the heat stove, where it had not yet been fully consumed.

Holmes made one more request of the old woman, "Where is the lumber room, madam? I should like to find a bag of some sort to transport this evidence."

The housekeeper led them down the hall and pointed a room at the end. Holmes entered and soon returned with a suitable canvas bag for their purpose. He assured the woman that the evidence collected would "surely convict the culprit," and the men left her, advising her that they would contact Forrester themselves in Glasgow.

Returning finally to the Edinburgh police building, the two investigators settled into chairs at Gibson's desk, where the constable questioned his old friend.

"What made you suspect Barclay when Mrs. Forrester said the culprit had a tenor voice? Barclay's more of a bass."

Holmes responded in the lecturing voice that I'd grown accustomed to over the years, "The panic of the moment generally causes the human voice to rise by an octave or two. A true tenor would have sounded more like an alto or even a soprano under those conditions. Thus, it was more likely to be the brother, rather than, say, Duncan."

Gibson nodded, wrote out a warrant for the arrest of Barclay Forrester, and had it dispatched to his counterparts at the Glasgow police headquarters.

Chapter V

"Well, Holmes, we've solved the attempted burglary of last night, but what of our larger case?" asked Constable Gibson as he leaned forward, his large hands folded on the desk before him.

In response, Holmes took his briarwood pipe and tobacco pouch from his pocket. Once he had it going strong, with a sweet aroma permeating the area about Gibson's desk, he then pulled another item from the canvas bag and tossed it in his friend's direction as he sat back in his chair, his long legs stretched to their fullest and languidly voiced his thoughts.

Gibson snatched the object out of the air and examined it briefly. "A knot from a thick board, probably oak. So what?"

"Look closely, man. There are yellow flecks of paint that match those found on the planks in Eyemouth. In addition, I found speckles of that paint on the floor of Barclay Forrester's lumber room. The brother must be in on the scheme. As to motive, I am as yet uncertain," he said. "But the facts suggest that Cecil Forrester wished to start a new life under a new name and cut all ties to his practice and his family. When we searched his rooms, it appeared that his most valuable possessions were missing. His closet was bereft of more clothes that would be needed for a weekend trip, as was his jewelry box of several pairs of cufflinks and tie pins. Not to mention his taking of his pistol.

"The paperwork missing from his office, along with mentions of persons and accounts without corresponding documents to attach them to any particular case, also gave rise to the specter of a secret client, or more likely, a secret identity. In particular, there are references to Rotterdam for no apparent case-related reason.

"Then there is the questionable Alick Lusk. As Lt. Commander Niven informed us, he is a shady character whom someone could buy off to take a detour or make an unscheduled stop. After dumping the so-called evidence of wreckage near Eyemouth, he could easily have changed course for the Netherlands, as Rotterdam is the largest port along Europe's western coast. An easy place to blend in and hide.

"Finally, during my enquiries among the boatyard shops, I found that a gentleman of Cecil Forrester's description had ordered a new life preserver. He told the maker it was for a boat he was buying. I believe it was to substitute for the one he would fling overboard where he had calculated the tide would take it into Eyemouth harbor."

Gibson whistled softly, "That's quite a tale, Holmes. If ye're right, how will we track down Cecil Forrester? Will he even stay in Rotterdam, or use it as a jumping off point to somewhere else on the Continent? And how does his brother fit in?"

Holmes sat up straighter, then crossed his right ankle over his left knee as he leaned on Gibson's desk with a sharp elbow, "I believe Cecil enlisted his brother's help with the promise that he would inherit what was left behind, including the income from Mrs. Forrester's own inheritance, which was divided between her and her cousin as separate sources of income from the McNab family estate. Somehow, Barclay Forrester realized he hadn't received all the papers necessary from his brother in order to cash in and pay off some immediate debts. Unwilling to wait until an official death notice released the inheritance, he broke into his brother's home in hopes that they would be there, since young Duncan was putting up quite a resistance at the office.

"I doubt the man had ever been to his brother's house when his brother wasn't at home. Thus, he assumed the doghouse in the backyard was the sleeping quarters of the retriever, not knowing that she slept indoors when her master was out of town."

"Well," pronounced the big Scot, "with the evidence we've got, Barclay will go to prison for sure. Perhaps he can be persuaded to give us the facts of his brother's scheme in return for some consideration."

Holmes tapped out his pipe and grumbled, "Barclay Forrester is a rogue without conscience. I've no doubt he would have turned his sister-in-law and her children out without a second thought. I should prefer to exhaust all our other avenues before making any sort of deal with the man."

"Can we prove a crime on Cecil Forrester's part?" countered Gibson.

"Not yet," murmured the detective. "But let us see what the morrow brings."

The next day saw the arrest and transfer of Barclay Forrester back to Edinburgh Gaol to await trial. Mrs. Forrester and her children were off to her cousin's home in London and Sherlock Holmes waited impatiently for answers to his previous telegrams. His hotel room was layered in a blue-tinged haze from the many pipes he had smoked, as his mind considered and discarded several scenarios which might explain Cecil Forrester's behavior.

At just after three in the afternoon, an answer from London arrived at last.

> *Agents report subject at Bilderberg Hotel, Rotterdam, under name Henry Boswachter. Boat anchored and set to stay in port for one week. Need evidence of crime to detain and extradite.*

Taking up this verification, Holmes immediately left for Forrester's office to consult with Duncan. The young man expressed even more shock than he would have had his employer's body been found washed up on some deserted shore.

"This is incredible, Mr. Holmes!" he cried upon hearing the news. "Granted, business is only marginal at the moment, but how could he leave his family behind? Mrs. Forrester is a charming woman, and the children are well-behaved and healthy. What could he be thinking?"

"His motives are not my concern at the moment," answered the detective. "I need to know if there is some law which can be invoked to force his return."

Duncan, running his fingers through his hair, began thinking out loud in a desultory tone.

"Hmm, he's not been gone long enough to be charged with family abandonment, and there's no proof he wasn't planning to come back.... Perhaps I can go through our current cases and see if he has progressed according to the contracted timetables. If not, we may be able to charge him with breach of contract, but that's only civil. You probably need a criminal charge to force an extradition."

Holmes nodded and placed his hand on the apprentice's shoulder. "See what you can find. I'll be at police headquarters."

Joining Gibson, Holmes and the constable continued discussing options for bringing Forrester home.

"I've dispatched a telegram to the Rotterdam police, informing them of the situation and giving them both Forrester's name and alias, as well as the hotel," recounted the big Scotsman.

"But unless he commits a crime there that makes him *persona non grata*, I'm not sure there's much we can do without getting his brother to implicate him."

Holmes mulled over their predicament as he and Gibson drank coffee at the constable's desk. Finally he put down his cup and said to his old school mate, "It's time to confront Barclay Forrester. But I believe our best tactic is to threaten rather than to bargain."

The two men stood to walk back to the cells when a messenger arrived with a telegram, which he handed to the constable. Breaking the seal on the form, Gibson read aloud for Holmes's benefit:

"It's from the *Koninklijke Marechaussee,* the Rotterdam police." Hr read:

> *Henry Boswachter found dead in hotel room. No foul play suspected but Lusk held for questioning. No other identification found. Autopsy to follow.*
>
> *Captain Jan Jensen, KMar*

"Well, that's an unexpected turn of events," continued the constable. "Any suggestions as to what we do now, Holmes?"

The detective pondered this new development for several moments before replying, "I believe we still need to confront the brother. Only now, I've a new tactic to use. Please follow my lead and do not mention that Cecil is dead."

The two men walked back to the cells with purposeful strides and had the guard let them in to Barclay Forrester's cell, where he lay on his bed.

Upon their entrance, he sat up and demanded, "This is false imprisonment! You have no cause to hold me here!"

Holmes leaned back against the bars, his long arms folded across his chest, and cocked his head at little man.

"We have proof you attempted to burgle your brother's house," he said, matter-of-factly.

"Impossible!" cried Forrester, "I wasn't there!"

"The dog, Pepper, would quite disagree," answered the detective. "She tore enough of your clothing off to match up with the garments you attempted to burn."

"Bah! One piece of cloth looks just like another."

"Not when you compare the dog's teeth marks. Besides, we have an eyewitness."

"That's ridiculous! If the dog attacked a prowler, it would have been in the front hall. My sister-in-law sleeps upstairs. She would have gone to the children at the sound of any intrusion."

Holmes smiled, "You are assuming that all were upstairs at the time. Being a bachelor, you are likely not aware of the irritating habits of young children who leave their rooms in the middle of the night in search of a drink of water or a need to use the loo."

"You'd take the word of a child over me?"

Gibson spoke up. "A child who would certainly know his uncle by sight."

"In the dark?" asked their prisoner, skeptically.

Holmes added, "You are also likely unaware that the light at the top of the stairs is perfectly position to reflect off the mirror downstairs. You believe your masked face protected you, but both your nephew and your sister-in-law recognized the distinctive ruby ring as the light reflected red on your left hand."

Barclay Forrester looked down at his empty hand, from which all jewelry had been confiscated. He said nothing, but the sag to his countenance revealed the sting of defeat he felt.

Holmes pounced upon this chink in the man's armour. "There is also the matter of your attempted fraud at trying to collect your brother's inheritance."

This new attack caught the culprit off guard. "Wha . . . what are you talking about? My brother's dead. The inheritance is mine."

The London detective shook his head and announced, "Your brother is currently in the Netherlands, being held by the Rotterdam police. He will soon be extradited back here, and I am sure he will spin whatever tale is most favorable to him, no matter where that leaves you."

The little man stood up in defiance at that scenario. "No! It was all Cecil's idea. He's been acting strange lately, though he puts up a good front for his wife. He kept saying 'they' were after him, and it wasn't safe for him to stay in Edinburgh."

Gibson demanded, "Just who are 'they'?"

"That's just it. He wouldn't tell me. He just kept insisting that the only way he and his family would ever be safe was to fake his death and move to another country. When he thought he was in the clear, he would send for Morna and the children, but until then they were to know nothing about it, for their own safety."

"There is nothing in his papers to indicate that anyone was after him," countered Holmes.

"All I know is what he told me," replied Barclay with pleading in his eyes.

Gibson was not satisfied, however. "Then why all the fuss at the office, and why did ye break into your brother's house?"

Forrester wrung his hands and looked at his captors. "Cecil wanted me to send him money to live on, but he forgot to give me the letter of authorization and his bank account number before he left. I tell you, he hasn't been thinking clearly. I had hoped I would find it amongst his papers."

"I've been through all his papers," replied Holmes. "There is no such document."

The brother raised his fists in the air in exasperation and cried, "I tell you it was *his* plan! I cannot explain it. I only agreed to go along with it because he felt so much in danger."

"Sit down!" ordered Gibson, looking down upon the smaller man. Slowly, Forrester obeyed.

Holmes added, thoughtfully, "We'll attempt to verify your story, Forrester. But rest assured, the truth will be revealed."

"Then I shall soon be free, Mr. Holmes, for that is what I've told you."

Chapter VI

Back at Gibson's desk, the constable turned to his friend and asked, "When did ye find out about Mrs. Forrester and the laddie seeing Barclay's ring?"

Holmes took out a cigarette and lit it, replying "They did not. It was a calculated bluff on my part, and Forrester took the bait."

The big man slapped his desk and let out a loud guffaw, "I suppose that bit about the dog's teeth marks was a lie also?"

"That," replied Holmes, "can actually be proven scientifically. I just haven't had the opportunity yet to make those comparisons. Remember, Gibson, when dealing with the criminal class you must be more clever than they. If that includes using their methods of prevarication, then so be it."

Gibson folded his hands and leaned forward on his desk. "How will we prove his story, what with Cecil being dead?"

"I have a thought, but it requires more research. The autopsy results will be critical." Suddenly, Holmes stood and announced, "I shall be at the university library. If you hear any more, you can reach me there. If not, I shall meet you for dinner at my hotel."

That evening, Constable Gibson found Sherlock Holmes sitting at a corner table with papers and telegrams next to his coffee cup.

"I see ye've been busy, Holmes."

"Testing theories, my friend," answered the detective. "Have you any news from Rotterdam?"

"No. I suspect the autopsy may take a day or two. No word on what they've done with Lusk. Do ye believe he's involved in Forrester's death?"

Holmes shook his head, "If my suspicions prove correct, Lusk may only be guilty of accepting an unusual commission. It's possible he may have even been unaware of Forrester's activities in throwing the life preserver and planks overboard, if he were busy at the helm."

"I don't know," pondered the constable as he accepted a menu from the waiter. "The timing seems awfully convenient."

Holmes lay his long fingers upon the stack of papers in front of him, "The timing may have been entirely up to Forrester, likely without Lusk even knowing it."

"Ye be talkin' in riddles, Holmes. What have ye found?" queried his old friend.

"Enough to make a special request of the Rotterdam coroner. The results may tell us all," was all the detective would say on the matter.

Frustrated, Holmes's fellow alumnus tucked his napkin into his collar and prepared to delve into his dinner. As he was cutting his meat, he asked one more question, "What of the paper ye found at Cecil's office? How does that fit in?"

Holmes smiled, "Again, a little prevarication on my part, just to judge his reaction. That paper was indeed an authorization letter signed by Cecil to allow Barclay temporary access to his brother's funds. However, until this cloud of suspicion dissipates, I think it is in the best interest of my client not to permit any such thing."

Gibson smiled, "Aye and the law would take a dim view of a suspected murderer being able to use ill-gotten gains for his defense. I think we can safely declare that letter as evidence until the investigation is complete."

Holmes raised his wineglass in appreciation of Gibson's grasp of the situation and the two drank a toast of silent agreement.

By the next afternoon, Holmes had pieced together an extraordinary and most unique hypothesis while sitting in Forrester's office with young Duncan. Armed with a myriad of facts derived from a new interpretation of certain papers and verification from Duncan of his employer's skills in certain areas, the detective now proceeded to Edinburgh police headquarters.

Finding Gibson at his desk, he started to announce his discoveries when the big Scotsman held up a new telegram.

"The autopsy results are in, Holmes," he declared. "Forrester died of a brain tumor."

"Located in the frontal lobe, no doubt," replied Holmes.

'Why, yes. How could possibly know that?"

Holmes sat at the side chair of Gibson's desk and proceeded with his findings. "As I told you, my new roommate is a doctor. As such, he leaves medical journals lying about, which I occasionally take up to read when the London press is lacking in anything pertinent to my profession. Remembering a recent article about brain tumors and their effect on personality, I researched the topic further at the University of Edinburgh's most excellent library yesterday.

"In my wire to the Rotterdam coroner, I suggested such a condition may have been a cause of death. I am gratified that my suspicions have proven correct."

"But what does it mean, Holmes?"

"Cecil Forrester was not responsible for his actions. The tumor affected certain cognitive areas of his brain and, while suppressing some, it also caused paranoia. He truly believed that he was in danger. The brother's story is very likely true. I found papers establishing multiple identities, and Duncan has confirmed that his employer was fluent in Dutch and German. No doubt, he would have left Rotterdam for Germany, leaving Lusk to tell anyone who asked that he was still in the Netherlands."

"Where does that leave our case, then?" asked Gibson.

Holmes leaned forward with his sharp elbows on his knees and fingers steepled in front of his lips. His countenance was almost prayer-like. But instead of supplicating to a higher power, his brain was calculating a variety of possible scenarios. Finally he focused on a singular outcome and sat up.

"Morna Forrester is my client. Barclay committed a crime against her, and I've no doubt would have committed even more reprehensible, if not illegal, acts, should he have gotten his hands on the inheritance. He needs to remain jailed for the time being, as his guilt for burglary is in no doubt.

"I presume the Rotterdam police will need an official identification of Cecil Forrester before they will return the body and issue a death certificate in that name?"

The constable nodded his head. "Yes. Either a relative or a British government official will be required to make a positive identification, I'm sure."

"Then I suggest we can use government 'red tape' to our advantage for once. With Barclay in gaol, Mrs. Forrester is the only next of kin who can identify her husband. I believe that I can persuade her to not be in any hurry to do so."

Gibson looked askance at his friend, "Why on earth would she not want to bring him home immediately for burial?"

Chapter VII

Back at Simpson's restaurant, Holmes looked across the table at Mrs. Forrester, and with one of those flashing smirks of his that one would miss if one blinked, he continued, "Because it was in her best interest to do so."

She nodded and he turned to me and declared, "You brought up the *'Married Women's Property Act'*, Doctor. Section 5 deals with the Husband's consent, dispensed with in certain cases. It goes something to the effect of:

> *Where a wife is deserted by her husband, a judge of the Court of Session may dispense, with the husband's consent, to any deed relating to her estate.*

"By delaying Mrs. Forrester's identification and having brother Mycroft tie up the government's expediency for three weeks, the Act went into effect. Her estate, and that of her deceased husband, remained in her control."

"What of Barclay Forrester?" asked my fiancée. "I've never heard of him before this."

Mrs. Forrester answered. "Brother Barclay agreed to sign a contract releasing any claims upon Cecil's estate in return for my dropping the burglary complaint against him. I gave him one-hundred pounds to assist with his debts, and demanded that he never contact me or my children again."

"What of that young Duncan fellow?" asked Mrs. Hudson, ever the mother hen.

Holmes replied, "Donald Duncan managed to keep Forrester's clients satisfied with his work, and is now a successful solicitor in his own right."

Mrs. Forrester picked up the conversation from there.

"And you know the rest. I moved to England to be near my cousin in Vauxhall, and hired Miss Morstan as governess for my children."

She looked at Mary, took her hands in both of hers and said, "The children and I are very sorry to lose you, my dear. But I could not be happier in your choice of husband."

They both turned and gazed upon me, with such love, admiration, and respect as I have ever had thrust in my direction. I'm sure my face was coloring when I was rescued by the voice of my friend as he stood with wineglass in hand.

"Friends, all, may I propose a toast?" said Sherlock Holmes in his most gracious tone. "To the future John and Mary Watson. Here's to the groom with a bride so fair, and here is to the bride with a groom so rare. Congratulations, my dear friend, whom I shall sorely miss. Miss Morstan, I do hope you will let me borrow your husband from time to time, for I am lost without my Boswell."

Such praise from my usually taciturn friend did not help my embarrassment. Then Mary replied, "I should not be so selfish as to deprive you of his talents, Mr. Holmes, so long as you promise to keep him safe during these 'interesting little problems' that come your way."

Holmes saluted her with his wineglass, replied, "My word of honor," and we all drank to the future, blissfully unaware of the joys, heartaches, and adventures that would come our way.

> *"I have come to you, Mr. Holmes," she said, "because you once enabled my employer, Mrs. Cecil Forrester, to unravel a little domestic complication. She was much impressed by your kindness and skill."*
> *"Mrs. Cecil Forrester," he repeated thoughtfully. "I believe that I was of some slight service to her. The case, however, as I remember it, was a very simple one.*
> *"She did not think so . . . ."*

The Sign of the Four

NOTES

1 – Watson will meet Gibson years later when he is Chief Constable for Edinburgh and requests Holmes's help in a case that is written up by the Doctor as "The Eleven Pipe Problem ", found in *Sherlock Holmes Adventures for the Twelve Days of Christmas* by Roger Riccard (Baker Street Studios, 2015),

2 – The typewriter, invented in 1874, would go a long way toward alleviating this issue. However, its commercial use did not become widespread until the mid-1880's.

The Adventure of Vittoria, the Circus Belle
by Tracy Revels

"It is disaster, Mr. Holmes! Catastrophe! You must come to my aid or all is lost – and not just for myself, but for more than a hundred poor souls who depend on me for their livelihoods. Name your price, sir, but drop whatever business you have and come with me to Oxford. There is not a moment to lose. When I think of what, even now, might be happening to my poor dear girl, it is more than my heart can bear!"

The speaker of these impassioned words, which had come between great sobs and hard gasps for breath, was a short and stout gentleman of some sixty years. He had burst into our rooms just as we settled at the breakfast table, a perfect cyclone of garish clothing and long, grizzled hair, reeking of gin, and none too steady on his feet. I had been on the verge of heaving him bodily through the doorway when Holmes halted me, intrigued by this ungodly apparition's mention of a single name: *Vittoria*.

"So the famous circus belle has gone missing," Holmes said, making an aimless ramble around the room as our visitor, at my friend's invitation, wolfed down the remains of our morning meal. "Surely, Watson, you have heard of the lady?"

I confessed my ignorance. Holmes waved me toward the Index. Our guest, who bore the rather unlikely moniker of Sebastian Marvela, spoke through a mouthful of half-chewed rashers.

"The finest lass who ever stood upon the sawdust! She is star of our show, the most talented thespian of our age! A wonder of the universe! She has performed before more crowned heads than the Swedish Nightingale! Given dozens of benefit concerts for orphans and their schools! And at least five gentlemen of noble rank and immense wealth have bid for her hand in marriage, yet she has turned them all down, for she belongs, body and soul, to our little family – *Marvela's Marvelous Menagerie and Circus*."

While the gentleman waxed eloquent, I quickly located the entry for Vittoria. It was at the bottom of a page, and revealed that she was a noted sideshow performer, famous for singing, dancing, playing the flute, and reciting Shakespearean sonnets.

"You have found her?" Holmes asked.

"I have. If you will forgive me for saying so, it seems she has a most unusual résumé for a circus performer. Surely a lady this gifted should be in the legitimate theater."

Marvela's face went crimson. Clearly, I had insulted his trade. Holmes, however, held out a placating hand to him, forestalling an outburst.

"If you will be so kind as to turn the page, Watson, I believe you will find her *carte de viste* pasted on the other side."

I did as Holmes instructed. A gasp of horror escaped my lips, and I nearly dropped the book on my toes.

"Good heavens! She . . . she is . . . ."

"The Circus Belle!" Marvela thundered, pounding a fist on the table. He winced. Clearly, his outrage had made him forget his obvious overindulgence of the night before, but the violent action had recalled it to him. "You must not judge her by her appearance," he whimpered. "A nobler soul has never lived."

Holmes strolled to my side. "Her condition is called *hypertrichosis*, I believe. It is fortunate that she lives in such an advanced age. Surely employment as a circus exhibit is better than execution as a werewolf."

I could not repress a shudder. The woman in the photograph was identifiable as a human female only by the shape of her evening dress. Her head and face were covered in long, tangled locks of hair, and wild brows sprouted out above her dark eyes. No lips were visible, yet I could easily imagine that if she were to smile, savage fangs would be revealed. Her gown was low, and her shoulders, bosom, and upper arms were all covered by shaggy fur. One foot protruded beneath the folds of the skirt. It too was hairy, with indecently long, canine-like nails that seemed to scratch the floor. I shut the book in a rush, but the image lingered. I feared that the beast-woman would follow me, howling for blood, into my nightmares.

"You say Miss Vittoria has disappeared?" Holmes said.

"No – she has been kidnapped! Abducted! Perhaps even ravished and murdered!"

Holmes crossed the room and poured more coffee. "Calm yourself, Mr. Marvela. We can make no progress until you gather your wits and tell us your story, from the beginning."

He groaned but nodded and, after downing another cup, began to speak with greater clarity and dignity.

"Vittoria is like a child to me, Mr. Holmes. I am, as you may have guessed – "

"Originally from America, but of Irish lineage, a former blacksmith, and a veteran of Union Army who spent much time in the southern states." Holmes made a quick motion to brush aside the man's astonishment. "It is as clear as your vowels, your thumbs, and the tarnished buttons on your coat. These things are as obvious to me as your stage name is ludicrous to your patrons. Continue."

Marvela swallowed. "Yes . . . and it was in Georgia that I found her, on a farm near the town of Valdosta. She was the youngest daughter of a family of what we called 'trash' people – poor, dirty, uneducated – who kept her locked away in a barn. I rescued her from that terrible situation." Marvela offered a sickly smile. "I paid almost a thousand dollars for her to . . . ahem . . . for her to become my ward."

The man disgusted me. "And she has been your prisoner ever since?" I snapped. "I thought the Americans had abolished slavery of all varieties."

Marvela waved a limp hand. "Of course she is not my prisoner. She has been free from the day she came of age – but I educated her, provided for her, brought her to Europe, and made her famous. She is a good girl, and would never willingly leave me."

Holmes had turned to a newspaper, flipping through it as if the gentleman's distress was invisible to him. "Yet now you have lost her. Please be precise as to the details."

"It was yesterday morning that she was abducted. We had made camp the night before in a field just outside of Oxford. Everything was normal, ordinary. We put up the tents and arranged our little caravan of wagons, fed the animals, and enjoyed our evening. Vittoria sang for us, some of those old and sad songs she learned from the Negroes in the South. But the next morning, she did not appear for breakfast. I thought nothing of it – she has the soul of an artiste, you see, and sometimes stays in her van until just before she comes on stage – and we had already experienced quite a shock that morning, for our oldest, dearly beloved lion, Leo, had died in the night. But, as we say, the show must go on! At one, we opened up our sideshows for the youth of Oxford, and we had quite a crowd of boys, all of them very excited to behold Vittoria. But when the curtain parted, she was not there!"

"You found signs of violence?" Holmes prodded, as our guest had once more lapsed into a fit of dramatic weeping.

"Yes. Her van is her private world, and someone had defiled it! The pillows on her bed were torn, the velvet curtains shredded, her lovely frocks ripped to shreds. Mr. Holmes, you must come back with me. You must find her! If you do not, the money we will lose . . . ."

"Calm yourself, sir. I need only a few more bits of data. Did none of your other performers or roustabouts witness this abduction?"

Marvela wiped his brow with a checkered handkerchief. "A few of them claimed to have seen dark figures lurking around that morning and to have heard a cry of murder. But they took these things in stride for, you see, we were adding a new scene to our performance." He fumbled in his pocket, pulling out a crumpled handbill. "A Wild West act! Half the cast is dressed as red Indians, the other as cavalrymen. There is a stagecoach, a robbery, and – "

"A rather noisy rehearsal," Holmes interrupted. "I take it the official forces have been consulted?"

"They have, but they were rude and dismissive, and said there was no real evidence the lady had not simply run away. As if she could, in her condition!"

"And what is happening at your circus today?"

"Nothing. I have given everyone the day off – though it will eat into my profits – but we must open tomorrow. After all, the show – "

"Very well, Mr. Marvela," my friend said, cutting off another flourish from his client. "My colleague and I will arrive on tomorrow's earliest morning train. Now, excuse me, but I fear I have another pressing engagement."

I knew Holmes had no plans for that day, but I played my part in the charade and, with some relief, saw the odious man through the door. When I returned, Holmes was studying the photograph of Vittoria.

"You must admit, this case will be unique," my friend said. I answered with a loud snort.

"Grotesque, you mean!"

"Not at all." Holmes held out the book with her picture. "She repels you?"

"Yes – though it is hardly her fault that she has such an unfortunate condition. However . . . ."

Holmes considered my silence. "You would prefer that she be hidden away in some institution? That she be forced to keep her talents, as well as her hirsute face, concealed behind closed doors?"

"You make me sound like a monster!" I objected. "I pity the girl."

"One wonders if we should," Holmes mused. His tone drew a sharp look from me. "But it is a capital error to theorize without data. Some research beyond the Index would be helpful. No, don't trouble yourself, Watson – this is a day for old books and yellowed newsprint. I shall be back before dinner."

Holmes clearly found information that was more interesting than food, for he did not return for dinner, much to Mrs. Hudson's irritation. I had retired and been asleep for more than an hour when the sound of footsteps in the suite alerted me to his return. Befuddled as I was, I decided to wait until the morning's train ride to Oxford to question him, but Holmes dismissed my inquiry with a grunt, pulled his cap over his eyes, and dozed throughout the entire ride to the station.

We disembarked at the celebrated university town and were quickly directed to a field on its outskirts. Marvela's circus was larger than I had imagined. A bright red-and-blue tent capable of housing several hundred people was it its centerpiece, and a series of smaller tents, each fronted by bright boards advertising some unique specimen of humanity, formed a pathway to the entrance. Despite the early hour, the air was already ripe with the smell of roasting peanuts. Stalls offering food and drink were being opened, and performers in all varieties of strange costumes were milling around. Substantial cages held sleeping tigers and a hefty bear, and I caught a glimpse of two elephants being fed their morning hay. However, the wild beasts were vastly outnumbered by ordinary horses. Nearly two-dozen were confined in a makeshift corral.

"Marvela's was originally an equestrian circus," Holmes said, breaking into my unspoken question. "He has attempted to conform his performances to the new mode, which emphasizes exotic animals and their trainers. However, a tragedy last year may have postponed this transition."

"An accident?"

"Yes. A trainer was crushed to death by an elephant."

I shuddered. "Are they certain it was an accident?"

Holmes turned his head. "What a suspicious mind you are developing, Watson! I fear I may have rubbed off on you, and not for the better. Indeed, there was some questioning of the event, as the trainer was involved in a romantic intrigue with a beautiful tightrope walker, much to the distress of her rather jealous clown husband. The performer spouses disappeared shortly after the trainer's death. But that is not our concern today."

I hesitated, watching as the denizens of the circus, the roustabouts, cooks, and performers went about their morning chores with no acknowledgement of the strangers in their midst. It seemed such an innocent place, a magic circle of childhood fantasies, especially as a calliope began pumping a merry tune. But what evil of the human heart might be hid behind such a bright façade, what hideous face lurked beneath this cheerful mask?

"Ah, I see our client has somewhat recovered himself."

Mr. Marvela was rushing toward us. He was now clad as a ringmaster, in a high hat and a bright red coat, with his yellow and blue striped breeches tucked into shiny boots. The costume made him only slightly less ridiculous than he had appeared the day before, but at least some of the puffiness had left his nose and he no longer smelled of gin. However, the garish grease paint that he had already applied to his face gave him the appearance of the cheapest and ugliest doll upon a shelf.

"Mr. Holmes, Dr. Watson – Welcome! You are just in time! We were about to begin our rehearsal for our western act, but I can halt it so you may investigate."

Holmes held up his hand. "I would not think of interrupting your company's work. Perhaps we may observe your new act now and speak with some of the witnesses to Vittoria's disappearance afterward."

"Oh . . . of course." Something about his moment of hesitation made me wonder if Marvela was about to demand we purchase tickets. Instead, he led us into the tent. The smell of sawdust was nearly overwhelming, mixed strongly with the sweat of animals and men. Marvela signaled for us to be seated on one of the rows of benches that surrounded the large ring. He picked up an oversized megaphone and barked orders. The few performers who had been lingering in the ring rapidly disappeared through another exit that was covered with a shimmering curtain.

"Ahem . . . and *now*," Marvela proclaimed, his voice startlingly altered as he assumed his ringmaster persona, "I give you the *greatest*, most *spectacular* performance of the age. Straight from the *American Plains* – innocent *settlers*, pursued by fierce *redskins*, and rescued by heroic – "

A shriek cut him short. In a storm of hooves and dust, an open wagon pulled by four shaggy ponies emerged through the curtain. The wagon was driven by a man wearing denim overalls and a huge, obviously false black beard. As he whipped his steeds, his beard whirled comically around his head. In the rear of the wagon were two clowns dressed as a woman and child. They screamed for help as their chariot made its first circle of the ring. At that moment, a host of purported Indians – young men costumed in buffalo robes, feathered headdresses, and red leotards – charged onto the scene, waving tomahawks and spears. Another circuit was completed, then another, the fierce Indians whooping for all their might and the buffoonish settlers squealing as they were chased.

Yet something was wrong. Marvela was stomping and sputtering impatiently. He raised his megaphone.

"Where the devil is the cavalry?"

He had barely spoken when a new figure shot into the ring. It was a young woman, slim, graceful, and confident, riding a splendid white stallion. She was dressed in a costume of fringed beige buckskins, and her thick auburn hair bounced in a loose braid down her back. She whipped a long gun from its holster on her saddle, pretending to pick off one of the attackers. He gave a melodramatic cry and hit the dust. The wagon drew to the center of the ring while the lithe Amazon continued her pursuit of the Indians. Round and round they went, and the lady, with each turn, performed some new stunt. She dropped below her mount's neck to fire her weapon. She stood in the stirrups. She even balanced atop the steed's rump to take aim at her moving targets.

For a finale, she somersaulted over the horse to confront the last Indian brave, who seemed poised to impale her with his flaming spear. Her gun fired a great cloud of black powder and the Indian toppled from his rearing mare with a savage shout, appearing to perish on the ground at the tip of the lady's dainty boot. She raised her gun above her head while the rescued "settlers" gave a cheer.

"Stop, stop! What was *that*?" Marvela cried, not requiring his megaphone to make himself heard. The dead tribesmen quickly rose all around him. Their leader, the last to die, pulled off his war bonnet.

"This is Laura Liberty! The Sharpshooter of San Francisco!" He grimaced in embarrassment. "Don't you remember, boss? You agreed to hire her three months ago. She's just arrived."

"I – yes, but – I thought the Sharpshooter of San Francisco was a man."

The young woman said nothing, though her face indicated she had heard such an objection before and did not appreciate its implications. The chief of the tribe turned to us and shrugged.

"I thought Liberty was a man as well – all the paperwork was signed with just an *L* for the first name. You can imagine my shock when this little miss stepped off the train late last night! But boss – isn't she wonderful?"

Marvela nodded. At that moment, Holmes began to applaud. The lady smiled with firmly pressed lips.

"She is indeed wonderful," Holmes said. "I suspect your patrons will be as surprised as you were, Mr. Marvela. She certainly adds an aspect of novelty to your circus."

"Yes, though . . . I hope she doesn't expect the salary I was willing to give Mr. Liberty!"

"As well she should not, for that would be unjust," Holmes said. I saw the maiden's tight smile slip. Holmes gave a nod in her direction, though he addressed his words to Marvela. "You should double it, sir. This lady is worth twice any man's value. Just think of all the tickets you will sell, and how the people will rush to see her."

The sharpshooter placed her delicately gloved hand to her face, but her amusement at my friend's audacity clearly shone in her beautiful dark eyes. Holmes spoke over the impresario's shocked stammering.

"Now, sir, I believe you have engaged me to find Miss Vittoria. Perhaps if you will be so good as to allow me to examine the lady's former residence? You may bring the witnesses to me there. I will interview them inside after I am done inspecting the scene of the crime."

Marvela nodded vigorously and dismissed his performers. A few minutes later, we were inside the wooden van that had served as Vittoria's home for years. The vehicle was so small that both of us were forced to stoop and take care not to collide with each other.

It was the oddest lady's bower that I had ever entered. Despite her deformity, Miss Vittoria had been the most feminine of creatures, surrounding herself with bottles of perfume, elegant hairbrushes, and pictures of theatrical beauties clipped from popular magazines and pinned to the sides of her small space. A gilded vanity was set to the rear of the wagon, and her narrow bed was adorned with silken coverlets. In contrast to its delicacy, however, the room showed signs of violence. The pillows had been slashed, their feathers scattered, and the beddings were torn. The dainty metal chair at the vanity was overturned, and the room was heavy with the scent of lavender, thanks to several broken bottles of perfume. An improvised rack held five evening gowns that had also been torn, their beads and bows ripped away and scattered on the floor. Holmes, as was his custom, examined everything with great care, and wedged himself down amid the floorboards with his lens. At his command, I took a seat upon the bed, trying to apply his methods in my mind.

"Ah – yes, just as I thought!"

"What, Holmes?"

He held out something to me. In the dim light within the van, I could scarcely make it out.

"A hair?" I asked, squinting at what he had placed in my palm.

"Yes, and a very telling one. Watson, will you alert Mr. Marvela that I am ready to interview his people? This van is perhaps a bit stifling. We should go outside."

And so, in the fresh air, seated in camp chairs, Holmes questioned a selection of the Marvela Circus performers. They were an odd and fascinating collection of individuals. The most common of them were two burly roustabouts, who said they had heard a cry of "murder" just as the rehearsal was taking place two days earlier.

"You did not find that a strange cry?" Holmes asked. The fellows glanced at each other, and after a bit of stammering, the larger of the pair answered.

"No, not since the boss was having all those wild Indians in the act. We just thought it was part of the show."

Holmes dismissed the workers. Next up was a tall, gangly man that Marvela proclaimed to be "The Human Skeleton". Indeed, he resembled a collection of sticks in a suit, with a cadaverous skull mounted above the collar. He introduced himself, very softly, as Paul Brown.

"Mr. Brown, what can you tell us?"

"Not much, sir. I saw some no-good looking fellows lurking around the wagons that day. But I was late to my stage, and I didn't say anything." He hung his head. "I wish I had."

"Can you describe these men?"

Brown shrugged. "They had on dark coats and their caps pulled low. But it was their manner, sir. Like they didn't want to be seen."

Holmes considered. "You could not make a guess as to their age?"

"No sir. I really didn't see them that well."

"But they were men, not youths?"

"I think so, sir."

Holmes sent him on his way. Our final witness was Mrs. Overton, a lady of ponderous girth. She made Holmes's portly brother Mycroft seem like a waif. Her stoutness was only emphasized by the gaudy raspberry colored frock that she wore. Unable to lower herself into the chair, she stood, swishing a bustle that would have filled half an omnibus.

"I saw three men hurrying away, and one of them had a big black bag over his shoulder. I've told this to the police already! I thought they were carrying off the lion that died in its cage the night before. I had no idea that Leo had already been buried."

Something about her tone caused me to lift my head from my notes. Mrs. Overton folded her massive arms across her chest, glaring at both of us.

"You didn't like Miss Vittoria, did you?" Holmes asked, with his usual perception into the human soul.

"I didn't kill her, if that is what you mean! But I will not lie to you – I won't cry because she's gone. It was 'Vittoria this' and 'Vittoria that', and 'Oh, Vittoria, she's so talented!' A dog who can play the flute, that's all she was or will ever be! Bah! I may be considered a freak, but I have more talent in my little finger than she did in her entire hairy body. Would you like to see my ballet poses?"

Holmes waved away the offer. "I think not. But you have been most helpful, and so I thank you."

With an angry huff, Miss Overton withdrew. Holmes asked me for my notebook, scribbled something on a page, then tore it free, disregarding my concern at having my property mangled.

"It is for a good purpose, I promise. Let us return to the tent."

Inside, Marvela was directing another rehearsal of his western show, but he brought it to a halt when we appeared. The performers gathered around eagerly as Holmes announced, in ringing tones, that he had solved the case.

"Mr. Marvela, it pains me to say this, but your Circus Belle is no more. Based on the evidence of the lady's van and the statements of the witnesses, I can tell you that you will never see Miss Vittoria again."

The entire company gasped. The clown who was dressed as the settler child began to weep.

"But – what has become of her?" Marvela asked.

"I recognize the signs of the gang led by Dr. William Wayward, the evil physician of Harley Street. He has a reputation for collecting people of, shall we say, distinctive medical abnormalities for his Museum of the Morbid. I doubt that your lady is alive now, if she was alive when she was carried from the circus. I hope you will all be on your guard, lest other members of your troupe find themselves spirited away to become permanent displays in Wayward's secret hall of curiosities."

There was a shriek and a loud thump. We turned to see that Mrs. Overton, who had slipped inside and been eavesdropping behind us, had fainted. Five of the Indians hurried over to fan her. Marvela's jaw sagged.

"My . . . my poor girl."

"I will continue my investigations in London and alert you should I learn more. In the meantime, Mr. Marvela, I suggest that you allow Miss Vittoria to live on in your fond memories of her, and focus on the continued success of your circus. Good day, and – oh, one thing." Holmes stepped forward and handed the note he had composed to the leader of the Indian tribe. "A few comments on your performance, sir. A critique, if you will, from one actor to another? Now, we bid you *adieu*. Watson, I believe we have just time to catch the eleven o'clock train."

We made a hasty departure, and within half-an-hour we were back at the station. I was burning with curiosity about this Dr. Wayward, of whom I had never heard before. Indeed, I was filled with outrage that a man of my profession could stoop to such a practice. Holmes, however, sent me into the station waiting room while he purchased the tickets. A few minutes later, he returned with a tray of coffee cups and sandwiches.

"We will hardly have time for this," I objected.

"Oh, I suspect we can devour this luncheon before the two o'clock train arrives."

"But you said – " Holmes was looking at me with twinkling eyes. I knew that expression of mischief. "What have you done?"

"Extended an invitation. Go on, Watson, have some coffee. It may take our guests some time to arrive."

"Guests?"

"Yes, two of the most intriguing individuals I have yet to meet. I may have deduced their actions, but it will be very interesting to hear their life story! Ah – I see they hurried behind us and have just walked in. Sir, Madame, won't you join us?"

Much to my surprise, it was the leader of the Indians and Laura Liberty, the Sharpshooter of San Francisco, who were timidly poking their heads into the room. Holmes waved them to the long benches where we sat.

"You truly won't tell what we've done?" the man, who quickly introduced himself as John Fitzroy, asked. The young lady settled onto the seat next to him. He had managed to wipe away most of his makeup, revealing himself to be a very handsome fellow, though a few red streaks on his brow and jaw gave him a fierce appearance. The lady, however, remained heavily painted and still clad in her distinctive frontier costume.

"Your secret is safe with me and with my companion. Tell me, Miss Liberty – how does it feel to be free of the persona of Vittoria, the Circus Belle?"

"It feels wonderful," she said. Her words were oddly accented. As she spoke, I caught the flash of sharp, almost wolf-like teeth. "Do you think I am wicked?"

"I think you are magnificent," Holmes said.

I wondered if the lady blushed beneath all her makeup. "Thank you, sir. I will tell you everything. Mr. Marvela bought me from my cruel parents when I was just a child. It is true that he provided me with books and tutors, so that I was as well-educated as a girl might be. And with him I have seen much of the world, and performed for many important people. But, Mr. Holmes, it came at a terrible cost! For every person who applauded, another snickered. Once, when I tried to take a walk in a park, my veil came loose and a group of young boys stoned me nearly to death. As I grew older, I began to long for love, as any woman would – but what hope could a freak like me have of ever finding a mate?"

"Marvela claims that men have proposed," Holmes said.

"Sick men," Fitzroy growled. "Men with strange desires. Some of them even offered to buy Vittoria – I mean, Laura – for an evening. To his credit, Marvela never forced them on her, but he promoted their disgusting proposals, had articles written about them, put it all on handbills. He used her pain and embarrassment to make money."

"You do not know how many times I thought of running away," the lady said. "But always my conscience stopped me. I felt I owed Mr. Marvela my life. I know I would have died in that barn in Georgia if he hadn't found me. And the world would not accept me as I was. So what could I do? I resigned myself to always being a lonely spinster . . . until John came along."

He reached out and gripped her gloved hand. "Laura may have had the face of a monster, but she has the heart and soul of an angel. I saw that from the moment I met her!"

Holmes nodded. "In my research, I read about her many good deeds, the charities for which she has given benefits. It must have been difficult to help others when you could not help yourself."

"Oh no," the lady answered. Her wondrous eyes glowed as she spoke. "Those were the only happy times, when Mr. Marvela allowed me to give concerts and donate the proceeds. I knew the little orphans and their schools would be aided. But always, for any good thing I did, he seemed to take the credit. It was all promotion for his freak, his . . . *belle*."

She fairly spat out the last word. Holmes leaned closer, his chin on his entwined fingers.

"Allow me to see if my deductions are correct. Mr. Fitzroy, you fell in love this lady and wanted to help her to live a normal life. But she insisted that her duty was still to the circus. Therefore, together, you came up with a plan that would allow her to achieve her freedom while remaining an important and profitable performer. Knowing that Marvela was about to incorporate a western themed attraction, you convinced him to hire a new featured player."

Fitzroy nodded. "I told him that the Sharpshooter of San Francisco was a star in America. Not to be unkind, but with the way Marvela drinks these days, I knew he would never check to see if I were lying."

"Meanwhile, you practiced your new act at night."

The lady who now claimed the name of Laura Liberty smiled brightly. "I have always loved horses. I used to ride as a child."

"She is fearless," Fitzroy added, with obvious pride.

"I have no doubt," Holmes said. "Then you took the boldest step imaginable. You enlisted a cadre of confederates." He turned with a wink. "Watson, surely you were not taken in by the vagueness of their stories. They were pat and flat, and hardly the intense – if perhaps exaggerated – memories that the sudden abduction of a beloved fellow performer would generate. All except for Mrs. Overton."

Fitzroy groaned. "I knew she would give us away!"

"Do not fault the lady. If anything, she behaved courageously by making herself seem villainous, jealous, and hateful, with a motive to have the Circus Belle removed from the scene. If Inspector Lestrade had been on the case, she no doubt would have been clapped in handcuffs – providing a pair to could be found to fit her! No, Mrs. Overton is as generous and brave as she is . . . stately."

Miss Liberty giggled. "She has been like a sister to me. She allowed me to hide in her van over the past two days. I do love her and would hate to leave her."

A train whistle blew in the distance. "And so, on the appointed evening," Holmes continued, "you caused the damage to the van and altered your appearance, being extremely careful to remove all the evidence of the shaved and shorn hair. Indeed, you were so precise that only a single clipped lock was visible to my glass. Of course, such an act of grooming presented you with a problem so – the lion?"

Fitzroy nodded. "It broke my heart a bit to give Leo his fatal draught, but in fairness he was old, blind, and clearly in pain. I think he is in a better place, if animals go to one, and his hair was exactly the color of Laura's. Nobody thought twice about it, when they found him in his cage."

"I see. And what are your plans now?"

"To seek a dentist," the lady said. "I think my new wig and my heavy make-up can continue to fool Mr. Marvela during the show. But until my teeth can be fixed, I will stay in my assigned van most of the time, pretending to be homesick!"

"And as soon as possible, we shall be married," Fitzroy said, lifting his lady's gloved hand to his lips and bestowing a passionate kiss on it.

"Then we wish you both the greatest happiness," Holmes said. "Dr. Wayward is, of course, an absurd invention – worthy of Watson's purple pen, no doubt! – but should your employer make any future inquiries, I will be certain to remain in desperate pursuit of him, in order to avenge the Circus Belle's abduction and possible murder. Come, Watson, I believe we can make the eleven o'clock train after all."

I can give a brief epilogue to this affair. For a few weeks, Marvela's ticket sales were enhanced by a new *tableau* called "The Cabinet of the Curious", in which all of his *outré* specimens were asked to hold static poses, as if they were exhibits in a museum. His western act, however, soon overshadowed this rather bizarre routine. Miss Liberty, The Sharpshooter of San Francisco, was a sensation, and even performed a special engagement of her trick riding routine before our beloved Queen, who rewarded her with a specially struck medal and a beryl broach. A short time after this command performance, Marvela succumbed to cirrhosis of the liver, and the members of his circus scattered to the winds.

Holmes, of course, insisted that I could never reveal the true identity or fate of Vittoria, the Circus Belle. Therefore, I have written this account purely for our mutual amusement, and not for publication.

To it I will attach one final note: Some years after the case, I came upon Holmes adding a new photograph to his index. It showed a striking family: The man was tall, broad-shouldered and resolute, the woman was slender and elegant, and their boy was as cherubic as could be imagined, except for the wild mane of hair that gave him the appearance of a baby werewolf.

> *I leaned back and took down the great index volume to which he referred. Holmes balanced it on his knee, and his eyes moved slowly and lovingly over the record of old cases, mixed with the accumulated information of a lifetime . . . "Vittoria, the circus belle" . . . .*
>
> "The Adventure of the Sussex Vampire"

The Adventure of the Silver Skull
by Hugh Ashton

I had spent a holiday of a few days in France, and had consequently not seen my friend Sherlock Holmes in that time. However, as I sat down to breakfast on the day before I was due to return to England, the manager of the Biarritz hotel at which I was staying handed me a telegram.

"*Thank goodness I have found you at last STOP Return to England and proceed direction to Baker Street, where I await you STOP Holmes STOP.*"

"Will there be a reply, *monsieur*?" the manager asked me solicitously. "It is pre-paid."

I scribbled the words, "*Coming at once,*" on a leaf torn from my memorandum book and handed it to the manager, together with the few francs which he and the rest of the hotel staff seemed to expect for every service. "I will be leaving this morning," I told him and ordered a cab to the station.

After enduring a seemingly interminable journey on the French railways and a squall which disrupted the Channel crossing, it was a positive relief to set foot on English soil once more.

On my arrival at Baker Street, I was not a little discommoded when Mrs. Hudson, answering the door, informed me that Sherlock Holmes was not in the house.

"He went out this morning," she told me, "and said he'd be back for dinner. I'll just let you into the rooms, Doctor, where there's a nice warm fire, and you can wait for him to return."

I passed the time waiting for Holmes attempting to deduce for myself what sort of case had prompted this imperious demand for my return, and at the same time had called Holmes away. A pile of newspaper clippings stood on a small table beside the chair where Holmes typically sat. I was surprised by their source, which was evidently the popular press, and their subject, which was the circumstances surrounding the scandal involving the card-room at the Tankerville Club, rumours of which had reached me even in France.

As I had heard the story already whispered in the smoking-room of the Hôtel de la Plage, the Earl of Hereford, Lord Gravesby, had won heavily at cards a few evenings previously. His opponent at that time was one of the Royal Dukes, Prince _____, and in the usual way of things, this would not have been of any great import.

However, the rumour was that His Royal Highness had, not to put too fine a point on the matter, accused Gravesby of having been less than honest in his play, and that he had been backed up in this accusation by his equerry, a certain Major Lionel Prendergast. Lord Gravesby, faced with this accusation, had hotly denied any such wrongdoing, and had consequently challenged Prendergast to a duel, etiquette prohibiting the participation in an *affaire d'honneur* by a member of the Royal family. Prendergast had declined to fight, instead demanding that the matter be brought before the Membership Committee of the Tankerville Club.

Opinion within the Club, it appeared from my perusal of the newspaper clippings lying beside Holmes's chair, was divided on the matter. On the one hand, there was talk that Gravesby had won more at cards than might be reasonably be expected from a player of his ability, and that the act of challenging the man who had made the accusation, regardless of any Royal privileges, was unworthy of a true gentleman. On the other hand, there were those who believed that Lord Gravesby had done no wrong, that His Royal Highness was stepping outside the bounds of decency by making his accusations, and that Prendergast was a coward and a poltroon for refusing the challenge.

My reading was interrupted by the arrival of Sherlock Holmes, who glanced at the clippings that I had been perusing.

"Well, Watson, what do you make of it all?" he remarked, in a conversational tone.

"I knew Prendergast well in my time with the Army," I replied. "I cannot believe some of the things that are written about him here."

"I am well aware of your acquaintance with him," replied Holmes. "That, after all, is the reason for my summoning you from your sojourn in foreign climes. I take it Biarritz was not too much to your liking, by the way. I would feel a little guilt should it become apparent that I had dragged you away from some budding romance or a similar situation."

I felt myself blushing. "Nothing of that sort, I assure you," I told him. "But I fail to see how my acquaintance with Prendergast may be of use to you."

"Major Prendergast has retained my services to determine the truth of the matter and to make it public. He will be visiting me here in a few minutes. In the meantime, I would value your comments as to his character."

"I knew him to be a solid character and a good soldier, albeit at times what one might term a rough diamond," I told Holmes. "I firmly believe that, if he gives you his word, it is to be trusted. When may we expect his visit?"

"In approximately half-an-hour," Holmes told me. "While we are waiting, perhaps you might care to tell me of whatever you know of Baron Maupertuis, who was staying in Biarritz while you were there."

"I hardly know the man," I protested. "I was introduced to him by a mutual acquaintance., and I fear that my impressions of him were hardly favourable. To be frank, he struck me as a common swindler."

Holmes chuckled. "As always, my dear Watson, your instincts, at least as regards personalities, are infallible. The Baron is indeed a swindler, though hardly a common one. He is, in my estimation, and that of half the police forces of Europe, one the of most accomplished members of his accursed breed. It would provide me with great satisfaction were I to be the one responsible for bringing him before a court of justice. His schemes are on a large – one might even say colossal – scale, and have been the ruin of many men and women whom I would otherwise have regarded as being intelligent."

"He has not been arrested, then?"

Holmes shook his head. "Sadly, no. He is a sly one, and usually works his nefarious deeds through confederates or cat's paws. Nothing can be traced to him – nothing, that is, that would serve as evidence in a court of law. In addition, he always contrives to be resident in a country other than the one in which his current scheme is operating. This presents several interesting conundrums from the legal standpoint." He broke off. "From the sounds downstairs, I believe our visitor is arriving a little early."

Mrs. Hudson knocked on the door, announcing that Holmes had a visitor.

"Show him in, Mrs. Hudson," Holmes replied, throwing himself into his armchair.

The man who was admitted to the room bore little resemblance to the strapping young officer I had known in India. While, as I had explained to Holmes, Prendergast had something of the bluff soldier about him, our visitor was epicene, almost effeminate in the delicacy of his features and the exquisite nature of his dress. A frogged frock-coat and a somewhat gaudy waistcoat and neckcloth formed the foundation of his appearance, which was completed by a top hat with an exaggerated curl to the brim, and a lacquered walking stick with a curiously worked silver handle in the shape of a human skull.

"Major Prendergast, I presume?" Holmes greeted him.

"Indeed not," was the reply, uttered in a fluting tone of voice. "I take it you are expecting him to pay you a visit?"

Holmes inclined his head by way of answer.

"I must request you not to entertain any belief in anything he may say to you."

"Indeed? And may I ask your interest in making this request?"

"I make this request as the result of the earnest wish – one might even term it a command – of the gentleman whom I have the honour of serving."

"This gentleman would be one who has an interest in this case, I take it?"

"Indeed so. You would be wise to take due heed of his wishes in this matter, given the rank that he holds and the influence that he exerts."

"I will treat your words and the wishes of your master with the consideration they deserve," Holmes told him. "May I have the pleasure of knowing with whom I am speaking, by the way?"

"I am merely a messenger. My name is of no relevance here. I bid you good day, sir." He sketched a faint half-bow as he left the room.

"Well, Watson," said Holmes, after he had watched our visitor's carriage pull away from outside our house. "What do you make of that?"

"It would seem that Prendergast knows something to the discredit of the Prince, does it not? But what will you do?"

"It is evident that our recent visitor and his master, whom we may well assume to be His Royal Highness, are unaware of the influence wielded by certain persons known to me within the government. Their power, though used discreetly, is nonetheless of sufficient potency to put a mere prince of the blood in his place. It will be interesting, at all events, to discover what Prendergast has to say for himself when he arrives here."

In the event, we had not long to wait. Prendergast entered the room, little changed from the time when I first knew him, save for a touch of grey about the temples, but appearing flushed and in a state of high excitement.

"My dear Watson!" he exclaimed. "This is indeed a pleasant surprise. I am more than happy to see you again after all these years. And Mr. Holmes, sir. Delighted to make your acquaintance. I look to you as my saviour."

"I hope that I may be of assistance to you in your troubles," Holmes said to him. "The problem would seem to be a relatively simple one."

"Alas, I fear that the issue has compounded itself since I first requested your help." Holmes did not reply, but raised his eyebrows in response. "I assume," Prendergast went on, indicating the newspaper from which I had been reading prior to the arrival of our previous visitor, "that you are acquainted with the facts of the case, as far as they have been made public." Holmes inclined his head. "There has been a shocking development. Lord Gravesby was found dead at the Tankerville Club yesterday. The newspapers have yet to be informed of this development."

"Dear me," Holmes tutted. "And the cause of death?"

"I can only repeat what I have overheard, which may or may not be accurate. I heard that he was found with a pistol ball through his brain – a pistol of an antique type, used for duelling, that is – with the weapon lying nearby."

"An antique pistol?"

"Indeed so. One of a pair owned by His Royal Highness."

"The case certainly would appear to have its points of interest," Holmes remarked. May I enquire what part you play in all of this?"

"The other pistol of the pair, as the police will shortly discover, if they have not done so already, is to be found in my room at the Tankerville, together with powder and ball."

"How did it come to be there?"

"Following the accusations of cheating at cards made to his late Lordship, you will be aware that a challenge was issued. His Royal Highness, had he accepted this challenge in person, rather than by proxy as he did, would have had the choice of weapons, and he felt that this privilege would be extended to me. He therefore made me the loan of these duelling pistols, which apparently are a family heirloom. Both pistols were in my room when I left it this morning."

"And now?"

"As soon as I heard the shocking news of his Lordship's death, I hastened back to my room at the Club where I am staying while I am in Town. I had been performing an errand of a somewhat confidential nature for His Royal Highness and was only informed of Gravesby's decease on my return. There I discovered the pistols' case opened, and one pistol missing, along with the powder-horn. There also appeared to be fewer balls than I remembered. My first instinct was to take the remaining pistol and its accoutrements and fling it into the Thames, but I considered that the Club servants might have remembered seeing it, and its disappearance would raise more questions than it would solve problems."

"Very well considered," remarked Holmes. "To my mind, you have done the right thing if, as I conjecture, you wish me to clear your name. Tell me, do you know if the police are on your trail?"

"I do not know, but I strongly suspect that they are," replied my unhappy friend. "How can they not be?"

"Before I proceed further in this matter," Holmes told him, "I would like to inform you of a singular event that occurred shortly before your arrival here." He proceeded to inform Prendergast of our visitor, and the warning that we had received. Prendergast heard Holmes with the greatest attention and sighed heavily at the end of the recital.

"Your visitor, I may inform you," he told us, "rejoices in the name of Sir Quentin Austin. He is a long-time intimate of His Royal Highness, and enjoys his full confidence."

"As do you?" Holmes suggested.

Prendergast shook his head. "You do me too much credit, sir. I was not brought up alongside the Prince, as was Sir Quentin, nor do I share some of their mutual tastes. No," he held up a warning hand. "I am not about to inform you of the nature of these tastes. Though they may appear shameful to some, they are within the letter of the law – in the majority of cases, at any event. In any event, loyalty to my Sovereign and her family, if not to my employer, would prevent me from providing you with further details."

I was intrigued, as I believe was Holmes, but we both refrained from making any further comment. At that moment, Mrs. Hudson entered, and announced that Inspector Lestrade was downstairs and wished to visit.

"By all means show him up, Mrs. Hudson," Holmes said affably. "I fancy we can guess the errand that has brought him here."

Lestrade gave a visible start when he entered and beheld Prendergast. "I was not expecting to find you here, sir," he exclaimed. "Though on second thought, perhaps it is a natural progression of events. I am sorry to have to do this, Mr. Holmes, to one of your guests, but – "

"Stop!" Holmes commanded him. "There is no urgency about this, I am sure, and I will stand surety that Major Prendergast here will be available if you need him in the future to assist you with your enquiries."

"As will I," I told Lestrade. "Major Prendergast is an old comrade-in-arms. Our friendship goes back many years, and I can assure you that he is a man of his word."

"Very well," said Lestrade. "I will refrain for now from making the arrest. But you are incorrect on one point, Mr. Holmes.

"Oh, and what may that be?"

"There is a great deal of urgency attached to this. Orders have come to us from the very highest levels that this case be solved and dealt with at the earliest possible opportunity."

"Then it is lucky that you have me on your side, is it not, Lestrade?" said Holmes, smiling. "I believe that, between the two of us, we will be able to satisfy the demands of the Palace in very short order, do you not agree? Pray take a seat and join our conversation? Watson, refreshment for our guests?"

I busied myself with the decanter and soda-syphon, and the conversation resumed.

"I must warn you, Major Prendergast," Lestrade began, "that anything you say now in this room may be used as evidence in court, in proceedings against you or others."

"I understand that."

A silence ensued, broken by Holmes enquiring of Lestrade, "You have discovered both pistols, of course?"

"Naturally. This, after all, is the reason for our suspecting Major Prendergast here."

"And there is no doubt in your mind that Lord Gravesby was killed by the pistol found nearby of which Major Prendergast has informed us?"

"None whatsoever in my mind."

"And that it is not a case of suicide, rather than murder?"

"With a bullet through the brain and the pistol on the other side of the room, some feet away, suicide would seem to be an unlikely possibility, Mr. Holmes," Lestrade smiled thinly.

"I see. And the place where he was found?"

"It is the Club room where he had been playing cards with His Royal Highness and Major Prendergast here on a previous evening."

"The game?" Holmes asked Lestrade.

"I beg your pardon."

"What game was being played?"

"I never thought to ascertain that," Lestrade confessed. "Is it of any relevance?"

"It was bridge whist," Prendergast informed us.

"Then it is indeed of relevance," said Holmes. "There are four players required for the game, one of whom at any one given time will be dummy. Since the dummy was obviously not Lord Gravesby who was being accused of foul play, rightly or wrongly I cannot say at this juncture, the accusation was made by His Royal Highness, who felt compelled to drag Major Prendergast, who presumably held a hand on this deal, into all this, there is a fourth person involved, who was presumably acting as dummy on this hand, and may well have been the one who first raised the alarm. Furthermore, I would assume that this person had the interests of His Royal Highness, rather than Lord Gravesby, at heart."

Major Prendergast started. "You are absolutely correct, Mr. Holmes. The fourth was Sir Quentin Austin." His voice appeared to me to quaver a little as he informed us of this.

"Indeed?" Lestrade asked in apparent surprise. "He was the source of the information about the pistol in your room, Major Prendergast. He was in the Club when I called to investigate, and he gave the information to me voluntarily."

"The snake!" exclaimed Prendergast in a voice of fury. "It was he who brought the pistols from His Royal Highness to my room at the Club. Naturally he would know where they were. But for him to inform the police of this – why, it is hardly the act of a gentleman. And together with his visit here earlier today—"

"What is this?" Lestrade enquired. Holmes informed him of the events prior to Prendergast's arrival.

"Before today, what was your relationship with this man?" Holmes asked my friend. "You have told us a little of his relationship with His Royal Highness. Can you tell us a little of his character?"

"I frankly confess that I have never liked the man," Prendergast told us. "He would not have lasted long in the Mess, Watson, I can tell you that. There has always been something about him that gave me the cold creeps. Nothing, I hasten to add, that can be precisely defined in public, but there is that in his nature which I find to be repellent. And indeed it was he who called attention to the alleged irregularities in play. You are perfectly right in your recital of the facts, Mr. Holmes."

"And you are unable to tell us whether those allegations made by His Royal Highness have any basis in fact?" Holmes enquired.

Prendergast moved uncomfortably in his chair. "I would prefer not to answer that question," he answered at length.

I noticed Holmes and Lestrade exchange glances. "You may be compelled to do so under oath when this case comes to court – either as the defendant in a criminal trial, or as a witness," Lestrade told Prendergast.

"Nonetheless I would prefer not to answer the question at this time."

"Very well, then. I think we may be able to infer something from Major Prendergast's answer, eh, Mr. Holmes?"

Holmes said nothing, but merely nodded his head.

"I fear I have said too much," Prendergast complained. "I pray you both that any conclusions you may have chosen to draw will go no further."

"I fear we are moving in deep waters, do you not agree, Mr. Holmes?" the police agent said with a touch of anxiety evident in his voice.

'Deep waters indeed. Perhaps we may view the scene together, Lestrade? Has the body been moved from there?"

"It was moved by the Club servants before we were called in," Lestrade told him ruefully. "If I have learned one thing only from you, Mr. Holmes, it is that evidence should be left undisturbed as far as possible until the investigation is complete. Other than the body, we have left the room as we first entered it, and gave strict instructions to the Club that no one was to enter, let alone move any object inside it."

"I am pleased to see that some of my seeds have fallen on good soil," Holmes smiled. "However, even without the body, it is possible that some useful data may be obtained. Major Prendergast, I do not think that your presence will be required at this stage, but undoubtedly I may wish to ask you further questions, without Inspector Lestrade here being present, as has been my practice in several past cases."

"I cannot say that I am happy with this arrangement, Mr. Holmes, but I am content to let you do so. You have always played fair with us at the Yard, and I do not believe this will prove to be an exception," Lestrade answered.

"Thank you. Watson, Lestrade, your hats and sticks, and then we shall be off to the Club together."

At the Tankerville, we were greeted by the Club Secretary, Brigadier Hetherington, who conducted us to the place where the body had been found.

"Who discovered Lord Gravesby?" Holmes asked him.

"Kenning, one of the waiters here. If he is here now, would you like to speak with him?"

"If it is possible, certainly I would." Hetherington called a Club servant to fetch the man. Holmes cast his eye about the room, where three chairs still stood around a card table. The fourth was overturned. "I take it that this is the chair that was occupied by Lord Gravesby?"

"We have every reason to believe so. The body was found on the floor beside it."

Holmes dropped to his knees and used his lens to scrutinise the carpet. "Do you happen to know if Lord Gravesby smoked cigars?" he asked Hetherington.

"Indeed he did."

"While he was playing cards?"

"Usually that would be the case, but I have every reason to believe that on the night which concerns us – that is to say, the night of the unfortunate incident in which His Royal Highness and Major Prendergast were involved – he did not."

"Oh?"

"His Royal Highness was suffering from a cough, and made it clear that he did not wish others to smoke in his presence."

"And on the evening when the body was discovered?"

"I cannot say. It may be that Kenning will be able to provide further information on that score."

"I see. And one final question on the subject. Do you happen to know if Lord Gravesby smoked Trichinopoly cigars?"

"Good heavens, no. He smoked Cuban Coronas. The Club used to keep a stock for his exclusive use. Ah, Kenning," he added as the waiter entered. "This gentleman here, Mr. Sherlock Holmes, would like a few words with you."

The waiter appeared to be ill at ease as he stood facing Holmes, his hands visibly trembling. "I didn't do it, sir," he stammered. "All that happened was, I came in here, and found him on the floor just there," pointing to a spot near the overturned chair.

"No one is accusing you of killing his Lordship," Holmes assured him. "I simply wish to know how you discovered him, and what you did then?"

"Well, sir, I had just finished tidying the smoking-room, putting the newspapers back on their racks and so on. Then I thought it was time to do this room, the second card-room, so I came in here and saw what I've just been telling you."

"You have two card-rooms?" Holmes asked Hetherington.

"We have three, as it happens. His Royal Highness always used this one, and we are careful that it should not be booked for use by any other members when he is in Town. He often comes here with no advance notice."

"I see," answered Holmes. "Kenning, what did you do after you discovered the body?"

"Well, sir, I thought he might have dropped off to sleep and slipped off his chair, like, or else, begging your pardon, that he'd had a bit too much to drink, which has happened in the past, sir, if you'll excuse me saying so, but there was no glasses or decanter on the table."

"No ashtray or signs of a cigar or matches?"

"No, sir. The table was bare. Nothing on it. I'd take my oath on that." Here the man paused, clearly relishing the importance that his recital was bestowing upon him. "Well, I bent over him and had a closer look, and he was stone dead, sir. His face was set all rigid, like, and when I turned him over, there was a hole in the back of his head, just there." He pointed to a spot on his own head. "I could see that at a glance, sir."

"Ha! You are familiar with dead bodies, then?"

"Indeed, sir. I served my time with the Gloucestershires before coming here, and I've seen my share of dead men. Good friends, too, some of them."

"Yes, yes." Holmes's tone was a little impatient. "And then?"

"I called for help. Nichols came, and I told him to go and fetch Brigadier Hetherington."

Hetherington nodded in confirmation. "Nichols brought me here, and I could see at a glance that his Lordship was dead. I told Kenning and Nichols to carry him discreetly to one of the bed-rooms, and I sent another of the servants to call the police."

"How long was it before the police arrived?" Holmes enquired.

"There was a constable outside the door who arranged for Inspector Lestrade to come here."

"I arrived as soon as I could, with Sergeant McIver – you remember him, Holmes, in the affair of the emerald earrings? – I would estimate I was no more than fifteen minutes from the time that I received the message," Lestrade told us.

Hetherington coughed discreetly. "Inspector Lestrade was here within twenty-five minutes of the alarm being raised, Mr. Holmes."

"And during that time, no one entered this room?"

A flush stole over the Club secretary's face. "I am afraid I am unable to answer that question, Mr. Holmes. My attention, and that of the Club servants, was taken up by Lord Gravesby, and the necessity of concealing the fact of his demise from the other persons in the Club at that time."

"There were many members, then?"

"Indeed there were many people there that night. The Worshipful Company of Confectioners were holding their annual dinner, and the usual number of members were present."

Holmes turned his attention back to Kenning. "The pistol here," gesturing to a flintlock pistol that appeared to date from the last century lying on a table at the other side of the room. "Was it there when you entered the room and discovered Lord Gravesby?"

"I'm afraid I couldn't swear to that either way, sir. You see, I was more concerned for His Lordship than anything else."

"Naturally." Holmes turned to Lestrade. "The cause of death is the bullet, I take it?"

"Surely you are joking, Mr. Holmes? A man is found dead with a bullet wound and a pistol in the room, and you question the cause of death? I know you have your fancies and your theories, but this beats all."

"Then I take it that the bullet has not been extracted? The *post mortem* examination has yet to take place, Inspector?"

"This afternoon, Mr. Holmes. I take it that you and Doctor Watson here would like to attend?"

"Who is performing the autopsy?"

"Sir Greville Patterson, if I recall correctly."

"Then there will be no cause for me to attend. Pray let me have a copy of Sir Greville's report as soon as it becomes available."

"As you will, Mr. Holmes, but I do not believe that it will shed any new light on the matter."

"My thanks." Stepping cautiously, and keeping to the edges of the room, Holmes moved to the side table near the door where the pistol lay. "With your permission, Inspector?" he asked, reaching for the pistol. Lestrade nodded silently, and Holmes picked up the weapon and raised it to his nose. "There is no smell remaining," he remarked, "such as I would expect from a weapon using black powder." He examined the flash pan. "There is no sign that the weapon has been fired in the recent past."

"What?" exclaimed Lestrade in confusion. "Are you telling us that this is *not* the means by which Lord Gravesby met his end?"

"Indeed I am," said Holmes. "You may verify this for yourself," he added, presenting the pistol for the police agent's inspection.

"Then we have more than one mystery on our hands. Who placed the pistol here, and how did Lord Gravesby die?"

"As to the first, I strongly suspect Sir Quentin Austin, presumably to place suspicion on Major Prendergast. I believe we will have to await the results of the autopsy before we know the answer to the second."

We left the Club in company with Lestrade, who seemed to be more than a little disconcerted by Holmes's findings. "So you believe Prendergast to be innocent?" he asked.

"Innocent of shooting Gravesby with that particular pistol, at any rate. Indeed, consider the evidence we have just seen and heard. Can we indeed believe that Gravesby was indeed shot?"

"I am not entirely sure why you should say such a thing. He is dead, at any event, no matter how he died," said Lestrade, thoughtfully. "I hope you are not disputing that fact. But, as you say, the *post mortem* examination may provide us with a few more answers."

"I think I will make my way to Barts and view the body before Sir Greville starts his work," said Holmes. "Watson, you will accompany me to the haunts of your youth? Lestrade?"

"Willingly," I answered him, but Lestrade declined the invitation.

"However, if you would be good enough to pass on anything you find, Mr. Holmes, I would be most obliged," he requested, and Holmes acknowledged this with a nod of his head.

We took ourselves to the hospital where I had trained as a student, and made our way to the room where Sir Greville Patterson plied his grisly trade.

"Ah, Holmes. Good to see you here. Shocking business, what? Watson, delighted to have another pair of hands and pair of eyes on this case. Shall we start?" He withdrew the sheet covering the cadaver. "I was informed that the cause of death was a bullet at the base of the neck. However, I perceive no exit wound. Watson, if you would, please?"

He and I turned over the body to expose the back of the neck, where a small hole was to be seen which lacked the superficial characteristics that mark wounds caused by projectiles fired from pistols or rifles.

"If I may say so, Sir Greville," I remarked. "That hardly appears to be a bullet wound. I have seen enough of such in my time with the Army."

"I agree," replied my medical colleague. "We can easily determine the truth or otherwise of your observation, Watson." A few minutes' work with the scalpel, and Sir Greville grunted. "You were perfectly correct, Watson. There is no exit wound, and no sign of any bullet in here. I detect some fracturing of the second and third cervical vertebrae, but it does not resemble that which would be caused by a bullet."

"As I thought," commented Holmes, who had been silently observing the proceedings. "We must seek another weapon. You are certain that this wound was the cause of death?" he asked Sir Greville.

"Certainly this injury was the cause of death. I would put the immediate cause as the extreme compression of the spinal cord caused by the pressure of the fragments of the vertebrae being driven forward by – by whatever it was that caused this." His tone, at first the confident manner of one of the foremost pathologists in the land, weakened and grew fainter as his doubts grew, in an almost visible manner.

"That, my dear Sir Greville, is my province," remarked Holmes cheerfully. "Yours was to determine the cause of death, and you have done so admirably. Thank you so much for your work here." He turned to go. "You will let me have the full report in good course? Come, Watson."

"In all my experience, I have never seen a wound like that," I said to Holmes as we walked away from the hospital.

"No more have I," he told me. "This has the makings of a most ingenious case, Watson. The only possibility that suggests itself to me is that the murderer held in his hand an object similar to a dagger, but with no edge, and a slightly blunted tip – you observed the distinctive characteristics of the wound, did you not? – and used it with sufficient force not simply to break the skin, but to crush the vertebrae and the spinal cord. Death must have been painless and instantaneous. There is a certain diabolical ingenuity here, as well as a powerful motive."

"I cannot conceive of such a weapon, or indeed, of the man who would wield it."

"Indeed. We would seem to be searching for a man of powerful build – a man of action."

"I hope that you are not suspecting my friend Prendergast," I told him.

"At the present time, noone and everyone may be suspected. But let us see Prendergast, in any event. It is best that we do not acquaint him with Sir Greville's findings, though."

We returned to the Club through the Park, and secured a quiet corner of the smoking room in which we awaited Prendergast.

On his arrival, I noted his drawn face, which exhibited a curious pallor. "Are you unwell?" I asked him.

"A bit worried, old man. What with the pistol missing from my room and turning up next to the body. Enough to give anyone a turn."

"I quite understand your concerns," said Holmes. "However, I do not think you need to worry yourself over that matter. However, I would appreciate your providing more details on Sir Quentin Austin – specifically on his appearance. For example, does he usually carry a stick, and if so, what kind?"

Prendergast appeared to be considering the question for a short while before responding. "I do not recall seeing him with such an article. I believe I would remember if I had done so."

"A lacquered stick, with a silver head in the shape of a skull, for example?"

Prendergast started. "You are describing a stick that is the property of His Royal Highness. It is a most distinctive article, and one of which he is most proud. I have heard it said that there is some secret about it, but it is not one to which I am privy. It may have been a gift from one of his female friends, perhaps."

"Very well. Another question about Sir Quentin. I observed when he visited us that he is a user of tobacco in some form. Perhaps you can enlighten me further as to the form in which he indulges the habit."

"He is often to be seen with one of those foul Trichinopoly weeds," smiled Prendergast.

Holmes clapped his hands together in an expression of delight. "Then the case is solved," Holmes told him. "When I have talked to the police, you will be freed from suspicion, and the culprit brought to justice."

"Sir Quentin?" asked Prendergast incredulously.

"It may well be he," answered Holmes. "I would advise you, Major, to return to your rooms and remain there until the police let you know formally that you are no longer under suspicion."

After Prendergast had left us, Holmes and I took a cab to Scotland Yard.

"But have you deduced that Sir Quentin killed Gravesby?" I could not but refrain from asking my friend.

"I have ," he told me. "No doubt you noticed his stick?"

"Indeed so. I could hardly tear my eyes away from that grotesque skull that formed the handle?"

"Tut. You did not observe the tip? The silver ferrule was stained with some dark substance that was certainly not mud, and could not have been, since we have had no rain in a week. Furthermore, the shape of the stick at that end, and therefore the ferrule, was not round, but octagonal. When we arrived at the Club, I noticed a peculiar indentation on the carpet, within one of the areas that had been stained with blood. That, too, was an octagonal shape. The cigar ash that I observed is the final clue that points fair and square, or should I say fair and octagonally?" Holmes gave a faint chuckle, "to Sir Quentin Austin as the murderer."

"I all seems too simple, Holmes. But you believe that that stick was the murder weapon? However, Sir Quentin seemed to me to be of too slight a build to inflict a blow that could cause the injuries we observed at Barts."

"That point had occurred to me also, and I confess to being a little troubled by it," Holmes admitted to me. "However, if we can convince Lestrade of the wisdom of interviewing Sir Quentin on the subject, I have little doubt that we will soon know the truth of the matter."

On hearing Holmes's words of explanation, Lestrade instantly sat up straight in his chair. "Why, thank you, Mr. Holmes. I will dispatch a constable to arrest him and bring him here immediately."

"It might be better if he were not arrested at this stage of the proceedings," Holmes suggested to him. "Let us hear what he has to say for himself first."

"Especially given his friendship with a certain personage," Lestrade added. "I see the sense in what you are saying, Mr. Holmes."

The constable was dispatched, and returned some time later with Sir Quentin Austin, dressed as we had previously seen him, and carrying the skull-headed stick on which Holmes had remarked.

Lestrade opened the questioning. "Sir Quentin, do you deny being in that card room at the Tankerville Club after the death of Lord Gravesby?"

"I do deny it," came the toneless reply.

"Then how is it," asked Sherlock Holmes, "that your stick still retains traces of blood on its tip, which were imparted to it when the stick was pressed into that part of the carpet where a bloodstain was present?" Sir Quentin looked down at the end of the stick with what appeared to be a genuine look of surprise and horror on his face. "Furthermore," Holmes continued, "traces of the cigar that you were smoking were present in that room, in the form of ash. We have established that while you were playing cards in that room on that night, you were not smoking."

Sir Quentin closed his eyes in resignation. "Very well, then. Yes, I was in the room after Lord Gravesby's death."

"For the purpose of placing the pistol that you had abstracted from Major Prendergast's room? For the purpose of implicating him in the murder?" Holmes went on.

"Yes," came the answer in a hushed voice. "It was the work of a cad, I know, but the alternative was worse."

"Such as being hanged for murder?" sneered Lestrade. "Sir Quentin Austin, I arrest you for—"

Holmes held up a hand. "Stop, Lestrade. Sir Quentin has not confessed to killing Lord Gravesby. With your permission, I would like to ask him a few more questions."

"Oh, very well," grumbled the police agent. "Since it is you."

"Sir Quentin," Holmes addressed the baronet, from whose face all colour had now drained. "However unpleasant or serious the consequences of your words, I strongly advise you to provide full and truthful answers to the questions I am about to ask you." The other nodded. "Very well. *Imprimis*, I believe that is *not* your stick that you are holding. Or, if it is, that it was only recently presented to you by another who was the original owner."

"The second of those statements is correct," was the reply.

"And I believe I know who presented it to you. Very well. Let us continue. Do you know the secret of this stick? Why it was given to you?" Lestrade and I looked at each other in puzzlement. Holmes's reasoning was beyond my comprehension, and from the look on his face, beyond that of Lestrade also.

"I believe I know why this was so," Holmes went on. "Will you do me the kindness of passing me the object in question?" Wordlessly, Sir Quentin complied with the request. "Observe the tip closely," Holmes requested us.

He held the stick horizontally, and we waited. Suddenly there was a loud click, and what we had taken to be the ferrule shot out from the tip of the stick to the extent of about two inches, with the velocity and force of a bullet from the mouth of a gun. "Imagine," said Holmes calmly, "that I had the tip of this pressed against the back of my victim's neck. Watson, what sort of injuries would result?"

"Those that we observed on Lord Gravesby," I answered.

"But how does this return to its former state?" asked Lestrade.

"By the very simplest of methods," Holmes informed us. He placed the tip of the stick on the floor and placed his weight on the handle, forcing the stick downwards. After a little exertion, the tip retracted, and another clicking sound presumably informed us that the mechanism was now locked into place. "And hence, gentlemen, the bloodstains on the tip of this stick when the murderer pressed the murder weapon into the carpet, at a point where it was soaked in the blood of the victim."

"What is this diabolical thing?" I asked.

"Behold the *Totenkopfstock*. A few of these were created at the end of the last century in Vienna for those involved in espionage and in secret government work. I believed them all to have been destroyed, but such is clearly not the case. The trigger to release this diabolical weapon is concealed in the eyeholes of the skull."

"My God!" breathed Sir Quentin. "I had no conception." His face, formerly pale, was by now ashen. "To think I have been walking around London with this— this monstrous thing in my hands. So I have been in possession of the weapon that killed Lord Gravesby without knowing it?" he stammered.

"Why do you think it was given to you?" asked Holmes. "As a reward for placing false evidence to condemn an innocent man? No, it was to absolve your master of any complicity in the crime. You are guilty, my man, of conspiracy to pervert the cause of justice, even if you are innocent of the killing itself."

By now, Sir Quentin, slumped in his chair, had his face in his hands, and appeared to be sobbing to himself. Between the sobs, we could make out the words, "I had no choice."

"I must warn you," Lestrade told him, "that anything you say will be taken down and may be used in evidence against you."

"No matter," replied Sir Quentin, recovering his posture, and addressing us with some dignity. "I am, as you may know, unmarried, and am likely to remain so for the rest of my life. I leave you to draw whatever conclusions you may choose from this statement. His Royal Highness drew his conclusions, and from then on, I was in his power, helpless to do anything other than what he commanded. The story of the card game at the Tankerville Club that you have read is a complete fiction. You have read, have you not, that His Royal Highness accused Gravesby of cheating?"

"That is so," Holmes affirmed.

"The truth is otherwise. It was Gravesby who accused His Royal Highness of double-dealing the cards. He, that is to say His Royal Highness, indignantly denied this, and he left the room, followed by Prendergast and myself, where we took counsel among ourselves."

"Was there any truth in the accusation against the Prince?" Lestrade asked.

Sir Quentin bowed his head. "I am ashamed to say that there was. It was not the first time that this had occurred. The Prince sent a Club servant to fetch a box from his rooms at ------- House.

"That containing the duelling pistols?"

"Indeed. When the servant returned with the case, His Royal Highness ordered me to talk to Gravesby, and prevent the facts from becoming public, as I am ashamed to admit I had done on previous occasions. In this instance, however, I was unable to do so, and reported as much to the Prince, who thereupon flew into a passion and stormed out of the room. He returned, some ten minutes later, informing me that Gravesby had challenged him in a duel. He had refused to accept, and had named Prendergast to take his place."

"Without consulting Prendergast? And did not Prendergast object?" I asked, incredulously.

Sir Quentin shrugged. "It is his way of doing things. Prendergast is a military man, and used to obeying orders. I believe that he would do anything in the world, if he were ordered to by a superior. His Royal Highness then dictated a note to me, addressed to Lord Gravesby requesting a meeting in the same card-room the next evening."

"That is to say, the evening that Gravesby died," Lestrade remarked.

"Indeed so. That evening, His Royal Highness and I made our way to the Club. While he went to the card-room where he'd arranged to meet Gravesby, I, as I had been instructed, met Prendergast and requested him to deliver a letter to Lady Thruxton at her home in Grosvenor Square."

"The purpose of the letter?"

"I believe it was merely a ruse to take him out of the Club for a short time. I then waited in Prendergast's room, and His Royal Highness joined me a few minutes after Prendergast's departure.

"'Take this, and place it in the card-room where it will be found,' he instructed me, opening the box containing the duelling pistols, and handing me one.

"Naturally, I expressed some question as to why this was needed, and he turned on me with a look of fury such as I had never before observed.

"'Your task is clear. Do this, or else . . .' he hissed at me. The message was clear. I would be exposed and shamed before the world if I failed to comply with his instructions. I therefore made my way down to the card-room, unobserved, and there beheld a sight such as I hope never to see again. Lord Gravesby was lying on the floor, blood seeping from a wound in the back of his neck. I could not think clearly, and merely deposited the pistol on the nearest possible surface. I left the room, and then realised that my master might have intended me to place the pistol in such a way that suicide would be suspected. I hasten back towards the room, but was prevented from entering by the sight of one of the Club servants moving towards the door. I therefore made my way back to Prendergast's room, where His Royal Highness awaited my return.

"'It is all done,' I told him.

"'Excellent,' he said, and that, Inspector, is when he presented me with this devil's tool here," indicating the weapon that Holmes had named as the *Totenkopfstock*.

"We left the Club quickly, without meeting anyone. Already, it was clear that Gravesby's body had been discovered – but who, I asked myself, would suspect a Royal Duke of any misdoing?"

"Who indeed?" replied Holmes. "And not only does he appear to have committed murder most foul to cover up his villainy at the card table, but he has attempted to lay the blame at the door of not just one, but two innocent men. What say you, Lestrade?"

"It's a puzzler, Mr. Holmes, and I don't mind admitting that the situation's a bit much for me. If it was anyone but His Royal Highness, we'd have the derbies on him by now. As it is . . . ." His voice tailed off. "As for you, sir," addressing Sir Quentin, "you're guilty of compounding a felony, obstructing justice, and I can probably think of some more if you give me a minute."

Holmes held up a warning hand. "Stop there, Inspector. Sir Quentin has given us an honest, and I believe a contrite, account of events. I do not believe that society has much to fear from him in the future. Rather, he has much to fear from society should these events be made public."

"That is true," Lestrade grudgingly admitted.

"You must retire from public life," Holmes told Sir Quentin. "I would recommend leaving the country. Paris, Aix, or Baden-Baden would be congenial, perhaps."

"He cannot leave England!" Lestrade exclaimed.

"He must. It is in no one's interest that Sir Quentin remains here. Believe me, Inspector, if you bring this man to trial, let alone his master, you will set the country by the ears. He must leave." He turned to Sir Quentin. "You have the money to do this?"

Sir Quentin shook his head. "I have little money of my own. His Royal Highness has been my chief financial support for the past few years."

"And he may continue to be so in the future, by the time we have finished with him," Holmes replied with a grim chuckle.

"What do you mean?" I asked him.

"I have alluded before to these matters," he said simply, but refused to elaborate more.

A week later, we were sitting in our rooms in Baker Street, and I was reading *The Times*.

"It says here, Holmes, that His Royal Highness is to leave from Portsmouth next week to serve as Governor of Grenada. Is this your doing?"

Holmes smiled lazily. "Not mine, but the work of others with whom I have been in contact," he corrected me. "However, it is at my instigation. We have also arranged that Sir Quentin Austin is to receive a generous annuity from His Royal Highness as soon as he is settled in Venice, which he has selected as his destination. Also a consequence of doings by those in Whitehall and the Palace."

"But how did you know that His Royal Highness was responsible?" I asked.

"Your friend Prendergast, though he was obviously not telling the truth when it came to describing the card game and the events surrounding it, was clearly truthful in other respects, such as the discovery of the pistol in his room. Sir Quentin Austin was my first suspect. I felt sure that the account of Gravesby's death we heard from Prendergast was incorrect when I remembered the blood on the ferrule of Sir Quentin's distinctive stick that I had observed previously, and I believed that the victim had been battered to death. My first sight of the body dispelled that belief. The *post mortem* puzzled me. A man of Sir Quentin's build and temperament could never have inflicted those injuries that we observed, but the evidence was strong that it was he who had placed the pistol in the room in order to falsely accuse Prendergast.

"Accordingly, I was forced to conclude that while he was not Gravesby's killer, Sir Quentin was in some way closely connected with the criminal, as you yourself will have remarked when you recall that he arrived in a carriage which bore the arms of His Royal Highness painted on the door. Prendergast appeared to have an easily checked alibi. His

Royal Highness was the only possible suspect remaining, and when I heard that the diabolical *Totenkopfstock* was the property of the Prince, I was convinced. A man who retains duelling pistols in a condition where they are easily made available for use might also possess some other objects of an equally nefarious nature. I must admit that the motive puzzled me a little until we had heard Sir Quentin's story at the Yard. The idea that the tables had been turned, and that the victim was the accuser and vice versa, so to speak, had not occurred to me. The Prince was obviously not about to let his propensity for winning at cards at all costs to be made public – we may assume that a large sum was offered by Sir Quentin to Gravesby which was refused – and not content with personally eliminating his opponent, he attempted to cast the blame on others."

"Monstrous!" I exclaimed. "Were it not for his rank . . . ."

"Indeed, Watson. But we cannot live in the land of make-believe. However, we have at least ensured that we no longer inhabit the same land as His Royal Highness." So saying, he took his Stradivarius from the wall, and proceeded to play a tune of his own composition.

> *"I have heard of you, Mr. Holmes. I heard from Major Prendergast how you saved him in the Tankerville Club scandal."*
> *"Ah, of course. He was wrongfully accused of cheating at cards."*
>
> John Openshaw and Sherlock Holmes –
> "The Five Orange Pips"

The Pimlico Poisoner
by Matthew Simmonds

"I shall call it 'The Strange Case of the Pimlico Poisoner'," I announced to Holmes, as we sat down for a late evening smoke.

"And who might that be?" drawled Holmes, as he slouched back in his armchair and sucked upon his unspeakable clay.

"How can you have already forgotten? You solved the case just last week! For heaven's sake, Holmes, sometimes I believe you are being deliberately obtuse."

"Oh, the business in Westminster," yawned Holmes.

"Pimlico," I interrupted. "Lupus Street, to be precise."

"Well that hardly matters now, does it?" Holmes sighed.

"You are incorrigible, but I shall ignore you, as you know full well to what I am referring. Barnes, the 'untouchable' criminal, undone by his own habits. Not the first to fall foul by such and surely not the last."

"An interesting exercise in inquiry, logic, and deduction I will concede, Doctor, but hardly one for your journals, I would have thought."

"On the contrary, dear chap, I believe that it demonstrates your powers at their absolute finest."

I

It was a cold and damp September Sunday morning when we were visited by Inspector Alec MacDonald. Holmes had feigned mild frustration at the inspector's unannounced visit, but I knew full well that he secretly cherished and eagerly anticipated these rare meetings with one of Scotland Yard's finest young minds.

"Here's one for you, gentlemen," began the inspector, stretching his long legs as he settled into a chair before the fire. "A group of men are enjoying a meal in a reputable restaurant in Pimlico. These are all men of a certain nature. Criminals, but of a high standing – the sort that order other men to endanger their lives and freedom with little risk unto themselves. They eat and drink for hours, and then, suddenly, one of their number collapses to the floor, mouth foaming and nose bleeding. In seconds he is dead."

"Stiffness of the body? Lockjaw?" I asked.

"Yes, strychnine poisoning for sure, Doctor," confirmed MacDonald seriously, his frown exaggerated by his large forehead and exuberant eyebrows.

"You say 'hours', MacDonald. Exactly how many?" asked Holmes, suddenly taking an interest.

"At least two, according to several witnesses. Barnes and his men arrived before seven and he dropped dead shortly after nine. And before you ask, they all ate and drank the same food, give or take. At least two others at the table, including his own son, Samuel, had the same courses and, according to the kitchen, none of the food was prepared separately. We have examined the kitchen and tested the remaining food and drink. Not a trace of the poison was found anywhere."

"But, surely, his own food was tainted?" I asked.

"That is the strangest part of all. His plate was thoroughly tested and we found nothing. We even had the good fortune to discover that the dish that contained his first course had not yet been cleared from the table. This was also clean, as was his cutlery, and all of the glasses. All were still present, none had been cleared away, or 'accidentally' smashed, which excludes that old trick."

"So, the poison was not introduced via the food or drink. That leaves us few remaining possibilities," stated Holmes, carefully tamping at his pipe.

"And what might these be?" inquired MacDonald, hopefully.

"Deserving of thought, Inspector. It is a shame that you have waited so long to consult me. I suspect there is little left undisturbed at the scene of the crime, but I would like to take a look anyway, if you would be so kind?"

Inspector MacDonald was only too happy for Holmes to view the scene and, less than an hour later, we arrived at Rattray's Restaurant on Lupus Street. MacDonald allowed Holmes to take the lead and gave him free reign to examine the restaurant, while the Scottish Inspector and I sat at a side table, gratefully accepting the owner's offer of fresh coffee.

After about half-an-hour, Holmes ceased his examinations and began to interview the staff. Another half-hour had passed before he finally joined us. He took up a cup of coffee and sipped at it for a while before speaking.

"I'm informed that there are unusual aspects to Barnes's wine. We need to know who supplied it. We need to identify everyone who handled it, from the docks to the table. We will start by ascertaining exactly who served the wine, and who originally placed it in the cellar."

"Well, I can answer one of those questions for you, right now," announced MacDonald. "Barnes was a careful man, as one who has made his way to the higher branches of the criminal tree tends to be. Ruffled feathers lead to later repercussions, if you know what I mean. It seems he had a great fear of being poisoned, and insisted on always opening his own wine bottles. He would only drink from those fitted with foil over the corks, and even then he would never open a bottle without first examining it closely for signs of tampering."

"But what about his food?" I asked. "Surely that is just as vulnerable."

"He always insisted that a lower member of his gang watched over the chef and then tasted any food that was presented to him. This, plus eating at only a few select and trusted venues, meant that he felt safe from any tampering of his food.

"And before you ask," continued MacDonald, "all of the serving staff have worked here for at least two years and are well known to Barnes and his associates. All are accounted for, and nobody has conveniently 'disappeared'."

"So, the crime is symbolic as well as purely criminal," Holmes declared, suddenly. "The killer chose the one method that Barnes had worked so hard to render impossible. This was not simply business – this murder was personal."

"Does it matter which it is, Holmes? We still have to find out how it was achieved and then find the villain," sighed MacDonald.

"It matters, Inspector, as although we are clearly dealing with a most clever and cunning individual here, the fact that we now know that the killing was personal increases our chances of catching the criminal manifold.

"We would be casting a very wide net indeed if we hoped to identify all of those in the underworld who might wish Barnes harm for criminal reasons," continued Holmes. "However, to find those wishing him dead for personal reasons will require fishing from a far smaller pool."

"Someone close to him? You don't think it could have been a family member?" I asked, quietly. "That would certainly make it personal."

"I still prefer the theory that it was a business rival," contradicted the inspector. "But, please, feel free to investigate your own suspicions, I am sure that you will, anyway." MacDonald's thick Aberdonian accent could not quite hide his mischievous challenge.

Once MacDonald had left us to speak with his officers, I rounded on Holmes.

"Holmes, in whose name are we acting here? I do not recall being officially engaged by either an agent acting for Barnes, or indeed the authorities," I questioned.

"Why, Watson, you are quite correct. Let me see," Holmes smiled, unexpectedly. "Should we act out of pure public spiritedness, or would you prefer a fine payday and the execution of an otherwise fine and honest individual?"

I have to admit to being so flabbergasted by this response that I was momentarily unable to speak.

"What on earth do you mean, Holmes?" I managed to splutter out, finally. "What can you have learned here that makes you believe that the killer could possibly be 'otherwise fine and honest'?"

"Oh, just the very basics. The killer's identity, the motive, and the method by which the aim was achieved."

Holmes shouted a farewell towards MacDonald and headed for the door.

"Time to head east," he announced.

II

We took a hansom and set off towards Westminster. We passed the Parliament buildings, drove alongside the river for a very pleasant mile or so, and then passed through the City until we reached Whitechapel, some forty minutes later.

"Please, you simply have to explain how you came to these incredible conclusions?" I begged, as we trundled over the cobbles.

"Not every case is a tangled web, Doctor. Sometimes you just have to know which strand upon which to pull and all will unravel."

"Yes, very poetic, Holmes, but please, for once, can you just tell me clearly and simply how you have reached your conclusions?"

"In this case, it was simply by asking the right questions of the right person," Holmes replied, impassively.

"But none of Barnes' gang were there, so whom did you question?" I asked.

"Do you remember the list of things that I wished to know, back at the restaurant?"

"Something about the wine, I believe. Who brought it and served it? But MacDonald told us that the wine was opened and poured by Barnes himself, and that he always inspected it closely for any signs of tampering."

"Despite your lack of confidence, I can tell you that I have also determined the course travelled by the wine, from delivery to the table."

"But I still do not understand how any of this is relevant," I muttered, weakly, feeling thoroughly stupid.

"Then let us alight here and find someone who can perhaps provide some illumination," Holmes replied, as we pulled up in front of a large house on the outskirts of the borough.

The building was substantial, of red brick and stone, and set back some ten yards from the street. The most striking sight, though, was the presence of two large men at the entrance, and one more at each corner of the grounds. The house was clearly under guard, and not by the authorities.

We approached the front gate and stopped before the substantial duo who blocked our way. Their low brows and piggy, inset eyes identified them as low-level thugs, hired for muscle rather than any genuine skill or ability.

"Gentlemen," announced Holmes, with a broad smile. "I am Sherlock Holmes and this is Doctor Watson. Perhaps you have heard of us?"

"Never heard of any Shylock, and it's too late for a Doctor," replied the goon to our left. "Haven't you heard? The Boss is dead."

"Wait a mo'," growled the other thug. "I have heard of you, Mr. Holmes. I once heard the Boss say that you were the most dangerous man in all London. He said that he went out of his way to avoid you at all costs." He seemed to step back slightly as he spoke, as if he was troubled by Holmes's very presence.

To my utter surprise, Holmes then appeared to confirm what the powerfully built man had said.

"Yes, I did have an accommodation with Mr. Barnes. As long as he kept his dealings to those already involved in the underworld, I would not interfere directly with his business."

"Holmes, I am outraged," I whispered angrily, my blood beginning to boil at the thought that my friend, whom I admired more than any other man, had come to an "accommodation" with a career criminal.

"Later, Watson." Holmes spoke with such seriousness and authority that I stopped immediately and pushed my disgust to the back of my mind, to be brought up at a more appropriate time.

"Could we please pass?" Holmes asked, returning very much to the issues of the present.

"I am sorry, but have express orders from Miss B. herself. Nobody is to be admitted, no matter who they are."

"Very well," sighed Holmes. "Watson, it appears we must return to Baker Street. We have nothing more to gain here."

We returned to our waiting hansom and set off towards home. We stopped in Westminster, as Holmes announced that he needed to post a letter. He did not return to the cab for nearly twenty minutes.

"It certainly took you long enough, Holmes. I assume it is going long-distance?" I snapped, with undisguised sarcasm, my mood still dark.

"Indeed. For the simple reason that I had, first, to actually write it." Holmes reply was cutting, and in my place I was firmly put.

"I am sorry, old man, but I am rather in the dark here," I admitted. "And now I find that you have been consorting with – no, even worse, actually making deals with criminal gangs. My head is spinning. Whatever would MacDonald think?"

"Mrs. Hudson will provide you a wholesome bite to eat, you will smoke a fine Havana, and then, I shall endeavour to explain all that you have inquired upon," Holmes replied, gently. He did not speak again until after we had pulled up outside 221b.

III

Mrs. Hudson was, once again, our guardian angel. A supper of cold cuts of ham and chicken was followed by a delicious fruitcake, laced liberally with fine Jamaica rum. After such a repast, it was impossible to continue harbouring a bad mood, and I retired to my armchair in far better spirits than before.

Holmes moved to his desk, opened a large drawer, and removed an elaborately inlaid Macassar ebony box, about twelve-inches-by-eight. The patterns covering its surface appeared strangely familiar, as if they might be half-remembered letters taken from an ancient alphabet.

He pressed a metal stud on the front and the lid swung upwards. I half-expected the box to contain a clue or even prove to be some fiendish apparatus connected to another case, but the reality was far from sinister. The interior was lined with a finely grained reddish-brown wood, probably cedar. The presence of a row of fat brown sticks confirmed that it was a cigar humidor. Holmes tilted the now fully open box towards me.

"Please take one," Holmes asked. There were perhaps eight cigars left inside the box, which would have originally held twelve.

I took one from the centre and gazed upon it. Five inches in length, broader than was usual, perhaps as much as a forty-six ring gauge. The outer leaf was perfect: Dark brown, lightly veined, with a subtle glossy sheen. I gave the cigar a gentle squeeze. It gave slightly but sprung enthusiastically back. Despite his sometimes less-than-conventional habits, Holmes had kept these cigars in perfect condition. I struck and applied a long match, taking a short initial draw to avoid any flavours being imparted from the sulphurous match head. The second pull confirmed what I had suspected: This was a very special cigar. Spices, coffee, chocolate, along with hints of whisky and molasses, all hit me in a wave of sensations. I laid it down for a moment as Holmes filled and lit one of his ghastly clays.

"This is incredible, Holmes. Where did you get these cigars?"

"From a Spaniard whose family farm tobacco in something called the *Vuelta Abajo*, if I remember correctly," Holmes began.

"In Cuba?" I asked, enthusiastically.

"I have no idea, Watson. By the time they arrived, I had moved on to other, more pressing matters."

"What did you do for this Spaniard for him to have rewarded you with such a fine gift?"

Holmes raised an eyebrow and looked at me, quizzically. "Why, I bought them from him, of course. From his shop – the tobacconist in St. James' Street."

I sighed, but decided to ignore Holmes, whether he was joking or not.

"Holmes, you promised to share with me what you have learned, and more importantly, how you justify conspiring with criminals. Please feel free to begin at any time," I suggested seriously.

"London is the greatest, but also the largest, city in the world. It therefore must encompass both the very worst of humanity along with some of its leading lights. The authorities can barely hold back the tide of crime as it is, and sometimes have to compromise to stop the flow becoming a full-scale flood. Accommodations are made, truces negotiated, agreements upheld. A state of anarchy benefits no one – not the police, nor the criminal underworld. As long as certain lines are not crossed – murder, excessive violence, or the involvement of victims above a certain class – then the authorities are prepared to turn a blind eye to some lesser crimes – protection, low-level smuggling, and unlicensed gambling."

"But these are serious crimes. They cannot be simply tolerated, surely?" I stammered in reply.

"Maybe one day the police will have the resources and the appetite to go after *all* criminals, but for now they must prioritise, and we must understand. I, however, have left Barnes' gang unaccosted for the simple reason that, until today, our paths had not yet crossed. He seemed to have taken this as some unspoken pact between us, but I can assure you, Doctor, that this was not the case."

"But that is not what you said back at Barnes' villa," I argued. "You confirmed exactly what the thug had stated – that you had a deal with Barnes."

"That, Watson, was merely an attempt to gain favour with the man at the door and then, hopefully, ingress to the house. It was a weak effort and it failed – badly, as you witnessed."

"Well, that certainly eases my mind, a little," I decided, after a long, reflective pause.

Although not entirely convinced, I had to give Holmes the benefit of the doubt. We spent the rest of the evening talking on unrelated issues, mainly news from home and abroad. It was only after I had bid Holmes goodnight and shuffled off to my bedroom that I realised that he had, yet again, skillfully avoided telling me anything of what he had actually learned regarding the case. I shook my head and sighed, then took to my bed, as confused as to the progress of the case as I had been at the start of the day.

IV

I tried to rise early the following day, but a combination of too much brandy the night before and the dampness in the air troubling my old wound made leaving my bed extremely difficult. By the time I sat down for breakfast, it was fast approaching ten o'clock. I apologised as Mrs. Hudson brought me hot coffee with my eggs and bacon. She managed a half-hearted "Tut" in admonishment, but the twinkle in her eyes gave away her true motherly feelings.

"Now, before I forget, Mr. Holmes told me to say that he hoped to be back before midday. He also said that if his guest should arrive before him, you were to keep her company until his return."

I offered my thanks and Mrs. Hudson departed, smiling. "Call down if you would like more coffee."

Left alone, I picked up the morning newspapers. The usual mix of politics, gossip, and crime were all present, but there was no mention of the Barnes murder. Considering that it had occurred more than thirty-six hours previously, I was more than a little surprised. It seemed that, for once, MacDonald had managed to avoid the story being leaked to the press. The presence of more than a few hardened, professional criminals would certainly have aided him in keeping the press at bay.

I spent the remainder of the morning reading and trying to catch up with my writings. As twelve o'clock approached, I began, involuntarily at first, to glance out of the window and listen for the approach of Holmes's mysterious visitor. At half-past the hour, I heard the front door open and I bolted up straight in anticipation, but a familiar step on the staircase informed me that it was Holmes, returned from his morning's investigations. His footfalls were remarkably light and unexpectedly rapid as he swept up the stairs. The door was thrust open, dramatically.

"Is she here?" demanded Holmes, his face flustered. He peered inside before relaxing and removing his coat and hat. He thrust his cane into the stand and sat down heavily in his armchair.

"You look like you have had a busy morning, old chap," I remarked. "Should I call down for coffee, or would you, perhaps, prefer something stronger?" I asked, gesturing to the drinks cabinet.

"I shall wait. Our guest will not be long." Holmes rose, chose a pipe from the mantel, filled it from the Persian slipper, and settled back into his armchair.

"For whom exactly are we waiting?" I asked, with more hope than expectation.

"What do we know about Barnes' killer, Watson?" replied Holmes, lighting his hideous, waxy black clay.

"Very little, really, I thought. A poisoner, certainly. Somebody with knowledge of Barnes' habits and movements, of course. Other than that, I can ascertain nothing."

"A good start, Watson, but you must deduce further. What do we know about poisoners?"

"Poison has been the favoured method of assassins since classical times, I don't see how that helps. But wait a minute – Is poison not also one of the methods of murder most favoured by women? Along with the use of knives, I believe, it accounts for the majority of homicides committed by the 'fairer' sex."

Holmes nodded slowly and deliberately.

"Are you referring to the 'Miss B.' mentioned by those thugs?" I suddenly understood. "Surely they must have been referring to a Miss Barnes, a daughter!"

"Precisely, Doctor. We all know about his son, Samuel, a nasty piece of work indeed, but he also has a daughter. Although she is far from well-known, her influence upon her father's regime was far from insignificant."

"Enough to have complete control over those thugs back at the house, at least," I agreed. "But why would she kill her own father? And how on earth did she do it?"

"I think I hear the vessel, within which our answers dwell, arriving as we speak," announced Holmes.

As I strained to register any sound at all, the doorbell rang and shortly after we heard light footfalls upon the stairs. The visitor knocked once only, but firmly. Holmes called and we watched expectantly as the door swung inwards.

In walked a young lady of perhaps five-and-twenty years. Her hair was blonde and held high at the front with innumerable pins. At the back, it hung low in a long, wide plait. Her eyes were bright sapphire, her nose a small nub above a wide, full mouth. She wore a satin dress of light blue, finely detailed with silver and gold embroidery. Across her shoulders was a stole of finest Russian mink. Around her neck, she wore a necklace of pearls and diamonds. As she moved into the room and accepted Holmes's offer of a seat, I noticed a strange dichotomy. Despite her expensive finery, she did not act as one of the higher classes – her movements were natural and unaffected. It seemed to me that she was more than a little embarrassed by her own appearance.

"Miss Barnes," Holmes began. "Welcome to 221b Baker Street. Please be assured that anything that you reveal here will be treated in the strictest confidence. I am Sherlock Holmes and this is my loyal friend and colleague, Doctor John Watson."

"Mr. Holmes, Doctor," replied Miss Barnes, quietly, "Firstly, let me tell you that I fully understand the situation in which I find myself. I make no apologies for my actions and am completely at your mercy."

I was stunned by this most unexpected revelation. Was this a confession of murder? What could possibly have made her admit such a thing? I looked towards Holmes, eagerly awaiting his response.

"Well, Miss Barnes, you are certainly as brave as you are intelligent and ingenious," Holmes replied, far from the response I had expected.

"But not enough to best Mr. Sherlock Holmes. Your letter gave me no choice but to come here and reveal all to you. My father was right about one thing, at least. 'Avoid Sherlock Holmes at all cost.'" Miss Barnes smiled as she spoke. She clearly meant these words as a compliment.

"What letter was this?" I asked, rather foolishly.

"Oh, I see that Mr. Holmes has not confided in you his scheme." Her smile was wide and honest. I noticed that her accent, although expensively schooled, still bore an echo of the East End.

"It was really most ingenious," continued Miss Barnes. "He wrote a letter explaining that he knew everything, what I had done, and how I had achieved it."

"And he sent this letter to you?" I asked.

"Oh no, that would have achieved nothing. I would simply deny all of his base accusations," smiled Miss Barnes.

"Then to whom did he send it?" I asked, now thoroughly confused.

"To her fiancé," interjected Holmes, abruptly.

I hesitated for a moment before asking her, "Why would he do such a thing?"

"Because he knew that I would intercept and read the letter. You must understand, Doctor, that I exist in a world of suspicion and mistrust. I must know all that I possibly can to survive, even it means spying on those who are closest. But it eats away at you, piece by piece, until all that is left is a hollow, paranoid shell. That is what my father became, and that is what I swore to avoid at all cost."

"I tried for years to persuade my father to leave this world and become an honest businessman. He could easily have done this, but he enjoyed the life he had made too much. All of his friends, family, and associates were criminals. Why would he ever leave this life? The fact that nearly half of his income was now coming from legitimate sources meant nothing to him. The lifestyle was everything."

"And then you met a man, an honest man," added Holmes, gently. "One with no connections to your world. You wished to marry him and leave the underworld forever,"

Miss Barnes nodded, sadly. "Father refused, of course. You see, he wanted me to take over from him. My brother Samuel may appear the very image of my father, but he is vain, impulsive, and lacking in thought. If he were put in charge, the consequences would be dire. All of the truces brokered by my father would be breached and chaos and violence would ensue. Samuel could be the figurehead and the strong-arm, but father needed a more cerebral presence behind the throne."

"Could you not have simply eloped with this young man?" I asked. "You are clearly not without means." I gestured to her diamonds and pearls.

"My dear Doctor, do not think I haven't thought this over a thousand times. Yes, we could have run, but he would have found us. He had ties to organisations across the globe. Where could we have hidden? The world shrinks with every passing year."

"So you decided that you had to take drastic action." Holmes's voice cut through the fog of speculation. "You decided to kill your father and let your brother take control. He would then be fully occupied in his new role, leaving you free to marry your fiancé and eventually disappear from the scene altogether. That the family business might slowly crumble, or die in a haze of flame and violence, was of little interest. You wanted no part of it." Holmes took a deep draught upon his pipe. He leaned back and sent the resulting smoke upwards, away from our guest.

"Well I do, finally, understand the reasons and motives behind this affair, but I still have one important question," I managed, after some thought. "How did you kill your father, Miss Barnes?"

"Watson!" barked Holmes, loudly. "That is hardly a question to ask a lady."

"I am sorry, but in the circumstances, I must know," I replied, tersely.

"Later, Watson. But for now, we have a much more important decision to make. What do we do with the information that we have gathered?"

I thought long and hard.

"We must inform MacDonald, of course. Remember Holmes, a man has been murdered. Whatever mitigating circumstances you think there may be, surely it is for a court to decide the fate of Miss Barnes.

"I am sorry," I addressed Miss Barnes, "but justice must prevail. I have the deepest sympathy for your plight, I just wish that you had approached us before you took such drastic action."

"Watson, you forget that we lack the most vital element of all," Holmes replied, sternly.

"Which is what?" I asked, genuinely surprised.

"Proof. We do not, in fact, possess any evidence whatsoever of Miss Barnes' involvement with the death of her father. Nothing she says, or has said, here can be used against her. We are not the police. As regards our clients' testimonies, our office is sacrosanct."

I sighed and sank back into my chair. "I suppose you're right. And I don't suppose that you are going to voluntarily confess to the authorities, are you, Miss Barnes?" I asked, resignedly.

Our guest smiled sweetly, but kept her own counsel. I imagined her sitting in a courtroom, that same innocent smile beaming towards the jury. If we presented what scant evidence we had so far accumulated, we would be lucky to escape without a severe reprimand from the judge himself for wasting the court's time.

"But I will not allow you to simply slip away and leave anarchy and violence in your wake," Holmes intoned, darkly. "You know full well what will come to pass if your brother alone takes charge of your father's affairs."

"What do you expect me to do, Mr. Holmes?" Miss Barnes replied, a hint of concern breaking through her hitherto confident demeanour.

"You must stay and take control of the family business. You will continue to take full charge until such a point is reached where more than half of your family's business is fully legitimate. You will then be free to sell these businesses and retire to wherever you so please, to live quietly with your husband, forever unaccosted by the authorities. Your brother can keep the remaining criminal concerns, as these should, by then, be too small to remain a major player in the city any longer. Any trouble he may then cause would be on a far smaller scale, which would be better for him and more manageable for those around him. Who knows? By then you may even have convinced him that running a legal business is a far more admirable path to follow."

"And if I refuse?" our guest asked, quietly but pointedly.

"Do not confuse my pragmatism with altruism, Miss Barnes," replied Holmes, coldly. "I want what is best for the city and society in general. This means avoiding a costly and bloody period of anarchy that would surely follow if your brother is allowed to run roughshod through the London underworld.

"You would do well, also, to bear in mind that in a single day I have discovered the method of your father's murder, the motive behind it, and identified his killer," Holmes continued. "Imagine what knowledge I might have after a whole week has passed."

This cold and sharp declaration certainly had the effect desired of it. The colour left the face of Miss Barnes in seconds. Her eyes widened in fear as, for the first time, she realised that she was dealing with a man of huge capability and almost infinite faculties.

"Then I have no choice but to agree to your terms. I shall legitimise as much of the business as I can and leave what little is left to Samuel."

All trace of good nature had left Miss Barnes. Her lips were now pencil thin, her jaw tight and her hands gripped her silk handbag with such force that her knuckles were as white as polished ivory. I thought to detect a slight shudder of fear in her shoulders as she rose to leave.

As she moved towards the door, her shoulders suddenly fell and she turned back to face us.

"I am sorry, Mr. Holmes. You are quite right. I have acted only selfishly and viciously up to this point. You have presented me not only a chance of redemption, but also a long-term solution to all of my problems. In truth, I should be grateful. Thank you Mr. Holmes, and thank you, Doctor Watson. I shall not forget you."

A smile flashed across her once-more pretty, placid face, and Miss Barnes departed. I was not entirely certain whether her last words were truly genuine or, rather, a subtle, passive form of threat.

V

Once our visitor had left, we called down for an early supper. After a simple repast, we retired to our armchairs where we filled our respective pipes and settled down for an evening of reflection.

"What will you tell MacDonald?" I asked, tamping down a bowlful of my latest Cavendish mix.

"I was rather hoping you might come up with some appropriate fiction that would satisfy the inspector," mumbled Holmes, as he drew upon his already lit pipe.

"Very droll, old chap," I smiled. "We can concentrate on Miss Barnes' promise to remain and legitimise the family business, stressing that this would avoid an otherwise very nasty period of transition. Then, along with the lack of any real evidence, MacDonald may be satisfied to let the matter drop. Unlike me, of course. Now you must tell me exactly how she committed this impossible murder, and how on earth you managed to solve it."

"As I told you, Watson, sometimes one simply has to ask the right people the right questions. In this case, it was the people behind the scenes that held the key to the puzzle. I began at the restaurant where Barnes died, interviewing the serving staff and the chefs. While you and MacDonald sat and enjoyed your coffee, I learned that Barnes had some very specific habits – habits which were later confirmed by visits to the other restaurants that he favoured."

"What were they?" I asked, intrigued.

"I also learned that Barnes' daughter had a secret fiancé," continued Holmes, ignoring me completely, "the identity of whom strengthened a theory upon which I was already working."

"Do you feel like sharing his identity with me?" I asked, sarcastically.

"His name is of no importance, Doctor. But his occupation was of the greatest interest. He supplied a large proportion of the wine that was consumed in the restaurants frequented by Barnes."

"So he poisoned the wine!" I exclaimed. "But how? Barnes only drank from sealed bottles."

"I now had two suspects, Miss Barnes and her fiancé. Either had easy access to the wine, but which one was responsible, and how was the poison administered? Remember, no poison was found in any of the bottles or glasses from which Barnes had drunk that evening."

"I am at a complete loss, Holmes," I admitted.

"Habits, Watson. When I questioned the serving staff from the restaurants concerned, I insisted that they recount everything, down to the most precise of details. One waiter recalled that Barnes had a rather unusual quirk. At the next restaurant, I made sure to mention this and it was confirmed, and then again at a third venue. By this time I had also discovered that young Samuel Barnes was wholly incapable of running the business and of Barnes' desire for his daughter to become his successor. From there it was then only a short step to developing a fully functioning theory."

"But how did she do it, Holmes?" I begged. "You are taking far too much pleasure in teasing me."

"The waiter had noticed that Barnes did indeed have an unusual routine. Whenever he opened a new bottle of wine, after examining it closely for any signs of tampering, he would pour a large glass. This could be for himself or somebody else at the table – there was no particular pattern here to his actions. Nevertheless, what he would do next was the same on every occasion. He would run his finger around the neck of the bottle, collect any drops that had spilled, and lick these from his finger."

"That is a pretty uncouth act, but then he was not exactly a cultured man," I commented, before appreciating the importance of Holmes's revelation. "Oh, I see," I stuttered. "That is remarkable, Holmes."

"Miss Barnes, either by herself or with the aid of her fiancé, had covered the necks of the wine bottles, and the foil around them, with poison. Every time he ran his finger along the neck and licked it, he would ingest both wine and this evil concoction. They then had simply to wait. A night would soon come where his intake would be fatal," explained Holmes.

"And any earlier symptoms of poisoning would be simply be put down to the effects of the alcohol. Fiendish and utterly ruthless. I am now not entirely sure that you have done the right thing by letting them go."

"What was the alternative, Watson? We have no actual physical evidence of their involvement. All of the bottles have been disposed of, the glasses washed clean. If the police did choose to interview Miss Barnes as a suspect, then she would surely disappear at the first opportunity, leaving us with chaos and potential anarchy as the family business tears itself apart."

"The lesser of two evils. I understand that now, but I am far from satisfied," I admitted, gruffly.

"Nor should you be, Doctor. For it is only when people like yourself stop caring, that the criminals have truly won," replied Sherlock Holmes, a dark cloud of pipe smoke teasing its way around his fine angular features.

> *Twice already in his career had Holmes helped [Inspector MacDonald] to attain success, his own sole reward being the intellectual joy of the problem.*
>
> *The Valley of Fear*

The Grosvenor Square Furniture Van
by David Ruffle

"Grosvenor Square, Watson!"

"What of it, Holmes? I know it to be a rather pleasant square, not two minutes' walk from the eastern edge of Hyde Park. I daresay I could give you a potted history if required, but of what significance is it? To you that is?"

"Really, my dear fellow, your lack of recall often amazes me. I am sure your potential readers would profess themselves equally amazed at the jumble of dates and times you accredit to our cases. For a man of words, I sometimes wonder if you have ever looked up the meaning of the word *chronology*."

"Be that as it may, you well know why certain dates and times have had to be changed, and names if it comes down to it. I have a duty to certain innocent parties to protect them from the glare of public scrutiny. Even the guilty have sometimes had their identities protected to accord their innocent families the same privilege. None of which explains your emphatic, 'Grosvenor Square'."

"Watson, Watson. It was only two weeks ago when I mentioned the case of the Grosvenor Square furniture van, and you evinced a certain curiosity about the affair and you were eager to hear the details. Perhaps you are not as eager as you appeared to be."

"I cannot recall the conversation at all, Holmes. Perhaps it may have been Mrs. Hudson who was suitably enthusiastic regarding the case!"

"Hah! Your pawky humour rises to the surface once more. I have never quite fully guarded myself against it. Allow me to prompt your faulty memory. The affair itself came to my notice three weeks ago. Indeed, a week before I broached the subject with you, Watson, in the course of a conversation that was apparently not memorable in the slightest. If you recall – Ah, no you don't. I received a message from Lestrade which expressed a desire for my assistance with a mystery regarding – "

"The Grosvenor Square furniture van, perchance?"

"Ah, it comes back to you now, does it"?

"Not in the slightest."

"From the outset, it promised to be a mystery like no other."

"How could you possibly deduce that, Holmes? Surely you had no data to go on at that stage?"

"Elementary, Watson. Lestrade's note to me stated it was a mystery like no other."

"Coming from Lestrade, surely that was no guarantee of any great mystery shrouded in impenetrable gloom. The inspector has been baffled on many occasions, and it is us who have been able to get to the heart of things."

"Us?"

"You can hardly deny the great help I have been to you, Holmes. My intellectual capacity may be below that of yours . . ."

"You will find no arguments in this quarter, Watson!"

". . . but even so, I can sometimes point the way as to the solving of a case."

"You certainly do. I readily admit that your errors of deduction can often guide me to the correct solution. For that I am of course grateful."

"That is rather akin to being damned with faint praise, I believe."

"It may have to suffice, my dear fellow. I hold you in high esteem for your willingness to assist me at any hour of the day and night. Your bravery is a constant reminder to me as to how fortunate I am to have you as a friend and comrade. But we digress from the point."

"Which point?"

"The Grosvenor Square point!"

"Where was I that day?"

"You spent that week ensconced at Lords, watching the Test match,. Australia being the foes. You did mention in great detail each day's play when you returned each evening, although oddly enough I cannot now recall any of those details."

"Ah, so the problem of memory and recall is not exclusively my own then."

"There is a difference. I chose to forget because I find it abhorrent to clutter my brain with details that are never going to be of the slightest use to me. A cricket Test match falls firmly into that category."

"Perhaps I chose to forget about Grosvenor Square, too."

"Then again, perhaps your faculties are failing through too much cricket-watching. Your impending nuptials may play a part in your absent-mindedness also."

"My faculties are perfectly in order, thank you. I really must correct you especially since I can do so on too few occasions: I did not spend the week at Lords. The match was over in two days, England suffering an ignominious defeat."

"Only two days? I stand corrected, it seemed so much longer with your re-telling."

"In the four completed innings, Australia was the only team who managed a score in excess of one-hundred. It was a very low-scoring affair. Even W.G. Grace . . . ."

"Yes, thank you, Watson. I do not see we have any need to dwell on the cricket any longer. For whatever reason, you were not available to accompany me to Grosvenor Square on the day in question. My first inkling as to the severity of the crime was the view of stationary traffic as I walked hurriedly down North Audley Street . . . ."

"I used to play billiards in a club on North Audley Street. Thurston was a member and I used to sign in as a guest. It was said the billiard tables were the finest in London – not that they ever noticeably improved my game. What was the name of it? Oh yes, The Cathedral Club. Why it was so called, I never did find out. Sorry, Holmes, I interrupted you. Please continue."

"I will endeavour to. As I arrived at the entrance to the Square itself, all I could see was a veritable of jumble of hansoms, carts, growlers, and the like along with many bystanders craning their necks for a view of the proceedings – "

"Of course, in the early days of Grosvenor Square, there would have been no such access. The whole square was originally surrounded by gates and railings with only the local residents having keys. They also were expected to finance the upkeep of the gardens and square. You may be aware of that, Holmes."

"I am aware of that fact, Watson. I am also aware of the fact that it would pay dividends if I were to recount the details of this case without drawing breath. It is apparent to me that this may be the only way to divulge the singular events in the Square that day. If I may be allowed to continue?"

"Certainly, Holmes. Forgive my interruptions; I will sit here quietly and give you my fullest attention."

"I threaded my way into the square and spotted Lestrade, who nodded to me and then shook his head solemnly as if to emphasise the nature of what had taken place. There were four ambulances in attendance, and at least thirty uniformed constables. Lestrade expressed a fervent desire that I could unravel the mystery before us. He was quite out of his depth – "

"As he often is, Holmes. A nice enough fellow of course, but I often wonder if he was cut out for police work."

"He suffers chiefly from a chronic lack of imagination. I never doubt his tenacity, for he is the epitome of a British bulldog who will hang on to his man, come what may. But I have always advocated that Scotland Yard detectives should spend such time as they have free in reading up old cases and learning from each one. After all, there is nothing new under the sun, it has all been done before."

"So I understand from your many statements to that effect. The problem as I see it, if indeed it be a problem, is that Scotland Yard detectives and presumably their provincial counterparts have very little time to be delving into the annals of crime. For the most part, they will have families to care for and food to put on the table and as such, their time will be taken up in earning their wages. I don't doubt, Holmes, that you are correct in your views, but not everyone has the time to spend on such researches or indeed are as single-minded as you are."

"Perhaps then, they should educate themselves as to their chosen profession before the acquisition of wives and children. Now, where the deuce was I? Ah, yes. Lestrade appeared to be more hot and bothered than usual . . . ."

"It was the second day of the test match then. It was a very hot day indeed. If you recall, I wore my new blazer which showed off the M.C.C. colours."

"I do recall, Watson and you may remember my surprise at you wearing something quite so garish. I believed it was in hardly in step with your personality."

"You believe my personality to be sombre? Or grey and uninteresting perhaps?"

"I merely remarked on it being unusually garish, it was no reflection on your disposition or temperament, my dear fellow. If I may continue without further interruption?"

"By all means, Holmes. Although something has just come back to me about that day at Lords. Many people that day – well a few anyway – on seeing my blazer immediately inquired as to the name of my tailor."

"No doubt with a view to avoiding him. The first thing Lestrade pointed out to me was that the van was empty."

"Empty?"

"Yes, entirely."

"Devoid of furniture?"

"That is the impression I am attempting to convey to you, yes."

"How did that come about?"

"That is what I will come to if I am ever allowed to complete my narrative. The driver and his mate were both being treated for wounds – one appearing to be much more seriously hurt than the other. The mate, who exhibited far less marks of violence on his person, had been telling his story to Lestrade, and I managed to persuade him to recount the events of the day to me also from the beginning."

"Leaving out no detail, however small, no doubt."

"Thank you."

"Well, I do know your methods."

"Even if you fail to apply them. The van belonged to the firm of Williams and Sons in Cheapside – "

"That takes me back."

"To where or what?"

"To my school days. When I first arrived in London, I was installed by my uncle at St Paul's School. The school was housed in a grand old building in Cheapside. I may have mentioned that fact before, of course."

"Many times. Watson. When you said just a few moments ago that you would sit quietly and give me your fullest attention, was that a statement of intent, or merely a remark intended to punctuate the conversation with no real meaning behind it?"

"Almost certainly the former, but your narrative so far does tend to invite interruptions. It is, if I may say so, not the most riveting account I have heard from you."

"That is hardly surprising, as I am only allowed to utter one sentence at a time before your interventions come along at regular intervals. The driver, a Henry Morton, was taken to the infirmary as a matter of urgency, and his mate, James Hallam, was taken into custody by Lestrade – "

"He was obviously – "

"Yes, Watson?"

"Nothing, Holmes, please continue."

"I searched through what papers there were in the van, pertaining to delivery schedules. It was clear to me that the first delivery point had not been reached."

"And yet there was no furniture in the van?"

"I believe I have already established that point."

"Indeed, you have, Holmes. I was merely reviewing the data to get it straight in my mind. One cannot make bricks without straw, you know."

"Thank you for your insight. A search of the van revealed nothing other than a few spent matches and curiously enough, a stuffed eel with a Roman coin in its mouth."

"How curious."

"Yes, which is why I advanced the use of the word 'curiously'. This set off a train of thoughts in my head, being vaguely reminiscent of the affair of the taxidermist and the archaeologist. You recall the affair, no doubt?"

"No."

"No matter. It is not germane to the solving of the Grosvenor Square furniture van affair, although it did give me pause for a moment. I made my way to Cheapside, in the hope I would find the answers I sought there."

"Could not James Morton have supplied these answers?"

"James Hallam, you mean. I had already ascertained that he knew nothing of the affair. His answers to my questions were honest and straightforward."

"Surely he could tell you who had attacked him and the driver?"

"It appeared not. The attack came out of the blue and he could give no description of the assailant. The visit to Cheapside proved most illuminating."

"In what way, Holmes?"

"That is what I am endeavouring to tell you."

"Can I urge you to somehow accelerate the process, I have an approaching appointment with Thurston."

"If it had not been for your constant prevarication and interruptions, you would have been in full possession of the facts of the case by now. My inquiries at Williams and Sons pointed me in the direction of a specialist importer of fine furniture who was located in Hackney. No doubt you have connections to the area of a personal nature you wish to regale me with."

"None that I am aware of."

"A blessed relief for the recounting of this affair. After taking refreshment, I proceeded to make my way to Hackney. The importers had their office in a somewhat dilapidated building, with a small warehouse adjoining that leaned to one side precariously. It was only at this juncture that I realised I had visited these premises before. This was long ago before my biographer came to glorify me. Watson, perhaps you could look at your watch in a more surreptitious fashion."

"Apologies, Holmes. Then what happened?"

"What happened is that you will go and play billiards and I will never mention the Grosvenor Square Furniture Van affair ever again. If you will excuse me, I have an experiment I wish to conduct. Good day, Watson."

Some time later, as I was writing an account of the adventure of "The Noble Bachelor", I felt a pang of disquiet that I hadn't given Holmes my full attention as he attempted to explain the affair. How to make reparation though? I hit on the idea of the following passage that, now and forever, will have to suffice for the adventure of the Grosvenor Square furniture van:

> *"I have very little difficulty in finding what I want," said I, "for the facts are quite recent, and the matter struck me as remarkable. I feared to refer them to you, however, as I knew that you had an inquiry on hand and that you disliked the intrusion of other matters."*
>
> *"Oh, you mean the little problem of the Grosvenor Square furniture van. That is quite cleared up now – though, indeed, it was obvious from the first. Pray give me the results of your newspaper selections."*

Dr. John H. Watson and Sherlock Holmes – "The Noble Bachelor"

The Adventure of the Paradol Chamber
by Paul W. Nash

The year 1887 was a busy one for Sherlock Holmes. He was engaged in a dozen cases of note, including the adventures of the Five Orange Pips and of the defeat of Baron Maupertuis, the Hoxton Devil, and the Amateur Mendicant Society, not to mention the very curious case of the Hollow Effigy, all of which are recorded in my notes (though some cannot be made public until the noble and gentle personalities involved have been forgotten). Perhaps the strangest case of the year, however, was that of "The Paradol Chamber". It represented a triumph for Holmes's powers of ratiocination, and marked for me the end of an old phase of life and the beginning of a new.

It began one balmy afternoon in July. Holmes was still in delicate health after his prolonged battle of wits (and fists) with the Baron, but he was in good spirits again after the black reaction to his herculean efforts of the spring, cheered by his successes and the recent Jubilee. We were both lounging in the rooms in Baker Street, Holmes toying with one of his musical compositions, humming short snatches to himself as he scratched with his pen, while I was absorbed in the latest outrageous tale in *Blackwood's*. Suddenly Holmes threw aside his manuscript and jumped to his feet.

"I had quite forgotten," he cried. "We are to receive a visitor this afternoon." He plucked a letter from the mantelpiece and threw it into my lap. I picked it up and read as follows:

Dear Mr. Holmes,

I am sure you will not mind if I call upon you this afternoon at four o'clock to discuss a little matter which has troubled me. My name will, I am sure, be known to you, but I do not seek any favour on account of my fame. Please treat me as you would any common client.

Yours most sincerely,

Beresford Lamb

"I received it this morning," said Holmes. "What do you make of it?"

Knowing my friend's methods, I addressed myself first to the physical characteristics of the letter. "Well," I replied, "it is written on very good-quality paper, with a broad-nibbed pen, in a round, confident hand. The writer has not commissioned a printed heading for his letter-paper, but has attached a copy of his calling card to the top of the sheet with a pin. The card gives an address in Endell Street and is somewhat pretentious in execution, with rather too many curlicues. I suppose Beresford Lamb must be well-to-do as well as being, as he remarks, quite famous."

"*Is* he famous?" asked Holmes. "I confess I had never heard of him before I read his name here."

"He is certainly known to me."

"Really? Is he, perhaps, a celebrated jockey or tipster upon the turf?"

"No indeed," I replied gravely, feeling that Holmes was chaffing me rather. "He is an author."

"An author? Of what cast?"

"He writes dramatic stories of crime."

"Not *reports* of crime? Surely, I should have heard of him had he been a recorder of criminal proceedings."

"No. His work is pure fiction. But I am surprised, nevertheless, that you have not heard his name. He has become well-known from these very pages." I raised the copy of *Blackwood's Edinburgh Magazine* that I had been reading.

"I see," said Holmes. "Have you read all his works?"

"Hungrily," I replied. Lamb was among the more successful of a group of writers who had taken to inventing bloody and unlikely tales of crime and detection in the past decade or so. I remembered with pleasure Mr. Collins's *Who Killed Zebedee* and Miss Green's *The Leavenworth Case*, and almost as fondly the serialisations of Dr. Casterman's cases in *The Cornhill* and those of "Lupus" in *Once a Week*. My black bag contained, at that moment, an unopened copy of *The Mystery of a Hansom Cab*, of which I had heard very good reports.

"Well," said Holmes. "We have a few minutes before our visitor is due. Perhaps you would tell me a little of Mr. Lamb's works."

"I have just finished reading the final part of his latest story," I replied, "and will be delighted to give you an account of it. It is a tale of love and attempted abduction called "The Adventure of the Paradol Chamber", and is the latest in a series of *The Chronicles of Lord Pinto*. This Pinto, the Viscount son of the Earl of Fullerton, is an amateur detective."

Holmes held up his hand. "A detective?" he said. "Like myself, rather than of the official variety?"

"Not quite. Pinto is a rich man who pursues detection as a hobby, while you are England's foremost professional consulting investigator."

I felt a little flattery would do no harm to my friend, or my narrative, at this moment. Holmes smiled with a mixture of pleasure and condescension. "Pray continue, Doctor," he said.

"Although Pinto is a noble amateur, I have noticed, once or twice when reading of his exploits, that there are echoes of your own work and methods. Accounts of your successes have been available in the public prints, and I am sure Lamb has taken a little inspiration from you." Holmes continued to smile.

"The story concerns a stage magician who calls himself 'Paradol'. He works with a young assistant on various astonishing illusions, and soon forms a powerful regard for the beautiful daughter of the owner of one of the theatres in which he performs. He pays court to this girl, but she spurns him and, in the way of such stories, her rejection turns his genius from light to dark, and he plots his revenge. The climax of his act is the appearance of The Paradol Chamber. This is a gaudily-painted vanishing-box, six feet tall and three feet wide, with a door on the front, which the assistant brings on to the stage. It is raised to a height of about a foot on four wheels, which allow it to move easily and the audience to see beneath it while the trick is performed.

"Paradol would invite a beautiful woman from the audience to join him on stage, and ask her to step into the Chamber. The door was then closed and the assistant would turn the Chamber round upon its wheels through three-hundred-sixty degrees to allow the audience to see the back and sides. All the while, Paradol would make exaggerated signs and passes as if conjuring powerful magic. He would then open the door of the Chamber to reveal that it was now quite empty. The audience would inevitably gasp. Then Paradol would bow and step into the Chamber himself and close the door. The assistant would repeat the revolution of the Chamber and this time when the door was opened the beautiful lady was standing again inside the box and Paradol had disappeared. This was the end of the act and, while the lady left the stage and the audience clapped loudly, the Chamber was wheeled into the wings.

"We are told how the trick was done. It was a very simple matter. The interior of the Paradol Chamber was covered with black velvet and was divided vertically into two compartments by a velvet-covered board which revolved on a central pivot. When the door was opened, only the front half of the Chamber was actually visible, but this was not obvious because of the blackness of the interior. The lady chosen from the audience was, of course, a confederate of Paradol, and once inside the Chamber knew how to revolve the central board and pass into the back compartment. When the door was opened, the audience could again see only the empty black interior of the front half of the box. Clearly, when Paradol himself entered the front compartment, the whole process was reversed and the two compartments changed places.

"So much for the trick as it was usually effected. But on one night Paradol practised a dramatic and potentially fatal variation." Holmes snorted. Perhaps I had grown a little caught up in the narrative and decided to continue it without embellishment. "He paid his usual lady accomplice to feign illness, and suggested to the theatre-owner that his daughter might take her place. To this he readily agreed, and the daughter was initiated into the secret of the trick. At the climax of the act she was picked out, seemingly at random, by Paradol and entered the Chamber. While the magician's assistant turned the box to show its faces to the audience, the young lady revolved the central board and entered the hidden compartment.

"But the ingenious Paradol had prepared the Chamber differently that day. He had drilled a number of holes in the floor of the hidden half of the Chamber, and beneath them fastened a shallow metal box stuffed with cotton-wool soaked with chloroform. The girl naturally fell into a deep sleep. Rather than enter the Chamber himself, Paradol then bowed to the audience, received their plaudits, and left the stage, while his assistant wheeled the Chamber after him. Usually the Chamber would be halted and opened as soon as it was in the wings, but now Paradol took charge of it and, with his assistant's help, wheeled it to the stage door, which he opened. Then he departed through it, quickly to return driving a small cart and pair. The Chamber was loaded into the cart and the magician drove off into the night with his sleeping prize."

"The next part of the story is a curious dream or vision which Paradol enjoys as he drives away, thinking of his new life with the young woman he has abducted. He fancies he will open the Chamber and take out her sleeping form and lay her on the bed in the cottage he has rented, to recover from the effects of the chloroform. When her head is clear, she will perceive her situation and give herself willingly to her abductor in marriage. Paradol will revert to his own name, which no one in the theatre world knows, and a priest will be called to conduct the service. Then he will choose a new stage-name and continue his career. But when he arrives at the cottage and opens the Chamber he finds it quite empty.

"In the third part of the story, Lord Pinto makes his appearance, called in by the theatre-owner to trace his missing daughter. The official police have, naturally, failed to solve the mystery and have suggested that the disappearance was merely a carefully planned elopement. Pinto begins his investigation and learns that the magician's young assistant has also disappeared. After much circumlocution, and not a few co-incidental discoveries, Pinto traces the assistant to a rented room where he is living with his new wife, the theatre-owner's daughter. It transpires that the assistant too had been in love with the girl and, perceiving at the last moment what Paradol was about, had rescued her from the Chamber while his master was fetching the cart and replaced her sleeping form with a couple of sandbags which were used in the theatre to secure scenery. Upon waking, she had recognized her rescuer, declared her love, and willingly run away with him, believing that her father would no more welcome as a son-in-law a young stage assistant than he would a mature stage magician.

"The story then turns to the pursuit of Paradol. Pinto gains from the assistant certain clues which allow him to locate the magician's cottage. He alerts the local police who meet him at the cottage, where they confront Paradol – and Pinto recounts, to the magician's astonishment, the full story of his abduction of the girl. When he has finished, however, Paradol asks the police inspector what crime he is going to be charged with, since there is no evidence of any of Pinto's claims and the girl was not, in fact, abducted by him but eloped with his assistant. The inspector scratches his head, but Pinto smiles and leads the party to an outbuilding where they find the Paradol Chamber, newly-painted in a different livery, but still the same machine. He produces a hand-bill for the magic act of one '*Eggestein the German Wonder*', and opens the Chamber to reveal the unconscious body of another young woman. It is her abduction with which Paradol is charged.

"Upon finding that he had been cheated of the prize for his ingenuity, Paradol's heart had turned quite to wickedness, and he had determined to use his skills to take possession of the most beautiful young women of the region, repeating his trick in local halls and theatres under a series of different names. At the last, he is led away to prison, and the girl wakes to find herself in safe hands, with no knowledge of the fate which she has so narrowly escaped." I paused and looked at Holmes, trying to gauge his reaction to the story. His face was quite impassive however, like a severe carving of granite. "I enjoyed the story very much," I said. "Indeed, I found it . . . thrilling. But, I admit, it is a ridiculous tale, full of melodrama and implausible detail."

"I disagree," said Holmes sharply. "It is certainly romantic and melodramatic, even grotesque, but not wholly implausible. I can see only one possible flaw in the logic of the tale as you have related it, and that is the question of the chloroform held in a box beneath the floor of the Chamber. Would such an arrangement have been effective? And would not the odour have alerted the young woman that she was entering a trap? But then, why would she recognize the scent of chloroform?"

I had not expected Holmes to consider the story quite so seriously. "Perhaps," I said, "you should read 'The Adventure of the Paradol Chamber' for yourself."

"Perhaps I should," he replied. "But all that must wait, for here, if I am not mistaken, is the creator of that story." The small clock on the mantel chimed the hour and, in the same instant, there was a ring on the doorbell. After a few moments, we heard the regular footsteps of our visitor, and momently there was a firm rap upon the door.

Holmes paused a moment then called out, "Come in."

A tall gentlemen in a long brown coat entered. His brown bowler was held in the long, elegant fingers of his left hand, and in his right he held a gold-topped cane. He must have been well over fifty years of age, but his hair was coal-black, and swept back from his face in a sharp peak which he must have smoothed down just before entering our door. His face wore an expression of alert interest, and his blue eyes were especially piercing and earnest. At Holmes's invitation he handed over his hat and stick, removed his coat, which Holmes also took, and sat down beside the empty fireplace.

"So," said our guest when he was settled, "you are the famous Sherlock Holmes?"

"I am he," replied Holmes. "And this is my friend Dr. John Watson, who is has occasionally been good enough to assist me in my cases."

Lamb nodded to me, then turned back to Holmes. "You will know my name, of course," he said. "Have you read my stories?"

"I have some familiarity with them."

"Very good. I have followed your career too, as far as I have been able, through accounts in the daily papers. I must congratulate you on your triumph in the case of the Baron and the British antiquities. I gather you saved the French government something like a million, and the Greek nation a similar sum, and ended by knocking the Baron down the steps of the British Museum when he took exception to your interference . . . ."

"The accounts of the Baron's downfall in the papers were, I fear, a little purple. But I can count the case among my successes. Now, what can I do to assist you, Mr. Lamb?"

"I have received a letter," he said, "which has troubled me. It came last Friday, and I have been wondering ever since how to understand it. This morning I decided my best course would be to show it to you."

Lamb took a sheet of folded paper from his pocket and handed it over. Holmes read it carefully, then took the sheet to the window and used his glass to examine the paper in the summer sunlight which shone in. Then he handed the sheet to me and, for the second time that afternoon, I found myself reading a letter addressed to another man. This time, however, the text was not a little shocking. It read in this way:

Mr. Lamb

You are a basterd and murderer! You are responsable for my Ellen's death, as sure as if you had strangled her with your own hands. She would never have left the comfort and safety of her own home and gone off with that man but for you and your wicked story of the Dashing Carman. Be sure, Mr. Lamb, that I will have my revenge, if it takes all my skill and cost my life. Yours is forfit, Sir, for the wickedness you have done.

Your most bitter and determind enemy

Tom Charlett

Having read the text, I studied the physical properties of the letter, attempting to follow the actions I had seen Holmes take. It was written with a sharp-nibbed pen with such force that at times the nib had quite broken through the paper, which was smooth and white, octavo in size. It had been folded twice, clearly for insertion into an envelope, since there was no sign of a seal, address, or stamp upon the back. I held it up to see the watermark and read "*JOYN*" and "*SUPER*". Holmes would surely have recognized this at once, as I did – as all that remained of "*Joynson Superfine*", the mark of one of the commonest writing papers in the Empire.

"Well," said Lamb at length. "Should I take it seriously? It seems a very bitter threat to me – and yet I cannot believe the writer is quite in earnest . . . ."

"Do you still have the envelope?" Holmes asked.

"Regrettably, I threw it away. I remember it was buff and was addressed to me, care of *Blackwood's* London office, using the same handwriting."

"What is this reference to your story of 'The Dashing Carman'?"

"Have you not read it, Mr. Holmes . . . ?"

"I regret not, but perhaps Dr. Watson?" He glanced in my direction.

"Yes, indeed," said I. "I remember 'The Adventure of the Dashing Carman' very well. It concerned the beautiful daughter of a cruel Banker, who was loved by an ugly Viscount, who was far above her station, and a handsome Carman, who was far below. Lord Pinto was consulted by the Viscount when the young woman disappeared. He discovered that she had secretly married the Carman and was living with him in a humble place. When the Viscount learned this, he attempted to murder the girl, which had been his intention all along, as revenge for her rejection of him, while her father hunted down the Carman with the same end in mind. Pinto saved them both, defeating the Banker – who was ultimately reformed – and the ugly Viscount, who ended by fleeing into the path of a locomotive at Paddington Station. I have noticed, Mr. Lamb, that your stories often involve a beautiful daughter, and an elopement."

"You are perfectly right," said Lamb. "My readers like nothing better, and I try to please them. The other factor in my stories is, of course, crime, most usually a murder or abduction, and here too I do my best to satisfy my public."

"How very admirable," said Holmes. If he was being sarcastic, Lamb did not detect it.

"You are most kind," he said. "And Dr. Watson – though he has omitted all the most interesting and original points in my story – has put it into a nutshell and touched upon the vital element – that this tale might be seen as an encouragement to a romantic young woman to defy the wishes of her father and elope with a good man of lowly station."

"What of the woman, this 'Ellen'?"

"I know only what can be inferred from the letter," said Lamb, "that she was among my readers, eloped, and was later murdered."

"And Tom Charlett?"

"A relative, I presume. Most likely her father. I have never met the man, and yet he blames me for Ellen's killing. It is perhaps one of the hazards of the occupation of writer, that some deluded person may read a great deal more into your words than was ever there. It is as if Macbeth were to be blamed for a case of regicide, or Mr. Dickens for a cruel gynaecide."

"Not quite," said Holmes. "I do not believe either Shakespeare or Dickens could be said to have encouraged murder. Both Macbeth and Sikes suffered for their crimes, while your story, if I understand it, might encourage not homicide, but elopement."

"You are quite right, Mr. Holmes. But what should I do?"

Holmes took up the letter again and peered at it narrowly. "Since we cannot know, at present, whether this letter is real or its writer's extremity of feeling continues, we must, I think, treat the threat as very serious indeed. For the time, Mr. Lamb, I would advise you to lock your doors securely and keep a pistol always to hand, to guard yourself most carefully and, if possible, never to venture from your house except in the company of some trusted male friend."

"Thank you, Mr. Holmes."

"There is one further course of action I should advise. You should take this letter, and your fears, to the official police. A very serious crime may be in contemplation, and the police would, I am sure, take these threats most seriously."

"I hesitate to go to the police, for I know what fools they are."

"I am surprised to hear you say so."

"As you know, my experience, reflected in my stories, is that there is nothing more slow-witted and slow-moving than the average British policeman. They are inclined, I believe, to see crime everywhere except where it is actually taking place, and to judge by the merest appearances all cases that come before them."

"There is some truth in what you say," said Holmes. "But not all policemen are such imbeciles, and a few, a very few, come close to being able in their profession. In any case, the official force can assign a man or two to your protection and can put the entire metropolis on watch for this Tom Charlett."

"Very well," said Lamb. "I will do as you ask. But I do not trust the police to get at the truth."

"I will do my best to find the truth," said Holmes, "both about the letter, and about the murder. Once the killer is apprehended, Tom Charlett will have a more just focus for his bitterness."

"Thank you."

"You will not mind if I keep the letter for a while?" said Holmes.

"Will I not need to show it to the police?" Lamb asked.

"If you tell them of its content, and that I have the original for safe-keeping, the police will take your story seriously enough."

Lamb rose and bowed to each of us in turn. Holmes put the letter away in his pocket-book then fetched Lamb's coat, cane, and hat. Without another word, the famous author left our sitting room.

"Well," said Holmes, "what do you make of our writer and his story?"

"It seems serious to me," I replied. "If this Charlett blames Lamb, however unjustly, then his life must be in danger."

"Indeed. That 'if' is a most important word. I cannot help but feel that we have had today, from start to finish, nothing but fiction. Yet parts of the story may be, indeed *must be* true. I did not mention the fact to our client, but I well recall the case of the murder of Ellen Charlett. It was reported early last week. As you know, I make it my business to keep up with the criminal news, and read especially the more sensational literature on the subject, though pure fiction concerning crime I have always considered beyond the pale. I docketed the crime and no doubt have a few notes upon it my index. Perhaps you would reach over to the shelf to your left and draw out the volume for '*C*'? Thank you."

I passed the heavy, green-bound volume to Holmes who turned through the pages slowly, smiling and muttering to himself. "Camden Theatre Mystery. Castle Graham Imposture. Cats, Seven Black. Cervical Vertibrae . . . Ah, here she is, the Charlett Murder, lying neatly between the Chadlington Horror and my late lamented friend Charlie Peace – a long entry for him, but only a scrap for the unfortunate Ellen Charlett." He passed the book to me and I found a very brief newspaper clipping from *The Daily News* of the twenty-seventh of June, 1887, which ran in this way:

> *The murder, by strangulation, of Miss Ellen Charlett, daughter of Thomas Charlett, master-tanner, of Clerkenwell has been reported this morning. Inspector Lestrade of Scotland Yard told* The News *that it was a simple case and he expected to announce the arrest of the killer imminently.*

"Well," said Holmes, "that gives a little useful information. Our friend Lestrade is on the case, and we have Mr. Charlett's address and profession. In the morning I will summon Lestrade and we can begin our investigation. But for now we may perhaps best occupy ourselves with a little reading. I will assay the final episode of Lamb's "Paradol Chamber" in *Blackwood's*. You may perhaps have some similarly uplifting work to occupy your mind."

I remembered the copy of Hume's *Mystery of a Hansom Cab* in my bag and needed no further prompting to draw it out and begin the story.

The next morning, Holmes's telegram brought Lestrade to our rooms, where he told us what he knew of the Charlett case. It seemed the manager of Willis's Private Hotel in Highbury had reported the death of a young woman in one of his chambers. Lestrade had been called in to find it a clear case of murder. The girl had been strangled with a bootlace. The hotel register showed that the room had been taken by "Mr. and Mrs. E. Smith", but of Mr. Smith there was no sign. His clothes and possessions were gone from the room, while the girl's remained. The body was identified as that of Ellen Charlett, the daughter of Thomas Charlett, who had reported her missing a few days earlier. Charlett believed his daughter had run away with her lover, an unsuccessful actor named Elias Smith, whom he had forbidden his daughter to marry. Lestrade sought a description of Smith, but Charlett had only seen him once, and that from a distance, as he had been afraid to come to the house. The hotel clerk and porter gave similarly unhelpful accounts of his appearance, as he had worn a long coat and scarf, though the night was warm. All Lestrade could gather was that Smith was tallish and of middling build. The inspector enquired around the theatres of the city, but no one had heard of Elias Smith, so that he must either have given Ellen a false account of his profession, or a false name.

"We are still looking," concluded Lestrade, "but I wish you would give me a hint or two as to how, or where, to look."

"I believe I can help you best," said Holmes, "by suggesting that you may never find Elias Smith, at least not alive."

"What, you mean that he has done away with himself?"

"Not at all. I think it quite possible that he too has been murdered, by the same hand that did for Ellen. I am reminded of a story I heard recently of a Dashing Carman whose beloved was the focus of a rival's jealousy and a father's anger."

"Why, yes. A rival for the girl's affections . . . or perhaps her father – he had cause to hate Mr. Smith, well enough, and perhaps his own daughter too . . . ."

"It is a thousand pities that I was not able to visit that hotel room myself after the body had been found. The killer must have left some marks. I suppose the room has now been cleaned and re-let, and the girl is buried?"

"Yes, indeed."

"What of her possessions and clothes?"

"She had little enough, but what she had is still in store at Highbury Station. There is a little jewellery, a book, a couple of magazines, some money, and several sets of clothes. You can see it all, all except her shoes. We never found those."

"That is a curious circumstance, is it not?"

"I thought nothing of it at the time," said Lestrade, "assuming Smith had taken them with him by mistake, among his own things."

"Possibly . . . Yes, Lestrade, thank you, I should like to examine the young lady's clothes and possessions."

"You can come to the Highbury Station, any time you like, and see them."

"Perhaps you would be a very good fellow and have them packed up and sent to me here. Thank you. Now, before you leave, I wonder if I might ask one more question? You mentioned that the lady had been strangled with a bootlace. What sort of bootlace?"

"A common brown bootlace," said Lestrade laconically.

"A *leather* bootlace?"

He brightened. "Why yes, I see. Thank you, Mr. Holmes. I am sure I would have thought of it in time, but I am most grateful for the hint all the same."

Lestrade rose and bade us farewell. As soon as he was gone, Holmes said, "I, too, must leave for a short while."

"Really?" I replied. "I believed you had quite made up your mind to solve this case without leaving your chair, as you have done once or twice before."

"I would like to get to Mr. Charlett before Lestrade arrests him. Perhaps you would pass me the *London Directory*? Thank you."

I handed him the great red book and he opened it near the beginning and turned over a few pages. "As I suspected," he said. "There is only one *T. Charlett* listed as a tanner, at No. 5 Ray Street, Clerkenwell."

"Would you like me to accompany you?" I asked.

Holmes shook his head. "Thank you, no. You would help me most materially by remaining here, in case there should be any correspondence or visitors to receive."

I thought this rather unlikely, but perceived that Holmes would rather make this journey alone. I was not entirely unwilling to fall in with his plans, as in truth I felt indolent that morning, and relished the opportunity to idle in our rooms for a few hours. The prospect of another chapter or two of *The Mystery of a Hansom Cab* had more than a little appeal. So I said farewell to Holmes and settled myself in my favourite chair with Mr. Hume's excellent story.

I was to be disappointed, however, in my fancy for a spell of idleness, for Holmes turned out to be correct in his prediction of both correspondence and visitors to our rooms. I had not been reading for more than twenty minutes when a telegram arrived. It was from Beresford Lamb, who wrote as follows:

New Development. Coming Baker Street Soonest.

I tried to settle to my reading again, but my concentration had been broken and I had hardly turned another page of the mystery before I heard a cab in the street, and within a minute the great author was again in our sitting room.

"Thank you," he said when I had taken his hat and cane. "Dr. Watson, I have received another frightful letter. Is Holmes not here to help me?"

"He will be back presently," I said. "Will you wait?"

"I wish I could speak with him now," he replied. "I have an appointment with my publisher in a quarter-of-an-hour and had hoped to see Mr. Holmes at once. May I leave the letter with you, and return later to discuss the matter with Holmes?"

"Certainly."

Lamb handed over a small buff envelope which had been rather carelessly torn open. It bore a penny stamp and Lamb's name and address in Endell Street written in what looked like the same hand as the letter we had seen the previous day.

"I must depart if I am to make it to Bloomsbury in time, and so I bid you farewell, Doctor. Please do read the letter. I will return after lunch to discuss it with Holmes." I returned his hat, coat, and cane to him and, with a nod of farewell, the author quitted our rooms.

I felt, a little ruefully, that it was my lot in this case to read important correspondence intended for other men, but I drew the letter from the envelope:

> *Bastard, prepare to meet your maker! So end all murderers! I see before me every moment the sweet face of that innocent girl whose life you have ended with as much certainty as if you had killed her with your own hands. Indeed, you did just that, albeit your weapons were pen and ink instead of the power your grip. Damn you for the Dashing Carman! Damn you! Your life is forfeit, and I will take it, for Ellen's sake.*
>
> *Your most bitter and determined enemy*
>
> *Tom Charlett*

I examined the thing closely. It seemed in every respect the brother of the previous letter. There was the same heavy pressure of the pen which had scored and torn the paper, as if the writer were squeezing out his fury through the nib, and there was the familiar watermark of Joynson. I put the letter aside, all thoughts of reading Mr. Hume's narrative now quite expelled from my head by the real mystery which lay before us. I turned the matter over in my mind, but as so often when I considered the tangle of evidence which Holmes seemed to cut through with such ease, I found only questions which I had no power to answer.

Holmes returned to Baker Street shortly before lunch. He threw off his coat and hat and wiped his face with his handkerchief. "I have endured two cab journeys," he said "and a painful interview with the bereaved tanner of Ray Street, on one of the hottest days I can remember. I have also smoked no fewer than seven cigarettes and my mind has turned upon our little problem."

"I have had a busy morning myself, having received Mr. Lamb. He has been sent another threatening letter, which he left with me, and promises to return to talk with you after lunch."

"Well, well," said Holmes rubbing his hands together. "How very interesting."

I handed over the buff envelope and Holmes examined it and its contents carefully for some minutes. Then he took out the earlier letter from Charlett and laid the two side by side upon the table, comparing first the paper, then the writing.

"Most singular," he said. "Now, before Mr. Lamb joins us, let me tell you of my little outing this morning. I found Charlett's tannery in Ray Street a very superior establishment. He is a tanner, leather-dresser, saddler, and felt-manufacturer. But he is a ruined man, quite broken by the loss of his daughter. He is certain that the stories she read of romance and elopement had a strong influence on her decision to defy his wishes with Mr. Smith, and blames these stories, their authors, publishers, and illustrators – he particularly derided the last for their depictions of pretty heroines in the arms of handsome soldiers and the like – for the loss of his daughter.

"But, although he knew well the story of the Dashing Carman from his daughter's effusions on the subject, I could not persuade him to name Mr. Lamb as the architect of his misfortune. I asked him plainly if he had written Lamb a letter, and he denied it. I contrived too to glance at some specimens of his handwriting, which was clearly different from that we see here." He indicated the two letters which still lay side by side upon the table. "Yet that may signify very little, for a man may write memoranda in a quite different temper and style from that he would use for a furious threat to a hated enemy. That he denied writing the letter is also far from conclusive. Our interview was interrupted, as I rather expected it would be, by the arrival of Lestrade and a constable who arrested Thomas Charlett on suspicion of the murder of his daughter and of Elias Smith. Charlett greeted this turn of events with horror, and I confess I felt considerable sympathy for him, for I had put the idea into Lestrade's head."

"I noticed your doing so," I said.

"I regret having added to his woes," Holmes replied. "But, since my return cab-ride and those seven cigarettes, I am all the more convinced that it was necessary."

"You believe him guilty then?"

Before he could answer there was a ring on the bell, followed by footsteps and a knock at the door. It was a fresh-faced police constable bearing a large cardboard box containing the clothes and other property of Ellen Charlett. Holmes wrote the lad a receipt and, when he had departed, slit open the box with his pocket-knife. The contents were very much as Lestrade had described them. The book he had mentioned was an edition of *Jane Eyre,* and the magazines were copies of *Blackwood's,* both including episodes written by Lamb. Holmes examined these objects and the girl's clothes with minute care.

"Look here, Watson," he said, pointing to the hem of a dark blue dress. I looked and saw, adhering to the fabric, a smear of white crystals.

"Salt?" I suggested.

"Possibly." He carefully scraped the crystals into an envelope with his knife, then re-packed the box, which he took through to his bedroom. "Now perhaps you would call on Mrs Hudson for a cold luncheon," he said.

After lunch, while we sat smoking, we heard again the doorbell and the now-familiar tread of Beresford Lamb in the passage. When the pleasantries were over, Holmes invited our guest to take a chair and asked him a somewhat surprising question.

"Why," he said, "did you think you could deceive Sherlock Holmes?"

"What do you mean, sir?"

"The letter you brought Watson this morning was a forgery, was it not?"

Lamb sighed. "I should have known better," he said. "But how did you know? I thought I had done it rather well."

"There are six points in the handwriting alone which mark the two out as different. The style of the second is more literary. But the most obvious suggestion that the two were not written by the same hand is that the writer has apparently learned to spell correctly in the few days between." Lamb looked crest-fallen. "Why did you do it, Mr. Lamb?"

"I confess I thought you were not taking the matter seriously enough. I detected some doubt, even levity, in your manner, and though I feigned as much indifference as I could, I have been very much afraid for my life, and felt that a second letter from Charlett would concentrate your mind and powers upon my problem. I am sorry, Mr. Holmes. I should not have done it."

"No doubt you should not have done it. But it is done. Did you do as I advised and tell the police of the letter?"

"I did, and they promised to protect me. A police constable has been stationed in Endell Street each night, and another will make a special patrol of the area during the day."

"That is good. But these precautions will now be withdrawn, for Thomas Charlett has been arrested for the suspected murder of Elias Smith and his own daughter."

"Then the case is solved?" cried Lamb.

"Not quite. Watson and I must find Elias Smith, dead or alive, to bear witness to the killer's guilt."

"I wish you the very best of luck with your quest," said Lamb. "But my own mind is quite at rest as a result of what you have told me. Thank you."

"We still have a good deal of evidence to collect and analyse."

"Indeed," I said. "Barely an hour ago we received . . . ." My words were interrupted by a low groan from Holmes, and I looked round in time to see him crumple sideways upon the table then crash to the floor taking with him a vase of flowers which Mrs Hudson had placed there that morning. I rushed to his side. He was dreadfully pale and my first thought was that the day's heat and excitement had been too much for him after the huge stresses of his recent cases. It took me only a few seconds, however, to realize what he was about.

"Is Mr. Holmes ill?" asked Lamb.

"I am afraid so," I said. "His health is still poor after his encounter with Baron Maupertuis, and I fear he has overstretched himself. He needs rest now. Perhaps you would leave us and I will help him to his bed."

The instant Lamb had departed, Holmes sprang up from the floor.

"I perceive you wished to stop me telling Lamb about the box of Ellen's things," I said, nodding towards the bedroom. "But why? Surely you cannot suspect Lamb? Is not forging this second letter just what an innocent, but terrified, man would do?"

"For the moment I will say only that I wish to keep Mr. Lamb innocent about the details of my investigation. My next task is to identify the crystals found on that dress, and I would ask you to leave me alone with my apparatus for a few minutes to achieve that end. Thank you."

I sat beside the fireplace while Holmes repaired to the stained table at which he conducted his chemical experiments and lit his burner. He took out the little envelope of crystals and began to work on them, first tasting a few on his finger tip, then placing a few more upon the handle of a spoon and passing it through the flame, which briefly turned purple. Then he mused for a minute or so, and finally ground up the last of the crystals and mixed them with two other chemicals drawn from his numerous bottles and jars.

"Come, Watson, and observe the final proof," he said. I stood beside him as he scraped the tiny mound of black powder he had made into the bowl of a spoon, and then touched a lighted match to it. There was a flash and a hiss, and a tiny genie of smoke rose from the spoon. It had an unmistakable odour. "*Et voilà tout.* Potassium nitrate."

"Gunpowder," said I.

"Quite. I knew it was a Potassium salt by the taste and purple flame. Presuming it was a common compound, it could not have been the chloride because that is hygroscopic and would not have remained as crystals, so it had to be the sulphate or nitrate. The easiest way to tell which was to make gunpowder with the sample – if it fulminated it was the nitrate and if it was inert then it was the sulphate. Saltpetre was, in fact, what I expected to find. But the test is proof positive. And now I must again leave you to amuse yourself for a little time, while I make a further enquiries. We may bring the business to a conclusion this evening, when I hope you will accompany me in the adventure. I will either return to collect you, or send for you, if you are you willing to assist me."

"I most certainly am."

"Until this evening, then."

It was a long and weary wait. The heat of the afternoon was oppressive, and though I tried to bend my mind back to *The Mystery of a Hansom Cab*, I was constantly distracted by thoughts of Ellen Charlett and her sad fate. I ate a little supper. Soon night fell. It was past nine when I finally heard from Holmes. He sent a telegram which ran thus:

Meet 17 Buckler Street Woolwich. Ten. Bring Revolver.

I collected my pistol, drew on my coat, and went out into the street to find a cab. When I arrived at Buckler Street it was a little before ten. The sky was still not quite dark, but the streetlamps were lit and I could see Holmes on the street-corner, apparently lounging against a pillar-box while he smoked a cigarette.

"You see there," he said when I had joined him. "That warehouse?" He indicated a brick-built building. I nodded. "I hope you will not mind breaking an entry in a good cause?" Again I nodded. "I have been watching, and there is no one there now, but we can expect our bird to return to the nest before too long, now that night has fallen."

The door of No. 17 was heavy and locked both with a padlock and a mortice-lock. Holmes produced a set of burglar's tools, and quickly picked the padlock and opened it. The mortice-lock proved more difficult, however, and he had to unscrew the plate of the mechanism before he could release it.

"It is important," he whispered, "that our man does not suspect we are inside when he arrives, so we must leave no traces. I will slip in and open that window. Then I will close the door and while I lock it perhaps you would re-fasten the padlock, then climb in by the window?" Yet again I nodded, though I did not much fancy the window, which was narrow and nearly six feet from the ground. Nevertheless, once I had completed my task, I managed to scramble up and squeeze myself in, and close the window behind me. I found Holmes working by a narrow blade of light from a dark-lantern, relocking the door from within by reconstructing the lock.

We were in a small store-room which appeared to be empty, save for a few piles of rotting timber, perhaps once floorboards or ship's timbers. At the far end was a blanket, nailed up as a curtain, and Holmes nodded towards this. Beyond was a doorway into a gloomy space which smelt damp and acrid. Once through Holmes said, "I think we might risk a light here, as there are no windows." He lit a dark lantern and the place was flooded with light. Ahead of us lay a short brick-lined corridor with three chambers leading off each side. We walked slowly along and Holmes directed his lamp into each in turn. In one was a workshop, with a carpentry bench, tools strewn about and planks of timber leaning against the wall. In another was a bed, with a night-stand and dressing-table. In the third was a desk bearing books, papers, and a typewriter, with a bookcase and two chairs beside. In the fourth was a modest larder of tinned and preserved foods, a table and chair, and some plates and cutlery. In the fifth was a motley collection of objects – two bicycles, various trunks and boxes, several children's toys, and a great stuffed bear. The last room contained, however, a truly astonishing sight. When Holmes swung the beam of his lantern into the space I could scarcely believe it.

"Good Lord," I whispered. "It must be the Paradol Chamber!"

Before us stood a wooden cabinet, six feet tall and three feet wide, mounted upon wheels. It was painted deep red and decorated in blue and gold, just as the Chamber had been described in *Blackwood's Magazine*. When we opened the door, we found the interior covered with black velvet. Holmes reached in and pushed at one side of the central panel, which began to revolve.

"Surely," I said, "There cannot be someone in there?"

"I doubt it," he replied, and was proved correct. The hidden compartment of the box was empty, but, when Holmes directed his lamp at the floor, we could clearly see the holes drilled there and I could detect still a faint odour of chloroform coming from below.

"What does it mean?" I asked.

"Little in itself," he replied. "But I believe we will find something more conclusive." We returned to the room which was equipped as an office and Holmes began to search through the papers, then the contents of the desk drawers. From the bottom drawer he drew forth a pair of black patent leather ladies' shoes. They seemed ridiculously small, like a child's.

"This, I think, will be enough to convict our man," he said. "And now, we must wait for him. You have your revolver? Excellent."

We took our places on the two chairs beside the desk, and Holmes shuttered his lantern. I feared we might be in for a long wait, but I was happily in error, for only fifteen minutes had passed before we heard the crunching of a key in the great lock and footsteps entering the outer room. Then a gas jet was lit in the corridor and a tall figure stood in the doorway before us. Holmes uncovered his lantern, and I drew my revolver. Beresford Lamb uttered a foul oath.

"I am afraid we have you, Mr. Lamb," said Holmes. "My friend has a revolver and will not hesitate to use it, and I have these shoes, which I am sure Mr. Charlett will identify as having belonged to his late daughter."

"May I light the gas?" said Lamb urbanely.

"I will do it," said Holmes. He did so and then shuttered the lantern again.

"Now my good friend Watson will remain here, keeping you covered, while I fetch those forces of law and order which you so despise. Did you lock the outer door behind you?" Lamb thought for a moment, then nodded. "Then be so good as to throw me the key – Watson, watch him!" Holmes caught the key and slipped past our prisoner into the corridor. A moment later I heard the outer door open and the sharp note of a police whistle.

Lamb smiled, then moved very slightly towards me.

"Remain perfectly still," I said. "Or I will shoot you."

"I doubt that," he said. "You are a man of feeling, unlike Holmes, who is a mere reasoning machine. You would not harm a fellow creature, especially one who is innocent."

"You are quite right," I replied. "I would not harm an innocent. But I do not believe you are any such thing."

"Oh, I am," he said. "I am the victim of a most unfortunate error on Mr. Holmes's part. I beg you to believe me. Whatever evidence he has found he has misunderstood . . . . You will admit that it is possible."

I felt that it was, but was in no mood to argue the toss so said nothing more.

"Now let me show you something, something which will convince you of my good intentions." He began to reach towards the left inside pocket of his jacket.

"What is it?" I asked.

"It is a letter from Ellen Charlett. The truth is that I did know her, as a friend. She wrote to me after one of my stories touched her, and we struck up a correspondence. Her letters told of how she feared the anger of her father and wanted to run away with Smith to a safe place. I helped her with money. But her father found her all the same. This letter proves it."

"Move your hand no further," I said, "or you will find yourself quite unable to move it." He ceased the gentle creeping of his hand towards his pocket. "If you are innocent, how did you come by Ellen's shoes?"

"I confess I took them from her room, but after she had been killed. I went to the hotel to give her money, and found that Charlett had been there before me and strangled her. I took her shoes for a base reason, I am afraid – I intended to plant them in the possession of her father, so that the evidence against him would be all the stronger. I wanted him brought to justice. Only let me show you the letter, and you will see it all."

I thought this story convincing. He could see I was wavering in my resolve, and his hand moved slowly again towards his pocket, while he smiled. His face was a picture of honesty and candour. But at that moment I recalled the shoes, how small and pathetic they had seemed, and I squeezed the trigger and fired.

I am a good shot, and the bullet caught Lamb squarely in the right shoulder. With a terrible cry he was thrown back onto the floor in the corridor. A moment later Holmes rushed in followed by a constable.

"I should not have left you alone, Watson" he said. "Are you hurt?"

"Not at all," I said. "Lamb told me he had a letter that would prove his innocence in his left breast pocket . . . ." Holmes reached gingerly into the pocket and drew out a small, pearl-handled revolver.

Lamb groaned. "Your friend tried to kill me," he said.

"Nonsense," said Holmes. "Had he tried to kill you he would have succeeded. Now stand up and let me search you while Watson keeps you covered. I do not think you will twice doubt his determination in the matter." Lamb dragged himself to his feet, and Holmes went through his pockets, removing nothing else but a leather-bound notebook and gold-plated fountain-pen.

"Very well," said Lamb. "You have captured and wounded me, and I will tell you all. But not before the police inspector arrives. I want my story properly recorded, and known across the world."

"I doubt very much that there would be a word of truth in your story. Let me propose an alternative. When the inspector arrives, I will tell your story and you will kindly correct me if I go wrong in any particular. Now sit here – Yes, against the wall – and I will hold the pistol while the Doctor examines you. Do I hear the delicate footsteps of the excellent Lestrade approaching?"

Indeed, there was a thunder of footfalls in the outer room and Lestrade and two further constables burst into the corridor. Lamb sat down against the wall and I gave Holmes the revolver while I examined the wound that I had inflicted. The bullet had passed through the shoulder-blade, shattering it and the collar-bone, and out the other side. The wound was not life-threatening, but was no doubt very painful and would leave Lamb with a permanent weakness in his right arm. I did not have my bag with me, so that all I could do was apply a compress with a clean handkerchief. Holmes handed the revolver back to me.

"So you've shot him," said Lestrade, stating the obvious. "Why?"

"Let me enlighten you," said Holmes. "It is a grotesque story which your constable may care to record, for it contains a full confession. Beresford Lamb was not given that name at birth, but assumed it as one of a number of personalities in his life of crime. It became, perhaps, his dominant persona. Lamb, the successful writer, the great man of letters, famous, and now rich too because of the popularity of his stories. He has recently bought a new house in Endell Street on the profits of his writing. No doubt he has a considerable talent with his pen, but what makes Lamb remarkable is that he bases his stories, as far as possible, on realities, and the feelings of his protagonists, especially his villains, upon his own feelings. He is a sensualist, and has, I venture to suggest, so little of what a normal man would call conscience as to be practically devoid of any such virtue. He is probably the third cleverest criminal in London."

"Twaddle!" said Lamb.

"And possibly the most remorseless. He has also, until now, been able to continue his career, and to write about his crimes quite openly, without detection. That is the genius of the man. His mistake, his final mistake, was to take on Sherlock Holmes. For that was what you intended to do, was it not?"

Lamb made no answer, but gestured towards the desk where we had found the shoes. Holmes retrieved from it a sheaf of typewritten pages.

"It would have been my greatest triumph," said Lamb. "Or rather, Lord Pinto's."

"I see the story is called 'The Eclipse of the Great Detective'. A very lively title."

"It is all written," said Lamb, "all but the last few pages, in which the famous consulting detective fails, and Lord Pinto succeeds."

"The crime," said Holmes, looking through the papers, "is the murder of Ellen Charlett. I see you have given her another name, as you have to your failing detective, but the circumstances are identical. A young woman, seduced by an intelligent older man who pretends to be a failed actor, persuades her to elope with him against her father's wishes. When he has her at his mercy in a cheap hotel, he strangles her and flees into the night."

"You could never have solved such a crime," said Lamb.

"I suppose you think that because you see me as a rationalist? For Sherlock Holmes, there must be a rational motive for every crime, while this murder was committed for no rational motive. It was not for gain, or love, or hate, or revenge, or even for expediency. Why did you kill Ellen Charlett?" Lamb was silent. "In the story, I suspect the motive was one of pure sensuality. Your heartless older man merely wished to know what it was like to have a young woman at his mercy, and to take her life with his own hands. He wanted the experience. And that was something you believed I could not understand. Sensual pleasure was part of your motive too – for we must not forget that this murder has been done twice, once in fiction and once in fact. You wanted the experience. I daresay you enjoyed it. But you had two further motives. Firstly, you wanted to live out, to *try* out, the plot of your story, and secondly, you wished to confound Sherlock Holmes.

"In order for the last motive to succeed, however, I had to be brought into the case, and that was why you came to me with a forged letter in your hand. I could do nothing else but investigate the case, and fail to identify the killer – yourself – while every false move I made was noted and ascribed to your Great Detective, whose defeat was the heart of your story."

"Quite untrue!" said Lamb. "The heart of my story was Lord Pinto's success."

"I knew I was being led a dance, and so I danced, and tried to perform in every way as you wished me to, even leading Lestrade to believe I thought poor Tom Charlett the true killer. I am heartily sorry that I had to do that."

"I am confused," said Lestrade. "If this Pinto solved the case in the story, would that not reveal who killed Ellen Charlett?"

A look of irritation came over Holmes's face. "The story," he said, "reveals only the name and nature of a fictional character who killed a girl for pleasure, and the cleverness of Pinto in his deductions. It would be clear enough that the case was based on that of Ellen Charlett, but this would hardly be the first time a story had been inspired by a real crime. I believe Mr. Poe wrote something of the sort forty years ago."

He turned again to Lamb. "You almost succeeded. But I had three clues that guided me, and one scrap of evidence you overlooked. The first clue was in the letter which you forged from Thomas Charlett. I had no way to prove it a forgery, but I believed it was."

"Come now," said Lamb. "You must admit that the letter was a masterpiece, a brilliant piece of both writing and forgery."

"You betray one of your greatest flaws, Mr. Lamb. You are conceited. The letter was good, but it was just a little too florid, too much the work of a man of letters, to be genuine, while at the same time the poor spelling and coarse language was too strong for a man of Charlett's education and standing. My second clue came when Lestrade told me the name of Ellen's lover, Elias Smith. I was reminded at once of another Lamb, the poet Charles, who assumed a pseudonym for his essays. What were they called, Doctor?"

"'*The Essays of Elia*'," I replied.

"Quite so. Lamb had suggested to you Elia, and Elia had suggested Elias. Perhaps it was merely the unconscious signature of a self-regarding man of letters. The third clue came with the second letter which you forged. This was a very clever strategy. Your intention was to bring me a letter which was sufficiently unlike the previous one to be detectable as a forgery. When I uncovered the deception, as you knew I would, your stated reasons for undertaking it would do nothing but guide me further from the truth, and quite convinced Watson here of your innocence. However, I saw something else in the second letter, which you may not have considered when you wrote it. Although it was obviously different in a number of respects from the first letter, it was also obviously similar in a number of ways. The hand and language were so similar – as they had to be, if I were not to see immediately that this was a crude fake – that I asked myself how, without the earlier letter before you, you had done it. At that time, you will remember, the first letter was safe within my pocket-book. You either had a truly remarkable memory for handwriting and words, or you had written both letters yourself. Although I could not prove it, I inclined to the latter opinion.

"The final scrap of evidence was a few crystals which I scraped from the hem of Ellen Charlett's dress. You removed her shoes from the hotel room because your feared there were traces on the soles which might lead me to you, but you missed a very small trace on the hem of the dress which, I will wager, Ellen wore when she last visited you here. The crystals turned out to be of saltpetre. Where would one pick up such a chemical except in a manufactory of gunpowder? There is only one such in London, and it is hardly likely Ellen would have visited the Royal Arsenal. I recalled, however, that some years ago the Woolwich Dockyard had been part of the Arsenal, but had been closed down and many of the warehouses let to private companies. In such a building, where munitions had been made and stored for decades, was it not likely that saltpetre would be found upon the floors, and picked up by the boots and skirts of a visiting lady? I spent part of this afternoon with the agent for the former Dockyard buildings, and learned that only one of them, No. 17, had been rented in recent years – to a Mr. Charles W. Holmes. Guessing a little of Mr. Lamb's manner of choosing his *noms-de-plûme*, I suspect the compliment was due not to me, but to the American poet and essayist. So Watson and I came here and found your second home, your lair, in which your crimes were planned, your devices perfected, and your plots written."

"You have not bested me," said Lamb. "I am still the better man. That you found me out was sheer luck, Holmes!"

"I would expect you to believe nothing else."

"What of the Paradol Chamber?" I asked.

"That was an example of Mr. Lamb's practical approach to the writing of mysteries. He conceived his vain-glorious magician, Paradol – we may perhaps detect another self-portrait here – but had to know whether his device would work in practice. So he built the Chamber. It was an easy task for one who had once worked as a carpenter."

"How the devil could you know that?" said Lamb.

"When I first shook your hand, I remarked how much larger and stronger the right was than the left. You had clearly not developed such musculature wielding a pen, and I deduced some physical labour. Carpentry was suggested by the fragment of your story which I read, in which the construction of the Paradol Chamber was described in very precise terms. I would further venture to guess that you have worked in the theatre, both as an actor – witness your recent performances in my sitting-room – and in other roles, perhaps as a scenery-builder." Lamb regarded Holmes with malevolence, but said nothing. "Perhaps you tested the Chamber on Ellen Charlett."

"I did!" said Lamb. "That was back in February when I had first made her love me, and was initially drafting that great story. I had just told her my real name – well, I had revealed that I was Beresford Lamb, the very writer she admired with such a passion. I swore her to secrecy, and she was willing, eager even, to step into the Chamber and try my experiment. It worked wonderfully. Within a minute she was quite unconscious and I could enter and draw her sleeping body out. You cannot imagine my delight. Ellen came back here many times after that, to serve me. 'The Eclipse of the Great Detective' required that we elope – which I effected easily – and that she be strangled by her lover – which was also a simple matter. I brought her here that evening, so that I could tell her the story of the great victory of Lord Pinto over Sherlock Holmes."

"Did you tell her that you intended to take her life?"

"No, though perhaps she guessed. Had I asked her consent, I am sure she would have given it and offered her throat gladly. But it was important to me that she did *not* give her consent."

"You know," said Holmes, "in some ways, the letters you wrote in the person of Tom Charlett were your most truthful expressions. When you told yourself, '*You are a bastard and murderer!*' and '*You are responsible for my Ellen's death, as surely as if you had strangled her with your own hands*', you were, for once, writing the literal truth."

"I should kill you for that," said Lamb in a low voice. "I regret that I will probably not have the opportunity to do so."

"Probably not," said Holmes. "After you had taken her back to the hotel and done the deed, you thought to remove her shoes, just in case they bore traces which might lead the police, or an astute sleuthhound, to your door. But you missed the smear of saltpetre on her skirt, and that was your undoing. I wonder if you had another motive for taking the shoes? Did you wish for a memento of Ellen? Or of your sensual experience in bringing about her end?"

"I will not answer that," said Lamb. "I see that the constable has been taking notes, and there will no doubt be an official report on the case, and perhaps a confession which I shall be called upon to sign. I will do so, but on one condition. That my story, 'The Eclipse of the Great Detective', be published in *Blackwood's* as it stands, with my confession included as its termination." There was a moment's silence. "I had hoped to write more stories. I had a dozen plots in mind – all ingenious, all delightful – but I have done enough that the name Beresford Lamb will live for ever."

Lamb would say no more, and soon afterwards was taken away by the police surgeon. He stood trial for the murder of Ellen Charlett, and was convicted, but his sentence was commuted to one of life imprisonment as the judge believed him a lunatic. Holmes believed differently. He thought Lamb neither mad nor wicked, but a curious anomaly of nature, a man born without a conscience who regarded his mind, imagination, and senses, as the centre of all things. The case had been a triumph for Holmes's powers. He had defeated a great intellect in a game played by his opponent's rules. Thomas Charlett was naturally released by the police, and attended Lamb's trial, but betrayed no emotion when the sentence was passed. It is said that Lamb continued to write in the asylum, but his stories were always burned on the orders of the Governor. "The Eclipse of the Great Detective" was never published.

For my own part, I returned to our rooms after the adventure, and picked up again *The Mystery of a Hansom Cab*. I read it to the end, but found it dull and flat after the excitement of recent adventures with Holmes. This set an idea loose in my mind. These stories, these tales of murder and romance, had always an emptiness at their centre. Even those of Beresford Lamb had proved unsatisfying, because they were, in the end, untrue. What if I could write stories, based not on imagination but on *fact*, on the adventures of Sherlock Holmes, which had often been reported in the press with such scant regard for the truth? Some few years before, I had written a memoir of my time in India and Afghanistan and of my return to England, which had been lost in circumstances associated with the case I later called "The Adventure of Nightingale Hall". I had included short accounts of three of Holmes's cases in that lost book. Perhaps now was the time to recall those cases, and seek to publish those accounts, and others. I certainly had notes enough, and fancied I could write as fluidly as Beresford Lamb, and a good deal more honestly. I decided then to try to publish an adventure or two of my own. It did not occur to me until some days later, when I had completed the draft of the first such story, to wonder what on earth Holmes might make of the idea.

> *The year '87 furnished us with a long series of cases of greater or less interest, of which I retain the records. Among my headings under this one twelve months I find an account of the adventure of the Paradol Chamber . . . .*
>
> Dr. John H. Watson – "The Five Orange Pips"

The Bishopgate Affair
by Mike Hogan

I stood at the window of our sitting room on a pleasant September day, sipping a last cup of coffee and idly looking down at the street below.

"I say, Holmes, there is a young lady on the opposite side of Baker Street holding a small child who – "

"She in the grey?" Holmes said from his chair by the fireplace where he read his morning paper.

"Yes. She is in obvious distress. I shall go down to her."

"No need," Holmes turned the page. "I saw her dithering on the pavement before breakfast. Give her time to make up her mind, and she will come up."

The lady looked up and met my eyes. Even from across the street, I could see her face was pale and drawn and that she was holding back tears. I put down my cup and strode to the door. In a moment, I had returned with her.

"May I present Mrs. Towers," I said, ushering the young lady into the sitting room.

Holmes frowned. "Perhaps the child might be deposited with Mrs. Hudson?"

"Holmes, she is a baby, not a parcel."

I led Mrs. Towers to our sofa, offered refreshment, which was politely refused, and watched with a benevolent eye as she settled back with her child on her knee, a quiet baby of a year or so in age. I had earlier elicited that the child's name was Violet.

Mrs. Towers wore a grey ensemble of coat and walking dress with a matching hat, ornamented with a red feather. Her face was oval, and on closer inspection wan, puffed, and marked with the damp traces of frequent tears. He eyes were red-rimmed, and as she blinked at us, more tears ran down her face.

I proffered my handkerchief, which she accepted.

"My father, Thomas Towers, has been arrested by the City Police," Mrs. Towers began when she had assembled her faculties. I pondered that her married name was the same as that of her father, while she continued. "He had spoken of you, Mr. Holmes, and I pray I may put the matter before you." She sobbed into my handkerchief.

"On what charge?" Holmes asked.

"Burglary of a jewellery shop," Mrs. Towers answered softly.

"The theft is all over the newspapers," I said. I picked up *The Daily Telegraph* that Holmes had dropped on the carpet and turned to the domestic crime page. "The safe at Barratt's, the jewellers on Bishopsgate by St. Katherine's Workhouse, was blown open with explosives early this morning and robbed of a thousand or more pounds worth of jewellery. The explosion smashed the window glass to smithereens and blew out the metal shutters."

I looked up as the baby whimpered. Mrs. Towers tended to her child, teasing her blonde curls.

"PC Hanson of the City Police arrived on the scene at the run," I continued, "and he found the safe burst apart, the door embedded in the far wall, and the room awash."

I frowned at Holmes. "Awash? There was no rain last night. Later in the article, the writer describes puddles of water, so perhaps a water main was cracked, and it drained away. He concludes that the matter is in the masterful hands of that scourge of the criminal classes, Inspector Athelney Jones of Scotland Yard."

"Ha!" Holmes cried.

"Barratt's." I frowned. "I looked at their display of watches in the shop window once when I was early for a train at Liverpool Street and I took a stroll along Bishopsgate, but I never entered the premises." I addressed Mrs. Towers. "What evidence is there against your father? Has he been in trouble before?"

"He has, sir."

"Towers," Holmes mused. "Is he Long Tom Towers, the cracksman?"

Mrs. Towers nodded, her eyes downcast.

"Long Tom," Holmes said with a smile. "One of the best yeggmen in the country in the seventies. I had thought him long retired. He originally used drills, levers, and wedges to get into safes. Vaults have become harder to crack over the past decade or so with various patented improvements, and it seems he has branched into dynamite."

"My father assures me that he has retired from all that," Mrs. Towers said in a low voice. "He is not an easy man, as you might say, and he has a temper on him, especially these recent months, but he has never lied to me."

"And Mrs. Towers senior? His wife?" I asked.

"Died in childbirth, Doctor, delivering me." Mrs. Towers' voice cracked, and her eyes flicked towards the child. "I was the apple of my father's eye." She turned to Holmes. "My father is innocent of this crime, sir. We do not have any savings, and I do not know what is to become of us. I can only throw myself, my father, and my daughter on your mercy." She bent forward, sobbing, and the child screeched in alarm.

"Watson!" Holmes cried, leaping up from his chair and retreating to his desk.

I conveyed Mrs. Towers down to the omnibus stand, and when I returned, Holmes was putting on his coat.

"You did not inquire about Violet's father, Holmes."

"If there was a husband to hand, I should have expected him to be here beside his wife." He pursed his lips. "An inquiry would have been indelicate."

The shutters that had protected the plate-glass windows of Barratt's jewellery shop on Bishopsgate Street were bowed and bent, the metal twisted and torn into jagged remnants.

A whistling young man swept up glass outside the shop, the fragments glittering in the sunlight, and a crowd of gawkers clustered on the opposite pavement under the stern glare of a mounted policeman.

A portly man in a tweed overcoat stood in the shop doorway, smoking and talking with a police sergeant. His grey hair spilled out from under the rim of his bowler hat, joining ample side-whiskers in a Burnside style that framed his flushed and heavily dewlapped face. He frowned at Holmes and me as we stepped down from our cab, and his brows knitted further as we approached him.

"You are, Mr. Holmes, the theorist," the man said in a husky, wheezing voice.

Holmes bowed. "And you are Inspector Jones, scourge of the criminal classes."

"I have no time for airy theories, Mr. Holmes. My feet are firmly parked on God's own earth." Inspector Jones sniffed and offered me his hand. "Athelney Jones, in charge of this case."

I introduced myself and Inspector Jones led the way into the showroom, a mess of shattered shelves and broken glass from empty display cabinets.

"Now, many a Yard man might take exception to your turning up out of the blue, Mr. Holmes," the inspector said, "coming uninvited, without an official position in the matter and poking in everywhere as you are wont to do, but I am not moulded of that clay. I welcome you and the doctor with open arms. Just so long as you do not interfere with official business and the solemn processes of the Law."

Inspector Jones waved a hand at the warped skeleton of a good-sized Milner's safe that stood in the window alcove. "A bad business, gentlemen." He leaned back against a broken counter, searched his waistcoat, produced a packet of cigarettes, and shook one out.

"I keep nothing hidden and everything lies open before you, Mr. Holmes. We have a broken safe and missing jewellery. And we have a suspect, Mr. Thomas Towers, known as Long Tom, as skilled a cracksman as you'd find in a day's walk. But he does not live a day's walk away, gentlemen – he lives a furlong or so down the road in Cowper Street. He's now contemplating his sins in the cells of the City Police at Bishopsgate Station."

Inspector Jones lit his cigarette from the end of the previous one and flicked the stub out the front door.

"Fast work, Inspector," Holmes remarked.

"That is my style, Mr. Holmes, as you may recall. I arrived here at six-thirty-seven of the a.m., and I made my arrest at seven-and-four minutes, the instant I was apprised of the near location of the culprit. I do not let the grass grow, sir."

The inspector puffed on his cigarette and gripped his hands together, his fingers intertwining. "I am weaving the sinews of my case into a tight web of circumstance."

"I do have some slight official standing in the case," Holmes said. "I have been engaged by Mr. Towers' daughter."

"I met the young lady." Inspector Jones laughed a wheezing laugh, his tiny, deep-set eyes twinkling below puffed lids and his jowls wagging. "You are her knight-errant, I make no doubt, Mr. Holmes!" His laugh became a prolonged fit of coughing. "But here," he wheezed as he caught his breath, "here are stern facts that you will have to face, sir. I accept no airy-fairy theories on *my* watch."

"Barratt's is a family owned firm?" Holmes asked.

"The premises are in the care of Mrs. Barratt in the absence of her husband," Inspector Jones said, puffing on his cigarette. "Mr. Barratt ran off with his Jezebel fifteen months ago, and his rejected wife carries the business on with the help of a manager, a Mr. Spinelli. Mrs. Barratt was asleep in bedroom above the shop when burglars entered and blew open the safe with explosives."

I frowned. "Mr. Barratt ran off?"

Inspector Jones blew a stream of smoke across the shop. "With his fancy woman, a shop girl at Whiteley's Emporium. You know the type, gentlemen." He sniffed. "Mr. Barratt is thought to be somewhere up Harrogate way."

"May I talk with Mrs. Barratt?" Holmes requested.

"The lady is in shock and has taken to her bed. Or more exactly, to her estranged husband's bed, as her own room is in disarray, broken windows and so forth." Inspector Jones pointed to cracks in the ceiling.

"The safe is in an odd position," I said. "It faces the shop window, where anyone could look inside or spy as the door is opened and closed. Was it shifted here by the blast?"

A pale-faced man in a dusty frock coat had been sitting behind one of the few undamaged counters, writing. He stood, handed Inspector Jones a sheaf of papers, and faced me.

"If I may correct you, sir," he said in English tinged with a faint Italian accent. "The safe is unlocked only once a day, before we open our doors for business and when the metal shutters are closed. The contents are on trays that are transferred to the display cases. After closing time, the reverse process is adopted: We close the shutters, open the safe and store the trays inside. At no point in the procedure may anyone outside view the contents of the safe."

Inspector Jones introduced Mr. Spinelli, the manager of Barratt's. Then he glanced through the papers he had been given and whistled. "The inventory lists items worth almost two-thousand pounds."

"There is, or *was*, a peephole in the outside shutters," Mr. Spinelli continued, "so the patrolling constable might check that the safe was unmolested as he passed on his rounds. I uncovered the peephole and lit two gas burners as my last act before locking up last night. The lights burn all night, illuminating the safe. The water or blast doused them, and I believe the first policeman at the scene turned off the gas."

"PC Hanson was three streets away, five minutes at the run," Inspector Jones said. "He heard the blast, sprang his police rattle, and sprinted here. He found the safe as you see it, and the window alcove flooded."

I frowned. "I wonder where the water came from?"

"How long is Hanson's beat?" Holmes asked.

Inspector Jones consulted his notebook. "Thirty-three minutes at regulation constabulary pace. Hanson stated that he passed the shop every half-hour, give or take, from the start of his beat till the blast, and he conscientiously checked the peep hole on each round, noticing nothing amiss."

Holmes scanned the floor. "You found no debris? No broken watch parts, or bits of jewellery?"

Inspector Jones snapped a finger at the sergeant, who showed Holmes two items on his palm.

"Just this length of fishing line attached to the curtain rod, and a candle stub in a corner," the inspector said. "Nothing else."

Holmes pulled out his magnifying glass and examined the items.

"The burglars cleaned the safe out, Mr. Holmes," Inspector Jones said with a wide grin. "They took the lot, two-thousand worth. My men are searching Long Tom's crib as we speak."

Holmes nodded slowly, then looked up. "The constable was here within five minutes, you say? Did he see anything?"

"He tried to get in through the shutters but could not. In fact, he cut himself on some shards of metal making the attempt and I sent him back to the station to clean the blood off his uniform. He states that he hammered on the front door until the boy opened up. By that time the devils were long gone, out the back."

"The boy?"

"Reece, the groom who sleeps in the attic above the stables. He was awakened by the blast, and he hurried downstairs in his night attire."

Holmes turned to Mr. Spinelli. "How long has Reece been in your employ?"

"He works for Mrs. Barratt, sir, not the shop. I believe Mr. Barratt took him on a year-and-a-half ago to tend his horse. Since then, Mrs. Barratt has purchased a carriage-and-pair, and the boy drives that."

"Perhaps I might have a word with Reece?" Holmes said.

The sergeant called through the front door and the fair-haired boy of perhaps eighteen or so came in from the street holding a broom. He shook his head. "Blimey, what a mess."

"Watch your mouth, young man," Inspector Jones snapped. "There's no call for language."

"I should like to establish a timeline, if I may, Inspector," Holmes said. "Perhaps Reece could re-enact the proceedings of this morning from the moment of the explosion?"

Inspector Jones wagged an admonitory finger. "*Charades*, Mr. Holmes?"

"Bang," I said, feeling foolish, as a police rattle sounded from the main house. I stood in the doorway of Reece's simple bedroom in the attic above the stables at the back of the garden. I checked my watch and made a mental note of the exact time.

The boy swung out from under the bedcovers, rubbing his eyes. He put on his boots, stood, reached into a wardrobe for his dressing gown, and slipped past me. He leaned over the baluster, peering down to the stable.

"The horses were frightened by the noise, so I spent a moment calming them, then went out into the garden."

"Do so, please," I instructed him.

Reece scrambled down the stairs to the stable. He stroked the horses' necks, then looked out of the stable door towards the main house.

"There was a deal of smoke," he said. "My first concern was for Mrs. Barratt. The back door of the house was open wide, so I ran across the lawn and upstairs. I knocked on her door and asked if she was well."

Reece loped across the lawn to the back door, and I followed him through the scullery and kitchen and upstairs. He mimed knocking at a bedroom door and murmured. "The mistress was distressed, and she asked for a glass of water."

He went to the bathroom and ran the tap. "I heard a hammering on the front door and a cry of 'Police!', so I jumped downstairs and opened the door to the constable."

I followed the boy downstairs to the hall where Holmes and Inspector Jones waited, each with his watch open on his palm.

Inspector Jones smiled. "Seven minutes and eight seconds, Mr. Holmes, from the blast to opening the door. Time for the villains to clear the safe and escape out the back while PC Hanson was hammering. They ran the few hundred yards to Towers' crib. I'll stake my reputation that the loot is hidden there."

Holmes nodded. "Assuming the thieves grabbed the jewellery and ran out the back door, where did they leave the garden?"

The inspector and I trooped through the house behind Holmes, followed by Reece and the police sergeant and out the back door. It was a fine autumn day with bright sunshine, wispy clouds high up and a slight wind.

We crossed a well-kept lawn to a fence perhaps five feet high. Beyond the fence was a narrow lane, not wide enough for a carriage.

Holmes looked thirty yards or so back towards the house, then to the stable block beside us. He faced the boy. "You saw nobody crossing the garden last night, no dark shapes or shadows?"

"No, sir, but I was focussed on the house. The wind was blowing this way and it carried with it the stink of chemicals and smoke. I guessed a gas explosion and thought the house was on fire."

"The thieves slipped out while Reece was upstairs tending to Mrs. Barratt," Inspector Jones said. "It was a dark night, with just a sliver of moon."

"Undoubtedly," Holmes said. He turned back to Reece. "The garden is very fine. Who looks after it?"

"Mrs. Barratt cares for the roses," the boy answered. "I do the heavy work, the weeding and the mowing. Mrs. Barratt is down on weeds, sir. She cannot abide a weed."

"You do a good job. And the roses are remarkably healthy. Did you do any gardening this morning or yesterday?"

"No, sir, not for a day or so."

"What are your plans for the empty flower bed against the wall by the back door?" Holmes asked.

Reece grinned. "More roses I expect, sir. Mrs. Barratt is main proud of her blooms. She has prizes from the Spring Show at Kensington Gardens."

Inspector Jones and the sergeant exchanged amused looks, and I avoided their eyes. I was always somewhat bemused by my friend's very occasional expressions of horticultural interest.

"Is that your shed?" Holmes asked, indicating a wooden shed by the back fence. Reece opened the door and Holmes peered inside. "Very neat."

Holmes smiled at Inspector Jones. "Perhaps another word with Mr. Spinelli?" he suggested.

The inspector, Holmes, and I returned to the shattered showroom, and Holmes questioned the manager about the contents of the safe.

"Full, sir," Mr. Spinelli answered, shaking his head. "Apart from our usual stock, I had just purchased an eight-hundred-pound collection of jewellery from a lady, the wife of a person of rank in reduced circumstances – with Mrs. Barratt's approval of course."

"Who knew of this purchase?" Inspector Jones asked.

"Just she and I, sir, aside from the bank and our insurers."

"All the articles in the safe were insured?" the inspector asked.

"Naturally."

Inspector Jones narrowed his eyes and turned to Holmes. "Don't you want to know where Mr. Spinelli was at three-ten this morning, Mr. Holmes?"

Holmes smiled.

"As I told you Inspector," Mr. Spinelli answered in a soft tone, looking embarrassed, "I was staying with a friend in a room above the bar of the Horse and Groom Pub by Lambeth North Station."

"I know the Horse well." Inspector Jones said with a grin. "And this was with a lady friend."

"Yes."

"You are a married man, Mr. Spinelli?" Holmes asked.

"I am engaged to a lady."

"To the lady at the Horse and Groom?"

"To a person in Napoli." He flushed. "I hope that my whereabouts last night might be kept from my employer, gentlemen. Mrs. Barratt is a lady with the very highest moral standards."

The door opened, and Reece poked his head in. "Miss Dennis is here, Mr. Spinelli."

"Miss Dennis is our clerk," Mr. Spinelli said. "She comes in for the afternoon and evening when the City offices close and most of our business is transacted. She lives at home with her mother. She is a drummer in the Salvation Army band."

"Do you wish to interrogate Miss Dennis, Mr. Holmes?" Inspector Jones asked. "As we know well, nine times out of ten there's an insider involved in a robbery. Common sense, sir! Someone told *someone* of the extra swag to be had after Mr. Spinelli's purchase."

Mr. Spinelli blinked at the inspector.

Holmes smiled. "I will leave the young lady to you, Inspector."

Inspector Jones, Mr. Spinelli, and the boy filed into the showroom.

"Come, Watson," Holmes murmured as the door closed behind them. "We have a few minutes to ourselves. First upstairs."

Holmes loped up the stairs and opened the door to the room above the showroom. I followed him. "Any observations?" he asked.

"A lady's bedroom, Mrs. Barratt's presumably." The room was dominated by a high, four-poster curtained in paisley fabric. The chairs and curtains and lampshades were frilled, and a great many pots and jars of beauty potions crowded the dressing table. Two of the window panes were boarded and cracks stretched up the walls.

"The scent?"

I sniffed. "Rather pleasant."

"A fine fragrance from *Molinard*. Milady does not stint herself."

He opened the wardrobe. "Silks, feather boas, hats of fashionable hugeness."

"I am uncomfortable, Holmes. Why are we here? What has Madame Barratt's boudoir to do with the attack on the safe?"

Holmes led the way downstairs, across the lawn, and into the stables. He stroked the noses of a pair of fine chestnut mares as he looked around a well-kept space with horse brasses decorating the two stalls.

"Keep still, Watson. I will have a quick look upstairs."

"I say, old chap, shouldn't we wait for the inspector?"

Holmes leapt the steep wooden stairs to the attic.

I turned and found myself facing the stable boy, Reece. "What a fine pair of horses," I said, for want of anything else to say.

"Mrs. B. and I got them from the Gypos' horse fair on the Downs."

"And the coach is, ah – "

"Carrington's of Brighton, sir. They do good work."

Holmes clambered down the stairs, passed the boy and me without a word, and strode across the lawn to the main house. I scurried after him, my face flushed with embarrassment.

I followed Holmes into the showroom, where he again questioned the manager. Inspector Jones leaned against a shattered counter with his arms folded, smiling a knowing smile. A young girl sat on a stool, sobbing softly.

"Did your insurance company pay out the value of the jewellery Mr. Barratt took with him when he disappeared?" Holmes asked Mr. Spinelli.

"I understand Mr. Barratt took nothing, sir. According to Mrs. Barratt, he was an Episcopalian and immune to greed. Not wishing to cause inconvenience, he stated in an official, stamped letter that he had passed the business to his wife, and he wrote that he and the shop girl would live on a small annuity he had from his parents. Mr. Barratt ended the letter, *amor vincit omnia*."

"You saw this letter?" Holmes asked.

"I did. And a Christmas card that I understood was postmarked from Harrogate."

"And how is the business faring without Mr. Barratt?"

"We have had our ups and our downs, sir," Mr. Spinelli answered, "mostly downs before I took over. Business is better now, but still not what it was, sir. One of our main lines is engagement and wedding rings, and some customers may have felt that, in the circumstances of Mr. Barratt's midnight flit with his amour, a ring bought here might be contaminated. All nonsense of course, but people are superstitious on such matters."

Mr. Spinelli considered. "And Mr. Barratt had many connections within the trade that Mrs. Barratt does not. She brought me into the business a year or so ago to remedy that deficiency, but it's slow going." He frowned and seemed about to say more.

"Go on," Holmes said. "This is a serious investigation, you must hold nothing back from the inspector."

"Mrs. Barratt and I sometimes do not see eye to eye on the necessary replenishment of stock. I was only recently able to persuade her to agree to a major increment of items for sale so that we can offer more variety and increase our turnover."

"Very laudable, Mr. Spinelli," Holmes said. "You joined the business after Mr. Barratt left. Had you had any previous correspondence with him?"

"No, sir."

Inspector Jones shook another cigarette from his packet. "You have met everyone involved, Mr. Holmes, aside from Towers. There are no live-in servants except the boy, Reece. A cook and servant girl come daily at eight in the morning. The business uses bonded district commissionaires for deliveries. So, there we are."

He lit his cigarette and smiled. "I do not see that your theoretical approach to the case has yielded anything of interest, Mr. Holmes. While good, old-fashioned police work has unearthed a motive – *greed* – a method – *explosives* – and a man – *Towers* – currently in jug."

He indicated the sobbing girl. "You don't want to talk with Miss Dennis?"

"No thank you, Inspector," Holmes said, returning the inspector's smile. "It's a fine day and the roses are blooming."

He turned to me. "A page from your notebook, if you don't mind. I must send a telegram."

"I am going to inspect Towers' crib," Inspector Jones said. "Would you gentlemen care to join me? We can stop off at the telegraph office on the way."

"I have reached two conclusions, Mr. Holmes," Inspector Jones said as we walked along Bishopsgate Street.

Holmes smiled. "I am agog, Inspector."

"The thieves struck on the very night that a new consignment of jewellery was put into the safe. That's too pat for my liking – Too much for me to credit. I do not believe in coincidences."

"But coincidences are always singular, Inspector. That's why they are called coincidences."

Jones ignored Holmes's remark. "Only two persons, Mrs. Barratt and Mr. Spinelli, knew of the purchase of new stock, but Miss Dennis was present when the items were delivered, unwrapped, and put away in the safe. She remarked that she was happy that the stock had been renewed, as she had worried that the business was failing and she might lose her position. You should have joined me in her interview, Mr. Holmes."

"You may be right, Inspector," Holmes said. "Mr. Spinelli was also concerned at the falling off of trade."

"Exactly. We thus have two possibles for the inside man – or woman. And Spinelli is an Italian. We know of their ways with the gentle sex."

"And connected with Naples," I added, "that nest of Black Hand *Camorristas*."

"And the second of your conclusions, Inspector?" Holmes asked.

"I believe Towers knows he has no hope of escape from my net, so he got his daughter to bring you in, Mr. Holmes, to muddy the waters."

We stopped at a pleasant house set back a little by a small front garden. A policeman guarded the open front door. Inspector Jones consulted with a spade-bearded sergeant in the hall.

He turned to Holmes. "My men have discovered no explosives as yet, Mr. Holmes, but we have found plenty of cracksmen's tools, as you can see." He indicated an open leather bag on the floor.

Holmes sniffed. "Broken and rusty. These implements have not been used in months, if not years. That accords with his daughter's assertion that Towers is retired."

"You do not give our criminals sufficient credit, Mr. Holmes. I am sure you will agree with me when I say that we English have the most inventive brains in the world. New devices and apparatus proliferate daily, gentlemen. Our cracksmen are *evolving* (if I may use a scientific term, Doctor). Where once your Yeggman would carry twenty pounds of chisels, augers, and drills, now his tools are a few sticks of dynamite and a box of detonators."

"Nevertheless, Mr. Towers kept his conventional cracksman tools."

"He had expended his dynamite! In my office I have gas lighting, all very modern and convenient, Mr. Holmes. But on my desk is a paraffin lamp, just in case, do you see?"

"You have an answer for everything, Inspector Jones," I suggested.

"It's my business to do so, Doctor."

The inspector led us through to the scullery, where from the windows we had a view of a large back garden.

"We are starting on searching the garden, but there are certain difficulties," he said.

I peered through the kitchen window. The police constables searching outside seemed to be hugging the garden walls and edging along them in a most peculiar fashion.

Holmes joined me at the window and laughed aloud. "Bee hives. Mr. Towers keeps honey bees."

Inspector Jones opened the kitchen door and revealed a triple row of bee hives stretching to the back of the garden where the grass gave way to bushes and trees.

"I shall remain here," Inspector Jones said, "to better co-ordinate our efforts."

"Fuss and feathers," Holmes said. He marched out of the door and I followed, not without a certain trepidation. Holmes ignored the policemen and weaved between the hives towards a small copse at the back of the garden surrounding a shed and tarpaulin-covered woodpile.

The hives buzzed ominously as we passed them, and in my anxiety, I almost bumped into Holmes as he suddenly stopped and glared about him.

"We might start with the most obvious place, the woodpile. If not there, or the shed, we must look at the hives."

I blinked at him.

"And from here on we must emulate the constables and proceed with cat-like tread." He walked slowly and deliberately to the shed, and I followed in his footsteps.

"Are bees disturbed by vibrations?" I asked.

"It's not bees I'm worried about." Holmes frowned at the policemen behind us, who were gaining confidence and poking in the bushes that lined the side fences of the garden with hawthorn sticks.

"No, this will not do," Holmes murmured "They will pulverise the neighbourhood, stamping about in their policeman's boots."

He called softly to the nearest constable. "You, what's your name?"

"Anderson, sir, City of London Police."

"Married?"

"No, sir."

"Good. Come here. I need you to be careful and quiet. Can you do that?"

"Because of the bees, sir?"

"If you like. Send your colleagues back to the house."

Holmes led the constable and me to the woodpile. He gently removed three logs from the pile, lay them on the grass, sat on them and lit his pipe. "Gentlemen, kindly remove each log separately in the manner I just showed you. Do not drop a log, because you may set off an explosion that will demolish the neighbourhood. Stop the instant you see or feel anything unusual."

"I say, Holmes – " I frowned at his pipe.

"The danger is from the police clodhoppers, not a naked flame and not the honey bees. The smoke will calm them."

Holmes blew a cloud of aromatic smoke into the air. "If stored for beyond a year, dynamite becomes highly unstable and weeps nitro-glycerine. It killed Emil, brother of Alfred Nobel, the Swedish chemist and inventor."

"I'd best remove my boots, sir," Constable Anderson said.

Holmes turned to me. "An intelligent thought, the first from the police all day. This young man will go far."

Anderson and I took turns gently removing logs from the pile.

"What makes you think that Towers hid his – " I froze with a log in my hands.

Holmes leapt up and carefully leaned past me. "A loop of fishing line has snagged on the log, or perhaps it was imperfectly attached. Do not move a muscle, my dear fellow."

Holmes knelt and gently brushed away leaves and debris, revealing the corner of green tin box or trunk below the logs.

"The line passes through a tiny hole in the lid." Holmes looked up at me. "A booby trap."

My eyes widened, and I felt beads of sweat on my brow.

"I'll get – " Anderson began.

"Do not move." Holmes peered closely at my log, then very tenderly he slid his index finger into the loop of fishing line and drew it slowly off the piece of bark on which it had caught. It moved smoothly for an inch or so, then snagged again, and I sucked in a sharp breath.

"Nearly there." Holmes smiled up at me. He drew the line off the log, but it was now looped around his finger. "You are loose. Put the log down," he murmured.

I lay the log on the grass, my hands quivering.

"Anderson, go to the hallway and look among Towers' burglary tools for a lantern," Holmes ordered. "Check it is filled. There will be a tin of oil in the scullery. Move carefully, but make haste. Do not get involved in explanations."

"What is the situation, Holmes?" I asked. "What should I do?"

"I believe this line is attached to a phial of nitro-glycerine. The intention was that a person picking up your log would jerk on the line, bump or shatter the phial, and detonate the explosives."

"My God – "

"I do not want to let go of this line until we see to what it's attached. Ah, here is Anderson. Did you light the lantern? Good man."

Holmes instructed me to clear the remaining logs away and gently lift the trunk lid and inch or so, letting the line run through the hole. Anderson directed the lamplight into the box, and I bent down and peered inside.

"The fishing line is connected to an empty phial," I told Holmes.

"You are sure?"

"Yes."

Holmes slipped off the loop of line and stood. "Interesting. A booby trap, but not set to explode. My theory is proven."

He leant down and slowly opened the trunk. "An empty phial and a broken stick of dynamite, weeping nitro."

Holmes turned to Anderson. "You'd best get your inspector to call in the Explosives Inspectorate Department. Colonel Majendie has vast experience with explosives in all forms."

The constable stalked away, picked up his boots, and jogged to the house.

Holmes and I walked back through the lines of hives. Was it my imagination, or were the hives buzzing at a shriller tone?

"Well done, Constable Anderson," Holmes said as we returned to the kitchen. The young constable, now booted in regulation manner, saluted.

"We are safe enough here for you to dance a victory dance." Holmes smiled. "It might disturb the bees, however, so let us slink away and leave the hives in peace."

Inspector Jones waited in the hallway. He took a gold necklace from his pocket and displayed it. "This was found hidden in the baby's cot upstairs." He waved a sheaf of papers. "It exactly fits the description by Mr. Spinelli of items stocked by Barratt's. And I believe you have found explosives, Mr. Holmes, further confirming my case against Towers."

"Then you will not mind giving me a chitty allowing me to interview your suspect in Bishopsgate Police Station."

Holmes and I sat on folding chairs in a narrow, whitewashed cell. Long Tom Towers sat on his bed opposite us, a grizzled man in his mid- to late sixties who had stood tall and erect as we entered.

"Well, Towers, I am sorry to see you in this situation," Holmes said. He turned to me. "Towers is a first-class Yeggman. I would aver that for twenty or more years, there was no one in the business at his level."

Towers smiled. "Kind of you to say so, Mr. Holmes. Those were good years for my profession, sir, before we lost our way with these new-fangled explosives."

"We found your cache, Towers."

Towers looked down at his feet. "I dabbled a year or two ago, but found explosives not to my taste, sir. The cache is not mine. I requested the owner to remove it."

"Nevertheless, I want you to blow a safe open for me, Mr. Towers. A hypothetical, theoretical safe, similar to Barratt's Milner safe, but entirely in our imaginations. I can assure you that whatever you say will not prejudice your defence against any charge you may face. In fact, it will be in your interest."

"I trust you, Mr. Holmes," Towers said, "but you have picked a bad lay. Barratt's is a family business with the owners living above the shop. We can't hammer and lever our way in, as the noise would deafen the owners. We'd need a long winter night to drill the safe, again with some noise. I'd suggest we tickle the lock."

"Pray use the water method."

Towers chuckled. "On a Milner?" He shrugged. "I know the theory, Mr. Holmes, but I have never put it into practice – I prefer my levers and picks."

"We are speaking theoretically."

Towers nodded. "I would begin by drilling a quarter-inch hole in the top of the safe. That's two-inch case-hardened wrought iron, so a long job, Mr. Holmes, requiring a ton of elbow grease, a ready supply of the very sharpest bits, the patience of Job, and in this case a monk's silence."

"The safe was facing a shuttered window with a peep hole for the beat constable to check on it every half-hour," I said.

Towers shrugged again. "You'd need regular breaks and a tot anyway. Just fill the hole with black putty, hide as the copper passes, and press on."

Towers sprinkled tobacco on a paper and began rolling a cigarette. "Once you have your hole through to the innards, you put a funnel in and fill the safe with water."

I glanced at Holmes. We had a reason for the water.

Towers chuckled. "But now things get tricksy. Nitro is fickle stuff, gentlemen, and needs featherbed handling. You tie fishing line around the lip of a glass tube – you can get various sizes of tube from a laboratory supplier or have some blown to order to fit your brace-and-bit."

He held up his cigarette to the guard outside, and on his nod, I struck a Swan Vesta against the wall and lit it.

"You pour the nitro-glycerine into the tube, keeping an even flow with no jarring," Towers continued, puffing on his cigarette. "It has the consistency of syrup, gentlemen. What you want is the gentlest of touches and not too much explosive or you'll disintegrate the safe and everything in it. Stopper the tube with a cork and gently lower it through the hole and into the safe – leave it hanging in the water at about in the centre line."

He blew a stream of acrid smoke across the room.

"Now, detonators. Simplest is tie off the fishing line, put a candle under, light it, and scarper. The line will snap in a few seconds, the tube falls to the bottom of the safe and, even if it doesn't shatter, the jar will be enough to set off a blast in nine out of ten cases. In the tenth case you are scuppered – you sit with your hands over your ears waiting for a bang that doesn't come. Disappointing. Then you must very, very gently pull on the line and try again. Delicate, dangerous work that a man who wished to live to a ripe age would not contemplate."

Towers blew out another stream of foul smoke, filling the cell. I coughed, reached for my cigar case, and offered him a Panatela.

"Thank you, Doctor." He stubbed his cigarette against the sole of his shoe and took the cigar, rolling it under his nose. "What I would do, faced with a modern Chubb safe, is slip the nitro tube in the safe on the fishing line, as I've said, but make up a thin tube of dynamite, about the size of a cigarette, I'd grease it to make it waterproof and insert it halfway through the hole in the safe top. Dynamite is nitro stabilised with washing soda and absorbed into *kieselguhr*, a powdered earth. It's safe to work with, though you wouldn't want to drop it, but it goes stale pretty quickly, especially if it freezes. The sticks weep nitro as they thaw, which is no picnic neither." He sighed. "I prefer the old ways. You might not get into the safe every time, but you keep your limbs attached to your body."

I lit Tower's cigar.

"Attach what length of fuze you want," he continued, puffing. "In this case I'd give the beat copper fifteen minutes to get as far away as possible, light a five-second fuze, and take cover. The dynamite sets off the nitro and the water acts as tamper, multiplying the effect and reducing the sound of the explosion."

"This method works with any safe?" Holmes asked.

Towers blew out a stream of aromatic smoke. "If you can make a hole in it, you can blow it. The pressures are enormous. No iron safe can withstand them. Maybe this new steel material will, but that's a problem for younger men."

Holmes smiled. "You seemed reluctant to use the water method on a Milner."

"Hammer to crack a nut, sir. I could open a Milner with a hat pin." He smiled. "Were I still active in the profession."

Holmes turned to me. "Cigar?"

"Thank you, no."

"That was a request, old man."

Holmes took the last cigar from my case and I lit it with a match.

"Would you use the water method on a safe full of jewellery and watches?" Holmes asked Towers between puffs.

"Of course not. It's good for banknotes or printed documents, anything uncompressible. Helps there's no flame. But the pressure wave would pulverise most gems, smash up the settings, and crush watches flat. Is that what he did?"

"Who did?" Holmes asked.

Towers frowned. "The burglar at Barratt's."

"The thief followed your water scheme, with one error and a small detail omitted."

"Serious now, gentlemen," Towers said. "I did not crack that safe. I swear on the grave of my beloved wife that I am innocent in this matter. If he used nitro and water on a Milner, the thief's no Yeggman."

"Your granddaughter is a bonny child, Mr. Towers," Holmes said as he examined the burning end of his cigar. "Her blonde curls are particularly fetching. And she has her father's blue eyes."

Towers was silent for a long moment. "He's no loving father to her, sir, and no husband neither. He was a bad 'un with my Alice. He put her in the family way, so I threw him out on his ear."

"You set a booby trap to deal with him when he returned for the explosives, but you thought better of it."

Mr. Towers hung his head. "I did consider a trap. I was furious for a time, but I am no killer. I insisted that he remove the dynamite, but I never set the trap. I left it empty as a warning."

"I strongly advise you to convince your ex-apprentice to go to the police and admit his part in the safe blowing," Holmes said.

"Then Inspector Jones would have both of us, Mr. Holmes. He and Jones can rot in Hell for all I care. He was a poor apprentice, too full of himself and not wanting to hear of skeleton keys and finesse. He just wanted to blow things up. And he betrayed my hospitality. I shall rely on you, Mr. Holmes, to see me right."

"Very well." Holmes stood, and Towers and I stood with him.

"Bees?" Holmes asked.

"I am partial to honey, Mr. Holmes." Towers smiled. "And the bees are a useful deterrent to your official colleagues." He flicked a glance at the police guard outside and lowered his voice to a murmur. "I leave a pile of junk in a leather bag for the coppers to snout out, but my working tools are distributed among the hives."

Towers frowned. "You mentioned an error and that a detail was omitted, sir?" he asked Holmes.

"I believe the burglar followed your method to the letter, Towers, with the exception that he used far too much explosive."

"And the detail he omitted?"

"The safe was empty when it was blown. There was nothing to steal."

A telegraph boy on his bicycle waited outside the police station, breathing hard. "Which, I was told at Barratt's the Jeweller that Mr. Holmes was at the police station, so I followed – "

Holmes snatched the envelope from the boy's hand. "Thruppence for the messenger, Watson."

He scanned the telegram flimsy. "No, a tanner or even a bob."

I passed the boy a shilling and he beamed a thank you. "Any answer, gents?"

Holmes waved him away. "Ha! Inspector Jones did not check Reece's wardrobe, nor the contents of his shed. But I did."

"And?"

"In the first, the wardrobe contains suits of the very finest Saville Row cut, dress shirts and ties, a moleskin lapelled coat, silk drawers, and a top hat."

"And in the shed?" I asked.

"All the obvious things to maintain a weed-free garden."

Holmes called a hansom from the stand outside the police station.

"Mrs. Barratt appreciates the finer things in life," he said as we set off. "Her dresses, shoes, and perfume all evince that. Reece told you that he and his mistress travelled to Brighton to buy horses and a carriage. Mrs. Barratt stayed at the Grand, the best hotel in Brighton."

Holmes passed me the telegram. "According to this report from the manager, Reece did not stay in the servants' quarters but in the hotel proper as Mrs. Barratt's nephew. Their rooms were on the same floor. He ate with her in the dining room, they danced to the hotel string quintet, and no doubt promenaded arm-in-arm along the sea front." Holmes smiled. "Thus the dress clothes and topper."

"It was only a few months after the boy's entry into the household that Mr. Barratt decamped," I said. "Did he know of the relationship between his wife and Reece? Is that why he left her?"

"I think not." Holmes smiled. "I believe Mrs. Barratt realised that things could not go on the way they were. Inevitably, her amorous relations with her servant would be discovered by her husband or one of their staff. She had to make a fresh start. Reece's appetites were doubtless becoming as expensive as hers, and I would wager from his manner that he was no longer willing to act the part of a menial."

I frowned. "I say, Holmes, you do not mean that Mr. Barratt – "

"I think it perfectly likely. The shed was well-stocked with arsenical weed killer bought from a local shop where the boy is, I am sure, a regular customer. If the husband was done away with, Reece is either a guilty accessory to the crime of murder, or an innocent dupe. In either case, he is in danger. I think it's high time we met Mrs. Barratt."

"The lady has recovered to a degree, Mr. Holmes, and she is in the garden taking tea," Inspector Jones informed us as we stepped down from our cab at the shop.

"I must impress on you, Inspector, Holmes answered in a stern tone, "that although Towers is an infamous cracksman, in this isolated and particular case, he is innocent."

Holmes bore down the inspector's expressions of disbelief. "I believe Mr. Barratt may have been murdered, poisoned through the agency of arsenical weed killer. Mrs. Barratt's barrister, who I have no doubt will be of the greatest eminence, will inevitably point the finger of blame at Reece, who as gardener has free access to the poison. I have just discovered that he and Mrs. Barratt had a potent motive."

Holmes handed Inspector Jones the telegram.

"May I suggest that your people investigate the rose beds, and a patch of raw earth by the back door, and that you retain an open mind on the question of Mrs. Barratt's involvement in the robbery? Long Tom Towers is innocent, and I will wager you *my* reputation that the contents of the safe were never stolen. They never left the premises."

Inspector Jones gaped at Holmes for a moment before he called his sergeant.

Holmes and I introduced ourselves to Mrs. Barratt. A tea table had been set up on the lawn under a large parasol and she sat in one of four rattan chairs.

She was an elegant woman, perhaps in her early forties, wearing a frilly afternoon gown and a veiled and ornamented hat slanted, Duchess of Devonshire-style, at a sharp angle. Her hair was black, framing a pale, oval face, lightly made-up. Her eyes were a deep, deep green, bright with intelligence and humour.

"I must have my cup of tea, gentlemen," she said after she invited us to sit. "My nerves are in shatters. My sweet little bedroom is wrecked, and just look at the shop. How could anyone *do* such a thing. It is barbaric."

"I believe I know how you discovered Reece's experience as a cracksman's assistant." Holmes said.

"What are you suggesting Mr. Holmes? Reece, a criminal? He is but a child. I do not believe a word of it." Mrs. Barratt pouted. "What an unkind remark to make at the tea table."

"Mrs. Towers visited you and informed you of Reece's background. She aimed to convince you that the boy had designs not on you, Madam, but on the jewels in your safe. She wanted you to throw the boy out, so he would make his peace with Mr. Towers and return to her and her child."

"I recall no such conversation, Mr. Holmes. This is all *so* silly."

"The police may be stupid, Madam," I said. "but you cannot pull the wool over the eyes of Mr. Sherlock Holmes."

"Can I not, Doctor?" Mrs. Barratt pursed her lips. "Can I not?"

She rang a small silver hand bell, and a maid appeared from the house.

"Two more teacups, and bring more hot water."

Mrs. Barratt smiled. "Reece? You tell me he is a wolf in sheep's clothing. I had no idea. Do you think he was the perpetrator of the robbery? Surely not! What suspicious minds you gentlemen have!"

She sipped her tea. "Now I come to think of it, there have been one or two little items missing from the shop recently. It would be so very sad if they were discovered among his things and, what with the burglary and so on, he was sentenced to a long term of penal servitude. He is a willing boy who keeps the lawn just so."

The maid returned with a tray, and we waited while she lay cups, saucers, and plates in front of Holmes and me and filled the teapot.

The maid left us, and Mrs. Barratt poured tea. "You intrigue me, Mr. Holmes," she said with a smile. "I will make you a bargain. You tell me your theories, and if you are off kilter, I will endeavour to correct you. But not a word to that bumbling fool of an inspector nor anyone else, on your word of honour as gentlemen. No hint, nor jot nor tittle, and I am yours to question as you will. If not, my lips are sealed."

"I do so promise." Holmes turned to me. "Watson?"

I stood. "I prefer to leave, Holmes."

Holmes leapt up and stood before me. "We owe it to Mrs. Towers to confirm the truth."

"But if we cannot speak – "

"Trust, my dear fellow."

I subsided into my chair and nodded reluctant agreement.

"One lump or two, Doctor?" Mrs. Barratt asked with an insolent flutter of her eyelashes.

I refused sugar, and I regarded my tea cup with not unwarranted suspicion.

"Mrs. Towers visited you?" Holmes asked, settling into his chair and sipping his tea.

"The girl came here with her whelp," Mrs. Towers answered. "She attempted to convince me that Reece had inveigled his way into my house in order to steal my jewels. I knew better, of course. I had taken him to my bed within a week of his employment."

"You gave Mrs. Towers the gold necklace found at the house."

"Of course. If necessary, it would prove an attempt to blackmail me over my interest in Reece." Mrs. Barratt chuckled. "In fact, according to the fat policeman, it neatly convicts her father."

She turned to me. "You haven't touched your tea, Doctor. Is it too strong? Perhaps more milk?"

"Thank you, I am not thirsty."

"Oh, look at you, gentlemen, with your sour expressions," Mrs. Barratt exclaimed. "How prudish you are. The girl is no *Mrs.* Towers – she is little Miss Alice Towers, daughter of a known criminal, delivered of an illegitimate brat, and no better than she should be."

She sipped her tea. "And I see how you regard me, Doctor. Mine is an ardent nature that my husband could not satisfy. He ran off with his floosy and good riddance." Mrs. Barratt chuckled. "She'll have her work cut out."

I stood. "Holmes!"

"And if Mr. Towers evades the stout arm of the Law in the person of Inspector Jones," Holmes said, "you will throw Reece to him by revealing his connection with Mr. Towers and his daughter." Holmes put down his cup and leaned forward. "The boy's fingernails are crusted with soil, yet he said he had done no recent gardening. He hid the jewellery last evening, after the shop closed."

Mrs. Barratt shaded her eyes and looked across the garden. "Why are the police grubbing in the rose bushes? I do hope they mind the lawn. I like to keep things just so." She turned to Holmes. "If Reece did take the jewellery, he deserves a heavy punishment. Imagine what other crimes he may have committed while under my roof. It does not bear thinking about."

Inspector Jones halloed from the rose beds. "Doctor Watson!"

I jogged across the lawn and looked down into a newly opened shallow grave in which a man's body wearing only a pair of drawers lay face-down. I knelt and examined the corpse. "Remarkably well-preserved for, what is it, a year-and-a-bit? The lack of external decomposition and bright-red skin are potent indicators for arsenic poisoning."

"Thank you, Doctor," Inspector Jones said, rubbing his hands together. "The boy has identified the body as that of Mr. Barratt."

Reece stood between two policemen, his face blanched.

"He led us to the loot in the unplanted bed by the back door." Inspector Jones sniffed a consequential sniff. "I told you, Doctor, that cold hard facts would bring a solution to the case."

I followed the inspector's broad-shouldered back to the tea table.

"Tea, Inspector?"

"Thank you, no. I must inform you, Mrs. Barratt, that we have found the stolen jewellery."

"How clever of you, Inspector Jones. All's well that ends well, then, apart from the mess in the shop." She rang the bell and summoned the maid.

"You may tell Cook to serve the scones."

"I must also inform you that we have found your husband."

"After all this time? I do hope he is well. In Harrogate, I presume?"

Holmes stood. "I would imagine that Mr. Barratt is remarkably well, or at least well-preserved. Arsenic in heroic quantities has that effect."

Mrs. Barratt lifted an eyebrow. "I do not understand your reference, sir."

"Mr. Holmes refers to the murder by arsenical poisoning of your husband, Madam," Inspector Jones intoned.

"Arsenic? I know nothing of arsenic. Is it used to combat weeds? The boy does all that sort of thing."

"I must arrest you, Mrs. Barratt, in the name of the Queen," Inspector Jones continued. "I take you in charge for conspiracy to pervert the course of justice. Further charges may follow as our investigation proceeds."

"Good day to you," Holmes said.

I bowed a stiff farewell to Mrs. Barratt.

Sometime later, after Holmes had lectured the police on causes and inferences, Inspector Jones shook our hands, then leaned back on his heels, beaming. "I had my suspicions of young Reece from the start, gentlemen."

I followed Holmes out through the house and onto the pavement outside.

"The masterful inspector is pleased with himself," I suggested.

Holmes shrugged. "Let him have whatever meagre glory may attach to this sordid little affair."

We climbed into a hansom. "Young Reece had been turned out of the Towers household for his attentions to his master's daughter," Holmes said as we settled on the bench. "He applied for the job vacancy at Barratt's. Perhaps he had designs on the jewels. Possibly he wished to start a new life. He was seduced, raised out of his sphere, taken to Brighton, and given a high time there. He was in the thrall of Mrs. Barratt, with expectations far above his station. He, and in both senses his mistress, concocted the burglary."

He tapped his stick on the roof of the cab. "Baker Street."

We set off with a jerk. "His seductress plays a long game," Holmes continued. "She ensures that while those around her may be in danger, she remains inviolate."

"What of the farewell letter, and the Christmas card?" I asked.

"The only person who saw them was Mr. Spinelli, who did not know Mr. Barratt's handwriting. Both were forged."

"*Amor vincit omnia.* Love conquers all, Holmes. What a depth of depravity."

"And greed. In five more years, Mrs. Barratt could have had her husband declared legally missing and intestate, sold the stock, and closed the business. She could not wait, and she desired both stock *and* insurance."

"And Reece?"

"My feeling is that she would have shed the boy on her way to Biarritz." Holmes replied.

I shook my head.

"Our work is done," Holmes continued. "The Law, in its Athelney-Jonesian solemnity, must run its course. There is no firm evidence against Towers once the explosives are connected to Reece except the necklace, which his daughter will attest was given her by Mrs. Barratt to buy her silence on Reece's background. We know it was part of her longer-term plan to implicate Towers in the burglary.

"Reece is guilty of complicity in the botched, faked robbery, but whether of the death of Mr. Barratt, I cannot say for sure. What do you think?"

"Mrs. Barratt is obviously perfectly capable of killing her husband, planting him amid her prize-winning roses, and faking the note and card," I said. "She is a Gorgon."

Holmes leaned back on the cab bench. "We will see in a month or two whether a British jury shares your opinion."

> "Why, of course I do!" he wheezed. "It's Mr. Sherlock Holmes, the theorist. Remember you! I'll never forget how you lectured us all on causes and inferences and effects in the Bishopgate jewel case. It's true you set us on the right track; but you'll own now that it was more by good luck than good guidance."
>
> Inspector Athelney Jones – *The Sign of Four*

The Singular Tragedy of the Atkinson Brothers at Trincomalee
by Craig Stephen Copland

What though the spicy breezes
Blow soft o'er Ceylon's isle;
Though every prospect pleases,
And only man is vile?

The words of the missionary hymn I had sung as a schoolboy in chapel came to my mind as I stood on the deck of a Royal Navy sloop, anchored just off the Port of Colombo. They were to prove singularly prescient.

Under more usual circumstances, the experience of feeling the warm, moist tropical breezes caress one's face is a sensuous joy. Yet on that night, more than twenty years ago now, I had a profound sense of foreboding.

"Are those the lights of Colombo Port?" I said to my friend, Sherlock Holmes, as he stood beside me.

"Yes," he replied, "the tugs will pull us into the wharf at first light. We will meet with the governor and the inspector-general of police tomorrow afternoon."

Here I must digress for a moment. In one of my first stories of the adventures of Sherlock Holmes, "A Scandal in Bohemia", I deliberately allowed my readers to conclude that I had not been present alongside Sherlock Holmes when he cleared up the singular tragedy of the Atkinson brothers at Trincomalee. In truth, I did accompany him on that adventure but refrained from having an account of it published.

Our world today is different from that of 1887. With the passing of our beloved Queen, we have also witnessed the fading of a world in which civility and gentility reigned supreme. So, with some regrets, I have accepted that the unseemly subject matter of the account you are about to read has become commonplace. Those of you who have so faithfully followed the exploits of Sherlock Holmes are entitled to know the previously undisclosed events that took place in the fall of 1887 in the far-off colony of Ceylon.

Sherlock Holmes had been sent to Ceylon by the Foreign Office and directed to investigate the tragic death of a Mr. George Atkinson at the hands of barbaric local thieves – or so it was reported.

There was some urgency to the assignment. We were immediately dispatched on the Condor Class Sloop, *Mutine*. It was a gleaming new ship-of-the-line that had been assigned to the China station and would drop us off in Ceylon on its maiden voyage. We had made our way around Gibraltar, past Port Said, through the Canal, and on across the Arabian Sea in remarkable time. Now, we were about to enter the capital of Ceylon, the gracious city of Colombo.

The following morning, we descended to the quay and were ushered immediately to a carriage that bore the crest of the Galle Face Hotel. We enjoyed our short ride through the Fort district and down along the Galle Road, with the wide vista of the Indian Ocean on our right. The hotel, a magnificent whitewashed colonial edifice, sprawled for nearly a block along the seaside. No sooner had we arrived but three fine-looking native men, all wearing uniforms fit for a maharajah, appeared to assist with our baggage. They all graciously placed their hands together under their chins, bowed, and gave us the traditional greeting of *Ayubowan*.

Once inside the majestic lobby, we were welcomed by an exotically beautiful young woman bearing a silver tray on which were small rolled towels. Whilst still proffering the tray, she also bowed and said, "*Ayubowan*." I took a towel and was surprised to find that it was damp, chilled, and scented with cloves. The feeling of it as I wiped my face, hands, and neck was beyond refreshing.

The setting, as Holmes and I relaxed in the shaded chairs on the hotel terrace, was as idyllic as I could imagine.

"I must say, Holmes. A man could become accustomed to a life in the tropics. An hour or two working in the colonial office in the morning, and the remainder of the day for taking the waters, playing cricket, and our every whim indulged by the natives. What do you say to that, my dear chap?"

"I would say," he replied, "that it is not without cause that wisdom tells us the devil finds work for idle hands."

"Good heavens, must you always be so cynical?"

I was having altogether too fine a morning to argue with him. My only other time in this part of the Empire had been miserable, and the contrast between my morning on the Galle Face and my time in Afghanistan could not have been greater. Therefore, I merely changed the subject.

"Very well, Holmes. Have you had any more insight about the George Atkinson chap?"

"Very little, except that the event must have been more significant than it first appeared. Otherwise, we would not be here. However, I am certain that soon we shall know more. We meet with the governor in two hours."

Having rested and been refreshed, we departed the hotel for the Queen's House. The gates and portico of the colonial mansion were guarded by a phalanx of soldiers in the dress uniforms of the Raj, and an impressive young fellow in a scarlet frock coat, complete with epaulets, braid, and turban, opened our door and escorted us inside. Holmes and I followed him up the wide marble staircase to a small terrace.

Seated at a table were two men of a certain age. Both were elegantly dressed, with one in a fine linen suit and the other in the buttons and braid of the highest-ranking officer of the colonial police force.

"Your Excellency," said the attendant, "allow me to present Mr. Sherlock Holmes and his colleague, Dr. Watson."

The chap in the white suit, Mr. Arthur Hamilton-Gordon, the Governor of Ceylon, gestured toward the empty chairs opposite him.

"Sit down, gentlemen. This," he said, pointing to the uniformed man beside him, "is George Campbell, our Inspector-General of Police in Ceylon."

"An honor to meet both of you," said Holmes, smiling graciously.

"Very well, then," said the governor. "Let us not waste any time with needless chit-chat. Inspector, would you kindly furnish Mr. Holmes with the facts pertinent to the tragic passing of Mr. George Atkinson?"

"Right. George Atkinson and his brother Geoffrey came from Westmorland. They both served a stint in the navy, and by chance were stationed in Trincomalee. They must have found Ceylon appealing, for upon their discharge they returned to Trinco and established a business of import and expor,t and have done rather well. They gave their time and talents to the local boys' school and helped manage the cricket and football teams. However, one night just four weeks ago, George Atkinson was returning to his home in a rickshaw from one of the local establishments when he was robbed and shot. That is the case, Mr. Holmes. What else do you wish to know?"

"Thank you, Inspector. Would you mind telling me a little more about the nature of their business? What was it they imported and exported?"

"Right. At first, it was anything they could acquire the rights to. Spices, lumber, tea, and so forth were sent out, and woolens, suitings, foodstuffs, and the like brought back in. Lately, however, they became quite active in bringing in workers from Tamil-Nadu in India. The trade in indentured labor has grown and has been quite lucrative."

"Yes, so I understand," said Holmes. "I also understand that the influx of these workers has led to some unrest in the Eastern Province. Is that correct?"

"Bloody right, it has. The city and the districts around it are a witches' brew of various groups of men, any one of whom would cut the throat of a chap from a competing group. There is a large contingent of Singhalese Buddhists. Next are the national Tamils who have been there forever. Most of them are Hindus, but many are Mohammedans, and there are some Christians. There is a handful if Burghers, mostly working for the Colonial Office, and a few Jews. It is quite possible that George Atkinson's murder was connected to his arranging of imported labor, but we have no way of knowing that. Anything else, Mr. Holmes?"

"Yes. You said that George and Geoffrey were brothers. Is it true that they were twin brothers?"

"Aye. They were alike as Tweedledum and Tweedledee. Identical in every way. Same speech, same mannerisms, same hairstyle, same way of dressing. I was told by my men up there that no one, not even their fiancées, could tell them apart."

"Their fiancées?"

"Aye, there are two lassies from Glasgow who came here not long ago as missionaries and are teaching in the Methodist Girls' College. Eligible bachelors and attractive British girls are both scare commodities out here, so, as you might expect, the two brothers began courting the two teachers. Within days, I was told, one of the girls was engaged to George and the other to Geoffrey. Which was to whom, I cannot recall, but within a month, one of the brothers was dead. You can ask for the report at the station in Trinco when you get there. Now, Mr. Holmes, is that all? I have a job to do here and prefer not to waste any more of my time."

Without waiting for an answer, he stood and bade goodbye to the governor and to us. I began to stand to leave, but the governor raised his hand.

"A few minutes more of your time, gentlemen. There are some other matters to impart before you go. Please, another cup of tea?

"I have," he continued, "a reliable source of data in Trinco. Major Robert Garton has retired early from the army and teaches in one of the schools there. Quite the excellent fellow. He will be available to you whilst you are doing your work. Ah, but you were asking, Mr. Holmes, about the fiancées."

"I was."

"Lovely young ladies, both of them. Their names are Morag Douglass and Elspeth Linton. Morag was engaged to George and Elspeth remains engaged to Geoffrey. I am sure you can appreciate that both of the ladies and the brother, Geoffrey, are devastated by what has taken place."

"Entirely understandable," I answered.

"You should be aware that Miss Elspeth's family name is not actually *Linton*. Her true name is *Lipton*. Are you familiar with that name, gentlemen?"

"The grocery man?" I blurted.

"The same. One of the wealthiest men in Britain."

"But he is not married," I said. "The press keeps calling him the Empire's most eligible bachelor. How can she be his child?"

Holmes gave me a sideward look and the governor a condescending smirk.

"Dr. Watson," said the governor, "we have an entire segment of our population here in Ceylon, the Burghers, who trace their European ancestry through several hundred years of Portuguese, Dutch, and British bachelors. Need I say more?"

"No," I said, blushing somewhat. "Then she must be an exceptionally wealthy young woman."

"Not yet, but upon her marriage, she will be. She has, however, kept her true identity concealed from the public, although it may be known to her small circle of intimate friends."

"That data," said Holmes, "does tend to thicken the plot somewhat."

"I am sure it does," said the governor. "Add to that the news that Thomas Lipton expects to visit Ceylon soon and has plans to invest up to one-million pounds in tea gardens. It will result in an enormous growth in our tea business – a splendid boost to the economy of the colony."

"And," added Holmes, "opportunities for fortunes to be made."

"Quite so. Now to make matters worse, I have received a constant stream of reports not only of dangerous events – two young students were recently murdered – but also endless rumors of nefarious activities. The entire area is not merely a morass of crime and political intrigue – It is also a cesspool of appalling, immoral activity. Now, gentlemen, I trust you can see why we are not treating this case as a run-of-the-mill robbery and murder. Your transport has been arranged to Trincomalee. You depart on the mail train tomorrow afternoon. Good day, gentlemen."

He did not bother to stand but merely nodded to the man-servant, who quickly came over and gestured to us to make our egress.

The following morning, Holmes met me for an early breakfast on the hotel terrace. After a delectable serving of coffee, fresh scones, and tropical fruits, I asked concerning his intentions for the morning.

"I will go to the offices of *The Times of Ceylon* and read the reports of the murders in Trincomalee. I should also send off some telegrams to Whitehall, but I will be back in time to get to the train."

At three o'clock, I took a cab to the Colombo Fort railway station and, as expected, found Holmes waiting for me on the platform of the overnight train to Trinco. The accommodations in the first-class section were comfortable, and the food in the dining car passably palatable as long as one was fond of curry.

A knock on the door of my sleeping cabin at six o'clock the following morning could not be ignored, and we arrived at the Trincomalee station a half-hour later. The small building was a far cry from the bustling one in the center of Colombo and, being the end of the line, the remaining passengers who disembarked with us were few.

"*Namaste*, gentlemen. I trust your travel was not overly difficult."

We were welcomed at the platform by a man who was dressed in the white buttoned uniform and helmet of the colonial police force.

"I am Captain Rajanathan Devasenapathy. It is my honor to welcome you to the Eastern Province, where you will find Ceylon's finest beaches and loveliest palm trees. Come, come. Your breakfast awaits you by the ocean. The fishermen have just brought in their catch, and you shall enjoy them along with the prawns, potato curry, dahl, and coconut water."

We climbed into the waiting, howbeit modest, police carriage and trotted a few blocks until we stopped at the edge of a long narrow stretch of gleaming white sand. Dotting the beach was a line of small, brightly painted fishing skiffs and beyond them stretched the vast horizon of the Indian Ocean. The hotel was also modest, and its restaurant was no more than a thatched hut with an open stove and a few rugged benches and tables. We enjoyed a traditional Ceylonese breakfast and several cups of the finest tea I had even been served. I would have been more than happy to while away a full hour chatting amiably with the captain, but Holmes was anxious to redeem the time and get to work. He put down his cup and stood up.

"There is work to be done," he said. "Forgive my impatience, but I suggest that we proceed to the police station. May I assume, Captain, that your office is our next destination?"

Reluctantly, I took one last swallow and trotted along after them. Once inside the small station, Holmes turned to the Captain.

"May I see your report on the incident?"

"Of course, sir. It is here on my desk, sir. I had taken it from our files in expectation of your visit."

"Wonderful," said Holmes. "Might you, by chance, also have files on the recent deaths of the two students from St. Joseph's College?"

At first, the policeman's face took on a look of questioning surprise, and then he slowly began to smile.

"I will be happy to provide those as well, Mr. Holmes. I was not aware that you would be making inquiries concerning that terrible event. We are at a loss to know what might possibly have brought about their killings. They were fine young lads, sir. Very good boys and promising young cricket players, sir. Their families have been in deep mourning, as has been the entire town. If there is any light you can share on what took place, we would be most grateful, Mr. Holmes, sir."

Holmes smiled again. "Captain, I notice that you have a set of stairs outside the building leading to a *godown*. Is it possible that you have a police morgue under your station?"

"Yes, Mr. Holmes, we do. And now you are about to ask me if we still have the body of Mr. George Atkinson there, and the answer to that question is yes, we do. And you will want to know how we have managed to preserve it now for four weeks. The answer to that is that I obtained an ice-making machine from one of the merchant ships in the harbor when I received a telegram from London telling me to keep the body preserved if possible. So please sir, come with me."

"You are most kind, Captain," said Holmes.

We descended a long staircase into a dark, chilly basement.

"Our morgue, gentleman," said the police officer, "is no more than the corner of this room. If we bring all of the lamps together, you should have sufficient light by which to see."

On a set of racks in the corner was a stack of long grey metal cases that seemed like those I remembered as issued by the military for transporting artillery. The captain requested our help, and we lifted one of them over to a table in the center of the room. Holmes and I stood back while he opened it and swept off a layer of ice. Inside was the reasonably well-preserved corpse of a young man. His appearance and dress said that he was English, and his frame that he had been an active athlete. There were no visible marks of violence anywhere to be seen.

"He was shot in the back of the head," said the police officer. "If you will help me, gentlemen, we can lift the body onto the table, and the doctor may look at him."

I knew full well what Holmes was interested in. As a doctor on the battlefield, I had removed countless bullets from all parts of the body, and my purpose now was to extract the one that had killed Mr. George Atkinson. I did so and handed the bullet to Holmes, who immediately extracted his glass and examined it.

"Did you observe any evidence of gunpowder on the hair surrounding the wound," he asked me.

"None," I replied.

"How interesting. Very well, Captain, you have been exceptionally helpful. We must now move on to interview those who were close to the victim."

"Of course, sir. Before you go, would you also be interested in examining the body of young Mr. Selvarasa Pathmanathan? He was one of the lads from the senior cricket team who was also murdered several weeks ago."

"Have you not," asked Holmes, "delivered his body to his family for burial?"

"No, and they are very very angry with me for not doing so. It is a terrible violation of their faith that they should not be able to lay him to rest. However, he was the second boy from the team to be killed, and I knew that there was something dreadful and evil in our midst."

We replaced the one corpse in its case and opened a second one. The body was of a man in his late teens. He had the same dark skin tone as the other men of this region and even at this many days after his death it was obvious that he had been a handsome young man prior to his demise. As requested by Holmes, I removed the bullet from his brain and handed it over to him. Without his asking me, I also confirmed that there was no evidence of gunpowder on this hair or clothing close to the wound.

"Would you mind," asked Holmes, "if I were to keep these two bullets for a day or two? They could be instructive for the case."

"Of course, sir. Please, sir," answered the captain. "is there anything else I can do to be of assistance, sir?"

"Yes," said Holmes. "You are no doubt a diligent police officer who has served Her Majesty for at least a decade. Am I correct in that assessment?"

The man smiled briefly and nodded his head sideways in the manner of sub-continent, indicating, "Yes."

"Indeed, sir. That is correct, sir. For fifteen years, sir. I have tried to do my duty in a responsible way."

"Then kindly tell me what conclusions you have reached concerning these murders."

"Oh, sir. It is not a good thing, not a good thing at all, to leap to conclusions when one has not acquired a sufficient amount of evidence."

"I could not agree more, but please impart to me such insights as you have. I would be most appreciative."

"Yes, sir. It has been like this, sir. The two students were both members of the senior cricket team, and both were fine students, very handsome boys, model students who had already passed their school-leaving certificates and had excellent prospects. At first, we assumed that there might be a connection to cricket, but that would be most unsportsmanlike, sir. Then we looked further into the affairs of the families. Both of the lads have uncles who own large tea gardens south of Trincomalee, and it was known that they were planning to become part of the consortium of plantations assembled by Mr. Thomas Lipton. His taking over the tea production of much of Ceylon has been met with fierce opposition, and perhaps their deaths were a warning to those who had thrown their lot in with Mr. Lipton's plans. But Mr. Atkinson had been murdered in the same fashion, and he had no connection to the tea plantations that we know of, so we are back to the school, as improbable as that seems. I fear, sir, that we have not been able to make any headway beyond that. Any assistance you are able to provide me would be very very helpful."

"I will help in whatever way I can, Captain," said Holmes. "Kindly permit me a request. I wish to conduct a close investigation of the residence and effects of Mr. George Atkinson. Would you be willing to authorize such an exercise? Perhaps you could join us whilst we do so?"

Again, the captain nodded his head sideways. "Yes, sir. All those requests will be arranged, sir. For now, sir, I have arranged for you to have a lunch meeting back at the hotel with Mr. Geoffrey Atkinson, his fiancée, Miss Elspeth Lindal, and her friend, Miss Morag Douglass. I interviewed each of them four weeks ago, but I am hoping that perhaps your skills will elicit some additional insights."

Holmes nodded his assent, then continued.

"Another question, if I may, Captain," said Holmes. "The governor expressed quite positive expectations concerning the plans of Thomas Lipton to expand his interests in the tea plantations. Yet you informed me that there is a strong undercurrent of opposition within the local populace to the prospect. Therefore, I am curious to know why it is that the governor holds one view and you another. Can you offer me any explanation for that, sir?"

"The governor," he replied slowly, "places great faith in the insights and wisdom sent to him by Major Robert Garton. Perhaps when you meet him, you should ask that question of him instead of me."

On the patio of the hotel, we encountered three young expatriates who had been waiting for us. The one male, a man wearing a short-sleeved white shirt, open at the neck, and white trousers, quickly stood up to greet us. The two young women with him remained seated but looked in our direction and smiled. Both were attired in light cotton dresses with sleeves that reached only their elbows and hems that stopped well above the ankle. One of them was a pleasant if somewhat plain looking girl, the other was strikingly beautiful.

"Mr. Holmes and Dr. Watson," said the captain. "Allow me to introduce you to Miss Elspeth Linton, Miss Morag Douglass, and Mr. Geoffrey Atkinson."

Introductions were followed by chit-chat concerning the climate of Ceylon, and the latest news about the Old Girl, our beloved Queen. The conversation was led by the vivacious efforts of the lovely Miss Douglass, whose lively banter, contagious laugh, and radiant smile could have turned the most tragic funeral procession into a birthday party. Then Holmes abruptly interrupted.

"I have no interest in whatever it is we are now talking about. We are here to ask questions about the murder of Mr. George Atkinson. As time is pressing, allow me to end the pleasant frivolity and proceed to the matter at hand."

"Oh, very well, if we must, Mr. Holmes," said Miss Douglass, accompanying her words with an exaggerated pout. "But as one who knew George and loved him dearly, I can assure you that he was full of the love of life, and were his ghost here with us and found us gloomy over his departure, he would terrorize us until we promised to laugh and enjoy our lives to the hilt as he did."

She laughed merrily again and took a large swallow of the mango juice that had been provided for her, and that was, I suspected, seriously adulterated with gin. She did not at all fit my image of a young Scottish Methodist missionary.

"As neither he nor his ghost is present," replied Holmes, "I shall continue."

"Oh, Mr. Holmes, please," came the plea, this time from Miss Linton. "You mustn't be harsh with Morag. These past weeks have been so hard on us, and I do not know what we would have done without Morag's indomitable spirit. My fiancé lost his brother, and I lost a dear friend. Morag has been our pillar of strength during these terrible times. And Morag, my dear," she spoke now to her friend, reaching over and touching her hand, "you must try to be serious."

Holmes harrumphed and for the next half-hour asked and received answers about the events leading up to and following the death of George Atkinson. Geoffrey had visited the tavern briefly that evening and had been notified around eleven o'clock by a local police officer when George's body had been discovered on the Kandy Road beside the Yard

Cove. He had run to the site and identified the body for the police. Then he had gone to the residence of Misses Douglass and Linton, arriving sometime just after midnight, and told them the tragic news. The three of them had remained together until the early morning, when they took a rickshaw to the police station. Miss Linton at first said that she thought she had been awakened somewhat later than midnight, but admitted that she had been in a deep sleep and could not precisely remember the exact times and conversations that had taken place.

None of the three had anything to offer concerning the deaths of the two students except to repeat the story we had already heard concerning the connection of their families to rival interests in the tea industry.

Holmes thanked them for their time and cooperation. We had finished lunch and now had an opportunity to talk between ourselves and the police captain.

"Captain, would you mind taking us over to the St. Joseph's School. I should like to have an opportunity to chat with this Major Garton fellow."

"Most certainly, sir. The school is not far from the hotel. We can be there very soon, sir."

As we traveled, Holmes turned to me and asked, "Watson, during your time with the B.E.F., did you ever meet Major Garton?"

"Never directly," I said. "I did hear about him and his reputation. Very highly respected, not just for his exceptional bravery, but he was one of the rare breed of officers who sincerely cared for the well-being of his men. Not that any officer does not have a responsibility to do so, but Garton went beyond that. Those serving under him did not just admire him, they loved him."

"How then did he end up as a school teacher in Ceylon?" asked Holmes.

"I cannot say. He was well on his way to general. Last I heard, he was posted in Somaliland and then he up and quit. I can only guess that during his posting here in Trinco, he fell in love with the tropics and decided it was a much finer life than the army. Perhaps he became enamored with a local woman. You know, Holmes, *cherchez la femme*, as they say."

"Ah, yes. One of the oldest and most certain motivations known to man. I must look into what happened."

The St. Joseph School occupied a full block adjacent to the beach and harbor and was nestled amidst a grove of palm and milkwood trees. I could see several long, three-story buildings, behind which lay a well-worn sports field. Our guide led us to the office of the headmaster and requested that a message be sent to Major Garton.

A tall, lean gentleman – somewhat taller even than Holmes – soon descended from the upper floor. He had a striking bearing and appearance. His posture was unmistakably stiffened by years of service in Her Majesty's armed forces. His face, tanned but now showing a few signs of age, was handsome to the point of aristocratic. His hair was wavy and still mostly brown, with some edges of white beginning to assert themselves. He was distinctly attired in a blue blazer, white shirt and tie, and spotless white trousers.

"Mr. Holmes, Dr. Watson," he said in a clear, authoritative voice. "I have been expecting you. Follow me, please. We can chat in the tea room."

He turned without waiting for us to respond and began back up the stairs. We followed him to the area of the school reserved for the staff and then out onto a pleasant terrace, where a young woman appeared almost immediately with a tray of tea and biscuits. The cups were filled to the brim and, fearing that I would dribble, I leaned forward to reduce the distance from the saucer to my mouth. I could not help but notice that Major Garton sat ramrod straight and lifted his cup fearlessly all the way from the table to his lips without the least sign of a tremble.

"The governor sent a note that you chaps were coming here. Whitehall seems to be stirring the pot over the death of George Atkinson. A terrible tragedy, I say. Now, I have half-an-hour before I have to get back to teaching my boys their maths. How may I be of assistance to you, gentleman?"

"The governor," said Holmes, "spoke highly of you, Major. He places great trust in the intelligence you forward to him."

"I am flattered, Mr. Holmes. It is no credit, however, to me. All that is required to command respect in that function is to send in the unvarnished truth and avoid ever playing favorites. My years in the services taught me that."

He then looked directly at me and smiled. "You also served, if I am not mistaken, Dr. Watson. Northumberland Fusiliers, was it not?"

"It was indeed," I replied, pleased that he remembered.

"Had a bit of a rough go at the end, did you not?"

"Very rough, yes. But that is now all behind me."

"And obviously doing well. I hear you went and got married to a Beauty. Well done, old chap. There are so many lads who go back home in pieces and never recover. It does my heart good when I meet one who has made a go of it."

"Kind of you to say so, Major," I said. Sensing the opportunity, I moved ahead to ask the questions that I knew Holmes was waiting to have answered.

"Do tell, though, Major," I said, "how is it that such a decorated soldier decided to leave the B.E.F. and toil for the good Lord in this forgotten corner of the Empire? I trust you will not take offense at my asking."

"Not at all. I did my duty shooting Ashantis in the Gold Coast, Zulus in the Cape, and no end of angry young natives in every post in which I served. One day, I looked down at the body of a lad I had shot dead outside the fort near Berbera. He was no more than fourteen years old. I had killed him. His dead eyes seemed to look into my soul and tell me that some day I would have to stand before Almighty God and account for what I had done. I have never been overly given to religion, but I had my own humble version of the road to Damascus, and decided there and then that I had had it with military life. I had spent some time at the garrison here in lovely Trinco and came back. The school was in need of a maths teacher and were kind enough to accept me. I have been living in paradise ever since."

"Yet you remain unmarried," said Holmes.

"As do you, Mr. Holmes," came the immediate reply. "I do not know about you, but there are some of us who are forever married to our calling."

"I am familiar with the predicament," said Holmes.

"I am sure you are. But come now, Mr. Holmes. You did not come all the way to Ceylon to inquire as to my marital situation. You wish to me to tell you what I know about the death of George Atkinson. Perhaps we should move on to that topic now before I rhapsodize endlessly about the beauty of Ceylon and the native Ceylonese."

"I concur," said Holmes. "So, let us begin by your telling me about the fellow who was killed, Mr. George Atkinson. What was he like? What was the nature of your acquaintance with him?"

"George was an excellent fellow. Every day he would quit his office by three o'clock and make a beeline over here to the school so he could direct the senior boys' football team. I had the task of doing the same for the junior boys' cricket team. We would see each other almost every day out on the pitch, sharing what is left of the grass. In past years, we had seen a bit of each other at one of the pubs near the harbor where the soldiers and seamen socialize, but of late he had been spending his spare time with his fiancée. Quite besotted with her, I gathered."

"Yes, and which one was she?" asked Holmes.

"George had fallen for Miss Morag. His brother, Geoffrey, was stuck with Miss Elspeth."

"Stuck with?" asked Holmes.

"A poor choice of words. Forgive me. Most ungentlemanly of me. However, any man can see straight away that Morag Douglass is as stunningly attractive a lass as a man could ever hope to meet. Dear Elspeth Linton is more on the plain side. Mind you, she is as sweet and kind a girl as can be imagined. Her heart must be made of honey, and perhaps that is why Geoffrey found her so good a prospect for a wife. Who can say?"

"And what about Geoffrey?" asked Holmes. "You continue to be on good terms with him as well?"

"As well as can be expected. I have seen very little of him since the death of George. The brothers were exceptionally close, and Geoffrey has taken George's death very hard. He still comes to the school to direct the senior cricket team, but I fear his heart is no longer in it."

"That is entirely understandable," said Holmes. "Perhaps we can now move to the night when George was shot. What can you tell me about that night? Do you remember how you spent the evening?"

"Quite so, Mr. Holmes. That is a small tavern on Orr Hill Road, not far from the Army base. I was there for an hour in the evening chatting with some of our boys. Geoffrey was also there, and we chatted briefly. We left at the same time, about ten o'clock. I took a rickshaw back to my home on this side of the harbor and he to his home on the other side. I did not see George at all that evening, and it was the following morning when I heard the terrible news. All I can say is that George must have been in the wrong place at the wrong time. This is a harbor city, Mr. Holmes. It is not safe, and he was in the foolish habit of traveling about the town unarmed."

"Thank you, Major," said Holmes. "Might you have any insights into the deaths of the two boys from your school?"

"You are referring to Selvarasa and Chandran? A terrible tragedy, indeed, Mr. Holmes. The police looked into that matter and concluded that it was connected to the rivalry within the tea planters' families. I am not privy to any news about the progress of their investigation. You will have to ask them."

"You knew these boys?"

"Of course, I knew them. They were members of the senior cricket team. Before moving up to that level, they had been members of my junior cricket team. Wonderful boys. Good natured. Splendid athletes. As I said, a terrible tragedy. But you must speak to the police if you wish to know more."

"Thank you, Major. There is just one thing that puzzles me, if you will permit my asking you."

"Carry on, Mr. Holmes."

"It concerns the plans of the Lipton firm to expand their activities here. The police captain has informed me that there exists considerable conflict amongst the local people. Yet you have reported to the governor that the expansion by Lipton would be a boon and welcomed by all. Would you mind telling me why you hold to your opinion?"

"Oh, come, come, Mr. Holmes. These native folks are beautiful in their own way, remarkably attractive. As much as I love them, you have to understand that the vast majority of them still bow down to wood and stone. They are a simple lot but exceptionally jealous of any success by those who are not of their particular tribe. I assure you, Mr. Holmes, the minute they see their pay-packet start to swell when Mr. Lipton beings to remunerate them, they will suddenly forget whatever objections they might once have held and band together as one people, even if it is to demand more pay. It is just how these people are, Mr. Holmes."

"Ah, yes. An interesting observation. Again, thank you, Major Garton. We have kept you from your boys for far too long. Allow us to wish you a good day."

"And to you too, sir. I trust you will enjoy your time in our rather idyllic corner of the Empire."

Captain Devasenapathy was waiting for us with his police carriage. Holmes imparted to him the gist of the conversation we had with Major Garton, tactfully omitting any colonialist references to the simplicity of the natives.

"Thank you, Mr. Holmes," said the captain. "This is very very helpful. Now, if you will come with me, I will take you to the residence of Mr. George Atkinson. If we move smartly, you shall have most of the afternoon to investigate his rooms before his brother returns. Come, come."

The two Atkinson brothers shared a spacious house a few blocks north of the China Bay sector of the harbor. The house was a neat as a pin, thanks in part to the diligent maid, but also reflecting a couple of young men who gave the immediate impression of being exceptionally fastidious. There was a large common area in the central front of the building, adjacent to a front porch that afforded a pleasant view of the harbor.

Holmes moved immediately into the room that the captain informed us had been occupied by George Atkinson. It was also as orderly and immaculate as any barracks inspected by a tyrant sergeant-major that I had ever been in.

"If you would, my good Doctor," said Holmes. "Please, start on the books. I shall inspect his personal effects."

It was a pattern of inspection that I had expected, and that was to become quite familiar in the years afterward. One by one, I took a book off the shelf and examined it, page by page. Anything that struck me as noteworthy, I noted.

Holmes slowly and methodically went through each drawer in the dresser, removing every item of clothing, jewelry, toiletries, and odds-and-ends. He had his glass at the ready and gave many of the objects a close look.

After an hour-and-a-half, Holmes departed from the bedroom and took a seat in the comfortable parlor. The captain and I followed him.

"Very well, Watson. Let us hear your report. Quickly through the mundane, and some detail on the anomalies, no matter how trivial."

"As you could see," I said, "there were three shelves of books, each of four feet and attached to his wall above the writing desk. Quite well organized, as might be expected. Perfectly aligned. The lowest shelf was entirely reference books related to the business of the Atkinson brothers. The second row, all in order by the last name of the author, held a fine selection of the best of England's writers. There were even a few from America.

"The top row," I continued, "held his memories from his boyhood. All his photographs, prize cups, and favorite storybooks. I suspect he brought a trunk full of these old friends with him and still read them during some of the long, warm nights here in the tropics."

"The anomalies, Watson, please."

'Ah, yes. Getting to those, Holmes. None of the business books on the lower shelf were inscribed or had nameplates inserted. However, stuck inside some of them were notes, copies of memos, purchase orders, and the like. Oddly, any of them that had a name attached were addressed not to George but to his brother. Nothing to report beyond that."

"How very interesting, Watson. Good work."

"Thank you, Holmes. Now it is your turn."

"As you have dutifully recorded, the fellow had an exceptionally orderly mind. I have gone through all of his belongings, and they are all arranged in a regimented manner . . . with two exceptions."

"Ah, ha," I said. "Then do deliver, Holmes."

"His shirts, sweaters, trousers, and jackets are all aligned perfectly. His handkerchiefs are folded in perfect symmetry and stacked as if a plumb line had been used on the edge. Even his cufflinks and studs are placed in a row along a uniform edge."

"Yes?" I queried.

"His socks and underwear were tossed all together in an unholy jumble."

"Goodness, a man cannot be expected to be utterly faultless in all his domestic habits."

"True, perhaps of you, and most certainly true of me. But not, I submit, of this man. Now, as to the second item, I examined his bank book. As I have observed before, a man may lie to the police, to his wife and children, to his closest friend, to his employer, and even to his solicitor. He cannot lie to his bank book. George Atkinson made scrupulous notes in his personal ledger accounting for every cheque issued and every deposit made. One of them, however, could not be accounted for."

"Indeed, and what was that?"

"He records that six months ago he paid for a wire of funds to W. J. Brooks of Northampton."

"The shoe people?"

"Precisely. It was for a new set of boots at a cost of two pounds, six. There was a later note confirming the delivery three months later."

"Yes, go on."

"Those boots are missing."

"Maybe he was wearing them when he was killed, and they are still on his feet in the morgue," I said.

"No, his body was wearing a fine set of brogues."

Once back on the hotel patio, Holmes turned to me.

"Watson, do you have your service revolver with you?"

"Of course. I never go east of Aldgate without it, and I most surely would not walk the streets of a backwater town unarmed."

"Excellent. Now come and stand here." He jumped out of his chair and went quickly to a place about thirty feet back from the low stone wall that bordered the patio. I followed and stood as asked, not having the foggiest notion what he was up to. He then ran out onto the beach and approached one of the many local vendors. He returned carrying two fresh coconuts. Carefully, he balanced one of them on the top of the wall.

"Now, my friend, please take out your revolver and see if you can hit this coconut from that distance."

"Holmes," I cried. "What in heaven's name . . . ?"

"Oh, Watson. Just humor me. See if you can hit it. I assure you, there is method in my madness."

I took out my Webley and aimed. The gun has only a six-inch barrel and is not accurate in the least at any distance more than twenty feet. I raised and fired. I missed, and the bullet proceeded unhindered to some distant splash in the ocean.

"Try again," shouted Holmes.

This time I pegged the coconut. A gun with a larger caliber might have splatted the target, but a bullet from a small revolver merely penetrated the side and lodged itself somewhere in the interior of the fruit.

"Excellent," said Holmes. "Just what I wanted."

He took the coconut and departed. That was the last I saw of him for the entire remainder of the afternoon and evening.

Early the following morning, I came out from my room in time to observe the glory of the morning sunrise emerge over the eastern horizon. Holmes was already sitting at a table, sipping a cup of tea and reading the previous day's Colombo newspaper.

"Good morning, Watson," he said, beaming. His face was smugly happy, a look I have seen many times in the years since that day when Holmes knew that he had solved a difficult case.

"Do have a cup and your breakfast, my dear Watson," he said, not bothering to put down the newspaper. "We are being joined at half-eight by the people we met with yesterday. Until then, kindly do not disturb me. I have some lines to rehearse."

I began to say something, but he held up his hand to indicate that I should be silent. I had no choice but to wait until he deigned to speak.

I ate my breakfast and sipped my tea in solitude, and then took myself for a stroll along the beach, returning to the patio at twenty-minutes-past-eight o'clock. Holmes was still reading and did nothing more than look up at me, smile, and return to the newspaper.

At half-past-eight, he rose and looked toward the door that led back into the hotel. Coming through it was the police captain, followed by Misses Elspeth and Morag, Mr. Geoffrey Atkinson, and Major Robert Garton.

"I have brought them all as requested, Mr. Holmes," said Captain Devasenapathy. His tone and the look on his face said that he was not entirely sure why he had been so instructed.

Holmes smiled and greeted our visitors.

"Really, Mr. Holmes," said Geoffrey Atkinson, "is this necessary? The ladies and the major have classes to teach, and I have a business to run."

"I assure you," said Holmes, "I shall not keep you for more than a few minutes. I have an obligation to report my conclusions to you before Dr. Watson and I depart this afternoon."

The major was the last to enter the patio and Holmes walked toward him. Suddenly, Holmes stumbled and staggered directly into Major Garton.

"Oh, I am so sorry, Major. My apologies, sir. I am terribly sorry."

His voice and face conveyed profound embarrassment, and the major forced a smile and muttered a few forgiving words. The seven of us gathered around one of the round tables and waited whilst the mandatory morning tea and scones were served.

"Mr. Holmes," said the major, "please get on with your report. *Tempus fugit.*"

Holmes stood, holding a small sheaf of papers in his hands, and began as if he were about to address the local parish council.

"Captain Rajanathan Devasenapathy of the Trincomalee Police, Major Robert Garton, Misses Elspeth Linton and Morag Douglass, and Mr. George Atkinson . . . ."

"Geoffrey, not George," I interrupted. "Holmes, George is the one that was killed. This is *Geoffrey.*"

"No, my dear Watson, it is not. The man sitting with us is *George* Atkinson. It was *Geoffrey* who was killed. Immediately after his tragic death, his brother assumed his identity."

"Oh, honestly, Mr. Holmes!" said whichever of the Atkinson brothers it was. "Where did you get such an absurd idea. I assure you that I am Geoffrey and always have been."

"No, George, you are not. You were the first to hear the terrible news about your brother, and you reacted as any man would. You immediately sought the company and comfort of your fiancée. For reasons that I am sure you know better than I, the two of you agreed that you would assume your brother's identity and act as if you were engaged to be married to Miss Elspeth Linton. Then you rushed back to your house and made such minor changes in your belongings as were necessary to support your ruse, and only then went to wake Miss Linton and share the tragic news with her of the death of George."

"Utter nonsense!" said George or Geoffrey. "You have no proof whatsoever of such lunacy."

"Ah, but there you are wrong, George," said Holmes. "When you switched your rooms and re-arranged your belongings, you knew that you could wear your brother's shirts, trousers, sweaters, and neckties, but you drew the line at wearing another man's socks and underwear. You exchanged those items in his dresser for the ones from yours, but you failed to replace them with the obsessive neatness that you and your brother practiced in all your belongings."

When he said these words, I detected a momentary flash of George's eyeballs in the direction of Miss Douglass. Holmes noticed it as well.

"Ah, allow me to correct myself. Your fiancée who was helping you and who is not nearly as compulsively fastidious replaced those items for you. Meanwhile, you exchanged a few of your daily reference books with those of your brother, but failed to remove the odd notes addressed to Geoffrey that were hidden between the pages. And, it truly is most unseemly to steal the boots from a dead man, even if he is your brother. Yet the new boots sent recently from Brooks are now adorning your feet . . . George."

"You are proving nothing at all. This is all piffle and conjecture. George bought those boots as a gift for me."

"Perhaps. Men give many types of gifts to other men, but gifts of footwear? Hardly ever. Regardless, it is difficult to get around the evidence of finger marks. It is a known fact that even twins who are identical in every other way do not share identical finger marks. Fortunately, both you and Geoffrey have an array of cabinet photographs, prize cups, and various odds and ends along your top shelf. The local police officers are collecting them as we speak."

"The local police," said George, "have no ability whatsoever to extract and examine finger marks. You know that as well as I do, Mr. Holmes."

"No, but Mr. George William Robert Campbell, the Inspector-General of the Ceylon Police, and two of his finest most certainly do have the required expertise. And they are on their way to Trincomalee also as we speak. Now, would you like to explain your reasons for disguising your identity, or shall I?"

"No, I will," came the unexpected response from Miss Morag Douglass. "It was my idea. We did it for the sake of my dearest friend, my sister, Elspeth. She is the most generous and kind and pure soul on earth, an angel. But she has a spirit like a frail reed that would have been crushed by the news of the death of the man she was pledged to marry. I could not let that happen to her. When we first met them, Elspeth and I flipped a coin to decide who would become smitten with whom. For her to marry George instead of Geoffrey would make no difference. She would have a loving husband and father of her children, regardless. Giving up my betrothed in return for the love she has given me for all my life was the least I could do. That is why I insisted that George become Geoffrey."

Miss Elspeth Linton had sat throughout this entire exchange in shocked silence, her face becoming paler by the minute. Now, she reacted.

"Morag! Oh, Morag. My darling, Morag!" Elspeth Linton cried out. "Oh, my sweet, sweet sister. You did that for me? Oh, my darling . . . ."

Miss Linton had risen from her chair and thrown her torso, somewhat awkwardly, against the sitting torso of Miss Douglass. She was now clutching her friend tightly and sobbing loudly. Miss Douglass was using her restricted arms to pat Elspeth on the back, much as one might burp a baby.

"Elspeth, my dearest, Please. I had no choice. I had to do it for you."

The scene was full of emotional intensity, even if not with convincing sincerity. Elspeth slowly disentangled herself from Morag's arms and, with the help of a firm upward push by Morag, staggered to her feet. No sooner had she done so than she swooned and collapsed back onto her friend's lap. I shouted for the hotel staff, who came running and immediately carried Elspeth Linton to an empty bed somewhere in the interior of the hotel. Morag made as if to follow her, but Holmes stretched a long arm in front of her body.

"The staff will look after her," he said. "Your presence is required here."

She glared back at him, but the police captain rose to his feet and gestured her back to the chair she had been sitting in.

"Let us continue," said Holmes. "I shall begin by acknowledging that Miss Linton is legally named Miss *Lipton*. Upon her marriage, she will come into the possession of a small but significant fortune. That fortune, Miss Douglass, would have been shared with you had Elspeth married Geoffrey, and you had married his twin brother, George. But when Elspeth suddenly lost her prospects for marriage whilst you remained engaged to the surviving brother, I assume you saw the shared enjoyment of that fortune vanish. Is that correct, Miss Douglass?"

"You may assume whatever you wish, Mr. Holmes," she said. "If you make your questions more explicit, I shall attempt to answer them."

"A point well taken. Very well, we shall move on to what you did to avoid your imminent loss. Were Miss Lipton to be married to a capable young businessman and you to his twin brother, you would all soon be managing the affairs of the Lipton enterprise, up and out of your missionary posting, and off to a villa and a fine life in Colombo. With one of the brothers dead and the region reeling from the murder of the two students, that lovely future position was put in jeopardy. So you did what any intelligent young woman would do, in addition to making sure that your dear friend would still be married and receive her fortune: You blackmailed the man who was relied upon to send reports to the governor – our friend here, Major Robert Garton."

Garton immediately stiffened in his chair. "Holmes, that is absurd. No one blackmails me, and no one has ever had reason to. Withdraw your accusation immediately!"

"I fear I cannot, Major. You see, you left yourself open to being blackmailed when you murdered Geoffrey Atkinson, followed by murdering two student members of the St. Joseph's senior cricket team. The secret of your abusing them for your sexual pleasure whilst they were members of your junior cricket team was confessed to Mr. Geoffrey Atkinson. He confronted you that evening in the tavern on Orr's Hill. You followed him and shot him, and the following day shot the two students."

"Enough!" shouted Garton. He leapt from his chair and strode over to Holmes. He towered over him and pointed a finger an inch from Holmes's eyes.

"You have slandered me, Holmes. I shall see you in court and, if you are man enough, I will see you immediately behind the hotel. Now get up and prepare to defend yourself!"

Holmes did not move but began to chuckle.

"Oh, dear me. Am I being threatened with fisticuffs? Why not, instead, threaten to shoot me with your service revolver, the one you used on all three of your victims. Oh, dear me, your revolver is no longer in your pocket, so I fear you cannot do that."

Instinctively, Major Garton shoved his hand into his jacket pocket. He then took it back out again, empty.

"You bloody thief. You picked my pocket when you bumped into me. Give me that revolver back immediately!"

"Mr. Holmes does not have your revolver, Major. I do," said the captain.

"Then give it to me. Now!"

"I am very very sorry, Major, but it appears that your gun is now considered evidence in the case of the murders. So, it must remain in my possession, not yours."

"You have no reason whatsoever to keep it and no reason for these insulting accusations. I demand the return of my gun and an immediate apology!"

"Captain," said Holmes. "Do you happen to have the two bullets that Dr. Watson extracted from the heads of Mr. Geoffrey Atkinson and one of the murdered students."

"I do, Mr. Holmes." From one of his pockets, he took out a small paper packet and from it removed two bullets and laid them on the table.

"And," said Holmes, "what about the bullet that Dr. Watson eventually managed to leave in the coconut? I gave that one to you also."

"It is here." From another pocket, he took out a packet, removed a bullet, and placed it beside the previous two.

"What can you tell me about the bullets, Captain," asked Holmes.

"They are almost identical."

"Dr. Watson," said Holmes, "kindly place your service revolver on the table."

I took out my gun and laid it on the table. It was a standard issue Webley, carried by tens of thousands of men who had served in Her Majesty's army. The captain laid the major's gun beside mine. They were identical models.

"There are at least a hundred of those guns in Trinco," said Major Garton. "This proves nothing. Now, end this nonsense immediately."

"Ah, yes," said Holmes. "There are many such guns. You are correct. But there is only one that is owned by the last man to have seen Geoffrey Atkinson alive; by the man who was accused of gross indecency by Geoffrey Atkinson; and by the man who has the rare skill to hit a small moving target from a significant distance. To that, Major, I would add that as we speak, the members of both the junior and the senior cricket teams are being removed from their classes at St. Joseph's and brought to a private location for questioning by the police. Once they know that you can no longer harm them, and they are advised of the consequences of lying to the police, I expect they will be quite forthcoming. What you considered to be your affection for them, a court would view quite differently. The game is up, Major. You may have served your country with distinction, and what you do in private by mutual agreement with a man or a woman is none of anyone else's concern. But throughout your career you took advantage of your position and betrayed the trust of the children and families you were called to protect. I advise you to obtain a good barrister."

"And I advise you to do the same," said Garton. "Enough of this bloody drivel. I have classes to teach."

He turned and began to leave the patio.

"Major Garton," said the police captain, leaping to his feet. "I am so sorry, Major, but I am afraid that you must come with me."

Three police constables had emerged from just within the hotel to block the major's path. They escorted him through the hotel and out to a waiting police carriage.

George Atkinson, claiming a need to attend to the stricken Miss Lipton, also departed.

That left me, Holmes, and Miss Morag Douglass sitting on the patio. Holmes stared at her, and she met his gaze, unflinching, and clearly not the least intimidated.

"Perhaps another cup of tea, Miss Douglass?" asked Holmes.

"One perhaps, yes. Do you have more questions before I leave?"

"I admit that admire your imagination," said Holmes, "even if your morals are somewhat suspect. However, would you mind terribly, as a favor from one imaginative person to another, explaining what took place that brought you to your current situation on a patio in Trincomalee? Your story, Miss."

"Have you been to the Gorbals, Mr. Holmes? The poorest, most utterly miserable part of the city of Glasgow? That is where and I were born and raised, and where I learned to look after myself. As a six-year-old school girl, I met another child, one who was kind and pure and generous beyond belief. My father had died in an accident in the shipyards. Elspeth Linton's father had abandoned her and her mother. The two of us became as close as sisters. Whatever Elspeth had, she would always give a portion of it to me. In turn, I protected her.

"We continued that way through our schooling. Then, one day, she confided in me not only the identity of her father but also that she was expecting to receive a considerable portfolio of securities and title to properties upon her marriage. I feared that once she was married to some ambitious and possessive young man, she would be forced to abandon me. So, I took her to a week of evangelical revival meetings and convinced her that God was calling us to go and serve on the mission field. Ceylon was her suggestion.

"Once here, we soon met the Atkinson brothers. At first, I had no use for Mr. Tweedledum and Mr. Tweedledee, but it came to me that here was a solution to my fears. If she were to marry one and I to marry the twin brother, we would be inseparable for the rest of our lives. Maybe we would become the wives of successful gentlemen, live in Colombo, and eventually move to Belgravia.

"It was all going perfectly until Geoffrey passed on to George what two of the boys on his senior cricket team had told him about Major Garton. George told me, and I urged Geoffrey not to make an issue about it. I had learned in the Gorbals that it is not wise to poke a bear. But Geoffrey was sure that an honorable soldier would never act against the law, so he confronted the major and immediately paid the price, as did both of the students."

"How," asked Holmes, "did you manage to avoid becoming the major's victim yourself? You blackmailed him to send highly biased reports to the governor concerning the potential of the Lipton plans for the tea industry. I suspect he did not take kindly to that."

"Oh, you can say that again. What I did, Mr. Holmes, was to furiously write out all possible accusations against the major, with detailed evidence, and make four copies. Three I immediately sent to solicitors in New York, Paris, and London with instructions to pass them along to *The Times* in both London and America and *The International Herald-Tribune* in Paris should they hear of anything untoward happening to me, or Elspeth, or George. Then I gave a copy to him. And, auch, he was not happy with me. I told him that I would not demand any money from him, as I would never stoop to blackmail, but that from then on, he had to be the biggest booster of the Lipton invasion of Ceylon that could be imagined. He could not very well let on that it was Geoffrey he had shot and not George. He complied. I had far more to gain by having his serve my purposes than having him hung.

"So, that is my story, Mr. Holmes. Now, if you will excuse me, I have to come up with a plan that will ensure that Elspeth marries and stays married to George, but I will need to find an exceptionally clever young man to be George's indispensable business partner as well as my husband. You would not happen to know any men who fit that description?"

Try as he might, Holmes could not resist smiling at her. "No, my dear, I do not and, if I did, I assure you, I would recommend that he never come to Ceylon."

She laughed, smiled radiantly, and departed.

Holmes sat in silence, absently smoking a cigarette.

"How," I asked him, "did you know about the Major's problems?"

"It was you, my friend, who put me on to it. A highly successful officer on his way to the top does not up an quit because of some religious epiphany. A telegram sent to Whitehall was answered immediately with the details of the litany of accusations that had been made against him."

We both sat in silence for several more minutes and were about to get up, pack our baggage, and prepare to depart when Captain Devasenapathy returned. He was looking horribly distraught.

"Good heavens, man!" I said. "What is it?"

He collapsed his body into one of the chairs.

"Major Garton had a second revolver on his person."

"Did he shoot your men and escape?" asked Holmes.

"No. He waited until we had placed him in a room in the station. Then he shot himself. Mayor Garton is dead."

For a full minute not one of us spoke. Then the captain stood, nodded a quiet good day to us, and departed.

"I suppose," I said to Holmes, "that it was a better way for him to go the way he did than face the shame and humiliation that would precede a certain trip to the gallows."

I could tell that Holmes wasn't listening to me.

"Watson," he said whilst looking out to the endless, beautiful expanse of the Indian Ocean, "when you were a schoolboy and had to attend chapel, did you ever sing a hymn that beings with the words *From Greenland's icy mountains*?"

"I did."

"Does not the second verse make some reference to Ceylon?"

"It does."

> *From time to time I heard some vague account of his doings . . . of his clearing up of the singular tragedy of the Atkinson brothers at Trincomalee . . . .*
>
> Dr. John H. Watson – "A Scandal in Bohemia"

Colonel Warburton's Madness
by Gayle Lange Puhl

I have written elsewhere of the fact I was twice able to bring to the attention of my friend Mr. Sherlock Holmes cases of interest to his extensive study of crime. One I published as "The Adventure of the Engineer's Thumb". The other I hesitated to release to the public because aspects of the story were personal to me. However, under Holmes's encouragement, I have decided to put down the facts at last, in order to clear the name of a courageous and honorable man from the dark clouds that formed about him during his last years.

My friend was away from London on that early spring day of 1888. He had journeyed to Madrid the week before at the behest of a high government official to investigate the disappearance of certain pieces of art from the Palmatoria Museo. The thief had been seen escaping by jumping from a second-story balcony. Soon afterwards, a small fire broke out in one of the galleries. The police were baffled, and so Sherlock Holmes was consulted.

Holmes had sent a wire that day that he would return the next morning. I was alone in our sitting room at 221b Baker Street when a young woman was shown up by Mrs. Hudson.

She looked up at me with bright, intelligent blue eyes. She appeared to be in her late twenties, below the average height, but with a determined air. She was dressed in a walking suit of dark green, with a wisp of a hat on her wavy blonde hair, and a package wrapped in brown paper in her neatly gloved hands.

"Doctor Watson? Doctor John H. Watson, who served at the fatal Battle of Maiwand in Afghanistan?"

"I am. But madame, you have the advantage of me."

"I am Miss Katherine Warburton, the daughter of Colonel Jeremiah Warburton."

I ushered her in at once. "My dear, I remember your father well. Please, sit down. The last I heard of the colonel, he had retired and moved to the family home in the Lake District."

She accepted the glass of brandy I offered her from the sideboard. I never claimed to have Holmes's skills at observation and deduction, but the signs of her having been on a long railway journey were evident in the state of her clothes, her obvious fatigue, and the ticket she had thrust halfway up the wrist of her left glove. At my remark, she patted the wrapped bundle beside her and tears welled up in her eyes.

"I come on a sad errand, Doctor Watson. My father devoted his life to Her Majesty's service. He endured many hardships over the decades and never faltered from his duties. But his final posting, to lead the 66th Berkshires during the second war in Afghanistan, broke him.

"He came back to our family estate at Lake Windermere a shell of the man who had left from home just three years before. He didn't move into the main house, which he as head of the family was entitled to do. Instead, he retreated to a small cottage on the grounds. He refused to accept visitors, withdrew from those who loved him, and seldom left his 'quarters', as he called the tiny cottage. My father was content to continue the arrangement, begun years ago, whereas his brother administered the estate as he had done during the colonel's long absences.

"The entailment with which the estate had been set up long ago specified that no female could inherit the land or property, and that it descend to the oldest surviving son. I am given a generous allowance, but everything will eventually go to my oldest cousin. Fenton was a brilliant success at university, and has since found fulfillment as headmaster of our local school.

"My father, meanwhile, settled into the life of a recluse. He seemed to tolerate my presence, but still at times refused to admit me. He became more solitary. He desired no company. Often, for days and weeks at a time, he would refuse the society of a single human being. The signs of deep melancholia were obvious. This went on for years. The only time he seemed even moderately cheerful was when he spoke of you, Doctor Watson."

"Of me?" I exclaimed. "I think we met only a half-dozen times, and then only briefly before the battle."

"Yes. It was about the only thing in which he showed any interest after his return. When your story about Mr. Sherlock Holmes came out in the *Beeton's Christmas Annual* last year, he bought a copy and read it over and over. It was the only thing he wanted to take with him and he was heart-broken when that one small kindness was denied."

"What happened to Colonel Warburton?" I asked. I remembered a stocky, bluff commanding officer with a flowing blonde mustache and a head of hair to match, his battle uniform always crisp and neatly ironed.

"His health, both physical and mental, has declined steeply during the past year. Finally, about three weeks ago, I was forced, on the advice of his doctor and my uncle, his brother, to sign the papers to have him committed to a private sanitarium in Carlisle."

I sat stunned. What a sad ending to a long and honorable career!

After a minute, I looked again at the young woman before me. She was watching me expectantly. There was something else she had to say.

"Miss Warburton, I cannot tell you how much your story upsets me. Is there anything I can do for you or your father?"

She picked up the paper-wrapped package. "I wish you to take his diary, Doctor. He had kept it for nearly thirty years, starting just before his marriage to my mother. He entered notes haphazardly, as his circumstances permitted. He continued his entries after his retirement to The Fortress, as our estate is named. Before his commitment, he was making wild and unbelievable accusations about the people around him. I thought that you, being a doctor, could study his record of his own decline and perhaps find out why his illness changed from a deep melancholia to a violent madness that endangered his own life."

"Why don't you give his diary to his own physician?"

"That would be my Uncle Isaiah. According to the quick reading I gave the last pages, he wrote harsh things about Uncle, and I am afraid he would not be impartial to the slurs. Uncle Isaiah has been ill, and I think the knowledge of his brother's accusations would further undermine his health."

"I am sorry to hear of your uncle's troubles, Miss Warburton."

"Yes, he was diagnosed last year. The disease is terminal and we are very upset. His older son Fenton has given up his own educational duties and moved into The Fortress to take some of the burden of running the estate from his shoulders. My other cousin, Farley, Fenton's brother, visits often from Durham, where he is at university. Besides, Father did enjoy your story, Doctor, and I think he would like you to have his writings."

What could I do but agree to take them? Miss Warburton refused any more help and announced she had made arrangements to return to Ambleside in Cumbria the next day. I insisted upon hailing her a cab. Then I returned to our rooms and contemplated the paper-wrapped bundle.

I reflected for a time upon Colonel Warburton's circumstances, the war, and upon the concerned daughter who had left his diary with me. Finally I drew the lamp closer and unwrapped the package.

Sherlock Holmes returned the next day. I had left the loose-leaf diary on my desk. As Holmes roamed about the room, touching items and looking through the windows into Baker Street, he spied the manuscript. He picked up the diary and flipped through the pages with a lazy curiosity.

"This is not your handwriting, Watson," he drawled.

"No," I replied. I told him the story of the diary and the daughter of my former commanding officer. "I have read it. As a military document it is interesting, spanning a recent period of time in British history. However, I found the most fascinating part to be what the colonel experienced after his retirement."

Holmes took the manuscript and settled into his armchair. He thumbed through the pages, giving particular attention to the last twenty. Those pages covered the last years before Colonel Warburton's confinement. He read those carefully as I lit my cigar and rang Mrs. Hudson for tea.

It was quite twenty minutes until Mrs. Hudson brought up the tea and Holmes spoke. He accepted a cup from me and I nodded to the papers now stacked on the table beside him.

"What do you make of it, Holmes?' I asked.

"As a history of a man's mental decline it has some interest, but I am more drawn to the crime it describes."

"Crime? The poor man relates from his perspective a slow slide into madness, but I saw no sign of crime."

"On the contrary, Watson, there is ample evidence of a crime, and a dastardly one at that."

"Please explain."

"You know I have little interest in military matters. Therefore I only skimmed through the accounts of his exploits on the battlefield. My attention was piqued by his description of Maiwand and its aftermath. Although the causes of the battle were later firmly established by a military investigation, Colonel Warburton blamed himself. Guilt crippled him, and shortly after the results became known, he retired. He retreated to the family estate in the Lake District. He refused to move into The Fortress, the main house. Instead he took over an old gamekeeper's cottage and shut himself away from the world."

"Yes, his melancholia was well-developed by then. His symptoms were typical, craving solitude, showing poor eating habits, exhibiting self-neglect, and lack of interest in things he normally would have enjoyed. Then he believed that his mind cracked after the sightings began."

"The sightings?" Holmes reached for his pipe.

"Yes, the delusions. He heard voices, saw spirits in the night, and experienced sleep walking. All signs of a deep mental upset."

"I think the clues he left in his diary do not support the idea that he suffered from delusions, Watson. I think he really experienced all those effects. I think someone close to him used his circumstances to drive him mad."

"That would be diabolical! If true, how can it be proven? To what purpose would such a thing be done?"

"Oh, the motive is obvious. The question is who and how, not why. Persecution like this cannot be allowed to go unpunished. We must go to The Fortress, Watson, consult with Miss Katherine Warburton, and investigate. I believe that you said she is returning to Cumbria today? Wire a message to be left for the young lady at the Ambleside Station and tell her we are coming along behind her, and then pack a bag. There is a train in two hours."

As the train pulled out of London and headed north, Holmes spent his time reading the Colonel's diary in more detail. I was happy to be on a case with Holmes again. Life had been too quiet while my friend was gone. Now he had asked me to join him to solve the case of Colonel Warburton's madness, and I felt that frisson of excitement that marked our unique relationship rush through my body again.

Half-way through the trip, Holmes set aside the diary and began to discourse on the history of British railways, Lake District cuisine, and the District's influence on literature.

At Ambleside, up the side of a mountain, we were met by Miss Warburton in a hired trap. The air was crisp with a bite to it, and I was glad we had brought our overcoats. We wound through the pretty little town with its narrow, twisting streets until we alighted at the Lake Windermere pier. There the three of us clambered into a dory manned by a sullen, bearded man in rough fisherman clothing. He took our bags and stowed them away. The man must have had his orders previous to our arrival, for he cast off at once and began rowing in a southerly direction.

"There is a road around the lake to The Fortress," said Miss Warburton. "But it is long and must make allowance for the terrain. I was about to leave in this trap when the postmaster caught me with your telegram. I arranged this because going by boat is much more direct."

Holmes pulled out his pipe and filled it with tobacco from his pouch. He blinked at the sight of the cold lake surface that stretched out for miles before us and the evergreen and oak forest that stood on either side. Hours had passed since we had left London and the sky was darkening. The sun had set before our arrival and twilight was upon us.

Miss Warburton introduced the fisherman as Mr. Bonner, a worker on the Warburton estate. He grunted and stuck to his oars. I asked him how long it would take to reach The Fortress. "It'll take as long as it'll take," he muttered, giving a sharp glance at my city shoes and soft hands. Sherlock Holmes shifted his feet and let his attention fall on Mr. Bonner.

"We are fortunate, Watson, to be under the care of Mr. Bonner, an experienced sailor and former member of the crew of the whaler *Bailey's Hope* out of Plymouth. I dare say that if we were suddenly attacked by a pod of narwhals, Mr. Bonner would know how to handle them."

Bonner never stopped rowing, but his bearded face turned to my friend and he frowned. "How'd you ken that, Mister? 'Tis true, every word, but I swear I never saw you before in my life, nor your friend, either."

Holmes chuckled. He would never admit it, but he loved dazzling people with his observational techniques. "The foul weather gear you are wearing is heavy duty and designed for Artic climes. The coat, hat, gloves, and boots are necessary for a whaling excursion, but very expensive for such berths as the Lake District offers. They are years old, a part of your original ship's kit. The name of the ship is tattooed on your left wrist, which was visible when you extended your hand to take our baggage. As to the narwhals, that earring hanging from your left ear is crafted from a bit of narwhal ivory. Did you carve it yourself, as some sailors do whilst on long voyages?"

Bonner's jaw had slowly dropped as he listened to Holmes, but as the question hung in the air he snapped it shut and bent again to his rowing. Holmes waited with an amicable air for the man's response, but nothing more was forthcoming.

Sherlock Holmes asked Miss Warburton about the occupants of The Fortress. Beside her uncle and his wife, their sons Fenton and Farley had apartments in the big house. Farley was about to take his diploma in engineering at Durham University. There were maids, a kitchen staff, a butler called Morell, and several men employed as gardeners and stable workers. It sounded like a large establishment. Miss Warburton admitted that her father had inherited the estate from a rich great-grandfather, who had secured the property in the late 1700's. The Fortress and the two-thousand acres that came with it had been in the family for generations.

Jeramiah Warburton had loved the military since he was a child. He enlisted in the Horse Guards in his twenties, and after he became the family patriarch, he had seen his brother through medical school, used his money to advance in the Army, and married late to Miss Katherine Murphy of the Sligo Murphys. She had died young when her husband was stationed abroad, and our client had been raised by her aunt and a succession of governesses.

After nearly an hour, our dory approached a pier that extended out from a rocky point crowned with the faded grey stones that supported the Warburton Fortress. Bonner slipped the boat into a covered boathouse and secured the lines. A winding staircase took us up to a path that led to the main house. In the dark of the evening, we could pick out the rough limestone walls glowing at the edges of windows lit by the gleam of oil lamps.

Holmes stopped suddenly and turned to Miss Warburton. "Who has had access to your father's cottage since he was removed to the asylum?" She looked at him in wonder. "Why, no one, Mr. Holmes. I locked the door myself and I have the only key."

"So the cottage is secure?"

"Quite."

Holmes nodded and proceeded to the front door. We were greeted there by the butler Morell, a silent man who handed off our hats and coats to an equally silent maid. We were greeted in the hall by Dr. Warburton, an imposing man with slicked back yellow hair, and his short, round wife. I viewed Dr. Warburton with interest. He leaned on a stick and was too thin, with yellowish, papery skin. It was clear to my trained medical eye that he was well into the final stage of his illness and did not have many months left.

"Katherine, we have been worried about you. How could you go down to London without telling your aunt and me?"

"I left you a note, Uncle Isaiah."

"Highly irregular, my dear. Are this the gentleman you mentioned you were going to consult?"

"Yes. This is Dr. John H. Watson and his friend Mr. Sherlock Holmes. This is my uncle, Dr. Isaiah Warburton, and my aunt Susan."

We nodded to the pair, neither of whom extended a hand. Our bags were dispatched to our rooms and, over a cup of tea in the library, Miss Warburton explained that we had accompanied her to The Fortress to examine Colonel Warburton's effects in order to form a theory as to why he became mad.

Dr. Warburton and his wife exchanged a glance. "I know you have been very upset lately, dear Katherine," cooed Mrs. Warburton, "but do you think this course is wise? Dear Jeramiah has been in his new home for nearly a month now, and he seems happy enough."

"That place may be the best thing for him, but I want to know *why* he became ill," said our client. "Do not interfere, please, Aunt. What do you suggest as our first move, Mr. Holmes?"

"The day is nearly spent and we have had a long trip. Let us repair to our rooms and rest. A little sustenance on a tray for each of us would be welcome, since it is past the dinner hour. Could that be arranged, Miss Warburton?"

The daughter of Colonel Warburton nodded. Her aunt, nominal mistress of The Fortress, tightened her lips but rang the bell. When the butler appeared, Mrs. Warburton gave orders, and then her husband escorted us to the curving staircase that led upstairs. Miss Warburton went to her apartment, while Holmes and I were taken to a suite of three rooms on the same floor.

The Warburton mansion was shaped like the letter *U*, two stories high, with the center block housing the main rooms and the wings containing several three or four-room suites. Ours consisted of two small bedrooms and a sitting room whose windows looked over a view of the lake, the water barely visible as the moon rose behind the building.

A maid appeared first, lighting the fires and turning down the narrow beds. Trays of food soon appeared. Mrs. Warburton may have had to obey the requests of the daughter of the house, but apparently she did not feel she had to extend the resources of the house to do so. Thin cold sandwiches were good enough for her uninvited guests, along with pickles and more tea. Sherlock Holmes surveyed the spread and laughed.

"Eat hearty, my friend," he chuckled. "If this is what we get for dinner, I cannot predict what our hosts might offer for breakfast. As for me, I am more interested in what is in Colonel Warburton's diary than in food."

As I ate what was before me, Holmes sat on the floor and divided up the pages of the manuscript. He set the main stack to one side and spread several pages out in a semi-circle before him. After the sandwiches were gone, I joined him. He took up the first page on his left.

"Here we have mention of the first time he heard a voice. It happened five months ago, during Christmas month. He was alone in his bedroom. He wrote that the voice was hollow and repeated the words, '*You know what you did. You know what you did.*' He searched the room and found nothing. He then went from room to room and discovered that there was no explanation for the voice. He dismissed it as some kind of recollection of the battle and went to sleep.

"That might have been it, but he heard the voice repeat those words twice during the next twenty-four hours, and frequently over the next months, always at night or in the middle of the night. He began to fixate on the words, wondering which of his many faults were being highlighted. He became anxious. He began sitting up late, waiting for the mysterious voice. It was one night while he sat looking out the sitting room window into the darkness that he first saw the floating figure."

"Yes. He was deep into the clutches of his delusions."

Sherlock Holmes picked up another page from the floor. "He saw a white, flapping figure moving under the trees between his cottage and the cliff. There was a waning moon and he saw it through the branches. Colonel Warburton described the figure as '*luminous and grey*'. It came from the north and vanished into the trees on the south. Soon after it disappeared, he heard the voice again, saying, '*You know what you did.*' He slammed the shutters shut and hid under his bedclothes until dawn.

He didn't sleep all night.

"He got little sleep, according to his diary, after that. The image kept appearing, irregularly, for the next three months. Frequently the voice was also heard. Sometimes it came soon after the colonel sighted the white figure. He began to fear that his mind was going. He didn't dare tell his daughter. He thought she would mention it to his brother and Isaiah would seek to put him away if he thought the colonel was crazy.

"He wrote that Isaiah was jealous of him because he was the first-born. He believed his brother was plotting against him and that he would snatch the first opportunity given to *'depose'* him. He knew Isaiah was ill, but wouldn't admit to himself how badly off he was."

"Paranoia can be a symptom of melancholia," I remarked.

"He also didn't want to worry his daughter. He loves her very much. He began to have suicidal thoughts." Holmes picked up another piece of paper. "He began to sleep more. He would wake up in places other than his bedroom. Once in the kitchen, once in the front hall. The culmination of these *'sleep walking'* episodes came when he found himself in the woods above the cliff outside his cottage. There was a storm that night, and he came to his senses soaking wet and covered with leaves and twigs. He made it back to his rooms without anyone seeing him, but the incident frightened him.

"He started to hide the kitchen knives all over the cottage. Miss Warburton noticed and quietly took them away. She found it increasingly difficult to hide her worries from her father. He could tell that from her behavior. Finally one night, he saw the white figure from the window while she was there. He crashed through the glass after it. She screamed for help and Bonner and Morell chased after him. They caught him on the edge of the cliff and dragged him back to the cottage. He made his last entries in the diary that night under guard. The next day his daughter, on her uncle's advice, signed the papers that put him into the asylum."

I shook my head. "A sad, sad case. He once was an honorable officer, a credit to his regiment. The breakdown of a mind is a terrible thing."

Holmes gathered up the papers and got to his feet. "I think we have done everything we can do tonight, Watson. Tomorrow we shall examine the scene of the crime."

The scene of the crime? I was not convinced there had been a crime. As I lay in my bed that night, I gazed out the window and watched the half-moon suspended in the black sky above. I remembered my old commanding officer, his bright blue eyes snapping in amusement at the banter at the evening mess, and the way he sat on his horse as he reviewed the troops. Finally I rose and drew the curtains to shut out the moon. Only then could I sleep.

The next morning began with a bright sunrise. Holmes roused me out and, fueled by only a cup of coffee, we joined Miss Warburton on the side terrace. The colonel's cottage was situated only four-hundred feet away, behind some outbuildings and a line of low shrubs. It was a one-story red brick building with a slate roof. When we stood on its tiny front porch, we could see the line of trees between the cottage and the shore cliff on the left.

Miss Warburton produced a key and unlocked the front door. Before us was a narrow hallway. A row of hooks held a coat and a hat, suitable for colder weather, on our left. Beyond that was an open set of pocket doors that led to a small sitting room, holding a number of books. A cast-iron fireplace stood to the right of the door. An overstuffed high-backed winged armchair was positioned by the window on the far wall. It offered a clear view of the aforementioned line of trees that led up to the cliff's edge. The walls held shelves of books covering the dull dove grey wallpaper. There was a wooden straight chair and two small tables bearing oil lamps. A faded blue rug took pride of place on the wooden floor. The front window looked over the path we had used to approach the house. Thick brick-red curtains hung at every window of the cottage.

To the right of the hallway was another room of the same size, also equipped with pocket doors, set up as a Spartan bedroom. It had a matching fireplace to the left of the entrance and contained little besides an iron bedstead, a chest of drawers, a small rug, and a battered military foot locker. The wallpaper in this room was a muted brown. A wash stand stood by the window on the right. That window looked toward the shrubs and sheds that separated the gamekeeper's cottage from the main house. The most notable item in the room was an odd-looking handcrafted Afghan rifle, most likely taken as a souvenir, that hung over the bedroom's front window. Afghan tribesmen were famous for the hand-forged rifles they created in the hills to fight their enemies. Beneath it was placed the foot locker. "*Col. J. Warburton*" was stenciled on the lid.

In the back were domestic offices, including a modest kitchen, pantries, a coal bin, and a back door that led to a walled kitchen garden. It was complete with a garden shed and a pair of apple trees set against the back stone wall.

Holmes lost no time. Pulling out his magnifying glass, he began to examine the contents of the cottage. He took the bedroom first. I kept Miss Warburton out of his way as he systematically covered every item the room contained. She was fascinated to see him at work – opening drawers, examining bedclothes, crawling along the floor and into the corners, lifting the lid of Colonel Warburton's foot locker and poking about in the contents. He examined the fireplace, looked under the drugget that covered the center of the room, and even peered through his lens at every inch of the brown wallpaper. He spent extra time on the wall against which the headboard of the bed was placed. I could see no reason why the paper there drew his attention. Finally he left the bedroom and moved on to the sitting-room.

Again he was very thorough. He searched that room by opening each book from the many on the shelves, again lifting the rug, poking his long fingers into the armchair's stuffing, and even checking the levels on the oil lamps. Again he paid particular attention to the wallpaper of the room. At one point he picked up a volume from the table closest to the armchair and handed it to me. It was the copy of last year's *Beeton's Christmas Annual* that Miss Warburton had mentioned as her father's favorite reading material.

I cannot describe the feelings that washed over me as I gazed on the cover of my feeble effort to tell of my friend's extraordinary powers of observation and deduction. We had had many adventures together since that first one. Some had gone well and others had ended in stalemate or failure. Yet the case I had entitled *A Study in Scarlet* still held a special place in my heart.

To think that my poor attempt at storytelling had comforted my old commanding officer! I tried to imagine him in his chair, holding the little volume and turning the pages as he read it again for the nth time. My heart grew warm as I thought of the old man, beset with fears for his own sanity, losing his worries by following our cab to No. 3 Lauriston Gardens, or trekking over the wild landscape of the American West in words that I had written down.

Sherlock Holmes had moved away from the armchair to check out more shelves of books. I laid the copy of *Beeton's* back on the little table with a humble heart. An author is always gratified to hear that his readers think highly of his efforts. In this case I felt unworthy. I moved away from the armchair and went out to the hall, where I paced up and down until Holmes had finished his labours in the sitting-room and moved on to the back of the house.

Here he was no less thorough in his investigation. Holmes peered into the pots and pans stored on the kitchen shelves, sifted through the stove's ashes, tapped the white-washed walls, turned over every lump of coal in the bin, and even used his magnifying lens to examine the cracks between the flagstones that formed the floor. Finally he opened the back door and walked outside. There he briefly searched the little garden shed, paced along the stone walls of the kitchen garden, and then circled the cottage. That last maneuver took a long time, as he poked and pried at what seemed every exterior brick within his reach.

I was used to his methods, but Miss Warburton grew weary as time passed. I urged her to re-enter the cottage while I made her some tea. By the time Holmes walked into the sitting room, she was ensconced in her father's armchair with an empty teacup at her side. Holmes brushed off my offer of refreshment for him.

"Perhaps you would like to stay here, Miss Warburton, while Dr. Watson and I continue our investigation," said he. "My next step is to examine the trees that stand between this cottage and the cliff."

"Oh, no, Mr. Holmes," she said brightly, rising to her feet. "Dr. Watson's tea has quite revived me. I am eager to continue."

The three of us crossed the grass and entered the little grove of oaks and beeches. I noticed nothing unusual. Holmes strode along, hands slapping the trunks, shoes shuffling through the grasses, with his eyes darting everywhere – to the left, the right, and particularly up at the canopy. At one point, he even shinnied up a bole and crept out on a limb to look at something on a budding set of branches that only his eye had seen. Miss Warburton and I remained below, craning our necks and watching as he scrambled from one tree to the next for several minutes. When he dropped to the ground and turned to us, he pulled out a handkerchief and wiped his hands.

"This has been a most interesting and fruitful exercise. I think the next step should be a visit with your father."

Miss Warburton looked surprised. She obviously had a number of questions to ask, but she had learned by now that it was futile to question Sherlock Holmes in the midst of his investigation. We walked back to The Fortress. As we entered the front hall, we were met by Dr. Warburton, his wife, and two young men, obviously also of Warburton stock. The men were putting on their overcoats as the butler Morell stood by with an armful of hats and scarves.

"Katherine, where have you been?" asked the older of the two men. Miss Warburton murmured introductions to her cousins, Fenton and Farley Warburton, the doctor's sons. "We were about to go out and find you. There has been most upsetting news from the asylum. Uncle Jeremiah has escaped!"

"Escaped!" exclaimed our client. She went pale to the lips and dropped into a hall chair.

"A telegram was received an hour ago from the institution's superintendent, Mr. Belloes," said Isaiah Warburton. "Jeremiah was discovered missing right before breakfast this morning. The attendants believe he ran away sometime after lights-out last night."

"Where is this institution located?" asked Sherlock Holmes.

"In Carlisle to the north," answered the doctor.

"Then he has had plenty of time to make his way back to The Fortress," mused my friend.

Miss Warburton raised her stricken face to all of us. "Why do you think he would come here?" she asked.

"Because here is his home," I answered gently.

"What are we to do? He must not be harmed!" Miss Warburton cried.

"Mr. Holmes, what do you think?" asked Dr. Warburton. "He is my older brother, but if he is unstable and offers violence to the women – "

"He must be tracked down and captured," declared Fenton firmly. "Mother and Katherine must stay in The Fortress with the maid servants. Father, you cannot walk far. You must stay with them. I will send Bonner down to the pier to watch for him there. Morell and the gardeners and stablemen can search the outbuildings and the fields, starting at the north edge of the property, closest to Carlisle. Farley and I will contact the local police. Mr. Holmes, you and your friend must guard The Fortress. In his madness, our uncle could be capable of anything. Above all, the women must be protected."

The Warburton men agreed at once. Within a few moments, the available forces had been thus dispatched and Holmes and I found ourselves alone in the deserted hall. The maids, along with Miss Warburton and her aunt, had found refuge somewhere upstairs. Before he joined them, Dr. Warburton instructed the butler to hand over the keys to The Fortress to Holmes. Out of Miss Warburton's sight, Fenton distributed rifles to his brother and the servants. Two horses were hastily saddled, and the younger Warburtons rode away in the direction of Ambleside.

"Do you have your service revolver with you, Watson?" asked Sherlock Holmes.

"Of course I do," I replied. "But Miss Warburton does not want her father harmed."

"There may not be the luxury of choice available to us, Doctor," replied the detective. "The Fortress is secure enough, but the Warburtons have forgotten something important. Follow me."

Still wearing our outside garments, we slipped through the front door and locked it. Then we silently crossed the distance between the main house and the Colonel's cottage. The door entering off the tiny front porch was easily opened under Holmes's sure touch, and we found ourselves standing once more in the little hallway.

"The Colonel, once away from the asylum, is more likely to return here to his cottage. As you said so eloquently to Miss Warburton, here is his home. We must be ready for his arrival. You will find a place of concealment within while I take up watch outside. It is most important that we find the Colonel before any of his family does."

Holmes put his finger to his lips and disappeared outside. I looked around the cottage. There were not many places to hide. The bed sat too low to offer any cover, nor was there any to find amid the other bedroom furniture. The back part of the cottage was too exposed for shelter. Finally I closed all the curtains, turned the high-backed wingchair so its back was to the sitting room, and seated myself there.

The fair morning sky had turned overcast, and in the small rooms, lacking fires and lighted lamps, the corners were full of shadows. The atmosphere grew even gloomier as the sun passed the meridian and crawled downward. The afternoon slowly advanced. The only sounds were the ticking of the mantel clock and faint noises of Lake Windermere's waters lapping at the bottom of the nearby cliff. I was comfortably seated in the depths of the high-backed wingchair, but the need for absolute silence was nerve-racking. My muscles, motionless and tense with waiting, felt like they were on fire. Involuntarily I remembered that last night before Maiwand, when the entire regiment was ordered to wait silently at arms before dawn broke and the Afghans came screaming down from the hills to begin their bloody slaughter.

It was almost with relief that I finally heard a faint sound from the back of the house. I could see nothing, but my hearing was excellent. There was the click of a lock. A door opened, then closed. Faint sounds of scuffling were heard. Footfalls came toward me. They did not come into the sitting room as I expected, but instead shifted to the bedroom. I could hear metallic clinking, then the unmistakable sound of a rifle bolt being drawn back. I gripped my revolver and leapt from my hiding spot to confront the intruder.

I only had time to glimpse a muffled figure standing in the hallway. At my sudden appearance, the figure turned and I recognized Colonel Warburton's Afghan rifle pointed at me. I raised my weapon but the rifle muzzle blazed and smoke filled the air. I felt a sharp, hot pain in my right lower leg as my own shot went wild. I fell to the carpet as the mysterious assailant dashed out the front door. Holmes had left it unlocked.

I tried to follow, but the pain of my wound made it impossible for me to stand. Blood was spreading across the floor. I grabbed my leg to compress the artery and felt my fibula shift. I fumbled for a handkerchief to stem the bleeding. Outside I could hear yells and footfalls. Time slowed down as I concentrated on my wound until Sherlock Holmes burst through the door, shouting my name.

"Watson! Watson!" Holmes first turned to the bedroom but when I responded with "I'm here, Holmes," he swiftly ran to where I was crouched on the sitting-room carpet.

"Watson! Believe me, if I had had any idea this would happen, I never would have sent you in here!" He dropped to my side and examined my injury. Gentle fingers added another handkerchief to the binding I had applied. He lifted me up to sit on the wooden chair. Holmes's face was white and strained, his eyes anxious. I wanted to reassure him, but for some reason I could not speak. I was growing weak from pain, loss of blood, and shock. I did not notice when others entered. Orders were given, and I was carried out of the gamekeeper's cottage and placed into a carriage. Before it left the cottage, I lifted my head and saw through the window the man who had shot me. It was Fenton Warburton, securely bound and guarded by a Cumbria policeman.

At The Fortress, where I was carried up to my room, Dr. Warburton examined my injury. The crude Jezail bullet had passed through my lower leg, just above the ankle, leaving a jagged, still-bleeding hole. My right fibula was broken, as I had thought in the cottage. The local doctor, a surgeon named Quimby, was called in. Anesthesia was applied. The last thing I remember was Holmes's worried face hovering over me as I counted down to blackness.

When I awoke the next morning, Sherlock Holmes was slumped in the chair next to my bed. It was obvious he had never left my side. When he saw that I was conscious, he gave my hand a warm squeeze. "I shall never forgive myself," he murmured, "for failing to see Fenton Warburton taking the colonel into the cottage after leaving you there." With that he got up and left, sending in the doctor.

I was told by the cheerful surgeon the operation was a success. My right leg was heavily bandaged but the pain was managed. After the breakfast things were cleared away, Holmes returned, bringing Miss Warburton, her uncle, his wife, and their son Farley. A moment later a knock was heard at my door and a familiar voice asked to enter.

It was Colonel Warburton.

He looked older, of course. It had been several years since we had last seen each other before the Battle of Maiwand. He was thinner, his hair was silvered at the temples, his step was a bit unsteady. Yet his blue eyes were bright and his handshake strong as he greeted me. Except for dark circles under his eyes, there was no sign of melancholia.

My exclamations of surprise were interrupted by Holmes, who bustled about finding chairs for everyone around my bed. When he planted his feet on the hearth rug and pulled out his pipe, I knew the time had come for his explanation of the case. Sherlock Holmes would not admit it, but he lived for dramatic moments like these, when he could expound upon his methods and astonish his audiences with the results.

Sherlock Holmes waved his pipe at the mantelpiece where Colonel Warburton's diary was placed. "I took an interest in this case when Dr. Watson showed me your diary, sir." he said to the colonel. "There are three ways that a man may be driven to madness. One is chemically, another is by defects of the mind, and the third is deliberately. The entries kept in that diary made it clear to me that neither defects of the mind or chemicals were responsible for the experiences that you had undergone in the past half-year. It was simple for me to pick out the clues that told me you were being persecuted. I determined that the danger had not yet passed, and so we made the journey up to Lake Windermere and The Fortress that same day."

He turned to the rest of us. "Miss Warburton allowed us to examine the colonel's cottage the next morning. The most interesting thing I found was that by the head of the bed in the bedroom and on either side of the sitting-room armchair were odd spots in the walls hidden behind the wallpaper. They were hollow spaces, just the size of a single brick. An examination of the outside of the cottage revealed that at each location the outer bricks had been pried from their places and then replaced. Behind the bricks, all insulation had been removed. That allowed someone outside the building to take away the brick and speak into the resulting opening in order to be heard inside.

"That explained the voices. It also established that there was a plot against Colonel Warburton. Imagination doesn't need to move bricks to be heard.

"The floating figure in the trees was also part of the persecution. Watson and Miss Warburton can tell you that I even went to the extreme of climbing the trunks and balancing on unstable limbs in order to scrutinize the bark of the branches at the top for marks left by a human hand. I found evidence that a wire had been strung between the oaks and beeches in order to convey a lightweight something to the cliff from the other end of the line. That explained the floating figure the colonel glimpsed through his window. It was, I surmise, a thin wire framework draped in muslin or a similar fabric. I might also remark that each time the phenomenon occurred it was at night, dark and very late. All the better to disguise the perpetrator.

"Many of the pieces of the puzzle were now in my hands. Motive had been obvious from the beginning. Colonel Warburton was the landowner of a considerable property. He had returned home with no interest in the estate and isolated himself from contact with his family. His brother, next in line, since the entailment didn't allow inheritance by females, was terminally ill and not long to live. I am sorry, Doctor."

Dr. Warburton shook his head. "It is true. Over the past year, I have had to turn over much of the running of the estate to Fenton. He has had full access to all estate papers and contracts."

"Therefore he knew best how much the estate is worth," said Holmes. "If he could connive to gain permanent control of its assets, he would prosper far more than working as a headmaster at a local school. Fenton Warburton was an intelligent and ambitious man. Since his own father was dying, he reasoned that only one life stood between him and great wealth. He was also an impatient man. He decided to take steps. If his Uncle Jeremiah was declared to be insane, there would be no question of his ever gaining back control of the estate in the future.

"The reasons for the colonel's melancholia were well known in the family. From his reading, Fenton found the most effective ways to feed his uncle's fears. The accusing voice in the night, only when he was alone, and the specter fluttering through the trees. Even the sleep-walking which was a side effect of the stress the colonel was under, all served Fenton's purpose.

"He felt triumphant after Colonel Warburton was admitted to the asylum. His plan had succeeded and now it would be only a matter of months before everything was his. Fenton is not a good man, and could not be expected to be a good son. With him, family considerations did not hold a candle to the possibility of profit. It was his nature.

"Then his cousin Katherine left a note and traveled to London in order to consult Dr. Watson, whose good friend was Mr. Sherlock Holmes. The family knew that because of Colonel Warburton's favorite reading material, the *Beeton's Christmas Annual*, which carried Dr. Watson's tale, *A Study in Scarlet*.

"Fenton, like many intelligent criminals, made the mistake of improving upon perfection. Confinement for attempted self-destruction suddenly was not enough. Colonel Warburton must be proven to be not only a danger to himself but to others. So Fenton devised a new plan. He smuggled his uncle out of the asylum the night we arrived and left him tied up and gagged in an outbuilding close to his cottage. He realized he was taking a chance of discovery, but why would anyone look in that storage area without a good reason? Fenton knew the staff at the asylum wouldn't discover that their patient was missing until breakfast. They would then spend some hours searching their own premises before notifying the family.

"In his confession after he was captured outside the cottage, he told how he watched as Miss Warburton, Dr. Watson, and I examined the cottage, the kitchen garden, and the line of trees from which he had previously removed his wire. The telegram arrived from Dr. Belloes, and it was time to raise the alarm.

"He assigned tasks for all the men that would scatter them over the property, but not toward the colonel's cottage. Fenton and Farley then took the overland route to inform the Cumbrian police, but he faked an injury to his horse before they had gone far. He sent Farley ahead while he turned back to the estate. He spirited Colonel Warburton out of hiding, carried him into the cottage through the back door, and left him in the kitchen while he went into the bedroom and loaded the colonel's old Afghan rifle with Jezail bullets from the footlocker. He planned to fire several shots toward the searchers outside, untie and leave his uncle in the hallway, and see that he was blamed for the attack. That would guarantee that Colonel Warburton would never be released from the asylum, and he would lose all rights pertaining to the management of the estate.

"Of course, the colonel would protest his innocence and tell his own story, but who would believe a crazy, homicidal old man?"

"Why shoot Dr. Watson?" asked Miss Warburton.

"Fenton Warburton admitted that the sudden appearance of my friend startled him and his finger slipped on the trigger. He never meant to hit anyone, just to fire the weapon enough times to make us think the colonel had gone completely mad."

"Well, he failed," said Isaiah Warburton. "I'm sorry, Jeremiah, that I ever urged Katherine to sign those commitment papers."

"You thought you were acting for the best," replied his brother. "Even I was convinced that I had completely lost my senses. I do not blame you for thinking the same. The question is: What do we do now?"

"That is the subject of a private family discussion," said Sherlock Holmes. "If you need the co-operation of Dr. Watson and myself in further dealings against Fenton, Miss Warburton knows our address in London. Meanwhile, as soon as Watson can travel, we shall return to Baker Street."

That is the story of Colonel Warburton's madness and the surprising results of Sherlock Holmes's investigation. Fenton was sentenced to a long term in prison for the attacks on the colonel and myself. Miss Warburton married the surgeon, Dr. Quimby, and they made Colonel Warburton their special concern. Colonel Warburton became interested in assisting his brother in the management of the estate which helped to lift his melancholia. Dr. Warburton's illness did take him within the year, but his son Farley proved to be an able administrator who became the rock of the family. As for me, for a time I limped from my wound, and even years later damp weather could cause my leg to ache. That was my souvenir from the adventure I always thought of as "The Case of the

Diary and the Detective".

> *Of all the problems which have been submitted to my friend, Mr. Sherlock Holmes, for solution during the years of our intimacy, there were only two which I was the means of introducing to his notice – that of Mr. Hatherley's thumb, and that of Colonel Warburton's madness.*
>
> Dr. John H. Watson – "The Engineer's Thumb"

... and ...

> *I made no remark, however, but sat nursing my wounded leg. I had a Jezail bullet through it some time before, and, though it did not prevent me from walking, it ached wearily at every change of the weather.*
>
> Dr. John H. Watson – The Sign of Four

The Adventure at Bellingbeck Park
by Deanna Baran

My friend Watson, upon his bereavement, had returned to the familiar lodgings at Baker Street which we had formerly shared prior to his marriage. But while some grieving men self-medicate with the bottle, or find solace in any other number of personal crutches, Watson went through a period where he buried himself in work, departing before the rising of the sun and returning long after its setting, which is no insignificant undertaking during the long days of summer.

That deliberate distraction is the only excuse I have as to why I must needs chronicle my own doings. For anyone familiar with the newspapers, August of 1888 had no lack of lurid and sensational goings-on splashed across the headlines, bold black type upon yellow paper, and those goings-on quite overshadowed anything else. But whilst the *outré* is most certainly within my purview, I do not have a penchant for sensationalism for its own sake. Rather, I look upon the strange and the singular of crime much as a medical man may find himself observing a peculiar series of symptoms. It is not the symptoms themselves that are of interest, but rather, they provide clues as to what to expect in a given series of circumstances, all the better to treat the disease underneath. But like most physicians, the overwhelming majority of my cases take place in private, dealing with the secret misdeeds of anonymous men, far from the scrutiny of the public. And lacking the company of my most valued ally, my isolation was felt; and lacking the company of my most enthusiastic chronicler, so many of my cases disappeared without a ripple into the shadows of the past.

And thus I take the time to jot down some facts of one such case during that August – not the sensational, but the surreptitious.

It began in Baker Street, as most of my cases do. I had finished a solitary tea, and was working in fits and starts upon a monograph regarding the microscope and its relation to crime. The bell heralded the arrival of a visitor. I had received his letter in the morning mail, and Mr. Thomas Deering was shown in.

"Pray seat yourself," I said, indicating the chair nearby. He set a large leather bag by the door – solid, well-made, straps, a brass lock – and sat, somewhat nervously smoothing his hands across his trouser knees in an unconscious fidget. A monogrammed signet ring glinted on his hand, but he was moving too erratically to get a good glimpse of the letters. By way of putting him at ease, I inquired, "You appear to have come straight from your cricket match. Did you win?"

"Quite! Er, rather!" he said, brightening up. "We won by a run. The jacket told you, I suppose? Or the bag of sports equipment? I haven't been back to my rooms to drop them off properly. I came straight here."

"I would be sadly ignorant if I did not recognize the colours of the Burleson Cricket Club," I said, gesturing to his summer suit, which he had not yet changed. The jacket with its bold sky blue and navy stripes and matching cap would have been acceptable either upon the stage or upon the turf, but in few other places. "But even had you come hatless and clad merely in white, your shoes are too sturdy for tennis, and golf does not require pads strapped to one's legs. Their presence has left behind distinctive creases in your trousers." It was unnecessary to allude to however one may discern a man who has spent the better part of the day outdoors in the August sun. Instead, I continued, "I am pleased that, whatever troubles you, it has not interfered with your ability to enjoy a healthy day of sport. This morning's letter was very vague. Many people are disinclined to put down in writing the specifics of their fears or suspicions. Now that we are in private, pray feel at ease, and elucidate."

"I need a cracksman to break into my grandfather's safe," said Deering abruptly.

"You're in the wrong neighbourhood to hire a task like that. Baker Street is hardly the equivalent of Grosvenor Square, but it is also hardly the equivalent of the Old Nichol. Wouldn't it be easier to politely ask your grandfather to open it?"

"He won't see reason, and will be robbed this week-end because he ignores my warnings. There's a grouse shooting party at his country house, Bellingbeck Park. Except the grouse shoot is merely a pretext. What's really about to happen is the field testing of a secret miniature camera."

I inclined my head slightly to encourage him to develop this point a little more thoroughly in his narration.

"It takes photographs, you see. From the air. It's a miniature camera, strapped to the breast of a pigeon. The pigeon is released. The pigeon flies home to its roost, with the clockwork automatically snapping an exposure every half-minute or so along the way until it runs out of film. The pigeon lands, the recipient removes the roll of paper film, and develops it. And you develop them in a dark room with a jolly old set of chemicals, and have a jolly old series of photographs of the terrain the pigeon flew over on its journey."

"A clever device," I said, with an approving nod. "I can see how it would be a valuable resource in wartime reconnaissance or aerial surveys of difficult terrain."

"Exactly," said Deering, sitting on the edge of his chair. His hands were now still. The monogram looked as though it read *TAD*. "My father is something of an inventor, having nothing else to do, being a younger son. He ought to race horses, or collect incunabula, or play cricket, or something. But no. He putters about, inventing tiny cameras to buckle on to birds."

"And so . . . ." I said, steering him back on course.

"Oh. Yes. And so this weekend's grouse shoot is actually a field testing of this secret camera. There will be about ten guests in attendance, most of them from the Ministry of Defence. But I suspect that one of them isn't Whitehall. One of the guests on the list is a certain Mr. Walter Rowland-Powell, which I don't believe is his real name, either. But I must say, wherever he goes, something goes wrong behind him. A fire breaks out in a library. A gun misfires. Things go missing – not plate or things of that sort, but things you can't tell the police about. People talk, yet he still gets the most plummy invitations. I haven't figured how he does it. And I'm afraid that my father's plans for his miniature pigeon-camera, kept in my grandfather's safe, are going to go missing. I thought it would be a great idea to break into the safe and secretly bear away the plans. Of course, it would be obvious if they just vanished. Rowland-Powell wouldn't find that satisfactory at all. Instead, what if they could be replaced with a false copy, something with a few subtle mistakes on it. Nothing noticeable, but something that would be utterly useless to a Foreign Power weeks later when knowledgeable people finally start studying the thing. But in between, after Rowland-Powell bears it away and everyone's left in his dust scratching their heads, I can say, 'Ha-ha! I knew this would happen. Here it is, safe and sound after all.' And then reunite them with the genuine article, drop the curtain, exit stage left, *et cetera*."

"It certainly sounds tidy, the way you put it," I said dryly. "It sounds as though all you're missing, in addition to your cracksman, is a draughtsman. Surely drawings of the sort you refer to could not possibly be copied in less than an afternoon – possibly longer, if neatness and accuracy are to be taken into account."

"I managed to waylay one of his later drafts before it was committed to the fire," said Deering carelessly. "It was the easiest thing in the world to change a few lines, alter a few figures. And the best part is, it's in the old man's own handwriting, so of course, no one would suspect. Because it's the genuine thing. Except it isn't."

"So you know what is to happen, and you know who is going to do it, and you know approximately when, and you have devised a plan to prevent this misfortune from occurring. And what you require is someone to physically undertake this adventure. I suppose you've thought that through, as well." I kept my voice as neutral as possible.

"In fact, I have," said Deering, leaning forward. "It would draw too much attention if I were to show up and say, 'Hello, all, here is my jolly old friend from school that I just happened to pick up and invite for a jolly old round of grouse-shooting, I hope you don't mind.' That wouldn't work, of course. We wouldn't have been likely to have met at school."

"No, I suspect I may have been a few years ahead of your time."

"Contemporaries. That's the word I'm looking for. No, that story wouldn't do. But. Who is invisible at a house-party? Why, you could be disguised as my *valet*. That would give you a pretext, and everyone would treat you as the most natural person in the world. Or like furniture, depending."

"Except for all those who are acquainted with your *true* valet, seeing that this is your grandfather's estate, at which you both have presumably spent significant amounts of time in the past," I pointed out.

"Yes, but I can concoct a story to explain his temporary absence," said Deering. "An ill mother. An aunt's funeral. Nothing that anyone will think twice about, because no one really cares about other people's relations. They just make the appropriate noises and get on with life. They'll accept you all right, and you just act as though you belong, and hey presto! You take a few minutes of your time in Wolverly's library, and if anyone catches you, explain that you got lost, but that won't happen, because all the guests will be shooting grouse, or playing with pigeons, and all the house staff has something better to do than standing around waiting to catch people meddling with Wolverly's safe."

"Has anyone told you what a reckless nature you have?" I asked.

"I'm a younger son as well," said Deering. "There are three men between me and the title, so I'd better learn to live by my wits! Too bad I can't make a career out of playing cricket. Or inventing tiny cameras for birds, for that matter."

"I may very well do it, just for the amusement," I mused aloud. "I pride myself on my acting ability. It would be a personal challenge to see if I could pass for a valet at close quarters amongst the natives. Your case has several points of interest. And it would only be for the week-end."

"We arrive Friday, around five o'clock, and leave Monday," said Deering. "My valet's name is Adams. I expect it would be easiest if they called you Adams for the duration of our visit. No use in your coming up with an alias, for you can't use your own name, and it will make your acceptance smoother." He scribbled an address on the back of an envelope from his pocket, and handed it to me. "If you'll come 'round my rooms at the Charing Cross Hotel, we can do this. You're a jolly sport. I'll pay you ten pounds for your effort, up front. I pay my man twenty-five-per-year – not bad for a weekend's work, eh!"

"I'm intrigued by this Rowland-Powell," I said thoughtfully. "I wonder if he's as much a rascal as you suspect. I've always wondered what makes men tick. Selling secret mechanisms to Unnamed Foreign Powers! I say, Mr. Deering. If you were to do such a thing, how would you go about doing it?"

Mr. Deering stared blankly at me for a full minute before responding, "I . . . I really have no idea."

"Not to worry," I reassured him. "It was merely a hypothetical question."

We arrived Friday by carriage. Bellingbeck Park was the estate of the Viscount Wolverly, Deering's grandfather. The title had been created somewhat more than a century ago, under King George III, who seems to have been prolific in creating viscountcies, most of which had gone extinct due to a lack of male heirs, according to what I could glean from my *Burke's* and *Debrett's*. Bellingbeck Park was a manor house which would have done a far more ancient lineage credit as a family seat. The second Viscount had been responsible for the illuminated fountains. The third Viscount had ambitiously introduced a Doric colonnade, two extra wings, and a Palladian façade. Wolverly, the fourth Viscount, seemed to maintain the manor in a workmanlike fashion, neither spending extravagantly to further develop its aesthetics, nor scrimping and allowing it to fall into disrepair.

I arranged with a pair of footmen to bring Deering's luggage up to his room through a back entrance, whilst he went to the front door to greet whomever was responsible for the welcoming of guests. I knew from my abovementioned references that there was no Lady Wolverly, nor any daughters. Deering was my client's mother's maiden name. I found it a point of interest that he should deliberately wish to obscure his true surname, when it could be found easily enough in print.

Wolverly, the current Viscount, had had two sons. His heir was in a regiment stationed somewhere along the Gold Coast, busily building the Empire in Africa rather than securing the family bloodline. His given name was Edward and his nickname was "Diver". An odd name for an Army man! His second son was Deering's father, with the given name of Ruford (and who went by the familiar moniker of "Rufftum" when amongst friends and family, I was advised). He would naturally be present at this display of his own ingenuity. Deering's own elder brother (Fitzgerald, called "Fitzy" by his inner circle) had been stationed somewhere in India since 1881. I had asked Deering was his sobriquet was when dealing with people on a first name basis, and he looked blankly at me and said, "My father calls me Thomas." But I was pleased that I had a rough sketch of the family tree and the relationships of those I was and was not likely to meet.

I unpacked his things as tidily as I could, and he shortly arrived, whereby I dutifully removed all travel stains from his person and made him presentable for tea.

"We're in luck," he said, as I brushed the dust from his coat. "Rowland-Powell isn't scheduled to arrive until luncheon to-morrow. We have a bit of time yet, although most of the other guests are arriving to-day."

Whilst he enjoyed tea with the guests in the shade of the Doric colonnade (courtesy of the third Viscount) (the colonnade, not the tea), I made my way belowstairs to the kitchen, where I doffed my coat, donned one of the men's aprons, and took up wiping dishes for the pantry-maid, much to her gratitude.

"You're a far sight more of a gentleman than Mr. Adams ever was, Mr. Adams," she said approvingly. It took no effort at all to get her to discuss the house party, but unfortunately, she had little information about Rowland-Powell, except for the fact that this was his fifth or sixth visit, he never brought his own man with him, and one of the footmen always valeted him instead. Everyone else had also been here before, at least once – neither Wolverly nor Deering's father were strangers to the higher circles of the Ministry of Defence. His last invention of interest to them had been two years ago, when he had created a patent camera disguised as a pocket-watch. Due to the small size and precise measurements, the plates were difficult to manipulate, and he had never attempted to commercialize his invention, but she had no doubt it was in frequent use in foreign capitals. It seemed that our Rufftum was in the habit of turning out intriguing knickknacks every year or two, usually involving optics in some fashion.

We made our way through the washing-up of cooking for the tea things, and then the dishes from the tea things. I helped the footmen put away the glass and plate, and determined which of them usually stood in to valet for Mr. Rowland-Powell on the occasions of his visits. I mentioned that I had heard gossip about how odd happenings followed where he went. The first footman recalled a wastebasket fire in his room, (fortunately contained), and the second football reminded him of the shooting accident when they had gathered to hunt hare. (No one died.)

I went up to help Deering dress for dinner, and then came back down to help wash the pots and pans for dinner preparation. During this period, the servants had their own dinner about an hour before the family and guests ate theirs. The butler and housekeeper presided at table. There were two other guests' valets, in addition to Viscount Wolverly's man, and it was amusing to see them referred to by the names of their masters. I had to conceal a smile when I asked Viscount Wolverly to pass the salt. Precedence was very strictly observed, again according to the hierarchy of one's master. There was some debate as to whether a General outranked a fourth-in-line for a viscountcy who was merely a Mister, but I humbly ceded the higher place to him. At the end of our meal, as one of the upper servants, I was permitted to retire with the butler and the other valets to the housekeeper's parlour for pudding and coffee and conversation.

One of the valets, referred to as General Rocker, mentioned that he was looking forward to tomorrow's shoot, with the prospect of grouse for dinner. He then proceeded to relay a humorous anecdote about something that had happened while loading General Rocker's shotgun for him while hunting partridge last February. Another valet, called Lord Robert White, brought up the hare shooting episode. "Mr. Rowland-Powell said Mr. Adams had bumped him and the shotgun went off," he mentioned in passing, and it took me a few moments to realize that the Mr. Adams to which he referred was my Mr. Deering, not Mr. Deering's usual valet.

The signal came, and we made our way upstairs to resume duties. I stood behind Deering's chair at dinner and waited on him patiently. I timed it – two hours for the gentlemen to make their way through dinner, before they finally retired for cigars and brandy in another room. I helped with the washing-up once more, and then went up to Deering's room to help him undress for bed.

"You realize, of course, what neither of us considered. I'm expected to stand with you while you hunt and load your gun for you," I said, reflecting on how it was possible to discard too much from one's mental attic. That I, the descendant of how many generations of country squires, should make such an oversight!

"Surely we can make a story to cover that, too," said Deering optimistically. "Perhaps you were in the Army, and had a bad battle someplace, and are suffering from nerves. Can't stand to be around explosions. Kandahar, perhaps. Or Maiwand. Can you pretend to have been in Afghanistan?"

"Can we fool the Ministry of Defence into believing I served in the Army?" I asked sardonically. "I haven't, you see, and military men of the sort you've collected here this weekend have a great nose for spotting civilian imposters. They're not as credulous as pantry maids. If one marches a valet in front of a pantry maid and says, 'This is my valet', why would she doubt? But if one marches a valet in front of a General and says, 'This man fought at Arzu,' he'll immediately ask for regiments, and commanders, and comrades-in-arms, and did I know so-and-so. That sort of charade would be quite impossible to sustain without significant research."

"Then perhaps you ought to come down with a cold," he suggested.

"In August?" I hung his suit. "Will you prefer a hot bath? A cold bath? Or a cool bath?"

"I'll save it for tomorrow," Deering replied. "We'll figure something out."

It was midnight before I retired to my third floor bedroom, where visiting valets were hidden away. Although I had originally approved of this scheme due to the brevity of its duration, I found myself wishing for an extra few days to observe the habits and the schedules of the manor's inmates. If the grouse shoot were to occur in the morning, and the field testing sometime after luncheon, that left precious little time to effect the substitution. However, there was nothing that said Rowland-Powell would strike on Saturday evening. Perhaps he would wait until Sunday, when the family, guests, and servants were at church. Or perhaps Sunday night would provide opportunity, as the week-end drew to a close, and anything gone missing would not be noted until it was too late.

I preferred to leave nothing to chance.

The plans were rolled into a short, tidy tube and tied with red tape, secreted at the bottom of my satchel. Deering had reluctantly given it to me as we had left London, although I would have preferred extra time before our house party to examine them myself. He would have kept them up until the moment of substitution, if he had had his way, but I explained that I worked alone, and my luggage was safer. Although a valet unpacks his master's wardrobe, there was always the chance an officious maid or footman would interfere, and stumble across the plans by accident. I waited until the house settled, then slipped from my room down to the ground floor, where Wolverly's library was located. Deering had described where to find the safe. It was hidden behind a large portrait of the first Viscount and his family.

Unrolling my case of instruments, I set to work.

There are two schools of thought in this line of work. The swiftest, easiest, and most straightforward method is to drill holes and punch tumblers. Obviously, when embracing this method, the miscreant does not care to disguise the fact of his presence. This is the method used when the thief has no intention of returning to the scene, such as in stealing piles of currency or bags of coin.

The alternate method involves tremendously more finesse. One must attempt to break into the safe, not through brute force, but as though one is the ordinary safe-owner opening his safe under ordinary circumstances. This is the preferred method in the pursuit of information, and when one wishes to disguise for as long as possible the fact that information kept in a secure location has been compromised.

It was this second method that I turned to as I began my work. My clamps, my drills, my punches, my augurs – these tools I ignored, as I set to work with the delicacy of a surgeon performing a critical operation. I looked the part as well, armed with a stethoscope, the better to magnify the clickings and movements of the tumblers.

There was no hurry, only infinite patience and tremendous concentration. All that existed was myself and the invisible tumblers, rolling here, clicking there. The combination dial twirled smoothly under my fingers at one point, and met with more resistance at another point. It took a combination of subtle internal sounds, the feel of friction, and the guidance of instinct and experience. The quarter-hours chimed distantly away in another part of the house, one after another, but I did not allow myself to heed them or be rushed.

With a gratifying sound of sliding steel bolts, the door swung open. I noted clear glass ampoules mounted in a bracket attached to the inside of the door. If I had forced my way in through the door, I would have triggered a cloud of gas, most likely phosgene.

Wolverly's safe was not as impenetrable as he would have liked, but his security measures were solid. I did not realize I had been holding my breath so long. I exhaled quietly, slowed my heartbeat to its normal pace, and willed my hands to be steady. I sorted through the papers in the safe, taking care to disarrange nothing. The small roll of plans for the camera was easy to find.

I unrolled the two plans, side-by-side, and examined them by the light of my shaded lantern. Deering was correct: They were nearly indistinguishable, yet were different enough that, with both copies present for a comparison, it was clear that the copy Deering had provided was an earlier, imperfect version in need of significant refinement.

Before I left, I took a jar of kitchen ashes I had slipped into my pocket earlier, and sprinkled them delicately around the front of the safe. Not enough to draw attention, due to the pattern of the carpet, but enough to notice if someone stood before the safe and tracked them round the room.

I made it back to my bed unchallenged.

The next morning, I presume I functioned as smoothly as normal, but my nerves were taut. Would anyone suspect the safe had been tampered with? It was not the first time I had done such a thing – there had been the case of the Buffini diamonds and retrieval of the compromising letters stolen from the Countess of Redmond – but I preferred a quick, anonymous escape once my purpose was achieved, bolting to my Baker Street burrow, rather than this foolishness of loitering about the premises for another three days and waiting for something to go wrong.

However, the whole household was excited enough about the grouse and about the trials that any missteps I may have made would have been attributed to my inexperience as a substitute valet. Although some gentlemen's gentlemen are noble creatures, the majority of them combine the two distasteful extremes of servility combined with foppishness. It is not the sort of career a man with ambition would embrace, and not the sort of role I would voluntarily assume for any extended period of time. I attended Deering as dutifully as a nursemaid. Servants do not wait table for breakfast, so I was free to proceed downstairs to listen to the servants' idle chatter and help where I was needed. When the house was full, all hands were appreciated, but it was not long before I was called away to the field to wrangle gun and ammunition for my temporary master.

Neither of us made reference to any nervous conditions resulting from previous war experiences, and the grouse shoot was a success in that grouse were shot, and the guests were all pleased in consequence.

Mr. Rowland-Powell arrived towards the tail end of the shooting. He stood around with his hands in his pockets and told news in an amusing way, and laughed at the stories of others. I observed him without appearing to pay much attention to anyone. There was nothing striking or alarming about him. His tailoring did not indicate especial wealth, his features gave no hints as to extremes of personality. He seemed more of the type of country squire who preferred to fish than to ride or hunt or shoot, and the sort of man who was moderate in his food and his drink. Perhaps it was the fact that he was such an ordinary individual that made him such a potentially perilous foe. One is not likely to hand over secrets to French anarchists or Dutch socialists or Italian adventuresses, but such secrets may indeed pass freely into the possession of 'one of us'!

There was only one exchange of any note during the shooting. Rowland-Powell, hands still in pockets, came sauntering around to see what I was doing with a basket of freshly killed grouse. "You're not his usual man, are you?" he asked in a friendly tone.

"I'm only temporarily engaged, sir, while his regular valet is indisposed."

"What do you do when you're not a valet?" he inquired.

"I write novels, sir," I said. "I'm writing one now, but I'm stuck on a bit. I have a character who I think is selling secret technology to Unnamed Foreign Powers. Things like submarine plans, or a new kind of rifle. I haven't decided. I say, Mr. Rowland-Powell. If you were to do such a thing, how would you go about doing it?"

He looked at me, then tilted his head back and roared with laughter. "What a question!" He raised his voice a bit to widen the conversation. "This valet's writing a book and needs help with his character." He proceeded to repeat the scenario to a few of his friends, who had stepped closer out of curiosity, while the others maintained their shoot. "If it were myself, I would probably wrangle an invitation to a gathering such as this, and then steal one of the cameras off the pigeon when no one's looking. Harness and all. Maybe even take the whole pigeon and not mess with straps and buckles. Shove it in a basket or something. I'd take it to German scientists – the Germans are good at that sort of thing – and let them deconstruct the mechanism to reveal its designs. Its inner workings. That sort of thing. Then they'd know how to make it themselves – and they would."

"That would be hard to do if it were a submarine, though," objected General Rocker. "You can't shove a submarine in a basket. Might be possible to wander off with a new kind of rifle. Depends on the security, and whether everyone standing around is a blithering idiot enough to allow you to do it."

"Oh? What would you do?" he countered.

"If I wished to betray my country's secrets," mused General Rocker, "I wouldn't worry about doo-dads. They're only good for the one time. I'd probably focus on code books. Get a nice tidy sum per page, and codes are always changing anyways. I suppose Foreign Powers can intercept telegraphs. There must be a way of listening in to the wires, though I couldn't explain how. But that's why we use the codes. It wouldn't be one big thing all at once – that's unnecessarily risky. But a slow, casual trickle of information any number of men might possess – that would be hard to trace to the source."

"If it were me," put in Deering's father, "I would take photographs. I wouldn't risk trying to mess with the real thing. I'd probably develop the plates of whatever was interesting, and send 'em through the post. Maybe stuck between the pages of a Bible. Or perhaps a good thick almanac, with squares cut out of its inner pages, to form a recess. Perhaps I wouldn't trust it to the post at all – you remember Richelieu's *Cabinet Noir*. I wouldn't expect good solid Englishmen to investigate the post of other good solid Englishmen, but you never know, with all the socialists and anarchists running about these days. Perhaps I would have a designated shop, like a bookstore, or a tobacconist's. And my contact would come in and deliver a key phrase, asking for something peculiar. Uncommon. 'Have you a history of the Seljuk Empire?' And that would be the signal, and the shopkeeper would give the countersignal, such as, 'No, but have you read about the Anatolian beyliks?' and they'd both know it was all right, and the shopkeeper would give him whatever object the photographs were parceled up into."

"Of course, that would mean taking the shopkeeper into your confidence," said Wolverly. "You don't want that at all. You don't want to be blackmailed once he starts wondering about mysterious packages he's supposed to pass. I would run an advertisement in the agony column, and leave it at that. Sign it '*Shuttlecock*' or '*Cheops*' or something. No one would waste their time following up with all those nonsense assignations that already clutter the paper. I'd drop it off in a remote location, like in a particular hollow tree somewhere, and when the advertisement appeared, my foreign contact would know to visit the hollow tree and claim what I had cached, and deliver it to his handlers. My money, of course, would be paid directly to my bank."

"Is there a way of tracing unusual bank deposits?" wondered Deering's father. "One would think there was, but I'm not sure if I've heard of such a thing."

"One would have to be sly about it, so as not to draw attention," said Wolverly. "That's the thing about greed. It makes one take risks one wouldn't otherwise. Not just having inexplicable sums deposited to one's account, but also not be rolling in wealth when everyone knows one's living on an Army pension and a handful of investments."

"Which is exactly why I was thinking of doing it by the page," agreed General Rocker. "Don't want to kill the golden goose with the golden eggs, or what-not. Just a slow, steady trickle of just a little extra. An extra ten, twenty, fifty here and there makes all the difference in the world. Especially if it came once, maybe twice a month."

"But there's also the ratio of risk-to-reward," argued Rowland-Powell. "If one is going to risk one's neck for treason, it isn't going to be for a five-pound note."

"Men have been killed for less," pointed out Wolverly.

The subject drifted into anecdotes of men who had met untimely demises in foreign quarters over trivial incidents. I glanced at Deering, who was standing unhappily in a knot of the other men who had continued shooting grouse throughout our discussion, but had kept shooting glances in my direction. Perhaps he was unhappy because he had not been able to give a sufficiently imaginative answer. Or perhaps he was unhappy because I had not reloaded his gun for him in the last ten minutes.

I got back to work, and was aware of Rowland-Powell's eyes upon me.

I, and the other valets on duty, were dismissed to pursue our own devices after luncheon. No one said so, but all knew they were going to test the miniature cameras. I spent an hour plucking feathers from birds for the cook, and got as much information as I could from her, which wasn't very useful. Afterwards, I excused myself, and vanished for a few hours inside Wolverly's library, hidden behind the drapery. It was not the best hiding place, as the summer drapes were hung, but no one entered the library at all, and I eventually was compelled to give up my vigilance as the party began returning to the house exhibiting all signs of high spirits.

I resumed my watch that evening, between the hours of one and four in the morning, but the library remained deserted apart from my presence. The ashes had remained undisturbed.

Sunday, the family, guests, and servants made their way to the village church. All were accounted for. No one left the service early or in a suspicious manner.

Each time we were together in private, as I helped him with his change of clothes or tidied his appearance, Deering repeatedly asked if I had been successful, and I repeatedly dissembled, never giving a straight answer or reassuring facts.

"The thing is to catch Rowland-Powell in the act," I explained to him. "If you allow him to run off with false information, he'll only do it again and again."

"Yes, but I'm more interested with protecting my father's invention, not in justice. You're a fool to think you'll actually catch him at it. He's far too clever for that." Deering had obviously grown irritable with my evasiveness. All signs of the fatuous man-about-town had been long since absent from his demeanour. He had not used the word "jolly" in my presence once since arriving at Bellingbeck Park. How true that a valet sees a man's character in a way an acquaintance cannot, I thought!

"Don't shout so, unless you wish to alert the entire house to your motivations," I said. "To-night is our last night. Surely he must make a move."

"Surely *you* must make a move," grumbled Deering. "I hired you to act, not to think."

"If you wished for a slave, you should have kept your genuine valet," I said. "But if you wish to protect your father's invention, I have the situation under control. You *hired* me to work in a way only I can, so you must *permit* me to work in the way only I can."

"My genuine valet didn't go to a school that taught how to force one's way into a safe!" he said. "I'm beginning to think you didn't, either!"

"What if you're wrong about this whole situation? What if Rowland-Powell never breaks into the safe?" I countered. "What fools we'd look then, having to explain to your grandfather why the plans in his safe were fakes, and how you ended up with the real ones!"

"I never said he was giving the plans to the Ministry of Defence this week-end," said Deering. "These were only trials this weekend. I expect the plans to be refined a bit here and there. I can easily put my father's originals back in his workshop, and he'll just think he was absent-minded and put the wrong set in Wolverly's safe. But I couldn't keep Rowland-Powell from stealing the real plans, which was why I paid ten pounds for you to help me with that part. Ten pounds!"

When we left Bellingbeck Park early after breakfast, Deering sat coldly ignoring me. He was deeply grieved at my inability to act, and perhaps moreso grieved at the thought of the loss of his ten pounds. He had wasted all of his harrangues and abuse whilst action was still an option. Now all that was left to him was sullen reproachful disappointment.

The trip back to town was conducted in similarly stony silence. We shared the carriage with four fellow passengers, whose presence constricted any possible conversation.

It was not until the train drew up to Charing Cross and we stepped upon the platform that I reached into my satchel and passed him the tube of paper, tied with red tape. "I was able to open the safe on Friday night," I said, handing it over to him. "Pray forgive my secrecy, but it was necessary to the way I operate. I may add, I noticed someone had stood before the safe sometime before two in the morning this morning, which is when I slipped down to the library. A man's shoe, I would say. Not a boot. I made sure to be with the footman when he cleaned all the boots this morning, but of course, since the second footman collected them last night prior to bed, it was unlikely to find any with ashes in the treads, as footwear collected at nine in the evening is hardly likely to stand in the library at midnight."

"I have no doubt it was Rowland-Powell," said Deering, his lighthearted nature settling over his features once more as he clasped the plans to him. "Either way, I'll be sure to find out what happened, and make sure these stay in the right hands. Bad of you to make me worry so, but jolly good of you! I ought to have had more confidence in your capabilities."

"This was rather a complicated adventure," I said. "Either way, I trust you to do the right thing. Will you be able to manage to get your luggage home?"

"Oh, yes. I'm sure Adams is around here somewhere, and he and the porter will organize it all. And I'll be sure to write and tell you all the jolly details. About the safe, not about my luggage," Deering assured me. With a jaunty wave, he disappeared into the crowd at Charing Cross.

I stood looking after him for a few moments, and then went to go retrieve my own bag.

Inspector Lestrade stopped by for tea two days later. "We caught them both yesterday, right as he was attempting to pass the information to his contact. A bench in Hyde Park, watching the swans. Very casual, but we caught them. The contact tried to run, but we had surrounded them and he couldn't get away. Thank you for the tip."

"I wouldn't have touched the thing, if he hadn't thought I was such a fool. My pride told me to show him otherwise. I suppose we all waste a lot of time on our pride – but it would have been a pity if the wrong people had access to such an invention."

"Once the idea behind it is known, I'm sure their own inventors would be able to make their own version, but it would take a year or two," agreed Lestrade. "At least we have protected our start. Amazing what some people will do."

"Money, was it?" I asked.

"Of course. *He* has no desire to apply himself in the service of Her Majesty's Army," said Lestrade. "He was comfortable with his lifestyle, which would be fine, as long as one possesses the income to maintain it. And debt drives a man to do things sane men wouldn't dream of."

Lestrade rose, thanked me again, and took his leave.

I looked at Watson's empty chair – he was busy attending a patient, of course – and I wondered if he had been home enough to remark upon my own absence. This was the part that I enjoyed the most, the casual *dénouement* and fitting together of all the pieces. His reactions were always thoroughly satisfying as I pointed out the twists and turns of the clues of my latest adventure. But one cannot explain things to an empty chair, and it is tedious to spell it out, for it is the antithesis of adventure and action. I chide Watson on his sensationalism, but it is better than the dullness I fear my own efforts approach. I have no doubt I will give him these notes when his grief is not so sharp, and he'll organize them into a more thrilling narrative.

The first issue, of course, had been Deering himself. His signet ring, however, had proclaimed another identity: It had been monogrammed *TAD*, with the central initial, of course, representing the surname. It had taken very little research to discover that Adams, the supposed surname of the valet, was actually my client's surname. This was borne out by the servants' hall referring to both him and myself as Mr. Adams, as servants are referred to by their master's titles and surnames. He expected me to be referred to as such, by people who did not know me, but knew, as a member of the family in such familiar circumstances, that he was unlikely to be addressed formally, and as a mere hovering hanger-on of the weekend's activities, he was unlikely to be addressed by the other guests, who were there for official business, not for pleasure. What he had hoped to gain by this bit of obscurity, I could not begin to guess. However, it was compounded by the fact that a gentleman, even one fresh from a day of cricket, would have no card on him to give his address, and that he would have to scribble on the back of an envelope to disclose his address. And when such an address was not the Burleson Cricket Club, of which he was a member, or any other club of which he may have been a member, but a railway hotel! It was clear he wanted to make it as labyrinthine as possible to track him down in the future. There were too many layers of obfuscation to take him at his word, and useless lies at that, as it turned out he truly *was* the grandson of the Viscount Wolverly, and the thing could have been done, albeit with some amount of effort.

From the first, I saw it as it was: Deering, or Adams, was trying to use me as a pawn. He knew his father had invented something of much value to any number of governments, but was unable to obtain a final draft prior to its being committed to a secure location. Rather than attempting to sell imperfect plans, he hit upon a plan by which he would enter upon an elaborate charade. He would allow me to steal the plans and substitute an inferior version, so that the substitution would not be noticed for some amount of time. When the substitution was remarked upon, as it invariably would be, suspicion would not fall upon Deering, but upon the stranger who had valeted him that one weekend. There would be no way to trace my identity, of course, as I had no identity separate from that of my master. Just as no one really cares about other people's relatives, as Deering was jaded enough to opine, I suspected no one really cares about the antecedents of other people's servants!

I had broken into the safe, but did not effect my promised substitution. I merely reassured myself on one or two points, primarily as to how easily the two copies could be told apart without having both copies together, and whether there were any obvious distinguishing characteristics which differentiated the two. Thus it was that I held off until the last moment to give Deering his own copy back, to minimize the amount of time he would have to examine it closely, as well as to minimize any chance of the true final draft being removed from the safe during the course of the visit.

The shoes that had trod upon the ashes had been Deering's slippers. The traces still upon the soles in the morning had not been hard to notice! He had paced in front of the safe, and perhaps tried the handle, but it had been of no use, and he had not wasted his time for too long.

The only variable I had left was the identity of Mr. Rowland-Powell. Inquiries had verified that Deering had told the truth on that point, as far as the number of odd goings-on happening when he was around. But a few discreet inquiries in certain channels had reassured me on that point, and some highly placed individuals had ordered me not to compromise his identity, or interfere with any work he might be undertaking, should our paths cross. It was no coincidence that he was at the trials at Bellingbeck Park, but he was authorized, approved, and vouched for at the highest levels.

I was particularly pleased by my hypothetical question, which everyone had answered very readily, almost as an intellectual exercise. But the guilty party, with something to hide! His brain had frozen and his glibness had deserted him when faced with a question he was not prepared to answer – yet not an accusation he would have no hesitation in denying.

It is not often that a criminal and a traitor not only invites me to become involved in his work, but pays me ten pounds to do so. But I had suspected Thomas Deering Adams was a fool from the moment he walked in my door.

"By the way, Sherlock, I expected to see you round last week, to consult me over that Manor House case. I thought you might be a little out of your depth."

"No, I solved it," said my friend, smiling.

"It was Adams, of course."

"Yes, it was Adams."
"I was sure of it from the first."

"The Greek Interpreter"

The Giant Rat of Sumatra
by Leslie Charteris and Denis Green

Sherlock Holmes and The Saint
An Introduction by Ian Dickerson

Everyone has a story to tell about how they first met Sherlock Holmes. For me it was a Penguin paperback reprint my brother introduced me to in my pre-teen years. I read it, and went on to read all the original stories, but it didn't appeal to me in the way it appealed to others. This is probably because I discovered the adventures of The Saint long before I discovered Sherlock Holmes.

The Saint, for those readers who may need a little more education, was also known as Simon Templar and was a modern day Robin Hood who first appeared in 1928. Not unlike Holmes, he has appeared in books, films, TV shows, and comics. He was created by Leslie Charteris, a young man born in Singapore to a Chinese father and an English mother, who was just twenty years old when he wrote that first Saint adventure. He'd always wanted to be a writer – his first piece was published when he was just nine years of age – and he followed that Saint story, his third novel, with two further books, neither of which featured Simon Templar.

However, there's a notable similarity between the heroes of his early novels, and Charteris, recognising this, and being somewhat fed up of creating variations on the same theme, returned to writing adventures for The Saint. Short stories for a weekly magazine, *The Thriller*, and a change of publisher to the mainstream Hodder & Stoughton, helped him on his way to becoming a best-seller and something of a pop culture sensation in Great Britain.

But he was ambitious. Always fond of the USA, he started to spend more time over there, and it was the 1935 novel – and fifteenth Saint book – *The Saint in New York*, that made him a transatlantic success. He spent some time in Hollywood, writing for the movies and keeping an eye on The Saint films that were then in production at RKO studios. Whilst there, he struck up what would become a lifelong friendship with Denis Green, a British actor and writer, and his new wife, Mary.

Fast forward a couple of years .... Leslie was on the west coast of the States, still writing Saint stories to pay the bills, writing the occasional non-Saint piece for magazines, and getting increasingly frustrated with RKO who, he felt, weren't doing him, or his creation, justice. Denis Green, meanwhile, had established himself as a stage actor, and had embarked on a promising radio career both in front of and behind the microphone.

Charteris was also interested in radio. He had a belief that his creation could be adapted for every medium and was determined to try and prove it. In 1940, he commissioned a pilot programme to show how The Saint would work on radio, casting his friend Denis Green as Simon Templar. Unfortunately, it didn't sell, but just three years later, he tried again, commissioning a number of writers – including Green – to create or adapt Saint adventures for radio.

They also didn't sell, and after struggling to find a network or sponsor for The Saint on the radio, he handed the problem over to established radio show packager and producer, James L. Saphier. Charteris was able to solve one problem, however: At the behest of advertising agency Young & Rubicam, who represented the show's sponsors, Petri Wine, Denis Green had been sounded out about writing for *The New Adventures of Sherlock Holmes*, a weekly radio series that was then broadcasting on the Mutual Network.

Green confessed to his friend that, whilst he could write good radio dialogue, he simply hadn't a clue about plotting. He was, as his wife would later recall, a reluctant writer: "He didn't really like to write. He would wait until the last minute. He would put it off as long as possible by scrubbing the kitchen stove or wash the bathroom – anything before he sat down at the typewriter. I had a very clean house." Charteris offered a solution: They would go into partnership, with him creating the stories and Green writing the dialogue.

But there was another problem: *The New Adventures of Sherlock Holmes* aired on one of the radio networks that Leslie hoped might be interested in the adventures of The Saint, and it would not look good, he thought, for him to be involved with a rival production. Leslie adopted the pseudonym of *Bruce Taylor*, (as you will see at the end of the following script,) taking inspiration taking inspiration from the surname of the show's producer Glenhall Taylor and that of Rathbone's co-star, Nigel Bruce.

The Taylor/Green partnership was initiated with "The Strange Case of the Aluminum Crutch", which aired on July 24th, 1944, and would ultimately run until the following March, with *Bruce Taylor*'s final contribution to the Holmes canon being "The Secret of Stonehenge", which aired on March 19th, 1945 – thirty-five episodes in all.

Bruce Taylor's short radio career came to an end in short because Charteris shifted his focus elsewhere. Thanks to Saphier, The Saint found a home on the NBC airwaves, and aside from the constant demand for literary Saint adventures, he was exploring the possibilities of launching a Saint magazine. He was replaced by noted writer and critic Anthony Boucher, who would establish a very successful writing partnership with Denis Green.

Fast forward quite a few more years – to 1988 to be precise: A young chap called Dickerson, a long standing member of *The Saint Club*, discovers a new TV series of The Saint is going in to production. Suitably inspired, he writes to the then secretary of the Club, suggesting that it was time the world was reminded of The Saint, and The Saint Club in particular. Unbeknownst to him, the secretary passes his letter on to Leslie Charteris himself. The teenaged Dickerson and the aging author struck up a friendship which involved, amongst other things, many fine lunches, followed by lazy chats over various libations. Some of those conversations featured the words "Sherlock" and "Holmes".

It was when Leslie died, in 1993, that I really got to know his widow, Audrey. We often spoke at length about many things, and from time to time discussed Leslie and the Holmes scripts, as well as her own career as an actress.

When she died in 2014, Leslie's family asked me to go through their flat in Dublin. Pretty much the first thing I found was a stack of radio scripts, many of which had been written by *Bruce Taylor* and Denis Green.

I was, needless to say, rather delighted. More so when his family gave me permission to get them into print. Back in the 1940's, no one foresaw an afterlife for shows such as this, and no recordings exist of this particular Sherlock Holmes adventure. So here you have the only documentation around of Charteris and Green's "The Giant Rat of Sumatra" . . . .

Ian Dickerson
February, 2018

The Giant Rat of Sumatra

BOB CAMPBELL (Announcer): Petri Wine brings you . . . .

MUSIC: THEME. FADE ON CUE:

CAMPBELL: Basil Rathbone and Nigel Bruce in *The New Adventures of Sherlock Holmes.*

MUSIC: THEME . . . FULL FINISH

CAMPBELL: The Petri family – the family that took the time to bring you good wine – invites you to listen to Doctor Watson as he tells us about another exciting adventure he shared with his old friend, Holmes. You know, *I* have an adventure to tell you about too . . . only it's a different kind of adventure – an adventure in good eating. And to experience it, all you do is serve a Petri Wine with your dinner – either a Petri California Burgundy or a Petri California Sauterne, I'm telling you, you have no idea how much a glass of that good Petri Wine can do for even the simplest war time meal. Take that Petri Burgundy for instance. Try it with a good home made pot roast or Swiss steak. A slice of that tender beef and a glass of that good Petri Burgundy make a flavour combination that spells delicious in any man's language. That hearty, full-bodied burgundy is a red wine really worth trying. And every bit as full flavoured is that swell Petri Sauterne. Petri Sauterne is a delicate white wine that can help make a simple seafood dinner a feast. And wait'll you try a glass of that Petri Sauterne with Southern fried chicken – Oh boy! Yes sir, with food, nothing can take the place of that good Petri Wine.

MUSIC: "SCOTCH POEM" by Edward MacDowell

CAMPBELL: Well, that's enough from me . . . how about you, Doctor Watson? I hope you have something very special for us in the way of stories tonight.

WATSON: (OFF A LITTLE) Good evening, Mr. Campbell. Don't stand there in the doorway as though you weren't sure of your welcome. Close the door and come and sit down and make yourself comfortable. You know I always look forward to these Monday evenings.

SOUND EFFECT: DOOR CLOSING

CAMPBELL: So do I, Doctor.

WATSON: (CHUCKLING) Yes, I think I can promise to make your hair stand on end with tonight's story. I call it "The Weird Case of the Giant Rat of Sumatra".

CAMPBELL: Sumatra – that's an island in the Far East, isn't it? Somewhere near Java?

WATSON: That's right, but the setting of my story tonight is India – India the exotic and mysterious. Holmes and I were in Calcutta waiting for a ship to take us back to England. The great man had just solved the strange mystery of "The Sacred White Elephant of Parbutipur".

CAMPBELL: "The Sacred White Elephant of Parbutipur"? That sounds intriguing. What happened there?

WATSON: (TESTILY) Really, Mr. Campbell. I can only tell you one story at a time. That adventure will have to wait for another of your visits.

CAMPBELL: I'm sorry, Doctor. Go on with your story of "The Giant Rat of Sumatra". You and Sherlock Holmes were in Calcutta waiting for a boat back to England, and that's where things started happening, I suppose?

WATSON: They did indeed, Mr. Campbell, though the whole adventure started casually enough. Holmes and I were staying at the Great Eastern Hotel, an imposing and colourful edifice overlooking Chowringee – the fashionable section of Calcutta. I'd been in India, you know, for quite a few years when I was in the Army and I rather flattered myself I could teach Holmes a thing or two about the country and its customs. But, somewhat to my chagrin, I soon discovered that Holmes was just as much as home in the country as I was. Perhaps even a little more so. On the night my story begins, Holmes and I had just finished an excellent dish of curried shrimps.

We were sitting at our table and I was inhaling the bouquet of a pony of Napoleon Brandy *. A native orchestra was playing soft Oriental music and I was feeling completely relaxed and at peace as we sat there. Suddenly Holmes spoke.

MUSIC: * SNEAK IN ON CUE. UP STRONG ON WATSON'S LAST LINE, THEN DOWN AND UNDER

HOLMES: (LAUGHING) Watson, d'you know my most treasured memory of our recent encounter with the white elephant of Parbutipur?

WATSON: I imagine it was when the Maharajah gave you that check for ten-thousand pounds.

HOLMES: On the contrary, Watson. It was the night you came into the palace in a great state of excitement after you'd shot at a tiger cub. You told us how a shotgun had come on to your veranda and that you had fired a double-barrelled tiger cub at it.

WATSON: (LAUGHING) Yes, I'm inclined to get a little incoherent when I get excited! Holmes – you remember in *The Sign of Four* how I got so flustered with Mr. Sholto that I cautioned him against the great danger of taking more than two drops of castor oil and then recommended strychnine in large doses as a sedative!

HOLMES: Strychnine can be a very efficient sedative. Well, let's get the bill. I'd like to take a walk through the native markets before we retire. See if you can attract the attention of our waiter.

WATSON: (CALLING) Waiter – Hey, Waiter!

WAITER: (THIS IS HINDUSTANI, BUT IS SPELLED PHONETICALLY) (FADING IN) *Bought atcha, hasoor*.

WATSON: We want the bill – (LABORIOUSLY) The – bill. BILL!

WAITER: (PUZZLED) *Kia munta, hasoor*?

WATSON: (GETTING ANGRY) The bill. Goodness gracious, they can't even speak English.

HOLMES: (DRYLY) Why should they? (TO WAITER) *Sahib-ke hissab dough.*

WAITER: (DELIGHTEDLY) *Hissab!* (FADING) *Bought atcha, hasoor.*

HOLMES: Watson, you're a perfect example of the insular Englishman. I'm surprised at you. I should have thought you've lived in India long enough to have a smattering of the language.

WATSON: (GRUMPILY) I do know the language – but up in the Northwest we spoke a different lingo. And where did *you* learn to speak Hindustani I'd like to know?

HOLMES: Three months in Parbutipur has given me a working knowledge, at least.

WATSON: Well, I must say . . . .

HOLMES: (INTERRUPTING) Look, Watson. Here comes the manager in a great state of excitement and he's making a bee-line for our table.

MANAGER: (FADING IN, EXCITEDLY. HE SPEAKS WITH CULTURED ACCENT) Excuse me, Mr. Holmes, but I understand your friend is a doctor?

WATSON: Yes, I am a doctor. What's the matter?

MANAGER: Could you please come to Room 106 at once? One of our servants has been bitten by a rat – a giant rat – and he's lying up there having convulsions.

HOLMES: Convulsions from a rat bite? Of course my friend will come up. Come on, Watson! Never mind your brandy!

MUSIC: BRIDGE

SOUND EFFECT: GROANING AND HEAVY BREATHING, OFF

MANAGER: Is he going to live, Doctor?

WATSON: Yes, he's going to live, but the poor fellow'll be very sick for a few days. Better take him to his quarters. I'll come and see him later.

MANAGER: Very well, Doctor. (FADING) *Addmee ko layjow* . . . .

SOUND EFFECT: SCUFFLE OF FEET . . . GROANS OF BODY BEING LIFTED IN BACKGROUND

HOLMES: (CALLING) Before you go, where is this . . . er, giant rat now? And where is its owner?

MANAGER: (FADING BACK) The rat is in the bathroom, there. We tried to get it back in its cage, but we were afraid to handle it. Mr. Jackson is its owner, but he hasn't come back yet. I'm afraid he . . . Oh, here he is now.

JACKSON: (FADING IN EXCITEDLY. HE IS AMERICAN, ABOUT FORTY-FIVE) What the devil's going on in my room? Who are all these people and why's that man being carried out?

MANAGER: I am afraid, Mr. Jackson, that your rat escaped and bit him.

JACKSON: (FURIOUS) Escaped? What d'you mean it escaped? It must be found. Why the blazes don't you train your servants to mind their own business?

HOLMES: May I suggest you calm yourself, Mr. Jackson. Your rat – so I have just been told – is trapped in the bathroom there.

WATSON: Mr. Manager, I suggest you don't stand there in the doorway. See that poor fellow gets to his bed immediately. He's very sick.

MANAGER: (OFF) Very well, sir. *Addmee ko layjow*.

SOUND EFFECT: DOOR CLOSES OFF

JACKSON: And who are you, may I ask?

HOLMES: My name is Holmes. Sherlock Holmes, and this is my friend Doctor Watson.

JACKSON: Sherlock Holmes! I've heard of you. Aren't you the English detective?

HOLMES: I am flattered that my fame has spread so far afield. But don't look worried, Mr. Jackson, I'm not in your room in any professional capacity. My friend Doctor Watson was called in to attend the bitten man. I am here because I was very curious to see how a rat bite could produce convulsions.

JACKSON: (RELAXING) Of course. I'm sorry, gentlemen, that I was so abrupt with you. The servant is going to live, isn't he, Doctor?

WATSON: Yes, But it was touch and go there for a while.

JACKSON: Thank heavens he's all right. And now if you'll excuse me for a moment, I'll place my rat back in his cage. He's a little hard to handle so I suggest you don't come with me into the bathroom.

WATSON: Good Lord no. Wouldn't dream of it.

JACKSON: But please don't go. (FADING) I'd like to have a chat with you.

SOUND EFFECT: DOOR OPEN AND CLOSE QUICKLY (OFF)

HOLMES: (LOW) Watson, that bitten man had all the symptoms of poisoning, didn't he?

WATSON: (LOW) Yes, he did. I can't understand it.

HOLMES: No. Rat bites might cause an infection, but never the symptoms that poor fellow exhibited. Hmm. Very curious. Why does our friend in there keep a rat in his hotel room?

WATSON: Heaven alone knows. Disgusting things, rats. Horrible to look at and they carry germs. I can remember once when I was . . . .

SOUND EFFECT: DOOR OPEN (OFF)

JACKSON: (FADING IN) Well, gentlemen, allow me to introduce you to the Giant Rat of Sumatra. Isn't he a splendid specimen?

WATSON: (NERVOUSLY) Are you sure that cage is properly fastened?

JACKSON: Don't worry, Doctor. He can't get out. What'd you think of him, Mr. Holmes?

HOLMES: I can't say I'm exactly a rat fancier, Mr. Jackson. But he certainly is a giant. The thing that puzzles me is that his bite has produced the symptoms of acute poisoning in that unfortunate man that was just carried out. How do you account for that?

JACKSON: If you gentlemen have a few moments, I'd like to tell you the story of that rat. I think it will help you to understand what's just happened.

HOLMES: I should be very interested to hear the story, Mr. Jackson.

WATSON: Yes . . . yes indeed.

JACKSON: Do either of you gentlemen care for a "chota peg"?

WATSON: Thank you. I think a scotch-and-soda would be very acceptable.

JACKSON: (OFF A LITTLE) How about you, Mr. Holmes?

HOLMES: Thank you, no. Alcohol is one of the few vices I don't indulge in.

SOUND EFFECT: CLICKING OF GLASS AND BOTTLE

JACKSON: Say when, Doctor.

SOUND EFFECT: FIZZING OF SIPHON

WATSON: Whoa! That's splendid.

JACKSON: Ice?

WATSON: (OUTRAGED) Ice? Good heavens, no! Filthy habit.

JACKSON: Here you are.

WATSON: Thank you.

JACKSON: Well, to begin. I am a zoologist. For years now I've been roaming the world in search of rare and valuable animals to add to my collection (WITH A LAUGH). I have a miniature zoo at my farm in Connecticut in the States and, without wishing to brag, I may say my collection is quite unique. A year or so ago, I heard of an obscure tribe of Pygmies in the jungles of Sumatra who worshipped rats – rats that were reputed to be gigantic. Naturally I was determined to try and capture one for my collection and so, last September, I sailed to Sumatra. To cut a very long story short, I lived with the tribe for some months and learned many strange things – one of them being the reason for the rat's giant size. It's rather a horrible one, Mr. Holmes. They feed the animals human blood.

WATSON: Good heavens! What a shocking thing.

HOLMES: Human sacrifices for a rodent, eh? Go on, Mr. Jackson.

JACKSON: I managed to gain the confidence of one of the tribesman and, with the aid of a considerable sum of money, bribed him to steal the rat you see there. I had no compunction in doing this, for their worship of the animals is barbaric and disgusting.

WATSON: Downright disgusting.

HOLMES: Quiet, Watson.

JACKSON: My interest was purely that of the collector. And so I slipped away from the village with my prize in a cage and caught the next boat for Calcutta. I wanted to talk to the curator of the Calcutta Zoo about buying a specimen of their Himalayan tree bear whilst I was there. But my erstwhile friends in Sumatra have not been idle. I've been followed. Two attempts have been made to take the rat back. One attempt has been made on my life already. I think what happened just now was a third attempt to steal the rat.

HOLMES: Very possibly, Mr. Jackson, but I still don't understand the symptoms of poisoning.

JACKSON: I think that what undoubtedly happened was that the man just carried out was attempting to drug or poison the rat so that he could handle it. Even a dead Sumatra rat is an object of veneration amongst the tribe. Probably he opened the cage and tried to feed the poison to the rat. Possibly the rat got some on his fangs and then bit him.

HOLMES: (LAUGHING) You should have been a detective, Mr. Jackson. That's an ingenious deduction . . . though I can't say I find it an entirely convincing one.

JACKSON: (SUDDENLY) Mr. Holmes, you're a famous detective. Would you undertake to guard me and the rat until I'm safely on the boat for America? I'd pay you a handsome fee.

WATSON: Why not, Holmes? It's a most interesting case.

HOLMES: (LAZILY) I'm afraid not, Mr. Jackson. I'm on a holiday now and I want to relax.

WATSON: Well, 'pon my soul. I've never heard you turn down a case like this before.

HOLMES: However, we shall be here for a couple of days yet. And Doctor Watson and myself are neighbors of yours. We are in Suite 109 . . . just down the corridor from you, so please feel free to call on us if you have any more trouble. And now, Watson, let's take that stroll. I want to observe the night life of Calcutta.

MUSIC: BRIDGE

SOUND EFFECT: INDIAN FLUTE PLAYING SNAKE-CHARMING THEME. BAZAAR AD-LIBS IN BACKGROUND

HOLMES: (KEENLY) Watson, observe the trance-like condition of that snake. See . . . the glazed eyes . . . the immobile body . . . Fascinating. Quite fascinating. The powers of music are often more potent in the animal kingdom than in the human.

WATSON: (IMPATIENTLY) Yes . . . yes . . . it's very interesting. You know, Holmes, I still don't understand why you turned down that

Jackson case. A scared rat . . . a man poisoned . . . it's just the kind of case that's always fascinated you.

SOUND EFFECT: INDIAN FLUTE CEASES

HOLMES: Give that fellow a rupee. He's given us a fine performance.

WATSON: (MUTTERING) A rupee. That's rather a lot, isn't it? Here you are.

SOUND EFFECT: COIN BEING TOSSED ON STONE

COOLIE: (OFF) *Salaam, Sahib. Burra Salaam.*

HOLMES: Let's explore the Bazaar a little further.

SOUND EFFECT: FOOTSTEPS ON STONE. INDIAN FLUTE STARTS IN BACKGROUND AGAIN AND FADES AWAY

HOLMES: So you're worried, my dear fellow because I didn't accept Mr. Jackson's commission?

WATSON: I'm not worried, Holmes. I'm just surprised.

HOLMES: Well, don't be, old fellow. I'm very much interested in the case. But sometimes one has a greater . . . ah, latitude of behaviour in a case when one is observing it from the outside. If Mr. Jackson thinks he needs protection, he should apply to the official police.

WATSON: But if you *are* interested in the case, why are we wandering through this bazaar? Why aren't we back at the hotel keeping an eye on Jackson and his wretched rat?

HOLMES: We *are* going back to the hotel, Watson. But first of all I have a visit to make. This apparently aimless troll is taking us to the Calcutta Zoo. I want to have a little chat with the curator there. You know Watson, I have a feeling that before this night is out, the giant rat of Sumatra will bite again!

MUSIC: BRIDGE

SOUND EFFECT: VIOLIN IN BACKGROUND IMPROVISING THE THEME WE HEARD FROM THE SNAKE CHARMER IN PRECEEDING SCENE

WATSON: It's nearly one o'clock in the morning. D'you think you ought to keep scraping away at that violin? There are people trying to sleep, y'know.

HOLMES: Nonsense.

SOUND EFFECT: VIOLIN BREAKS OFF MELODY

HOLMES: Confound it! What can't I capture that snake-charming melody?

SOUND EFFECT: VIOLIN PLAYS AGAIN

WATSON: Holmes, did you learn anything from the curator tonight? I listened to your discussion, but I'll be hanged if I could understand a word either of you were talking about.

HOLMES: You're a medical man. You should at least have found it as understandable as I did.

WATSON: I'm a simple General Practitioner. When you stray off into the subtleties of Oriental poisons and the anatomy of rodents, I'm out of my field and I don't mind confessing it.

SOUND EFFECT: VIOLIN COMPLETES THEME, THEN FINISHES WITH A LITTLE FLOURISH

HOLMES: (EXCITEDLY) That's it! At last I've got it.

SOUND EFFECT: VIOLIN BEING PLACED ON TABLE

HOLMES: Now I can go to bed.

WATSON: Well, thank heavens for that. (YAWNING) I must say I'm ready to turn in myself. You still haven't answered my question, Holmes.

HOLMES: Hmm . . . question? What question?

WATSON: I asked whether you learnt anything from your discussion over at the zoo tonight?

HOLMES: Oh yes. I learnt a great deal. A very great deal. In fact I may say that –

SOUND EFFECT: PIERCING MALE SCREAM (OFF)

WATSON: Good Heavens! D'you hear that? That came from Jackson's room!

HOLMES: Quick, Watson!

SOUND EFFECT: RUNNING FOOTSTEPS. DOOR OPEN. FOOTSTEPS ON SLIGHT ECHO

HOLMES: (BREATHLESSLY) Have you got your revolver with you?

WATSON: (PANTING) No . . . shall I go back for it?

HOLMES: Never mind, I have mine. Here we are –

SOUND EFFECT: DOOR WRENCHED OPEN, ANOTHER PIERCING SCREAM. FOOTSTEPS CEASE. SCRABBLING AND YELPING OF RAT

JACKSON: (HYSTERICALLY) Back! Get back there!

HOLMES: Watson! See what you can do for that poor fellow there. I'll take care of the rat.

JACKSON: (VIOLENTLY) No, Mr. Holmes! Put that revolver away! I'll get the rat back in the cage, but don't shoot it! It's too valuable.

HOLMES: (GRIMLY) You'd better hurry then. Here . . . throw this bedspread over it!

SOUND EFFECT: AGONISED DEATH RATTLE OF DYING MAN

WATSON: Holmes . . . the man's done for.

SOUND EFFECT: YELPING OF RAT SUDDENLY STIFLED. THE CLANG OF A CAGE DOOR CLOSING

JACKSON: There! The rat's back in the cage!

HOLMES: Just in time, Mr. Jackson. I was about to bring your pet's career to an abrupt end.

SOUND EFFECT: LAST SPAMS OF DYING MAN

WATSON: The man's dead, Holmes. Poor devil . . . look at that expression on his face . . . the contorted features . . . the staring eyeballs . . . the arched back.

HOLMES: Exactly. All the symptoms of strychnine poisoning! Mr. Jackson, I'm afraid your chances of taking the rat back to America are very slight. I think you'll find the police will insist on killing him and performing an autopsy

MUSIC: CURTAIN

CAMPBELL: Well . . . so Holmes is now turning the case over to the Indian police. We'll find his motive for doing so in just a few seconds when our story continues. Meanwhile, I'd like to remind you that the best time to begin a good dinner is before the beginning. While you're waiting for dinner to be ready, try a glass of Petri California Sherry. Petri Sherry is one of the most famous of all sherry wines . . . and rightly so. Because Petri Sherry has a perfect color, a wonderful aroma – "bouquet" the experts call it – and as for its flavour – well, Petri Sherry has a flavour that comes right from the heart of luscious California grapes. And say – if like most men – you like your sherry dry . . . well, you certainly ought to try a Petri pale dry sherry. That is something! And remember – you can serve Petri sherry proudly . . . because the name "Petri" is the proudest name in the history of American wines.

MUSIC: "SCOTCH POEM"

CAMPBELL: And now back to tonight's new adventure of Sherlock Holmes. Doctor Watson and his famous friend are in Calcutta awaiting a boat to take them back to England. Whilst staying at the Great Eastern Hotel, they have become involved in the strange case of the Giant Rat of Sumatra – a rat whose bite is sudden death. As we rejoin our story, Holmes and Watson are seated in the bedroom of Mr. Jackson, the owner of the rat (FADE) awaiting the arrival of the police . . . .

WATSON: Two-thirty in the morning and still the police haven't arrived.

HOLMES: Patience, Watson. They'll be here.

JACKSON: This is terrible. Mr. Holmes, you really think they'll kill my rat?

HOLMES: It's hard for me to predict what the police will do, but personally I can see no alternative. The rat has bitten and killed one man, and severely poisoned another. The cause of death looks like strychnine poisoning. It seems obvious that if the rat bite did kill the man, the first thing to do is to dissect the rat and discover how it was able to deliver this lethal bite.

WATSON: What d'you mean "if" the rat bite killed him? We know it did.

HOLMES: We know it bit him.

JACKSON: What is your theory, Mr. Holmes?

HOLMES: I never theorize. By the way Mr. Jackson – being a zoologist you are naturally familiar with the *Tamana* . . . the *Tamana* . . . the Darjeeling snow bird?

JACKSON: Oh, yes . . . Yes, of course.

HOLMES: There's an excellent specimen that's just arrived at the zoo. We saw it earlier on today.

WATSON: Darjeeling snow bird? I don't remember any –

HOLMES: (INTERRUPTING) You never remember anything, my dear fellow. Mr. Jackson: The man who was killed here in this room tonight. Have you ever seen him before?

JACKSON: Never.

HOLMES: Are you still of the opinion that he was employed by the tribe in Sumatra to recapture the sacred animal?

JACKSON: I can't think of any other motive.

SOUND EFFECT: KNOCK ON DOOR

HOLMES: Ah . . . that must be the police now.

JACKSON: (CALLING) Come in.

SOUND EFFECT: DOOR OPEN

SINGH: (OFF. CULTURED, SLIGHT ACCENT) Mr. Jackson?

JACKSON: Yes . . . that's right.

SOUND EFFECT: DOOR CLOSE

SINGH: (FADING IN) I am Inspector Singh of the Bengal Police.

JACKSON: Sit down, Inspector. These two gentlemen are Mr. Sherlock Holmes and Doctor Watson.

SINGH: Mr. Sherlock Holmes? I am very honored to meet you, Mr. Holmes. We in the Indian Police service are very familiar with your brilliant work in Europe.

HOLMES: Thank you.

SINGH: Also your recent handling of the case of the white elephant for the Maharajah of Parbutipur. I am flattered to be associated with you in this case.

HOLMES: I'm merely a spectator, Inspector. Pray proceed as though I were not present.

SINGH: Thank you. Mr. Jackson, we have just performed an autopsy on the man bitten in this room tonight. He died of strychnine poisoning. Naturally, we shall have to kill the rat and perform an autopsy on it too.

JACKSON: This is dreadful! The rat is worth thousands of dollars to me.

SINGH: (STERNLY) Undoubtedly the dead man's life was worth even more to him. No, Mr. Jackson, your rat will have to die. I shall return within the hour with the necessary authority to take the rat for dissection. Before I leave, I'd like the exact facts as to the tragedy tonight.

HOLMES: (YAWNING) I think if you'll excuse me, gentlemen, I'll turn in. Are you coming Watson? It's a quarter-to-three in the morning.

WATSON: (SURPRISED) Yes, I suppose so, though I must say I'm surprised at your leaving . . . .

HOLMES: There is nothing further we can do. Inspector Singh is in efficient command. Good night, Inspector. Good night, Mr. Jackson.

SOUND EFFECT: FOOTSTEPS

WATSON, SINGH, AND JACKSON AD LIB "GOOD NIGHTS"

SOUND EFFECT: DOOR CLOSE. FOOTSTEPS ON SLIGHT ECHO

WATSON: (CUE) Holmes, I just don't understand your handling of this case. Walking out just as the police walk in.

HOLMES: Don't you, Watson? There was nothing more to be learned in there – merely a recapitulation of what we already know. Come into the room and I'll tell you my plans.

SOUND EFFECT: DOOR OPEN AND CLOSE. FOOTSTEPS STOP

WATSON: (MUTTERING) I'll never get any sleep tonight.

HOLMES: Perhaps not. But think of the satisfied sleep you can have on the boat – when the case of the Giant Rat is solved.

WATSON: Good Lord, Holmes. You think you've solved it?

HOLMES: Almost, my dear fellow. Almost. There is just one more thing to be done . . . and it's a job for you.

WATSON: Of course, Holmes. What is it?

HOLMES: I must examine that rat before it is taken away. You must get Jackson out as soon as Singh leaves. I don't care what excuse you make, but get him out of the hotel for half-an-hour.

WATSON: Of course I'll do it. But I say, Holmes . . . be careful when you get near that rat.

HOLMES: Don't worry, old fellow. I've learnt quite a bit about the behaviour of rats from our visit to the zoo today. Also, you will observe that pair of leather gloves lying on the table there. No, I'm taking no chances. Within an hour from now, I think I can promise you the solution to the case!

MUSIC: BRIDGE

WATSON: Well, Holmes, I got our friend Jackson to come out and have a drink with me. He's gone back to his room now. Did I give you enough time?

HOLMES: You've done splendidly Watson. Splendidly. I have completed my examination of the rat and laid all my plans, and there's no time to waste. Better bring your revolver.

WATSON: Revolver? What do I – ?

HOLMES: Don't argue. Do as I say. This is a matter of life and death.

WATSON: Oh, all right. Here it is on the table.

HOLMES: Now follow me . . . .

SOUND EFFECT: FOOTSTEPS . . . DOOR OPEN AND CLOSE. FOOTSTEPS CONTINUE

HOLMES: Quickly, Watson . . . in here . . . .

WATSON: But this isn't Jackson's room . . . this is 104.

HOLMES: This is the room next to his. It's empty and I have obtained the key. Come in.

SOUND EFFECT: KEY TURNING IN LOCK. DOOR OPEN AND CLOSE

WATSON: What on earth are you up to, Holmes?

HOLMES: You'll soon see. We open those French windows . . . .

SOUND EFFECT: WINDOW BEING OPENED

HOLMES: So . . . and what do we find?

WATSON: By Jove! A balcony!

HOLMES: Exactly. A balcony that extends under Mr. Jackson's window. Now slip off your shoes, Watson, and keep your voice down. Come on. We'll have a grandstand seat. And keep your revolver handy . . . Here we go . . . .

SOUND EFFECT: FAINT SHUFFLE OF FEET. SOUNDS OF EXERTION

HOLMES: (AFTER A PAUSE, WHISPERING) Here we are, Watson. This gives us a view of the whole room.

WATSON: (WHISPERING) Yes. There's Jackson sitting facing the door . . . and the rat's beside him on the table. I hope that cage is securely fastened.

HOLMES: Shh . . . Here comes Inspector Singh now. We've timed this perfectly . . . keep your eyes peeled . . . .

WATSON: (AFTER A MOMENT) Singh's got the warrant. They seem to be arguing about it . . . Singh's moving towards the cage . . . . (EXCITEDLY) Look! Jackson's opening the cage Great heavens! He's thrown it on the floor! The rat's loose!

HOLMES: (GRIMLY) Exactly! And here comes Jackson now! Grab him, Watson! He's trying to get out this way. I'll get the rat!

SOUND EFFECT: WINDOW OPENED VIOLENTLY. SOUND OF RUNNING FOOTSTEPS. HOARSE SHOUTING. YELPING OF RAT

WATSON: (FADING A LITTLE) No you don't, Jackson!

SOUND EFFECT: STRUGGLE

JACKSON: (OFF A LITTLE) Let me go!

HOLMES: Look out, Singh! Move away from there!

SOUND EFFECT: REVOLVER SHOT. YELP OF RAT (OFF)

HOLMES: (FADE IN) And that, I think, is the end of the rat. (CALLING) Watson, bring Mr. Jackson back in here.

WATSON: (OFF) Come along.

JACKSON: (FADING IN) This is all a ridiculous mistake!

HOLMES: Inspector Singh, I don't know whether a pair of handcuffs is part of your regular equipment?

SINGH: Yes, Mr. Holmes.

HOLMES: Then I suggest you slip them on our friend Mr. Jackson here. He's your murderer.

SOUND EFFECT: CLICK OF HANDCUFFS

JACKSON: I'll get you for this, Holmes! You see if I don't!

HOLMES: Hardly. The gallows will get you first.

SINGH: But Mr. Holmes, I don't understand how you solved this case.

WATSON: Nor do I. Will you stop keeping us in the dark any longer, Holmes, and tell us how the devil you know that Jackson is the murderer?

HOLMES: With pleasure. Let me first slip on these leather gloves. Even in death our rat can still be extremely lethal. Now, gentlemen, to be technical, here is the weapon that was used to commit the murder. This rat. First of all let me point out the fang here. It's really an extremely clever piece of dental work. The center of the tooth has been drilled hollow and in the cavity has been inserted a tiny hypodermic needle – a needle containing strychnine. On biting anything – a natural impulse in a rat – the needle would puncture the skin, injecting strychnine, and so producing immediate death. Ingenious isn't it?

WATSON: But why should he have done that? I say, Jackson, did you go to all that trouble just to protect the rat from the vengeful Sumatra tribe who were trying to recapture him?

SINGH: Mr. Jackson, I must warn you that anything you say will be taken down and may be used in evidence against you.

JACKSON: I'll tell you nothing. Ask Mr. Sherlock Holmes. He seems to know everything.

HOLMES: Certainly I'll tell you. Your guess isn't a bad one, Watson. The rat was equipped with a device for protecting itself from capture – but not from a Pygmy Tribe in Sumatra who worship rats. That was a colourful story invented by Mr. Jackson. There are no Pygmies in Sumatra, but there are Pygmies in the Andaman Islands some three-hundred miles away. If you read your papers thoroughly, you will recall that some five weeks ago, the famous Hapang diamond was stolen from the head of the idol worshipped by the Andaman Islanders.

WATSON: Good heavens! But where is the diamond now?

HOLMES: If you will observe the underside of the belly of this rat, you will notice this large bulge. When you perform your autopsy, Mr. Singh, you will find the Hapang diamond cleverly inserted between the skin and the flesh of the dead rat. A very ingenious safe for your treasure, Mr. Jackson – a safe that defends itself with a bite of death. But I'm afraid you reckoned without meeting Sherlock Holmes.

WATSON: Look out! He's going for the window!

JACKSON: (FADING HYSTERICALLY) You'll never get me! Never!

SOUND EFFECT: CRASH OF GLASS, FOLLOWED BY FADING SCREAM

WATSON: Great heavens! He's gone. Through the window and over the balcony. Poor devil!

HOLMES: (STERNLY) I should save your sympathy, Watson. A man who kills with a rat must expect to die like one!

MUSIC: UP TO STRONG FINISH

CAMPBELL: Well, Doctor Watson, you promised to make my hair stand on end and you've certainly succeeded! That's quite a story. But I still don't understand when Holmes first became suspicious of Mr. Jackson.

WATSON: (CHUCKLING) Nor did I. But coming home on the boat, the great man told me a lot of illuminating facts. For instance, d'you remember his asking Jackson if he was familiar with the *Tamana* – the Darjeeling snow bird?

CAMPBELL: Yes, I do. And Mr. Jackson said that he *was* familiar with it.

WATSON: Exactly. (LAUGHING) *There is no such bird*! Holmes invented it! So of course he knew at once that the man was no zoologist.

CAMPBELL: (LAUGHING) Well Doctor, to tell the truth, I didn't know that Holmes had invented the Darjeeling Snow Bird, so I guess that proves I'm no zoologist either.

WATSON: Well, you don't profess to be – you're a wine expert.

CAMPBELL: Now wait a minute Doctor – don't get me wrong. I never said I was a wine expert. I judge wine just like anybody else does. I taste it . . . and if the wine tastes good – well, then I say it's a good wine.

WATSON: That sounds like good common sense.

CAMPBELL: And I say that Petri Wine is good because the Petri family knows how to make wine that's really delicious. That's because the Petri family has been making wine for generations. And ever since they started their business, back in the last century, they've kept it in the family. Therefore they've been able to hand down from father to son, from father to son, all they've ever learned about the art of wine-making – that fine art of turning plump, sun-ripened grapes into clear, fragrant, delicious wine. And because the making of Petri wine is a family affair – naturally the family takes a great deal of pride in every bottle of wine that bears their name. That's why – even today – when the demand for Petri wine is so great, Petri Wine is still made in the same, old-fashioned, unhurried way. So if you want a wine to serve with your meals, or a wine to make a refreshing wine and soda – no matter what type of wine you wish – you can't go wrong with a Petri Wine, because Petri took time to bring you good wine. And now . . . .

WATSON: I know. You want me to give you a hint about next week's story. Next week, Mr. Campbell, I have a strange story for you. It takes place on a lonely island off the Cornish coast – an island containing a lighthouse – a strange bird, and a . . . an extremely frightened politician . . . .

MUSIC: UP TO CLOSING

MUSIC: "SCOTCH POEM"

CAMPBELL: Tonight's Sherlock Holmes adventure is written by Denis Green and Bruce Taylor and is based on an incident in the Sir Arthur Conan Doyle story *The Sign of Four*. Mr. Rathbone appears through the courtesy of Metro-Goldwyn-Mayer and Mr. Bruce through the courtesy of Universal Pictures where they are now starring in the *Sherlock Holmes* series.

MUSIC: THEME UP AND DOWN UNDER

CAMPBELL: (OUT) The Petri Wine Company of San Francisco, California, invites you to tune in again next week, same time, same station.

MUSIC: HIT JINGLE

SINGERS: *Clink, click, clink*
An icy drink
A drink for summer time
Is wine and soda, half-and-half
Made with Petri Wine!

CAMPBELL: Yes, Petri Wine made by the Petri Wine Company, San Francisco, California . . . .

SINGERS: *Pet – Pet – Petri Wine*

CAMPBELL: This is Bob Campbell saying goodnight for the Petri family. Sherlock Holmes comes to you from the Don Lee Studios in Hollywood. (CUE) This is MUTUAL!

> "Matilda Briggs *was not the name of a young woman, Watson," said Holmes in a reminiscent voice. "It was a ship which was associated with the giant rat of Sumatra, a story for which the world is not yet prepared."*
>
> Sherlock Holmes – "The Sussex Vampire"

The Vatican Cameos
by Kevin P. Thornton

Although I no longer shared lodgings with my friend Sherlock Holmes. I tried to stop in and see him at least two or three times a week. When he was busy he was less a worry to me. As long as his brain was occupied, he would not lapse into some of his more laggard ways. I also conspired with Mrs. Hudson to try to make an event of at least one of those visits. For all that Holmes was disinterested in whatever form of nourishment was placed in front of him, he had eminent connections in the countryside, and quite often I would be informed of the arrival of a treat – one time there was a basket of oysters, another a leg of venison.

So it was that evening. It was the beginning of the year, with the cold nights setting in. The fog of the city settled around one as a vaporous cloak and the bite in the air made a hansom cab the preferred means of travel. We had dined on two well-hung end-of-season grouse, gamy and tender, accompanied by a pot of stored root vegetables: Potatoes, turnips, and carrots with onions. The entire repast was washed down with some excellent Riesling from the Hochheim region that Holmes seemed able to obtain at will.

I was reluctant to leave, though I knew I should get home to my wife. It had been a while since adventure had taken me away from her as in the early days, and I was a little wistful of those more carefree times. Holmes may very well have read my mind, for as I was shrugging into my coat and hat he called me to the window.

"Pray tell me," he said. "What do you make of that man across the road?"

"He is dressed in quality clothing," I said. "Obviously well-to-do. I would guess his attire to be Savile Row. Maybe out for a stroll after a repast such as ours. He may even be coming from the Park."

"Really, Watson, you amaze me. Your eyes see what mine see, but your mind and the grey matter therein does not connect in the same way. About all that you had correct was that he is well-dressed, which tells me that he is a servant at an establishment where they place much standing on propriety. He is not, as you suggested, a gentleman out for a stroll. He is not dressed for the cold or an extended walk in this weather. No, this is a man sent to us in a hurry by cab. There is adventure in the air. Do you think you can send a message home to say you may be some time yet?"

I nodded my assent. "Dash it all, Holmes. How do you know all this about the man? You barely glanced at him."

"Ah. Well that is because I recognize him. His real name is Sergeant Jontellier Barkoven, formerly of the 5th Brigade, Royal Artillery, but you must never call him such. To the few who know him, he is the front door guard and gatekeeper of the Diogenes Club, and as such he goes by the name '*Epicurus*'."

I looked at my friend in astonishment. "Holmes, did you just play a joke on me?" My answer was his continued smile, which I had put down at first to the hock. "Your good humour has to do with where Epicurus works. Whatever message he brings comes from Mycroft, and his puzzles are always intriguing."

"Indeed," said Holmes. "And he has not even entrusted it to a message by wire. My brother is obsessive about secrecy, but he is also parsimonious, so this presupposes derring-do and intrigue. This adventure will be a challenge, Watson, you mark my words." He rubbed his hands together in delight.

"Barkoven," I said. "It is an unusual name. I remember him from when it was gazetted. He won the Victoria Cross at Isandlwana. He's a brave man, and lucky. Most who win that august honour do so posthumously."

We were interrupted by Mrs. Hudson, showing in our visitor. Now that he was closer, I could see that he was not a gentleman, but far more. He came from that special breed of men that are the backbone of the Empire. Tough, resolute, and convinced of his role in life. I had served with such men in the Army, and there are none finer. Epicurus was in his early thirties and was lightly scarred about the face, as if he had fallen prey to sharp weapons. He was solid and had hard, working hands. Wordlessly, he handed a message to Holmes, who read it quickly and passed it to me. "'*Go immediately to Our Lady of Victories, Kensington*'." And it was signed '*Mycroft*'.

"We must depart," said Holmes. "Did you ask you cab driver to wait?" Epicurus nodded, and without further discussion we left.

"Do you know this church, Holmes?"

"I do. It is the Pro-Cathedral for the Archbishop of Westminster, Cardinal Manning, and the London base of the unofficial yet influential Papal Envoy, Cardinal Luigi Antonio Tosca. Tosca was sent here twelve years ago after Cardinal Pecci was elected Pope Leo, for his own safety I believe."

"What do you mean?" I said.

"Tosca needed to be protected from his friends. There is a story from the conclave that Tosca was Papabile, likely to be voted the next Pope, until he ceded his support to Pecci. His supporters felt betrayed. They saw Tosca, who was from a high-ranking family, as the man who could help them reclaim their lands lost with the Papal States. When he failed them, as they saw it, they were unhappy and threats were made. Pecci, on becoming Pope Leo XIII, moved him to London."

Holmes must have seen the look on my face. "Is there something wrong, Watson?"

"In all the years I have been your friend, I never knew of your interest in Papist politics. Indeed, rarely have I ever known you to be interested in anything not relevant to the most immediate matters at hand. It is as if you have been hiding an entire facet of yourself from me." I tried not to sound regretful, but sometimes being the great man's confidante was trying, and to find that there was a part of his life closed off from me was irksome.

If Holmes noted I was vexed, he said naught. He turned to Epicurus. "My brother told you to go with us. Do you know why?"

Epicurus shook his head.

"No matter," said Holmes. "Doubtless he thought your indomitable nature would be an asset."

"And his conversational skills," I said. "The man has not said a word since we met. Is this more of the Diogenes Club? I know they place great value on silence, but surely they cannot restrict their staff outside their place of work."

"They don't. Just as the club itself is named after Diogenes the cynic, whose philosophy is replicated by the curmudgeons within the walls of their club, the position of Epicurus is so named because, as one of the outward facing members of staff, he is expected to converse with the outside world. In comparison with the members, Epicurus is a chatterbox."

"But Epicurus was a philosopher of joy and bonhomie," I said.

"I suspect it may be the only time the Diogenes Club has ever attempted anything humorous," said Holmes. Epicurus sat, rocklike, as we rode through Hyde Park towards the Kensington High Street. If Holmes knew why his brother had sent him with us, he did not say, and indeed the mystery of why we were going to the church seemed to envelop us in the back of the cab.

We were met at the door by a man of the cloth and a man in a suit of good cloth.

"Stoutbridge," he said. "Foreign Office. This is Monsignor Della Chiesa. Please come in."

The Monsignor looked ascetically Italian. In a different light he may have been mistaken for a relative of Holmes, until he spoke, whereupon his accent marked his Latinate origin. He looked worried. Stoutbridge on the other hand seemed impatient, until my friend stepped into the light.

"Why, Mister Holmes," he said. "I was not made aware of your impending arrival."

"Arrival into what precisely?" I asked.

"Patience, Watson," said Holmes and he made towards the back of the church as if he knew where he was going.

There were two rooms behind the altar. To the left lay the sacristy, the room where the vestments and accoutrements of the church where stored and where the celebrants prepared for service.

The other room was much larger. Like the sacristy, it had the strong outer walls of the church on two sides and a high, vaulted ceiling which extended back from the church. The other two walls were interior, one shared with the sacristy, the other with the interior of the church. It was ungainly in size, too big to be a room of comfort, too small for a meeting room. It felt like a shop storeroom, and it had clearly been used to keep leftover material from the church construction. Ominous statues lurked in one dim corner, and there were boxes stacked in several places and a shelf laden with supplies.

There was a table in the middle, and on it a sturdy wooden packing box. It had leather handles attached, as if the maker knew the contents would be heavy and wanted to make the burden easier.

There was a chair next to the table, and a short rotund man sat there. He wore a fiery red cassock and sash, with black shoes and socks. He had a red *zucchetto* on top of his bald head as well as a wide-brimmed *galero* next to him on the table. His complexion matched his dress, and I thought briefly that he looked ready to explode from pressure, so red was his face. Monsignor Della Chiesa rushed to his side.

"Eminence, you look unwell." The Monsignor turned to us and clicked his fingers. "Fetch some water."

Nobody moved. Holmes walked over to the stone wall and examined it. "Stoutbridge," he said. "Give Cardinal Tosca some of your brandy. Come, come. There is a flask inside your jacket. It will be more useful than the Monsignor's request."

Stoutbridge did as he was asked. The Cardinal took a decent swallow and it seemed to do him some good.

"Now, your Eminence," said Holmes, "pray tell us why we are here."

Cardinal Tosca held up his hand, motioning for some more time, and Holmes replied, "No, I'm referring to Cardinal Manning. You may leave the safety of your dim corner sir, and come and join us in the light."

There was a moment's hesitation and then one of the dim statues moved, revealing itself to be the scrawny figure of the Archbishop of Westminster. This once-rugged man, who had played cricket for Harrow and Balliol in his youth, was a shadow of the healthy sportsman he had been. One needed no medical degree to deduce that Cardinal Manning had been unwell for a while, and he did himself no favour with his fashion sense. Unlike the flamboyant scarlet of the Italian prelate, Manning wore a plain black cassock and sash, and the only indicator of his rank as a Prince of the Church was some delicate red piping on the sleeves and hems. The darkness of his cloth seemed to consume him, as did the hollowness of his gaunt face. His eyes, however blazed briefly with anger and colour before a more Christian-like demeanour came over him.

"Your brother speaks highly of your talent for intrusiveness," he said. "Despite Cardinal Tosca's protestations, I insisted they send someone to get to the bottom of this."

"Yet you wanted nothing official," said Holmes. "There are no police here. Indeed, the only government presence is Stoutbridge, who is no high flyer at the foreign office." As if to prove the point, the comment sailed over the Whitehall man's head.

Manning said nothing, gazing evenly at the gathering.

Holmes gazed at Tosca. "Very well, then. What is missing?"

"*Dio Mio*! How do you know it is something missing?" said Tosca. "It has only recently happened. And nobody else knows."

"There are two reasons why people hire me in dark of night. Murder or theft. There is no dead body, ergo *quod erat demonstrandum*. As to knowledge of the event, at least eight people know so far. Stoutbridge, Della Chiesa, Epicurus, Cardinals one and two, Watson, Mycroft, and me. This will spread the longer we wait and whatever you want kept secret will be impossible to contain. If no one will tell me what is missing, I'm afraid that I can't help." He walked over to the crate and looked in briefly. "My word," he said. "Are these the cameos?"

Even Manning was surprised. "What could you possibly know of them?"

"That is of no consequence," said Holmes. Pointing at the gap in the box, he said, "Is there only one missing, or are there other surprises lurking?"

"I'm impressed, Mister Holmes," said Cardinal Manning. "Even knowing of your distant relative in the church, I am still intrigued by your ability to render something out of nothing." He gestured towards the crate as if blessing the room and paced gently back and forth. "These are cameos like no other ever seen. Unlike the oval charms that some ladies purchase while visiting the Riviera, these are historical renditions of history rendered nearly two-thousand years ago."

"Like the *Grand Camée de France*," said Holmes.

"Indeed," Manning replied. "Until these were recently found in the vaults in Rome, the *Grand Camée* was considered the best example of its type. It celebrates a point in Tiberius Caesar's reign when the dynasty seemed established, as the young Nero is a prominent part of the artwork."

"And what do these cameos display?" askedHolmes.

"We don't know," said Manning. "At least not with any certainty. They were undiscovered until a year back, when they were found by a monk in an obscure part of the Vatican archives. Normally they would be studied with great intent and diligence for many years before they would ever see the light of day, and while our own scholars have some theories, they are not definite as to what exactly is depicted."

"Then why are they here?" I said.

"They are an act of good faith," said Cardinal Tosca. "Once they were discovered, I was able to prevail upon the Holy Father to have them transported to the British Museum so that they could be shared with the British public, even as the scholars from both lands investigate them."

It was a clever idea. The Roman church had a foothold in our society but were still viewed with some suspicion. Sharing such undiscovered greatness would stand the Papists in good stead.

"Tell me what transpired," said Holmes.

"The crate arrived today," said Monsignor Della Chiesa. "It was carried in by two men and placed on that table. Then, when they left, the Cardinal and I opened the crate to ensure the contents. That was when we found that one was missing."

We all peered into the crate. The two remaining cameos were each made of a glasslike substance and were some eighteen inches by twelve in length and breadth, while an inch thick. Holmes picked up the bill of lading and I read it with him. It showed a delivering weight of the crate as a hundred and twenty pounds. He turned to Epicurus, whispered to him, and watched him leave whence we had come in. When Holmes turned back to us, the bill of lading was no longer to be seen.

"This time tell the truth please, Monsignor." There was an uneasy silence. "Very well. When you opened the box, all three of the cameos were there. You then left the room, and when you came back one was missing."

The Monsignor's fallen expression said it all.

Cardinal Manning filled in the gap. "Now that we have tried your way, Don Luigi, maybe we can do this properly?" He turned to Holmes. "Monsignor Della Chiesa is very loyal and is trying to protect the Cardinal."

"Indeed," said Tosca, "and I allowed myself to be persuaded." He stood up and stretched himself into a man of importance. "These cameos are most important to me and to the tetchy relations between the church and your country. What has happened here must be covered up. We need to let the British Museum know that there are only two cameos and that the other will not be coming."

"I care not for your games," said Holmes. "I want only the truth. Somebody here is going to tell me what happened."

"What makes you think something did?" said Manning. He asked out of the genuine curiosity of a scholar.

"Because you do not hunt a rabbit with an elephant rifle," I said. "If it was merely a missing cameo during the delivery, you'd have called the police, not my colleague. That you have arranged for his services means that only his services will suffice. Otherwise it would be excessive."

Holmes nearly smiled. "Thank you, Watson. That was an eloquent *précis*."

"I alone was here," said Tosca. He was interrupted by the return of Epicurus, who handed Holmes a note. Holmes read it then placed it in his pocket.

Tosca continued. "I wished to check the cameos for myself, make sure they were not damaged. I opened the crate and saw that one was missing."

"No," said Holmes. "Epicurus here has just verified with the shipping company. The weight of the box they delivered is consistent with how heavy three cameos and a crate would be. Each cameo is about thirty pounds, and the crate would be similar. A hundred and twenty pounds all told. This box is a quarter lighter, I'll wager. Epicurus?"

Epicurus picked up the box by the handles, tested the weight in his arms, and then put it down. "Eighty-eight, mebbe eighty-nine pounds."

"Which means that the box came here with all three of them packed, and one of them went missing in this room."

"And why should we believe this man's parlour trick?" said Stoutbridge, pointing at Epicurus.

"Because he's a Gunner." I said. "He served in the Royal Artillery and had a distinguished career, winning medals and fame, including the highest glory of them all. But even more importantly, the men who man the guns learn about weights and measures. It is their life, and if they are wrong it is their death. After a thousand loads, most gunners can tell the weight of a charge to the nearest half-pound just by picking it up and putting it in the cannon. If he tells you that box weighs eighty-eight pounds now, you may trust him."

"Don Luigi misinformed you, because the truth is so much stranger," said Cardinal Manning.

"*Non mi dire!*" said Tosca. "It is such a strange tale I feared you would not believe me. It is true they were delivered here for our inspection to make sure they had travelled safely, and the cathedral has this safe storeroom where they could be kept overnight. There is only one entrance, and only one key. I opened one of the cameos and laid it out on the table, but the exertion was too much for me. They are heavy, and as you can see, well wrapped. I left the room, locking the door behind me."

"You are sure of that?" said Holmes, interrupting the Cardinal.

"I am sure," he said.

"And when you came back, it was missing?" Holmes seemed disinterested, and as Tosca was answering he whispered to Epicurus, who again took his leave.

When Tosca had finished lamenting the loss, Holmes addressed Manning. "And it was you, Eminence, who decided to call for diplomatic help instead of the police. No doubt you have the ear of half the cabinet and all the Mandarins of Whitehall, my brother included."

"You are correct, Holmes. I walked in on Don Luigi as he was unlocking the door. We discovered the theft together. Don Luigi did not want a fuss, but I insisted. Eventually we compromised. No police due to the diplomatic delicacy. But how did you deduce that?"

"You are English, sir, and your sense of fair play shines through your cloak of religious purpose. You are a man who will always try to do what is right, but you are worried that you may damage the career of your friend Tosca, as well as embarrass the Pope. So you called in a favour. What you could not have known is that you are the only one playing fair this evening. No one wants this solved, least of all Cardinal Tosca." He chose this moment to walk away in a flurry of coat and hat, leaving me to flounder in his wake.

"Then what will you do?" said Manning to his departing back.

"I will solve it," he said, "and then we will see what the politicians and bureaucrats think when they are faced with the truth."

"What is going on Holmes?" I said as we settled into the cab.

"We are in the middle of a delicate game, Watson. There is much afoot."

"And a locked room mystery as well," I said.

"The room was locked," said Holmes, "but there is no mystery. There is, however, more to this than stolen artwork. Let me drop you at home, lest your wife worry about the company you are keeping. If you wish, come round in the morning. We shall break our fast together and then there is someone I want to meet. I think you will find him interesting. He is a distant cousin, and by some way the most intelligent man in the country. Even Mycroft will attest to that."

"I thought the Diogenes Club would be our next stop?" I said. "Your brother put you up to this after all."

"Yes," said Holmes. "Then he sent the drunken halfwit, Stoutbridge, to represent the government – surely a sign they wish to have nothing to do with this. There is no point talking to Mycroft. Whatever game he's playing has already run its course in his head. Now he's waiting for the pieces to fall into place."

"But he also sent Epicurus with us," I said. "As if he knew we would need him. Why would he do that?"

"Aside from his ability as a scale? Epicurus is also brave and resolute. I do believe that he was sent with us as a protector. Mycroft, in his own unfeeling manner, used Epicurus to warn us that the solution to this theft is fraught with danger."

"Where is Epicurus? Where did you send him?"

"Outside, to stay and watch the cathedral. I shall ask Wiggins to relieve him later."

I would have asked why, but Holmes lent back into the cab with a look I knew so well and he said nothing more save, "Good night, Watson," when he dropped me at home.

The next morning, I arrived at 221b Baker Street early to find Mrs. Hudson waiting for me at the door. "There'll be no breakfast here," she said. "He's been up all night, pacing and slamming books. He'll be rushing you out the door." My stomach rumbled in protest then she pressed a packed meal in a bag into my hand.

"Thank you, Mrs. Hudson," I said. "You are a wonder."

"I know," she said. "Just because he ignores food doesn't mean *you* have to."

Holmes appeared at the top of the stairs. "Ah, Watson, let us away. This promises to be an eventful day."

Thirty minutes later, delayed by traffic that seemed to be growing worse by the day, we arrived at the back of St. Paul's Cathedral.

"I must admit," I said to Holmes, "that of all the places I could think of to visit in this most Catholic of mysteries, Wren's house would have been low on the list."

"You are aware," said Holmes, "of the movement of several high church Anglicans in the last few decades to the Roman church."

"Somewhat," I replied. "Cardinal Manning was one of them. He was married and at one point the Archdeacon of Chichester. His conversion was one of the most famous."

Holmes raised an eyebrow in query. "Mary dabbles in religious matters," I said. "I may have glanced at some of her newspapers from time to time. Er, who are we here to meet?"

"Even though some left the church, they did not leave their friends." The voice, rich and plummy, came from a tall, sallow man. He looked as though a sharp breeze would bowl him over, but there was no mistaking his authority. Canon William Church, in his position as Dean of St Pauls' Cathedral, was one of the highest ranked members of the Anglican hierarchy in the land. "Sherlock, I hope you are well. And this must be your friend, Doctor Watson. Do come through. Your cousin is resting in the antechamber."

My surprise was complete when we went into the room. Even though he was dressed in none of the finery of his two fellow Princes the day before, it was still an incongruous sight to see a Cardinal under the roof of the Anglican Bishop of London. All three men must have seen my surprise.

"Poor Doctor Watson, Holmes has told you nothing," said Reverend Church. "You were right to say so, John. Sherlock is a rapscallion of the highest order. Permit me then. Doctor John Watson, please meet my friend and Mister Holmes's cousin . . . ."

"Cardinal John Newman," I said. "As I live and breathe. My word, sir. It is indeed an honour."

And it was. Newman was a giant of the century. A poet spoken of in the same breath as Keats or Byron, a philosopher, a theologian, a man of letters. His reach was vast and his intellect as keen as any in history.

"This man," I said to Holmes, "this giant of a man – is your cousin? And you never thought to mention it?"

"We are distant cousins only, my dear Doctor Watson, through our French antecedents." Cardinal Newman's voice was reedy and thin. It made one want to lean closer to hear what he had to say. He also looked unhealthy, with a thin face and long bony fingers. Either asceticism was a hard road or the sanctified life was not without its trials, for it seemed every high ranking church member I had recently met was on a short road to meet their maker.

Holmes looked around the antechamber. It was quietly resplendent, a room fit for a Prince. "If you are visiting here, do you know any of what is happening with your fellow Princes? The Vatican Cameos."

"I know, since I first mentioned them to you some weeks past, that they have been sent here, shrouded in secrecy, as a sop to the British Government. As if sharing secrets will make us all great chums." Newman gestured as if conducting grand affairs of state. "It will not. It was a mistake to send the cameos, and Tosca may yet pay for the missing one with his career, such as it is."

"Why did Tosca allow Pecci to become Pope, when he had it in his hands?" asked Holmes.

"I was not there," said Cardinal. "If you already know that much about what went on in a secret conclave, then I suspect you and Mycroft have better sources than I. However, I believe that, when faced with the possibility of the chair of St. Peter, Tosca stepped back for the good of his church. He is an honest though weak man, and I think he realized, for once in his life, how much of his career had been created by others who used him. Stepping away from the most powerful position in Christendom defined his goodness, but also marked him for vengeance. His former backers have long memories. They wanted to control the church through him, have access to the church finances, and try to reclaim portions of the Papal States lost in 1870. Pecci, Leo XIII, is a tougher nut to crack."

"So it is about more than church politics," I said.

"It must be," said Newman. "The cameos are about more than revenge on Cardinal Tosca. That is not the Italian way. If it was important for Tosca to be punished, he would have been found hanging from a bridge over the Tiber. No, this is about something far weightier, I fear."

"What do you know of these enemies of his?" said Holmes.

"That they have motives far beyond the spiritual, and that Tosca is naïve," said Newman. "Manning as well. When a thing is too good to be true, it almost always is."

He sighed and lent back in his chair. "The French cameo depicts a point in history that allowed historians to conclude certain things about that time. To commission a cameo was a long and expensive business, so great care and much consultation would have gone into its characterization. It is therefore deemed to be more historically accurate than any other form or depiction of the times. They were also fragile, so any that survived are assumed to have been well protected – not just as art, but as a sign of the times."

"So where have the Vatican Cameos been for the last two-thousand years?" asked Holmes.

"Exactly," said Newman. "What do they depict that has left them hidden for so long? What is their message, and why have they appeared now?" He paused to sip some water, which had the effect of strengthening what he had to say. "Europe and the world have been sitting on a powder keg since Napoleon. There are at least five major powers wrestling for the conquest of the globe, and the might of America will also feature in that struggle sooner rather than later. All it will take is one incident, a death at the wrong time or even a diplomatic disagreement, and that powder keg will start burning."

"And you fear the cameos and their historical context," said Holmes.

"I pray I am wrong," said Newman. "I fear I am right."

Holmes used the Dean's servant to send some messages. We waited for the replies. I could see that Holmes was restless. The Cardinal left for his room to rest.

"He is in the habit of staying here among friends when he comes to London," said Holmes. "He finds the machinations of Manning tiring."

The servant returned with the replies. "It is as I thought," said Holmes. "My brother is now showing an interest. He will meet us at the Pro-Cathedral, as will their Eminences Cardinal Tosca and Manning."

The ride across the city would normally have been pleasant. The driver took the direct route and we passed by much of what marked London at the height of its worth. Holmes, however, was preoccupied. As we rode down the Mall and passed Buckingham Palace, I asked him, "What could possibly be so important in those cameos?"

"Superstition," he said, before retreating into his thoughts.

Epicurus met us just inside the church. "No one has been in or out the room."

I looked around. There was no easy observation point in the church of the storeroom door. "How can you be so sure?" I asked.

Epicurus looked puzzled, as if the question demeaned his word. "I stood in front of it. Wouldn't let them, until now."

"Thank you," said Holmes, and we went inside.

They were all gathered in the storeroom, except for Stoutbridge, whose dim presence was no longer needed. There were extra chairs now so the *dramatis personae* could all be seated. Everyone had separated. Mycroft to the left, Manning in the middle, Tosca to the right, with Della Chiesa behind him. I took a seat near the elder Holmes. He turned and smiled, a rare occasion.

"Doctor Watson. Glad to see you. Whenever you are near, I feel my brother is better behaved."

If Sherlock Holmes heard the exchange, he chose to ignore it.

"I believe we are here only because of Cardinal Manning. If he had not chanced upon Cardinal Tosca and the missing cameo so soon after the discovery, we would not be here. Cardinal Tosca was in the process of covering up the story of the cameo and another few moments leeway would have meant none of this would have happened."

He paused for a second and looked at Tosca. "You would do well to dismiss your assistant. This will not aid his career in the church. He is better off not knowing."

"You know?" said Tosca. "But how could you?"

"I suspected," said Holmes. "Now I know."

Mycroft harrumphed. "Monsignor Giacomo Della Chiesa is being trained for higher roles." He said. "I believe he is leaving here soon to be the personal assistant to Cardinal Rampolla, the Secretary of State." He saw the surprise – and then momentary delight – on the young man's face before he resumed his diplomatic mien. "You didn't know," said Mycroft. "No matter, the announcement will be in three days. They are grooming you for high office, young man. Whatever sins are hidden here will be a lesson for you as well. Let him stay."

"Continuing," said Holmes. "Cardinal Tosca was sent here to get him away from Rome, where he had many enemies. Then he was offered this diplomatic coup, to mend fences with the British people by sharing an exciting new secret from the Vatican Archives. What he didn't realize is that very often a secret is hidden for a reason. Have you looked at the other two cameos?"

"Yes," said Della Chiesa. "They are similar style to the *Grand Camée de France*, except of a slightly later period. The French one shows the family and important officials of Tiberius Caesar. The two that I have seen here this morning would seem to be similar in design. The first is of Caligula. He was the successor to Tiberius and it is unfinished, although there was room for the horse. It is likely incomplete because he was mad and only lasted three years as Emperor. The other one may refer to the time of Claudius Caesar and it is complete, which points to his thirteen years as Emperor."

"*Va bene,*" said Tosca. "We are finished here. The third one was stolen. The exhibition is over, and we shall return these two back to Rome." He stood up as if to leave until Holmes's voice stopped him.

"There was no theft," he said. "No locked room mystery and no crime committed." He walked over to the shelves and moved away parcels of cleaning cloths and solvent. Then he picked up a rectangular parcel and placed it on the table.

"You had no time to hide it and when you tried to come back, you were stopped by Epicurus. You must have known then couldn't get away with it. Had you been innocent, you would have protested such treatment. You didn't, which confirmed my suspicions. Whatever is on this cameo is so frightening that you felt you had to hide it, and when Cardinal Manning insisted on calling for an investigation, your story became more unwieldy."

"Please," said Cardinal Tosca. "I beg of you. Do not unwrap it. There were only supposed to be three, which is why I started to look at them. When I saw it, *Madre di Dio*, I did not know what to do. The scandal it will cause!"

But Holmes would not be stopped. He unwrapped the third cameo, leaned over it and looked closely at the depictions. Mycroft joined him.

"I see," Mycroft said.

"Indeed," said Sherlock. "This is now more within your realm than mine. I bid you good day. Watson, with me."

"But?" I said.

"Now, please. We must leave at once."

I was seething with anger, curiosity, and frustration. Being Holmes's friend was often interesting and seldom quiet, but it could also be tiresome.

Before I could say anything, Holmes spoke.

"Please, my friend. Give me this ride to think of all the possibilities. I have just made a monumental decision and I need to reconcile myself with my actions. Let us return to the rooms at Baker Street. It is early enough, but I think it will be time for a glass of port when we arrive, and I shall tell you all."

I honoured his request, as disgruntled as I felt. We went straight up the stairs, and Holmes waved at the cabinet. There was a fine bottle of malt whisky gathering dust and I chose that instead for both of us. I don't think that Holmes noticed.

"What if you discovered a piece of information so terrifying that you truly could not even envision the consequences?" he asked. "A cameo so divisive it could create the war to end all wars, could set brother against brother, nation against nation, continent against continent."

"Holmes, whatever you saw could not possibly be that bad. You glanced at it for barely a moment."

"Watson, I am no expert in the iconography of early civilization, but what I saw, if true, would change the world."

I waited, dreading his answer.

"The last cameo appears to follow the sequence. It is from the time of Emperor Nero and it is the reason why the entire set was hidden. Like the others it can be dated, and it shows the Emperor standing next to a figure with holes in his hands and a crown of thorns. There is a woman with him and a child, and the scroll above their heads says *Iesus Nazarenus, Rex Iudaeorum*."

"'*Jesus, the Nazarene, King of the Jews*'," I said. "Oh my word." I moved away from the fireplace and sat down, trying to comprehend the implications. "It must be a forgery."

"Think of the provenance," said Holmes. "Even if it is eventually proven to be fraudulent, the story will be out there that the church hid it for two-thousand years, unwilling to test the core beliefs of their religion. And what if it is not a forgery? What if that cameo is taken as proof that Jesus had a family and children, and didn't die? The date marking on that cameo shows it to be in the ninth year of the reign of Nero. That would be around about 64 A.D.

"Thirty years after the crucifixion," I said. "It would mean that all of Christianity would be a lie."

"Exactly," said Holmes. "And that is why, despite my better judgement that the truth must always win out, I took us away and left it to my brother to resolve. This was never about revenge on Cardinal Tosca. Cardinal Newman was right. This way is not the Italian way. This was about the destruction of society. Whoever did this wanted to change the world, and didn't care how many people died to make it happen."

"Surely it wouldn't be that bad?" I said.

For perhaps the only time in my life, I heard my friend utter these words: "I don't know." Then, "But when you have all these raging empires ready to go to war, and possibly the only thing holding them back is their professed faith in a religion that has sustained society for two millennia . . . ."

"What happens if you take that away?"

"Indeed," said Holmes. "And in this incendiary political climate no one needs to find out."

"What about Cardinal Newman? Will you tell him?"

Holmes drank again from the whisky glass. It did not seem to be relaxing him. "John Henry Newman has spent a lifetime justifying the cause of Christian faith. He has not long to live, and I am not the person to ruin what is left of his life for him. There are times, Watson, when the truth is too terrifying to be told."

"I never thought I'd hear you say that," I said.

"Neither did I, my friend. Neither did I."

POSTSCRIPT

Cardinal John Newman died later that year, on 11 August, 1890, thankfully never knowing the truth about the matter which would have shaken the Church to which he'd devoted his life

Two weeks after the events described here, there was a small announcement in *The Times* of the cancellation of a display of church artifacts at the British Museum, as the ship that was transporting them had sunk with seventy-two souls on board. Mycroft had taken a disaster already extant and used it to bury the truth of the Vatican Cameos.

In 1914, many years after the events in this story, Giacomo Della Chiesa was elected Pope. As Benedict XV, he watched from the sidelines of St. Peter's in Rome as every Christian country in the world tried to rend civilization asunder. His diplomatic and humanitarian efforts, though largely fruitless, drew praise from all who met and knew him. He died in 1922, having seen Christianity fail, and like all who knew the truth of the cameos, wondering if it ever existed at all.

Signed: *Doctor John H. Watson*

. . . I was exceedingly preoccupied by that little affair of the Vatican cameos, and in my anxiety to oblige the Pope I lost touch with several interesting English cases.

Sherlock Holmes – *The Hound of the Baskervilles*

The Case of the Gila Monster
by Stephen Herczeg

During my friendship with Sherlock Holmes, I have, on numerous occasions, found myself over-awed by the breadth of knowledge that resides behind those aquiline features, and also been humbled by his immense understanding of all things medical. At times I have been left mouth agape in surprise as some esoteric piece of information springs forth from that immense intelligence.

These incidents have been quite frequent and ego shattering, but none so much as the time Holmes solved the mystery surrounding a death from the bite of a Gila Monster.

It was a wonderful spring day and I was enjoying a late afternoon cup of tea in the back garden behind my Kensington practice. I had seen numerous patients all day and rewarded myself with some peace and quiet. The serenity was sadly broken by the appearance of my beautiful wife, Mary, at the rear door.

"Sorry to bother you, John, but we've received a late patient. I suggested that she return in the morning, but her manner was ever so compelling that I thought it best if you see her now," she said.

I stood up and replied, "Quite alright, dear. It will probably be nothing, but I would rather quieten her fears now than allow any to develop further overnight."

I moved to the door, but Mary placed a hand upon my chest stopping me short. She glanced over her shoulder then leaned in close to me, whispering, "She's a formidable lady. If I was to have an opinion, I would think that her problems are all in her mind. But of course, you are the doctor."

I smiled and patted her on the shoulder. "I'm sure they are, but I've never met a patient that could pull the wool over my eyes."

Mary allowed me to pass and I stepped through into my consulting room. My patient spied me and immediately stood up to greet me.

My wife was right. The lady before me was an astounding specimen. She stood just short of six-foot high and was quite rotund as well. She wore an extremely tight-fitting black tulip skirt and a matching black blouse wrenched over her enormous bosom and brought in tight at the waist. Her hair was pulled back into a high bun, giving her face a fierce expression, even at rest.

She had the look and presence of a private school governess. My only thought was pity for her students.

Her face split into a fierce smile and she said, "Dr. Watson, thank you so much for seeing me at such short notice. I have to apologise, but I didn't know where else to go."

I bade her to sit and took my seat behind my desk.

"What is it I can help you with Mrs, ah . . . ?"

"Bell," she answered, "Mr. Moira Bell. I live not far from here on the edge of Regents Park with my son."

It was then that this remarkable woman lost all composure and showed that underneath her gruff exterior was someone full of emotion and love. As soon as she mentioned her son, a torrent of tears poured forth from her eyes and she sobbed uncontrollably into her sleeve.

I jumped up, raced around the desk, pulled a clean kerchief from my breast pocket, and offered it to the distraught woman. She took it, wiped her eyes, and then blew her nose into it. As it was an inexpensive silk kerchief, I decided to let her keep it.

I quickly found Mary and asked her to brew some tea while I attended Mrs. Bell.

The troubled woman finally calmed down once the offer of a cup of hot tea was made. She began to tell me her tale whilst sipping the brew.

She was a local resident who lived in a line of properties that edged onto a lovely part of Regents Park, not far from the London University College. Her family had possessed one of the three-storey Georgian houses for well over a hundred years, and she had inherited the lease on the passing of her father almost thirty years previously.

She lived alone with her grown son, Julius, as her husband had died in the Afghan war. I told her my own war tale and was able to provide a larger level of empathy towards her because of it.

She went on to explain that her son was a Professor of Zoology working at the University College. He possessed a rather large and exotic collection of snakes and reptiles, which he kept in a room on the second floor.

"A herpetologist?" I asked.

"If you insist," she answered, indicating to me that she had no real interest in her son's profession. "It was those damnable lizards that caused all this trouble."

I pushed her for more information and was finally told that her son had been arrested for manslaughter. A man named Hyram Shrubb had forced his way into their home and had died as a result of being bitten by one of her son's lizards, a Gila Monster from America.

I frowned internally at this revelation. Gila Monsters are venomous, but to my knowledge are they rarely deadly. Most victims are usually left with horrid wounds caused by the strength of the jaws rather than from the venom.

At the remembrance of her son's current whereabouts, she began to sob all over again without revealing any other pertinent details. I quickly went to her aid to calm her once more and prescribed a relaxant to help her sleep that evening. I also suggested that a friend of mine might be able to shed more light on the facts of the case and help to unearth the true nature of this horrid affair. She then admitted that it was my friendship with Holmes that had led her across town to see me.

Once she was calm again, I helped her out of my rooms after securing her address and said that I would bring Holmes to her home at precisely eleven o'clock the next day.

Through a veil of drying tears she agreed, thanked me for my service, and marched off home.

As I watched her go a small thrill went through me. I know that my good friend Holmes requires constant stimulation of his mind to keep the *ennui* at bay, but during these quiet times I find myself in such a need as well.

This case also promised the need for a high level of medical knowledge, and there was hope that the depth of my experience would be of use to Holmes.

Sadly, that was not to be.

I arrived at the front door step of Mrs. Bell's home on Cumberland Terrace at a few minutes of eleven. The day was quite warm and I found that I had underestimated the walk and was awash with perspiration.

I had removed my hat and was mopping my brow with a fresh kerchief when I noticed Holmes walking towards me. He was elegantly dressed as always and tapped along with his cane. He had left his hat at home and showed no sign of being overheated.

"Good morning, Watson, and what a wonderful morning it is!" he said, admiring the building before us. "Poisoning by venomous lizard. Not a regular occurrence in London, one would think."

"Indeed."

We both studied the house before us. It was part of a long series of terraces flanking this side of the park.

"I took the liberty of walking around the back of the houses. There's an alleyway running along the buildings used by the night soil men and a gate through which one can access the park. Very convenient for a quiet evening stroll or for accessing the rear doorway unseen," he said.

I nodded in agreement, unsure of what he meant.

We turned to mount the steps to the front door but were disturbed by a commotion next door. Two men were struggling to manhandle a settee down the steps and into a large cart parked by the roadway.

I turned and watched their antics just as the lead man slipped off a step and tumbled to the pavement below, bellowing in pain. By the time I reached him, he was sitting up and holding his right ankle.

"I'm a doctor. I can help if you like," I said.

"Ow! It's my ankle! I nearly broke it!" he cried.

I gently pulled his hands away from his foot and straightened his leg out. The ankle was certainly swollen. I moved the foot about, which elicited more howls of pain. To stop his moaning, I lowered his foot and spoke to him.

"I don't think it's broken," I said as I reached into my pocket for a card, "but you certainly won't be doing any more furniture moving today. I suggest you make your way home, rest, and put some ice on it to take away the swelling,"

He took the card and I continued. "Come and see me tomorrow – or better yet, the next day. I'll be able to tell how badly damaged it is by then. Meanwhile, stay off it."

"I'll 'elp 'im get 'ome," his friend offered.

Another man emerged from the doorway with an angry expression on his face.

"Here, what's all this laying about then?" he asked.

I stood up and addressed him.

"I'm afraid your man has had a rather nasty tumble. He's sprained his ankle or worse. I'm a doctor, and I've told him to rest up for a couple of days before coming to see me about it."

The man was indignant.

"I can't wait up for him to get better. I need this place emptied today," he said.

He pointed to the man on the ground, "Get up, Harry, or you're fired!"

Harry's eyes lit up in fear. He tried to pull himself up, but screamed in pain as he put weight on his leg and collapsed again.

"I think that answers that question, then," said Holmes.

The angry man turned to face the detective.

"And what do you care?" he asked.

"Nothing, really. I'm just a casual observer, but anyone can see that if this man is not fit to work, then the work will not get done."

The angry man turned back to Harry, ready to blast him again.

"And why are you in such a hurry?" asked Holmes.

The angry man turned once more, "What's it to you?" he said.

"Just a casual observer," repeated Holmes evenly.

"Well, if you have to know, this whole place," he indicated the line of terraced houses, "Is going to be pulled down and replaced by nice, new, modern houses."

I was horrified.

"Why destroy these wonderful buildings? Who would do such a thing?" I asked.

"I think the answer to that, Watson, is pretty much under your nose," said Holmes.

I looked at him and saw that he was staring at the wagon behind me. I turned and read the side board of the cart. *Shrubb Brothers.*

"I've never heard of them," I said.

Holmes smiled at me, that smile I had seen far too often for my own liking. I'd missed something again.

"I think you'll find, Watson, that one of those brothers is exactly why we are here."

I once again urged the injured man to rest, much to the annoyance of his employer, and then joined Holmes on the neighbouring door step. Holmes smiled at me and indicated the door.

"Well, it's your case so far, Doctor," he said.

I stepped up and lifted the heavy knocker. I rapped only once before the door was unlocked and opened. It revealed a sallow-faced young maid. She looked at us wide-eyed through the crack in the door.

"Can I 'elp you, sirs?" she asked.

"Yes. Dr. Watson and Mr. Sherlock Holmes, to see Mrs. Bell. We are expected," I said.

"Oh, yes, sirs. Please come in," she said as she backed away and opened the door for us to enter.

We stepped into a small entry hall that proved a little too tight for both Holmes and I together. The maid squeezed past us, locked the door, and withdrew the heavy iron key. She moved to a nearby wall stand and hung the key on a hook next to its twin. A third hook remained empty, so I placed my hat upon it. The maid once again moved past and motioned for us to follow her into a room off to the right.

"Does that key unlock the rear door as well?" Holmes asked.

The maid was surprised by the question and shrank back slightly. "Yes. Yes, it does," she said.

Holmes simply nodded.

We entered the small reception room and found Mrs. Bell sitting by the window, reading the day's newspapers. She looked up and brightened when she saw me, and then eyed Holmes with a curious lift of her eyebrow.

"Mrs. Bell, I'd like to introduce my good friend, Mr. Sherlock Holmes. I've described the scant details of your son's case to him, and he is very interested in hearing more to see if he can indeed provide help."

Mrs. Bell began to rise from her seat. Holmes gallantly tried to stop her with a gesture, but was too slow. He was taken aback when she rose to full height and met him almost eye-to-eye, something that happens rarely for Holmes, especially with women.

Mrs. Bell held out her hand and said, "Mr. Holmes, I am very pleased to meet you. I am Moira, but I do prefer Mrs. Bell in deference to my late husband."

A small grin came to Holmes's mouth as he shook hands with the dominating presence that was Mrs. Moira Bell.

"Please tell me all about your son's troubles, Mrs. Bell," he said, indicating her chair. Holmes and I took seats on the small settee nearby. My friend sat back and steepled his hands before his face, his standard pose when absorbing facts provided to him.

Mrs. Bell began her tale.

"My son has been charged with the manslaughter of a very nasty man, Mr. Hyram Shrubb. My son, Julius, lives here with me and is a Professor of Zoology at the University College, just down the road. He specialises in the study of lizards and snakes."

"Herpetology," Holmes said, "Yes, Dr. Watson informed me. To be honest, that was probably what piqued my interest the most. I have heard a lot about your son and would dearly love to meet him. I can assure you that I will do all I can to clear this little matter up for him."

Mrs. Bell continued, "Oh, thank you. Well, this Mr. Shrubb turned up on our door step one day and barged past my poor Milly uninvited."

"Your maid, I presume?" asked Holmes.

"Why, yes. I'm sorry. He stormed into this room and blurted out his introductions, and then laid out an offer to buy the lease on my house. I was far too perplexed at his gruff manner to even consider such a request unannounced. I sent him away without another word, but he didn't leave it there. He turned up several days in a row, but Milly, God bless her, held her ground and wouldn't let him in. After the seventh time, he arrived when Julius was home, so I agreed to meet him again and hear him out."

She took a deep breath before returning to her story.

"We met in here with tea and biscuits to present an amiable setting. Mr. Shrubb called himself a 'property developer'. He is purchasing all the houses along this street with the idea of demolishing them and building a new set of larger terraces to serve the officers of the nearby Regents Park barracks. Julius became very nervous at this talk. Our house has been in my family for over a hundred years. Julius was born here. He's never known another home. He's a good boy and would never hurt a fly. He needs this house, as it's near to the University which is his life, and he needs the space to store his collection."

Holmes sat forward, a slight glint in his eye, "I take that to be his collection of reptiles," he said.

"Yes," she continued, "My Julius has a large collection of reptiles upstairs, with some very rare breeds that even the London Zoo doesn't possess." She made a slightly disgusted face. "I never go in there myself. Dreadful things," she finished.

"And that's where the Gila Monster is housed," asked Holmes, sitting back and resuming his contemplative pose.

"Oh, yes. That's also where everything went wrong."

"Go on."

"Well, I told Mr. Shrubb that there was no way that I would even contemplate selling. Julius was much relieved. Mr. Shrubb tried to offer more money to persuade us, but my mind was made up. I don't need any money, as my poor unfortunate father, God bless him, was well invested. I shan't be in need for the rest of my life and neither will Julius. Mr. Shrubb left in quite an angry mood and I hoped that would be the last we saw of him."

"But it wasn't," I said.

"No. Not at all. That meeting was a fortnight ago. Earlier this week, I was at my bridge club, Milly was out at the grocer, and Julius came home early to feed his collection. He stepped in through the front door and heard screams coming from the second floor. He ran upstairs and found Mr. Shrubb lying on the floor with Julius' favourite – his Gila Monster – clinging to his arm. Julius went to his aid and managed to pry the lizard away from Mr. Shrubb's arm. He then put the reptile away, latched up the case, and then attended to Mr. Shrubb. My dear boy managed to bring the man down to this room just as Milly returned. They both helped to tend his wound and call him a hansom. He kept blubbing that he found the door unlocked and was looking for me. He stumbled into the reptile room and was attacked by the lizard. The last they saw was his slumped form in the seat of a hansom, taking him to Dr. Brown's surgery around the corner in Robert Street. Frankly, no one thought any more of it until the police came two days ago and took my poor boy away. Manslaughter, they said, caused by the lizard bite. They blamed Julius for leaving the cage open."

"Hmm," said Holmes, "I think I'd like to see this reptile room and then, Watson, I think we should pay a visit to Dr. Brown."

The reptile room was more crowded than I had presumed. It was located in what was a rather large second floor bedroom, but it seemed to shrink when filled with a dozen or so large wooden framed enclosures with glass sides. Each had a glass lid and held a single specimen.

Holmes moved around the room, a look of delight on his face as he stared into each of the reptile tanks. He stopped by one and studied it.

"Ah," he said, "*Vipera berus*. The common adder. The kingdom's only venomous snake, but really quite shy and harmless."

He moved on to another that contained a brown snake lying on a flat rock.

"*Naja haje*, the Egyptian Cobra, also known as the Asp. It was this snake that was thought to have been used by Cleopatra to commit suicide. Very good, very good."

He moved on and stopped by another enclosure.

"Ah, and here is our little mischief maker himself."

Inside the glass cage was a fat, squat lizard with a pink and brown mottled body and black face.

"*Heloderma suspectum*, the Gila Monster. Native to the southwestern United States and northern Mexico. I'm not sure if I'm more impressed in seeing it, or the fact that Professor Bell managed to find one and keep it alive."

He studied the cage and unlatched two slide bolts near the top which caused the front to fold down. The lizard hardly moved with the door open and simply looked at Holmes for a moment before falling back to sleep.

"Hardly the vicious killer of legend, hey, Watson?"

"Is it still alive?" I asked.

Holmes chuckled and relatched the door.

Just then the room's door opened and Milly walked in with a tray of food scraps. She saw the two of us and a slight shocked look came to her face.

"Oh, I'm sorry gentlemen. I can come back and feed these beasts later."

"Never mind that, Milly. Please ignore us, will you. Go about your chore," said Holmes.

Milly moved to the nearest cage and opened the top. She dropped some scraps inside and the resident lizard wandered over to eat. She replaced the lid and repeated the exercise with the next few tanks.

Holmes watched with interest.

"Milly," he asked.

The young maid almost dropped the tray in shock. She turned sheepishly to face the detective.

"Yes, sir?"

"I assume that Professor Bell usually feeds the reptiles."

She nodded.

"Since he's indisposed you've taken up the challenge."

Again she nodded.

"I noticed that you only feed them through the top of the enclosure. Do you ever need to open the front?"

"Oh, no, sir. Julius, er, the *professor* always uses the top. 'E would only open the front if 'e was moving the animal to another enclosure, and then 'e would use those."

She pointed at a pair of thick leather gloves hanging from a peg on the wall.

Holmes studied the gloves, looked back at the Gila Monster sitting on its rock, and then turned to me.

"Watson, it's time to visit Dr. Brown."

We were shown into Dr. Brown's room just as his last patient before lunch left.

Behind the desk sat a man of about sixty years of age with a ramrod-straight posture. He was quite bald but possessing of a luxuriant grey moustache and a monocle held in with his right eyebrow.

A quick look around his room showed the standard paraphernalia of a modern doctor. A full sized human skeleton hung from a frame in one corner. A gurney sat against one wall with a curtained area for undressing next to it. On the wall behind the desk was a small but marvellous collection of artefacts from the east.

A Ghurkha knife stood on a stand in the middle of a mantle-piece that framed the grate of a small fireplace. On the wall to either side were framed copies of the doctor's professional certificates and a letter with the seal of Her Majesty. I strained to read the letter, but only made out a comment about service to the Crown. It looked very similar to the one that I had received.

"Let me introduce ourselves, Dr. Brown. I am Dr. John Watson, and this is Mr. Sherlock Holmes," I said. I pointed to the Ghurka knife and asked, "You served in India?"

He looked around for a moment and turned back with a smile of fond remembrance, "Yes," he said, "I was an officer in the Indian Army for more than twenty years." He studied me for a moment, "And yourself? You have the air of a military man as well."

I nodded with a slight bow. "In Afghanistan, until I was injured."

He looked at Holmes, taking in my tall companion's presence for a moment before directing his enquiry at the detective.

"Sherlock Holmes. I have heard of you, sir, but never believed I would find myself in any need of your services, so forgive me if I am surprised to find the reverse."

A small smile crossed Holmes's face. "Let us not take up too much of your time," he said, "A couple of days ago, you received an emergency patient by the name of Hyram Shrubb."

The doctor nodded, "Yes. Lizard bite. Very strange and nasty."

"I know it may constitute a breach of privacy, but could I enquire as to how you treated the bite?"

"Well, I don't wish to let out my secrets, as it wasn't something well known among British doctors."

"Could it have been with the administration of a weak mix of strychnine?"

The doctor looked aghast. "How in the blazes would you have known that?" he asked.

I was just as shocked. "Yes, Holmes. How?"

Holmes's face possessed that smile generally reserved for me when I've been surprised by one of his deductions. He took a deep breath and enlightened us.

"Dr. Brown, before you even spoke, your Ghurka knife told me that you lived in India. I presumed that you would have served as a doctor for most of that time."

"Yes," said Brown.

"Mr. Shrubb presented to you with a bite from a Gila Monster. He may not have known the actual species, but you would have seen fang marks and much damage caused by the bite. I expect that you would have treated him as if he had been bitten by a venomous animal."

"Well, yes. Once I treated any infection, I naturally took the precaution to treat for poison."

"And coming from India, where the standard procedure for cobra bite is to use strychnine, a treatment developed in Australia in the 1850's to care for bites from their local snake population, as it contains species far deadlier than the cobra of India."

"Yes. Correct again. Amazing. You got all that from a Ghurka knife?"

"You would be amazed what information Holmes can gather from the smallest of sources," I said.

"Thank you, Watson," Holmes said. "By the way, Dr. Brown. Do you know that your patient, Mr. Shrubb, died the very next day?"

Brown's face dropped in complete shock.

"What? That's impossible. Once I administered the strychnine and settled him down here for a little while, he was right as rain. I loaded him into a hansom and sent him home. I'm flabbergasted."

"Quite so, but I would have experienced the same reaction if I were in your place. I do give you my promise that we will return and explain what happened when I have solved it myself, which will be quite soon," said Holmes, "I thank you for your time, Doctor."

He spun on his heal and spoke to me.

"Watson, if you will, I think we should take a visit to Scotland Yard. We need to see the unfortunate Mr. Shrubb."

Martin, the young mortician, looked up as Holmes and I entered. He was just finishing his lunch and had probably expected a little peace and quiet. He stood up quickly and addressed us.

"Dr. Watson, Mr. 'Olmes. I wasn't expecting anybody today. What can I do for – "

He was cut off by the arrival of Inspector Lestrade, who seemed a bit flustered. He carried the small note from Holmes that had been passed to him by the desk Sergeant on the floor above.

"Ah, Inspector," said Holmes, "I believe you will find the following of interest."

"Why did you drag me away from my luncheon to come down to this God-awful place?" Lestrade asked.

Holmes ignored the question and instead addressed Martin.

"If you would be so kind to please direct us to the corpse of the unfortunate Mr. Hyram Shrubb, Martin."

Martin put his sandwich down and pulled the napkin from his collar before skirting a few gurneys and stopping before one covering a large bloated body.

"'E's a big 'un," he said, before pulling back the sheet to reveal the corpse below.

"Thank you," said Holmes. He bent forward and looked at the man's face, studying the mouth and nose while making small humming noises to himself – something to which I have long become accustomed when Holmes investigates. He pulled out his glass and had a closer look at the man's nose. I did find this particularly odd, as I could see the bite mark on the man's left forearm quite clearly.

Finally, Holmes moved away from the man's face and studied the bite. From where I stood, I could see that the flesh on the arm had been ravaged by multiple teeth marks. The lizard had latched on with considerable force and thrashed about before being pulled off. There were two larger holes on opposite sides of the bite which were deeper and more pronounced. I took these to be the venom-bearing teeth.

Holmes's examination of the bite was remarkably short as he moved away from the area and fixated on the man's upper forearm. I could see more puncture marks, which I presumed were from the injections administered by Dr. Brown.

Holmes rose and stood staring at Shrubb's corpse for a moment before turning back to Martin.

"The Coroner hasn't performed an autopsy," he said.

It was more a statement than a question.

Martin replied, "No. No, 'e 'asn't. 'E said that we know 'ow the man died, so no need to mess 'im up any more."

Holmes's face screwed up. I knew that he viewed such actions and sloppy, as they restricted the amount of information that could be gleaned.

"Why do you think that would be important?" Lestrade asked, "We know it was the lizard, and we know that this professor was the lizard's owner. Case closed."

A short flash of fury leapt to Holmes's face before he replaced it with calm. I believe that Lestrade barely missed a thorough lecture.

"Because, Inspector, this man is extremely obese. I dare say a good shock of any sort could have caused him to keel over. Also, do you not think it would be a good idea to ascertain the amount of venom in his system? I've seen the lizard in question. Unless it had friends working with it, then it wouldn't have been able to generate enough venom to kill a man of this size."

With that, he placed his lens back in his pocket and abruptly departed, speaking over his shoulder as he did.

"Thank you, Martin. Your help has been admirable. Inspector, I think you should meet Watson and me at the house of Mr. Hyram Shrubb and his brother in two hours. I will announce my findings there forthwith. Please bring Professor Bell, for he has nothing at all to do with this unfortunate event and you can release him afterwards."

I gave thanks and said my goodbyes before following after Holmes.

We took luncheon in The Rag nearby in Pall Mall. My status as an ex-serviceman held me good stead amongst the military folk that inhabited the place, and Holmes was always welcome once his identity was known, even though he'd never served Her Majesty in the armed services.

Throughout the meal, I kept prodding him about the solution to the case. His only answer was to smile, nod, and say, "All will become clear." A most infuriating affair it was. He seemed more intent on studying the diners at several other tables, most of whom wore very high-ranking insignia on their jackets.

"My word, this is a very prominent gathering for this time of day," I remarked.

"Yes," said Holmes, "One would almost imagine that we are centralising some of our garrisons in preparation for another campaign."

"I'm sure it's nothing to do with war, Holmes. Just a gathering of officers."

Holmes simply smiled.

At a little after two, we were the first to arrive. Holmes went straight to the door and knocked. It was opened by a pasty-faced doorman, who eyed us with slight suspicion.

"I am Sherlock Holmes and this is Dr. John Watson. We should be expected."

The doorman nodded and replied, "Yes, sirs. Mr. Shrubb was informed of your imminent arrival. He has seen fit to meet with you in the parlour."

He stepped back and allowed us to enter. The foyer was quite luxuriant with deep-grained woods and leather. The doorman led us down a short corridor and into a spectacular room lined along every wall with book cases, each crammed with leather-bound volumes in nearly perfect condition, and a small number of display cases holding an assortment of bric-a-brac.

Both Holmes and I were quite taken aback by this room. Neither of us has any expectations of such a place in a house occupied by a pair of bachelor property developers.

It was then I noticed a man sitting in a high backed chair towards the far end of the room. He was the spitting image of his brother, but lacking most of the weight. For a split second, I imagined the Holmes brothers, with Mycroft lying in the Scotland Yard morgue and Sherlock sitting before me.

"Gentlemen," he began, "Welcome to my home."

He rose and stood a good two inches higher than Holmes. He made his way towards us and held out his hand to me first.

"I am Aubrey Shrubb," he said and took my hand.

"John Watson," I replied.

He turned to Holmes and repeated the action, remarking, "And you would be the famous Sherlock Holmes."

"I'm sorry about what happened to your brother," said Holmes, shaking and finally releasing Shrubb's hand.

"Yes, damnable strange way to die, that. Who would have thought such an intelligent man would allow his creatures to run free and attack any innocent person who happened upon them? Very negligent, it would seem."

"That is partly why we are here. Mrs. Bell has asked me to investigate a little further and determine just how your brother came into contact with the lizard, and what happened afterwards."

"I think the police have worked all that out, haven't they? He was bitten by a venomous lizard and it killed him. Case closed."

"Forgive my cynicism, but the police are likely to take the most obvious answer when investigating a strange case such as this. I much prefer to look at all the facts and evidence before jumping to conclusions."

The sound of the door knocker filtered in as the second group of guests arrived at the Shrubb residence.

"Ah, speaking of the police," said Holmes.

Moments later, the doorman showed a slightly aggrieved Lestrade and a very perplexed and dour looking man, who I assumed was Professor Bell, into the parlour.

Shrubb took one look at Bell and asked, "What is *he* doing here?"

"I thought it best to have the professor here to provide any expert information concerning the Gila Monster, and to be on hand to defend himself if required," said Holmes.

"Hmm. I only agreed to this because your note said that you had new information that would shed light on Hyram's death. I was hoping that you would find something to convict this man with murder rather than manslaughter," Aubrey said, his contempt for Bell on show as he spat out the word man.

"Well, it could go either way," said Holmes, "To move things along, would it be possible to see your brother's rooms? My understanding is that he had a suite of apartments on the second floor, and that he was found in his own drawing room."

"Yes. The rooms are as he left them. I haven't had the heart to let the help tidy up yet."

The second floor was a large and sumptuous collection of rooms styled in a more minimalistic way than the parlour below. I assumed that they reflected the less austere tastes of the younger and larger of the Shrubb brothers.

The climb up the stairs also left me a little breathless and I wondered how a man of Hyram Shrubb's girth would have found the journey. It was later that I discovered there was a lift, which explained quite a lot.

Aubrey Shrubb led us down a short corridor and into a large but modestly decorated drawing room. There was a sizeable wooden desk at one end, with a small collection of leather bound volumes on a set of shelves behind it. I pulled a book down and looked closer. They were mostly books relating to the history of London's property transactions. It seemed this room doubled as Hyram Shrubb's office, or else his work was also his hobby.

I turned back from the shelf and found Aubrey directing Holmes to a large chair in the far corner. The elder Shrubb brother pointed to a stain on the carpet and spoke.

"My poor unfortunate brother was found face down here. His last act was to expel his luncheon – hence the stain. I did allow the maid to clean the results after the police allowed it."

Holmes turned to Lestrade and said, "Did your men take samples for examination?"

"Why?" Lestrade asked.

Holmes closed his eyes for a second, pursed his lips, and said, "Because it would have been a trivial exercise to determine the contents of his stomach, revealing how much venom was in his system, and also what else may have been ingested."

"Right," said Lestrade.

Holmes turned back to the scene and moved to a small table next to the sitting chair. Opening the drawer, he pulled out a bottle of white powder and a half-full syringe containing a clear liquid. Holmes picked up the bottle, uncorked it, and dabbed a small amount of the powder on his finger. He tasted it, nodded, and smiled. I questioned him as he put the bottle down.

"What is that?"

"My old friend – though a lot more concentrated than my favoured seven-per-cent solution," he said.

"Cocaine?" I remarked.

Aubrey piped up with a hint of offence. "What my brother did in his own house is none of your business!"

"Indeed," said Holmes. "But it must be taken into consideration with all the other evidence."

He turned and scanned the room, seeking out *minutiae*. His eyes fell on me, and then the desk. He strode over and stood behind it, opening the top drawers and rifling through them.

"Hello, what the blazes do you think you are doing?" yelled Aubrey, "That's Hyram's private business!"

He started to move towards Holmes but Lestrade placed a hand lightly on his shoulder.

"I'd let Mr. Holmes finish, sir. If there's something that we've missed, then he is most likely to find it. I'm sure he's not interested in any private affairs of your brother's."

With that, Holmes finished looking through one of the bottom drawers and stood up with holding his prize – a large iron key.

Professor Julius Bell yelled out in surprise, "That's our missing key! We thought that Milly had lost it. She got a right dressing down from Mother. No wonder she cried so much. I had to console her for hours."

Lestrade turned to look at the professor, who suddenly realised he'd said too much. A sheepish look came across his face.

"Well, she was very upset," he added.

All eyes slowly returned to Holmes, who placed the key in the middle of the vacant leather desk pad. He looked around all of the faces full of anticipation and smiled. "This, gentlemen, is the vital clew for which I have been searching."

"But what does it mean?" I asked.

He ignored me and turned towards Shrubb.

"Mr. Shrubb. You and your brother are highly successful property developers, a new occupation that takes the city's old and derelict districts and renews them for the next generation and in turn attracts a tidy profit. Is that not right?"

Shrubb nodded, "Yes, why?"

"Your brother wasn't used to failure, I think. He studied the city and chose the best locations for these developments – hence his detailed volumes of property transactions and locations in London. A well-versed man in that field, I would presume."

"Yes. He was the educated one. He found the properties and I organised the workmen and ran the operation."

"So, his latest venture was to revitalise parts of Regents Park, with the view of establishing residencies for the officers of the nearby Regents Park Barracks and the new garrisons that will be moving there soon."

"We had already convinced most of the residents to depart, and were almost ready to demolish."

"But one held out."

"Yes. Mrs. Bell wouldn't sell. Even when we made a higher offer than to any other resident."

Holmes held up the iron key.

"And that's what drove your brother to purloin this key and gain access to the Bell residence when he believed all to be away."

"How dare you besmirch my brother's good name!" said Aubrey as he stepped towards Holmes.

Lestrade intercepted him and posed a question of Holmes. "How can you be sure that Shrubb took that key from the Bell residence?" he asked.

"When we arrived, we noticed that there were only two keys on the rack near the front door. Professor Bell has told us that there was a third which seems to have gone missing. Mr. Shrubb was found inside the house when all occupants had left. I would say that his claim that the door was unlocked was a fantasy. With this key, he could have entered from the front or back, as both doors use the same lock."

"Why did he break in?" asked Lestrade.

"Ah, well, that's where I must presume a little, until of course more evidence is unearthed that proves me incorrect. The sticking point of the sale of the house was Professor Bell's residency at the University College. His mother would not have them move. The facts as they stand point to Mr. Shrubb entering the house with the express purpose of removing one of the venomous reptiles and probably placing it in Mrs. Bell's bedroom."

"Preposterous!" said Aubrey.

"Possibly, but if Mr. Shrubb could cause a ruction between mother and son because of the reptile collection, then he may have thought he could convince Mrs. Bell to sell up."

"Yes, Mother is proud of my work, but she doesn't like my collection," said Julius.

"But that lizard bit him. It's obviously vicious and," Aubrey pointed at Julius, "*he* is responsible!"

The professor looked shocked at the accusation. "I would never – " he started before Holmes cut him off.

"You have no need to apologise, Professor Bell, I have seen the lizard in question and it is a somewhat sedentary beast. Can you explain to us how and why the Gila Monster in question would act the way it did?"

Julius Bell's posture changed completely as his professional stature was called upon.

"The Gila Monster, especially the male that I possess, is rather slow and sluggish. They generally don't attack unless provoked."

"If someone were to pick one up, would that be enough to elicit an attack?"

"Possibly, especially if it was handled roughly. A Gila Monster will bite and latch on for dear life then thrash around until they subdue their pray," Julius said, "That was how I found Mr. Shrubb. My lizard had bitten him on the wrist and clamped its mouth shut with some force. I had to remove it with a stick."

"But it wouldn't attack unless picked up or moved?"

"Yes, that's right."

I felt I had to step in and clarify things. "So, what you're saying is that Mr. Shrubb stole a key from the Bell's household, and then came back when they were away and tried to pick up a venomous lizard to put it in Mrs. Bell's bedroom, but was himself bitten."

"Precisely. We already heard from the maid that the cases are rarely opened fully, so the lizard had to be extricated from its confinement, which probably aggravated it enough to attack," said Holmes.

"That doesn't excuse this man!" said Aubrey Shrubb, pointing at the professor. "He kept dangerous reptiles in his house, waiting to leap on unsuspecting victims and kill them."

"Yes," said Lestrade, "Regardless of whether Mr. Shrubb entered illegally, he was still killed by the professor's lizard, which is manslaughter under the eyes of the law."

"Ah, but did the lizard kill him? What say you, Professor?"

"As I explained to the police, it's simply not possible for my Gila Monster to inject enough poison into a man of Mr. Shrubb's size to kill him. Even if he had ingested the entire poison sack, he would simply have been rendered prostrate for a matter of hours and lethargic for a good week."

"Quite so. That was also my estimation. If the neurotoxic poison of the lizard didn't kill him, we should then look at the treatment," Holmes turned and addressed me directly. "Watson, of the doctor's use of strychnine in treating the lizard's venom?"

Searching my memories, I stated, "Strychnine is itself a poison, but like many poisons when administered in small doses acts as a stimulant. I've never come across its use in this way, but I would assume it is used to stimulate the nervous system to counteract the retardation effect of the neurotoxin."

"Exactly. And what of cocaine?"

"Again, another stimulant. The two together would engender an extremely vigorous reaction from the heart and respiratory system." I clicked my fingers as the penny dropped. "By God, Holmes! I see where you are going."

Lestrade looked as lost, as always. "What are you suggesting?"

I continued, "The dual actions of the strychnine and cocaine on a man of Mr. Shrubb's size would have put such a strain on his heart that it would have seized, if not burst."

"And as I found out in the morgue, Mr. Hyram Shrubb was a very habitual cocaine user, with many injection marks in his left forearm."

Holmes pointed at the syringe.

"I'm sure that if we test the contents of that syringe, it will be a very highly concentrated dose of cocaine. I would presume that Mr. Shrubb was in intense pain from the lizard bite and mixed himself what he thought a heavy dose of pain relief, but to his poor luck, turned out to contain the seeds of his own demise."

Aubrey Shrubb stepped forward and said, "Are you saying that my brother accidentally did it all to himself?"

"Yes. Through his actions, your brother paid the ultimate price."

Holmes turned to Lestrade. "I would think that the death should be put down to misadventure. I'm sure that the Bells would be most happy to remain out of any further enquiries."

Lestrade nodded and gave Aubrey Shrubb a look of contempt which made the taller brother shrink back. "I'll do that, but I'll be making some notes about the practices of Shrubb Brothers for future reference."

He turned and stormed out.

Aubrey Shrubb looked apologetically at Professor Bell and tentatively held out his hand. The professor took it in his own and gave it a perfunctory shake.

"No hard feelings, I hope," said Shrubb, "I can only apologise for my brother's actions, but can assure you I knew nothing about them."

Julius eyed him with suspicion before begrudgingly nodding his acceptance and turning to leave.

"Professor," Holmes said.

Bell turned and saw Holmes holding the iron key.

"Yours, I believe," he said.

The professor walked over and took the key, saying, "Thank you, Mr. Holmes. I can't tell you how much that I'm in your debt. I'm sure my mother has made some recompense offer, but I would be prepared to increase whatever it was."

Holmes smiled, "No need for that. This has been a most interesting day and has broken the monotony with much verve. There is only one reward I would be most interested in seeking."

"Name it, sir, please."

"I would love to return to your reptile room and discuss all things herpetological with you, at your leisure."

The professor's face lit up with glee.

"Oh, any time, sir, any time! I would also be delighted for you to attend my lectures at the University College whenever you have the time.

From what I've seen and heard today, I believe that there are things I can indeed learn from you."

"I'm sure we can both benefit," said Holmes, "I will check my calendar and take you up on your offer."

Still beaming, the professor pocketed the key, turned on his heel, gave one last desultory look at Shrubb, and exited.

Shrubb's face was aghast with all that had happened. He looked around his brother's room as if every artefact held a level of danger and betrayal in his mind. He finally stepped towards Holmes.

"I am in awe of your deductive skills, sir, and owe you an apology as well. I truly believed that young man meant ill to Hyram. I was possibly blinded by a brother's love, but now see what Hyram was up to. Sadly, his actions have left me with several terraced houses that serve no purpose in my business – business that I will need to re-examine in case there are other occurrences of this kind."

He turned, shoulders slumped, and trudged out of the room. I watched his tall figure reduced by bereavement and betrayal and almost felt a touch of sympathy towards him. I told Holmes as much as we stood alone in the dead man's parlour.

"I wouldn't be too sad for him, Watson. His pride has been damaged more than anything else. I don't think the loss of his brother will affect him too much. It's more the damage to his reputation that worries him. With all that's happening in this city at the moment, I'm sure a person like Mr. Shrubb will recover and build an empire with a renewed vigour. I just hope he refrains from utilising the devious methods of his kin."

> *I leaned back and took down the great index volume to which he referred. Holmes balanced it on his knee, and his eyes moved slowly and lovingly over the record of old cases, mixed with the accumulated information of a lifetime. ". . . Venomous lizard or gila. Remarkable case, that!"*

Dr. John H. Watson – "The Adventure of the Sussex Vampire"

The Bogus Laundry Affair
by Robert Perret

The Foreign Office had rewarded Holmes handsomely after a bit of diplomatic business in Woking, and so it was that he had spent the better part of a month loitering around Baker Street. I have had no small part in making the public aware of the fruits of Sherlock Holmes's prodigious industry, but he spent as much time in the valleys of exertion as he did at the peaks. He had thus languished in a blue cloud of tobacco smoke, calling for tea to be brought to the divan and toast to be brought to the settee. We were just reaching the tipping point I often feared, where his torpor would trickle into ennui and the needle would follow, and so I was much heartened when a constable appeared in the doorway to fetch us to Inspector Lestrade.

Holmes waved the policeman away. "If it were anything of interest, Lestrade would have come himself."

"He is detaining a caravan and refuses to leave it," the constable said.

"Why ever not?" Holmes sighed. "Surely such a task is a particular speciality of patrolmen such as yourself."

"He doesn't trust anyone else to do it, on account of there is no cause, sir."

"Lestrade is detaining a tradesman without cause?"

"Inspector Lestrade believes there should be cause, sir, but there isn't. That's why he requests your presence, Mr. Holmes – in order to find it."

"'The Case of the Lost Cause', Watson. I'm afraid it is over before it begins."

"Why not, Holmes?" I said. "If it is nothing, you get to tweak Lestrade's nose. If it is something, all the better."

"I suppose."

"You'll come then?" asked the constable.

With a melodramatic sigh, Holmes stood from his seat and systematically stretched each muscle until he was as limber as a prize fighter. While this went on, I donned my own coat and hat and held Holmes's at the ready. I had expected a carriage outside, but instead we were led on foot, the constable unerringly choosing the most sinister alley, the most forbidding passage, the most forsaken common, and soon we were deep within a London that I had never seen. The buildings were ramshackle piles of bricks and boards peppered with grim faces peering from the darkness within. Refuse seemed to grow like a mold upon the place, and living ghouls shuffled about, now gawking silently at the interlopers. It was as savage as the wilds of Afghanistan and it was less than a mile from where I lay blissfully next to my wife each night. My hand drifted to my pocket, but I had not anticipated the need to bring my Webley. I reconsidered the constable, but found little hope that he could protect us should these people become violent.

Ahead, I heard the familiar bellowing of Lestrade, and when we turned one last corner we saw him standing knee-deep in a pile of clothes which appeared to have spilled from the back of the caravan. A scrawny fellow paced back-and-forth while protesting to Lestrade his right to conduct legal trade. Two more men of remarkable stature stood silently in the background. They turned towards us with the blank eyes of sharks as we approached. Normally, toughs like these would be wound up for a fight, but these two seemed completely indifferent to our presence. In their pugnacious assessment, we did not rate as a threat, and I was forced to agree with them. This expedition had gone very poorly, and I silently assigned much of the blame to Lestrade, who had drawn us into this sinister tableau without consideration or warning.

"Mr. Holmes at last!" Lestrade cried. "Will you look at this? Do you see?"

"There is nothing to see, Inspector," I said. "It is just laundry."

"Precisely!" exclaimed Lestrade.

"Did you expect to find something else when you waylaid a laundry van?" Holmes asked, prodding at a pile of cast-off garments with the toe of his boot.

"Don't play coy with me, Mr. Holmes," Lestrade said. "If I can see it, you can too."

"See what?" I said. Our presence seemed to have renewed the interest of local denizens, and we were slowly being hemmed in by the gathering crowd.

"The laundry!" Lestrade said.

"Yes, Inspector, we all see the lovely laundry." I said. "Well done. Perhaps it is time to put in for a holiday."

"Don't be too hasty, Watson," Holmes said.

"You think there is something to this, Holmes?"

My friend shrugged. "You know my methods."

I could feel dozens of pairs of eyes watching me now. I cleared my throat and drew myself up before stepping through the cast-off clothing with as much dignity as I could muster. I walked 'round the carriage, kicking the wheels and buffing the painted name on the side with my cuff. I took the cart horse's head within my hands and examined its muzzle, as if that would tell me something. While it was true that I was playing for time in hopes the solution would leap to my mind, I was also watching the disreputable men who had been arguing with Lestrade. It was a feint I had seen Holmes use many times – poking and prodding in hopes of provoking a reaction from the criminal. The small man simply sneered and his comrades remained stoic in the face of my investigation. I walked around the far side of the cart and finally looked inside. It was a largely open space with shelves lining the sides, and a simple plank for a bench at the extreme end. It appeared that Lestrade had done a through job of dumping the van's contents out on the rutted street.

"Everything seems to be in order, aside from the laundry itself being upset," I said.

"Indeed, I'm afraid the quality of the laundering puts our own habiliment to shame." Holmes picked up a shirt and brought it close to his face.

"I believe our charwoman is thick as thieves with Mrs. Hudson, so there's little hope on that front."

"At the same time, Mrs. Eddels is quite discreet and circumspect, which suits me better than a pristine collar. There is another reason why this laundry is remarkable."

Following Holmes's lead, I plucked a white cloth from the ground, which turned out to be a lady's underbodice. Fighting back a slight blush which I knew would win Holmes's contempt, I held it up to examine it. It was so flawless as to be practically new, though I did detect a faint scent of lye. I continued staring at the delicate thing, my mind churning for any useful observation that I might offer.

"It's not anything about the laundry!" Lestrade bellowed. "It is that it is here at all! Do you think any of these blighters is paying for first-class laundry service?"

Indeed, most of those watching us were in filthy tatters and rags.

"I say!" I turned toward the small man, who was now twitching. "Where were you taking these things?"

"My clientele list is private!"

The two hulking men had now developed the clenched posture I most associated career thugs. Lestrade had been onto something.

"I've yet to see the laundry cart manned by three," Holmes said.

"I need protection in places like this," the small man said.

"If your business was legitimate, it would be cheaper and easier to avoid this kind of place altogether," Holmes said. "Finally, I've never seen a launderer dressed so poorly."

"Indeed?" asked Lestrade.

"For in that trade, the commission is also the collateral. Within a matter of months, any practitioner will have developed a most enviable wardrobe from those items left behind or left unpaid for."

"Maybe I'm too honest for that," the small man said.

"Ha!" Holmes replied. "I'm afraid both the inspector and the doctor are correct. At the same time, everything and nothing are amiss here. You'll have to let them go, Inspector."

"That's not what I brought you down here for. Constables have seen this caravan all over London in places it oughtn't be. They are up to something and I mean to prove it."

"I concur completely, but there is nothing more to be gained here. Send them on their way."

"Much obliged, Mister Holmes," the small man tipped his hat. His companions scooped the errant laundry into the back of the wagon and the whole enterprise trundled off.

"Shouldn't we follow them, at least?" Lestrade asked.

"They won't do anything incriminating while we are trotting after them. Besides, the laundry's address was painted right on the side of the van. Keep an eye on Upper Camphor Street, Inspector."

"That's it?"

"I'll make some inquiries of my network. I have the feeling we see that petite gentleman in cuffs yet."

"You had better be right," Lestrade said, spinning on his heel and disappearing into the murky byways beyond.

The constable quickly trotted away behind him. Holmes and I were suddenly very much alone beneath the weight of a hundred feral gazes. I brought my shoulders back, hoping to look as imposing as possible. Holmes took a moment to survey the crowd before smiling to himself and, much to my surprise, moving to throw open one of the dilapidated doors on the edge of the square. The action sent a ripple through the onlookers. Holmes stepped through and now I was left on my own. To follow Holmes in would be to make myself subject to whatever might lie inside, and perhaps worse, it would likely trap us in. Yet I didn't much fancy my chances of retracing our path here, nor of being allowed to egress unmolested. I made up my mind and strutted right into that mysterious void whence Holmes had disappeared. I was relieved to see there was a bolt and, as quickly as I could, I closed the door and shot it home. Rarely in London does one experience true darkness, but in this place it was absolute.

"Holmes?" I rasped.

There was a burst of light in the distance, which after a moment I reconciled as a struck match held by my friend.

"This way, Watson, but carefully."

"Are you mad?" I protested. "It will be trivial for that lot to wait us out. Or worse, break down the door. We could have made it out the way we came in."

"Many of those poor souls are little more than animals, relying on instinct. The moment they saw us as prey, they were not going to let us go. We may have gotten a block or so, but they would have gotten us before we left their territory."

"Let's hand over our valuables and be done with it. Better that than our lives."

"I fear it would not be so simple. The calculations of life and death are different here than what we are accustomed to."

The light between Holmes's fingers fizzled, but I had a bearing now. Carefully I slid my feet forward until I could see his shape in the void.

"What do you mean to do then?" I asked.

With a horrible wrenching noise, Holmes pried up a section of the floor. A fetid earthy breeze now washed over me.

"London is a city built on a city built on a city," Holmes said. "In these raw places, the strata are thinnest."

"How did you know to look here?"

"The masonry is characteristic of the old wards. These secret passages were common means of circumventing quarantine during plague. The resurrection men made free use of these contrivances as well. I have an atlas of that macabre trade back at Baker Street."

The door by which we had entered splintered and buckled, casting an ominous pillar of light into the room.

"Quickly!" Holmes hissed.

I scuttled through the opening and Holmes followed, letting the trapdoor close as quietly as possible.

"How far do these tunnels go?" I asked.

"They are the streets of Old London, so as far as we need them to."

"Have you been down here before?"

"Not in some time."

As my eyes adjusted, I was surprised to find myself in a brick lined passage, and indeed the building above appeared to be an extension, almost like a turret.

"All of this is just laying abandoned down here?"

"It is not abandoned by any means," Holmes replied. "I suggest we step quickly."

We walked for several minutes through eerie silence before Holmes tugged at my sleeve and led me up an almost impossibly tight stairway, which let out upon an alley. Following the city noises to the street, I was amazed to find ourselves in front of Grant and Son.

"Holmes, I had my watch repaired here just last year!"

"You might have done as well fixing it yourself," Holmes scoffed.

"Do you think they know?"

"I shouldn't think so. Open portals like this are well-kept secrets. There are a thousand of these, long-since boarded up and bricked over. Only a scant few remain passable."

With that we made our way back to Baker Street, Holmes turning the curtain in the bow window to signal the Irregulars that they were wanted. By the time we had our tea, Samuel had appeared. He was chief among the Irregulars, a post that seemed to change every few years as the unfortunate children progressed from street urchins to whatever fate lay before them. I know that Holmes would discreetly exert his influence on behalf of those he felt held the most promise. He charged the boy with observing the laundry wagon, and most of all putting a name to the driver.

Shortly thereafter, Holmes noted that there was no immediate action to be taken and he suggested that I return home.

"If I keep you past your curfew," he observed, "I'll not see you again for a month."

With assurances he would not do anything that would put himself in jeopardy without summoning me first, I went home with my head spinning and an unquiet feeling in my stomach. Thus it was that I expected the worst when my wife prodded me awake to tell me there was a policeman at the door. It was the constable who had come to Baker Street yesterday.

"What is it?" I cried. "What has happened?"

"I'm meant to fetch you to the police morgue, Doctor Watson."

I clutched at the doorway as the world seemed to tilt suddenly.

"Is it Holmes?" I gasped.

"Of course, sir," the constable replied.

"*Of course, sir?*" I bellowed. "Of course it is, that dashed fool! I knew I should never have left him alone last night! Curfew, indeed."

"Are you coming to see the body, Doctor Watson?"

"Certainly, though his brother Mycroft is his next of kin. Probably can't pry the man away from Whitehall, even for this."

"I wouldn't know about that, sir."

This time there was a police carriage, and we rode in silence, for I was adrift on a sea of remorse and self-recrimination. I was a bit taken aback to see that it was business as usual at the Yard. Holmes had not been one of that fraternity, but I would have thought him dear enough that his passing would warrant at least a pause in the business of this place.

"Ah, Doctor Watson," Lestrade said as I descended into the morgue. "Have a look, won't you."

The inspector's glib manner rankled me, but every thought was stilled by the rough white laundry sack sat upon the exam table at the center of the room. The tiled floor felt as if it dropped out from beneath me as I stepped forward, and my hands trembled uncontrollably. Close upon it now there was the unmistakable odor of human death. I fumbled at the neck of the bag as I tried to open it. Steeling myself, I uncinched it and cast a steely gaze upon the tragic contents.

"This isn't Holmes!" I said.

"Of course not," Holmes laughed. "Why would it be?"

I turned to see my friend perched on a stool at the coroner's desk, papers adorned with dark smudges spread out before him like painter's palettes.

"The police came and told me I had to come down here to see a body," I stammered. "I was told it was you!"

"It was Mr. Holmes that *sent* for you, Doctor," the constable offered.

"I insisted upon it," Holmes said. "As per our agreement."

"I thought . . . you were . . . I've got my nightshirt tucked into my pants like a fool."

"I didn't want to say anything," Lestrade said. "Since you have fallen back on writing, I thought you might have gone a bit eccentric. Hard times can do that to a man."

"I have not fallen back on writing," I said. "I'm quite successful, I'll have you know. Never you mind. Is there reason beyond abuse that I have been dragged out of bed?"

"I don't think you can complain about having been drug out of bed mid-morning," Lestrade muttered.

"Was the message not clear?" Holmes asked. "I would like you to examine the body."

"That is what I told him," the constable said.

"My dear Watson likes his intrigues," Holmes said. "Does this poor fellow remind you of anyone?"

"It is a bit hard to get at him like this," I said. "May I cut the bag?"

"Of course," Holmes said. "It has revealed to me all of its secrets."

"Hold on a minute," Lestrade said. "I'm the Inspector here and that's my evidence."

We stood about for a moment.

"I suppose the next step is to cut open the bag," Lestrade conceded.

Holmes produced a jackknife.

"No need to dull a scalpel," he observed.

The blade was more keen than any I'd ever wielded. The rough cloth parted like water, and inside was a man curled into a ball, packed in tight with fresh laundry.

"A transient, like the ones we saw earlier?" I said.

"So it appears," Holmes replied.

"Body snatchers?" Lestrade asked.

"I think he was alive when he was stuffed in the bag," I said.

"I agree," Holmes said. "This man suffocated in the bag."

"How?" Lestrade asked. "He looks hearty enough to me, and I don't see any sign that he struggled."

I pulled back his eyelid and say the trademark dilation and glassiness. "This man was plied with laudanum."

"Poisoned?"

"Surely the effect was meant to be purely soporific," Holmes said. "It is a needlessly complex scheme otherwise."

"Slavery, perhaps?" Lestrade said. "Selling off transients to foreign merchant ships and the like."

"True press ganging is rare anymore. A penny of opium would save you a pound of bother. Observe your fingers, Watson."

The grime on the man's face had easily transferred to my own. It was less ground-in grit and more like a paste.

"Makeup?" I conjectured.

"Expensive makeup at that. I've narrowed the source down to a couple of likely candidates. Note also his shoes. While somewhat worn, they are expertly constructed – in Naples if I don't miss my guess – and that pair is worth as much as every other shoe in this building combined. I'll hazard much the same can be said for his undergarments. We've all seen our fair share of the disenfranchised. Apply your senses once again, gentlemen."

We all stepped forward to look at the figure now laying slack upon the table.

"There's no smell," I said.

"There is a bit of an odor," the constable replied.

"Of death, but not of vagrancy," Lestrade said.

"While his costume looks the part, the clothes he is wearing are as cosmetic as his face."

"You are thinking of Neville St. Clair," I said. "The man with the twisted lip."

"There are superficial similarities," Holmes said, "But also significant points of departure. St. Clair essentially lived a double life.

When he was Hugh Boone he was a vagabond – his clothes were filthy, his weather-beaten features were real, and so were the begged coins in his pockets. This gives every indication of pure costume."

"Perhaps a pantomime," I said.

"I commend that possibility to your attention, Lestrade. It might explain the makeup, and the laundry service, and perhaps even the strange locations we know that laundry van to have been."

"You sound unconvinced, Mr. Holmes," Lestrade said.

"That eventuality does little to explain how this man came to be suffocated in this bag."

"Those theatre folk get up to all sorts," Lestrade offered.

"I leave it in your dogged hands then, Inspector. I can suggest a few cosmeticians who might have concocted the makeup. Kindly leave my name out of it, as I still avail myself of their services on occasion."

"And you, Mr. Holmes?"

"I want to know what this laundry business is all about. Leave that to me for the time being."

When we returned to Baker Street, we found Samuel waiting on the stoop.

"Did Mrs. Hudson leave you out here on the street?"

"If I go in, she makes me scrub every inch of myself until I shine like a penny."

"That sounds quite beneficial to me," I said.

"Right, well, if you live out here, it ain't a favor. Besides, then she just sets there and looks at me all queer, like I'm going to make off with the silverware if she takes her eyes off me."

"I'm afraid she has had some experiences along those lines," Holmes said. "The Irregulars have come in all stripes, like any other men. What did you discover?"

"The bloke's name is Peter Grande. He's a sharpie from down south."

"Peter Grande, eh?" I said. "A pseudonym surely. He's not any taller than Samuel here."

"Still," Holmes said, "it is something with which we can work. Anything else?"

"That laundry van don't go where it says on the side. It spends the night in a warehouse down in the docks."

"Slavers after all," I said.

"It don't go the right way," Samuel said.

"It doesn't?" Holmes replied.

"They pick up the laundry in posh places like Chelsea and Kensington, but they deliver it to places like Barking and Islington. Then they take it back again, one bag at a time."

"We saw the back of the wagon," I said. "It was stocked full of laundry."

"I'm telling you they only ever touch the one bag."

"How can you be sure?" Holmes asked.

"Because it is heavy. They've two large lads carrying it, and between the two of them they still staggar about."

"The bag is always heavy?" Holmes asked.

"As far as we can see."

"It begins to take shape," Holmes said. He pressed a handful of coins into Samuel's hands. "See that your comrades are well compensated."

The boy scampered off and we continued inside. "What is taking shape, Holmes?"

"Clearly the bogus laundry service is being used to transport people back and forth, but I now suspect it is with their consent. You were very near the mark when you suggested that there was a bit of theatre at hand."

There came a knocking at the door. Moments later, Mrs. Hudson appeared on the landing. "One of your gentleman friends, I presume, Mr. Holmes."

"Thank you, Mrs. Hudson. Please send him in."

The figure that replaced her in the doorway was almost comic in his appearance and tragic in his mein. He wore a collection of the finest cashmeres and silks I had ever laid eyes upon, but in a riot of colors and patterns, like he was the King of the Fortune-tellers. Likewise, his hands were gnarled and cracked, yet his swarthy face was as cleanly-shaven as a politician.

"Now this," Holmes said, "is a genuine launderer."

"You must be Mr. Holmes," the man replied. "My name is Aldridge."

"Please, Mr. Aldridge, have a seat. I take it that recent events are far beyond what you bargained for."

"Ha, I certainly wouldn't call it a bargain, Mr. Holmes. It seems that you know all, just as they say."

"It is a simple enough deduction when a man shows up on my doorstep the same day his business is implicated in a murder. You know that things look bad for you, and you fear that the police will find just enough to stop looking once they have you in cuffs."

"A murder?" Aldridge cried.

"Did you not know that a dead man was found in one of your laundry bags early this morning?"

"Oh, this is terrible news!"

"But news to you nonetheless. Why are you here, if not for that?"

"There is no use in trying to hide any of it now," Aldridge said. "I am afraid I am at the mercy of very bad people, Mr. Holmes."

"Including Peter Grande."

Aldridge was completely shaken by the mention of that name.

"It is true, Mr. Holmes, Grande is the devil in my home. My family have been in the laundry business for generations, but times are changing and we needed to change with them. We were no longer able to make a living with only a handful of workers, each with only a handful of clients. Laundry, like all things, is becoming a business of scale. We needed a commercial building, and washing machines and wagons and horses and so on. We took out a small loan and were able to quickly pay it back."

"From a private financier?" Holmes asked.

"English banks still see me as a foreigner, although my British roots run as deep as yours. With our contacts and reputation, we quickly needed to expand our business again, and then again. It was this third expansion that was our misfortune. We were successful enough that our benefactor accepted shares in the business as collateral. I was blind to the conflict of interest in that arrangement. I thought we both only benefited if the laundry business was successful. My whole livelihood was wrapped up in it.

"Of course, to Lord Mickleton – my creditor – my business was but one small cog among many. I honestly believe that he managed events so as to ruin my business. I found I was unable to make good on my debts, even as I was busier than ever. As one default followed another, my business fell under his control. Suddenly he had his own men running their own side business, but with my name plastered all over it. That was when Peter Grande appeared. He slinks around my family, making thinly veiled threats towards me, and taking an interest in my wife and my daughters that I can only describe as loathsome. Yet I am shackled to the whole business."

"Why have you have chanced coming to me?"

"Mr. Grande has a strange venture indeed," Aldridge said. "I've justified looking the other way because it has been harmless, up to now."

"What has happened?"

"While I'm not sure I fully understand it, I know Grande was secreting people in and out of certain neighborhoods. To what end I'm not sure, but he used my carriages to do it."

"Why would he do that?"

"I'm speculating, of course, but I can tell you no one looks twice at a laundry cart, and we go everywhere in London."

"Surely not everywhere," I said.

"You would be surprised at the strange little hideaways the well-to-do have secreted away all over."

I thought about Holmes's claim to have five or six boltholes about London. I could not imagine him sending out for laundry service, but then again, I was certain that Sherlock Holmes did not do his own washing. What an interesting profession laundry suddenly became to me. Holmes smiled behind his tented fingers as if he were reading my thoughts.

"In any event, one of my tasks was to clean Grande's special laundry. The bag associated with his personal business. Every week or so there would be a collection of rags covered in filth and paint, and I would personally launder them."

"But not today."

"Grande's special van just went out last night. It shouldn't have been back for days. When I asked why it was here, he told me to mind my own business, so I left it alone, but the situation nagged at me through the night. I came in early to take a look at the wagon and I found the smoldering remains of a fire in the street."

"He burned the wagon?" I gasped.

"No, but in the coals were remnants of clothes I had never seen before. A young woman's clothes. Why would Grande be burning those? If nothing else, they would be worth a few pounds. They must be evidence of a crime. Now you tell me there is a dead man? It must be true. Grande has done something awful and I am ruined!"

"Have you seen Mr. Grande, since? Or his colleagues?"

"No, Mr. Holmes, but I came here straight away."

"Return to work under the pretense that you know nothing, or failing that, that you only know what rumors you have heard being called out by newsboys. Cooperate fully with the investigation, but leave your suspicions with me. You only know Lord Mickleton and Peter Grande as unpleasant business partners. We'll look into the possibility of a missing woman."

"Thank you, Mr. Holmes!"

After Aldridge had retreated I turned to Holmes. "What are you playing at?"

"As it stands, there is an exposed incident, and a secret one. The first was clumsy, the second calculated."

"You hesitate to say murder."

"I think the nature of the first incident is unresolved. However, the disposition of it is suggestive. I'll wager that Peter Grande is not a squeamish man. Had that body been a victim of his, I doubt we should have seen it again. He is already in the human smuggling business. Yet that dreadful sack was found discarded on the side of the road."

"Was it? Then why is Lestrade so sure it came from one of Aldridge's wagons?"

"Witnesses saw the bag being dumped from a moving carriage with Aldridge's name on it."

"That does seem a bit sloppy."

"So sloppy that I'd assume it was a frame-up without Aldridge's own testimony. No, I think Grande's helpers panicked when they found that the man had died and dumped the sack from the back of the wagon while Grande was up top driving. By the time Grande realized their horrible mistake, it was too late to recover the body. So he burned what evidence that he could and hoped that no one was the wiser."

"What of the woman?"

"We know nothing of her or that she existed. A challenge even for me, but certainly far beyond Lestrade, and so there is no need to tip our hand. It seems that Lord Mickleton, who is behind all of this, is a cunning villain, and I mean to catch him wrong-footed. While all eyes are looking one way, we shall look the other."

Soon we were outside the address that Samuel had provided. I tightly gripped my Webley in my pocket, but Holmes assured me the place would be abandoned. While at first glance it matched the slapdash riverside constructions around it, the windows had been newly boarded up and the doors were perfectly plumb in reinforced jambs. Holmes approached and began feeling his way around the door. With a shake of his head, he then began knocking along the wall.

Looking up and down the street, I quietly freed my gun from my coat. I expected a gang of surly toughs to come bursting out at any moment. Instead I watched Holmes make his way around the corner before stopping to kneel down. He hooked his fingers under the lower edge of the siding and began wrenching at it. After a few sharp tugs, the board worked free. We heard muffled screams inside.

I rushed forward and the pair of us made short work of the next few boards, allowing us to enter. The low hole we had just made was the only source of light. I was momentarily startled when I saw a figure lurking with a gun on the far side of the room before I realized that I was seeing myself in a mirror. At the rear of the space, a woman was bound to a post. She thrashed and wheezed at us, and I slowly approached her while making calming gestures. Holmes had turned to the doors, throwing the bolts and lifting the cross-arm. When he pushed it open, the light revealed a strange place.

It was primarily a stable, with hitch and tack, mounds of hay, and a trough still full with water. And yet there was a corner laid with a fine oriental rug, and upon that two polished wardrobes and a vanity that might have come right from the Savoy. No less than four gas lamps surrounded the small space and several canisters were piled high. I put my Webley in my pocket and again made calming gestures towards the lady. Gently I slipped the gag from her mouth and she drew in great gasping breaths.

"Where is he?" she demanded.

"Who?" Holmes replied.

"My fiancé, Ronald Sumerton. He was with me."

"I'm afraid – " I began.

"I'm afraid you are the only person here," Holmes interrupted. "Do you know how you came to be here?"

I worked at the knots of the rope as she spoke.

"No. Well, I know a bit."

"Please," Holmes gestured.

"Ronald hired a driver to take us on a trip," she said with a moment of hesitation.

"Was this your intended destination?" Holmes gestured. The woman's gaze drifted to the floor. "A strange kind of elopement," he added.

"How did you know?"

"When a young man and a young woman run off in secret, what else can it be?"

The rope fell to the floor and she followed. Holmes offered his hand. "Miss . . . ?"

Her jaw clinched for a moment but then she said, "Vidalia Hayes." She rubbed her arms to work blood back into them.

"Miss Hayes, why did you resort to this most unusual scheme?"

"I don't see how that is your concern, Mr. . . . ?"

"Forgive me. I am Sherlock Holmes, and this is my colleague, Doctor Watson."

"Is this part of it? Ronald was so secretive about it."

"Part of what?" I asked.

She screwed up her face before saying, "Thank you for your assistance, gentlemen. I hope I can rely upon your discretion."

"There will be no worries there, love," a voice said from the doorway. "Dead men tell no tales."

Grande was there, laughing, flanked by his fellows.

"We just wanted to see to the girl. What a pleasure to find a plump hare caught in the mousetrap. It weren't nothing to buffalo the Yard, but Lord Mickleton was concerned when he heard Sherlock Holmes was involved. Turns out you were just smart enough to get yourself killed. Ta." With that he struck a lucifer and tossed it into the hay. As I stomped at that, the doors were thrown closed. Holmes threw himself against them to no avail.

"Barred from the outside somehow," he said.

We could hear the popping and cracking of burning wood.

"They've set the place on fire," I said. "Are they mad?"

One of the beams above us shuddered and collapsed.

"A question for another time," Holmes replied. "Quickly, back out the side!"

We turned just in time to see a flaming bottle shatter in the gap we had created, igniting the whole opening.

"There must be another way out!" Holmes declared. "A rat like Grande never traps himself in a dead end. That's it!" Holmes threw back the corner of the rug, revealing a trap door.

"This must be part of the show!" Vidalia said. "Look, this is really unnecessary! Just take me to Ronald."

"This is no show, Miss Hayes!" Holmes said. "Down you go!"

She was poised to continue her protest but Holmes swept her up and leapt down into the darkness. I grabbed the nearest lantern and followed, closing the door above us. I lit the wick and we moved further down the tunnel, fearing a fiery collapse. We found ourselves entombed in dirt.

"This makes the last passage look absolutely palatial."

"Most of the network looks like this," Holmes said. "No one is paving the warrens of sailors and fishmongers. Quickly!"

Where the other tunnel had seemed almost sterile, this one was fecund, a riot of roots and mosses and stagnant puddles beneath our feet.

"It is a funny thing how our steps echo down here," I said.

"What's that?" Holmes asked.

"I mean, the dirt floor, all the foliage, should act as dampeners, but our steps are echoing up and down the tunnel."

"Those aren't echoes," Vidalia hissed.

"But that would mean we're . . . surrounded," I sighed.

Almost as if sprouting from the walls, dark figures emerged at the edge of the lamplight, both before and behind us.

"Who are you people?" Vidalia cried. "What do you want?"

"You shouldn't have come here," said one of the figures, with an accent I couldn't quite place.

"We don't want to be here!" Vidalia said. "There is a madman chasing us!"

The shadowy figures guffawed.

I had my revolver pointed at the group behind us as Holmes squared off against the shadows in front.

"We don't want any trouble," I said. "Just let us go and we'll not trouble you again."

I found my arm wrenched around hard and my wrist on the point of breaking. My hand went involuntarily slack, and Peter Grande suddenly had me at the mercy of my own weapon.

"How?" was all I could muster.

Then they were upon us, and I soon found myself pinned to the earthen wall while Holmes was being dragged to the floor. For a moment, I was agog at the possibility that all of our adventures should end under these truly bizarre circumstances when Vidalia suddenly sprung into action, seizing my Webley from an unwary Grande. She waved it around frantically.

"You let me go! You let me go this instant!"

"Don't shoot!" I pleaded, but to no avail. Grande grabbed at the gun and she pulled the trigger, missing over his shoulder but deafening us all in the confined space. My attackers dropped away and I cupped my ears, staggered by the concussion. Vidalia was scrambling down the tunnel wildly. "Don't shoot!" I begged again. She tripped and, in a complete panic, let off three more shots. My stomach churned and my vision swirled. Holmes was able at last to lunge forward and disarm her. I turned to see Peter Grande looming with a knife. Reflexively I put my knuckles to his jaw and he dropped. The four of us appeared to be alone in the tunnel now. Holmes was saying something to me but I couldn't hear over the ringing in my ears. He gestured at Grande and I nodded before slinging the man over my shoulder. It was no minor effort to haul him out, but Holmes soon had us above ground again, where the area was crawling with police on account of the fire. The villain was in metal cuffs before he awoke.

At Scotland Yard, Holmes explained how Peter Grande, working for Lord Mickelton, had contrived the unique scheme to secretly move people around London, carrying them for hire in hidden laundry bags – both for legitimate and illegal purposes. He broke the sorry news of her fiancé's death to Miss Hayes, relating how the the accidental smothering of Ronald Sumerton, innocently attempting to get her away from her parents, had resulted in all the events that followed, including her subsequently being kept prisoner. He could be inimitably sensitive and kind when the occasion called for it. I think Miss Hayes already had her suspicions, for she showed great resilience upon learning the truth. She was adamant upon the point of not returning to her parents, but Lestrade would not hear any objections and had soon sent a constable to fetch them. While he was out of the room, Holmes whispered to her and then demanded loudly to speak directly to the Commissioner. In the resulting confusion, Vidalia slipped away.

"This is unbelievable, Mr. Holmes!" Lestrade said when he discovered the subterfuge. "I'll have you in stocks for this!"

"On what basis?" Holmes asked. "Miss Hayes is an adult who has committed no crime. She was under no obligation to stay here."

"So you send her out on her own, do you? She doesn't know her way about out there. She won't last a week. And what of her parents?"

"What of her parents? Do you not find the lengths to which she went to escape them suggestive? And yet you would condemn her to return to their dominion?"

"What do you know of parents and children, Holmes?"

A wry smile crossed my friend's face. For all I knew about his parents, he and Mycroft were orphans. Had he too escaped his familial shackles?

"In any event," Holmes said, "she is no longer present." He produced a calling card. "I will meet with the parents tomorrow and we will see where the business stands."

"But they are on their way here now."

"I will meet with them tomorrow or not at all. Only I know of Miss Haye's whereabouts, and even then only for the moment."

As we exited the Yard, Holmes waved away my many questions, asserting simply that all would be clear soon, and entreating me to be present at Baker Street at the appointed time tomorrow.

The next morning found Holmes draped across his favorite chair with an impish glee twinking in his eye. Mr. and Mrs. Hayes were stomping around the sitting room, taking turns in hurling invective at Holmes. Near the door shrugged a sheepish Inspector Lestrade, who I imagine had spent much of yesterday enduring a similar onslaught. At long last the pair seemed to run out of steam.

Holmes flicked open *The Daily Mail*. "I see here you have offered a reward for the safe return of your daughter."

"What else can I do?" Mr. Hayes bellowed. "A perfectly respectable girl goes missing for days, presumably in the clutches of this blackguard Ronald Sumerton. The police finally rescue her and you, a charlatan and a cad, secret her away. I can't poke my nose in every dark corner of London, and clearly men of your ilk cannot be trusted. Fifty pounds will buy me every pair of eyes in the city, and I consider that cheap."

"It is a certain kind of father that spares his wallet when searching for his daughter," Holmes said.

"Don't you judge me, Mister Holmes! I'm a businessman and I'll pay what it takes to see the job done and not a penny more."

"May I ask why, in your opinion, Miss Vidalia ran away?" Holmes asked.

"She's a foolish girl," Mrs. Hayes said. "She always was. Got swept away with her romantic notions, no doubt. I shudder to think what abuse she has suffered at the mercy of that man."

"That man paid for his love of your daughter with his life," I said.

"I consider that cheap, too," said Mr. Hayes.

"I take it you had notions of a less romantic nature," Holmes said.

"I had the opportunity of a lifetime to expand my Oriental trade. Those foreigners still practice their savage ways, you know. A well-placed marriage in Calcutta is worth more than catching the eye of some dangling whelp from the peerage."

"An arranged marriage, then?" I asked.

"Of course. She knows not a soul on that Dark Continent."

"That sounds little better than servitude to me," I said.

"Now see here! I am a preeminent merchant in this town, and you will recognize your place, sir."

"The language in your advertisement suggests that any person responsible for the safe return of your daughter is eligible for the reward," Holmes said.

"So it is about money, after all," Mrs. Hayes clucked. "It always is with these types."

"As much as it rankles me, I will honor the reward should you effect a reunion with my daughter," Mr. Hayes said.

"I would like that affirmation in writing, witnessed by Inspector Lestrade here," Holmes said.

"The impertinence!" Mr. Hayes bellowed.

"As a businessman, you should have no objection to the formal observance of the particulars of this transaction."

"You are testing my restraint, Mr. Holmes," Mr. Hayes said.

"Let us just be through with this," Mrs. Hayes said. "Write the agreement."

"What do you have in mind then?" Mr. Hayes said.

"Nothing particular onerous," Holmes said. "Simply, '*I, Harold Hayes, affirm before witness that I shall honor my pledge of fifty pounds to any person who affects the return of my daughter, Vidalia Hayes, promptly and without reservation'.*"

"Fine, fine," Mr. Hayes said, writing the document out upon my desk.

"Inspector Lestrade, if you would be so kind as to set your signature as witness and keep safe the document."

"You are playing at a strange game, Mr. Holmes," Lestrade said as he complied.

"Do you have the cash?" Holmes asked.

"We don't walk around with that sum upon our person!" Mrs. Hayes said.

"It is held in an envelope at the National Bank, available upon reliable demand from the manager."

"The paper made us do so before it would print the advertisement," Mrs. Hayes said.

"Very good," Holmes said. "Everything is satisfactory," he called out.

After a moment of confusion, Vidalia appeared, down from my old room.

"She was here all along in this unsavory bachelor's flat!" Mrs. Hayes sobbed. "We are ruined!"

"Actually, Madame," I said, "I was as surprised as anyone to find Miss Vidalia at my own lodgings yesterday evening, taking tea with my wife, who has more of a sense of humor about such things than she must. She spent the evening quite secure in a private room of my house. My maid could testify to as much, as could my wife."

"But of course neither will," said Holmes, "for your daughter's conduct is no longer any of your concern."

"Dash it all, Vidalia, you are coming home at once!"

"I loved him, father," Vidalia said. "And he loved me, more than I thought I ever deserved. He is dead now, because of some dreadful mishap, but as far as I am concerned, you forced us into it, and you killed him."

"Be reasonable, dear," Mrs. Hayes said. "We'll talk about it when you are less hysterical."

"I will not!" Vidalia said. "I have made my own arrangements for my future, and I do not believe you shall hear from me again."

"What do you mean, dear?" Mrs. Hayes said.

"Inspector," Holmes said. "Will you see that Miss Hayes receives her reward unhindered, please?"

"Reward?" Mr. Hayes scoffed. "What reward? The girl walked in her of her own accord."

"And thus met the terms of your offer," Holmes said. "Miss Hayes, I call to your attention that it is rather difficult to recall a person from a ship that is already underway, and I have noted upon this timetable some likely prospects departing within the day." He pressed a scrap of newspaper into her hand. "*Bon voyage*, Miss. I regret that sorrow will be your traveling companion, but I hope a well-earned peace will await you in your new life."

A single tear fell down her cheek. "Thank you, Mr. Holmes."

Lestrade held the door for her and then they were gone. The elder Hayes quickly recovered and made to follow but with a spritely dash I filled the doorway.

"Get out of the way," Mr. Hayes said.

"Won't you have some tea before you go?"

In response, he seized my lapels and attempted to pull me off my feet. Having learned a trick or two from observing Holmes, I slipped his grasp and he himself ended up on the floor. Graciously, I extended my hand to assist him up, but he smacked it away and clamored up the wall.

"You haven't heard the last of this," Mrs. Hayes said as the pair scurried out.

"We weren't able to give her much of a head start," I observed.

"It will be enough," Holmes said. "Lestrade is nothing if not stalwart in upholding the law, and I dare say my own name will carry some small weight with the banker."

"Still, was it wise to advise Miss Hayes of her escape plan right in front of her parents?"

Holmes smiled. "I quite enjoy the thought of Mr. and Mrs. Hayes turning the port of London upside down in an effort to shake out their daughter."

"She will not be there?"

"Indeed, what I passed to her was in fact the schedule of trains that will take her north where she can be on a French ferry before her parents are the wiser. From there, I suggested that North America or Scandinavia were both places relatively friendly to independent women."

"Do you think she'll manage the trick?"

"I expect the memory of her beloved Ronald will carry her through the next few trials."

I regret to say that despite Peter Grande's best efforts at condemning the man who came up with the scheme of moving people around in laundry bags, Lord Mickleton escaped the inquiry mostly unscathed. In protesting his innocence, he disavowed his interest in Aldridge's business, and the eccentric launderer was so grateful he offered his services to us *gratis* in perpetuity. As I suspected, Mrs. Hudson had soon told Mrs. Eddels, who made it clear upon her next visit that she had seen far too much of Holmes's dirty laundry for him to ever consider giving his business elsewhere. Nonetheless, it was some small satisfaction to me whenever I saw one of Aldridge's wagons trundle by. As for Vidalia Hayes, I never heard another word about her. However, I did notice that Holmes's case notes for the matter moved from his cabinet to his lumber room a few weeks later, which I took to mean he considered the Bogus Laundry Affair settled.

> *"He is a big, powerful chap, clean-shaven, and very swarthy – something like Aldridge, who helped us in the bogus laundry affair."*
>
> Inspector G. Lestrade – "The Adventure of the Cardboard Box"

Inspector Lestrade and the Molesey Mystery
by M.A. Wilson and Richard Dean Starr

Chapter I

1881
or Ten Years Before the Present Time

"The evidence is nigh," said Inspector Felix Windsow, evenly. "When it is at hand, we *shall* come inside. Of that I can assure you."

Windsow stood close to the gate with his hands shoved deeply into the pockets of his coat. Sundridge stood opposite him, his face just a short distance from Windsow's. The two men were separated from one another by nothing more than the gate's thick, cast-iron bars. That, and a sense of mutual hatred that was nearly palpable in the frosty morning air.

Barrett, with his partner Walsh, stood some distance back from Windsow and watched the two men with fascination. It was, he reflected, like witnessing two lions facing off across a pond on some distant African plain.

"It is no use, Inspector Windsow," said Sundridge. "You were permitted to come onto the property when there appeared to be some possible reason to search the grounds. The only way you shall cross this gate now is if I invite you, and that I shall *never* do. In point of fact, sir, the groundskeepers are still cleaning up the muck your people left behind!"

"I shan't require your permission if I have evidence of your participation in the murder of Dr. Nowak," replied Windsow. "One scrap of it, sir, is all that I shall need."

Although Barrett could not see the face of his superior, he knew that the grizzled old Inspector was glaring as only he could. The man's eyes, Barrett knew, could be as cold and as sharp as an ice spear hanging from a country eave.

"If you insist on wasting your valuable time," Sundridge said, the mockery in his voice clear, "then I wish you good hunting . . . *sir*."

Barrett was astonished by the man's cheek. It was bold of Sundridge to challenge an officer of the law, especially one so respected as

Windsow was known to be. Still, Sundridge was a man designed by nature to overpower his opponents through implication of force, if not outright power.

The former barrister was six-feet-two inches tall at least, his head fully-crowned by hair that was still dark despite his threescore years. He had whet his teeth upon court litigation and listening hard to the workings of the guilty and the innocent. Yet, with Pounds Sterling having been the primary measure of his worth at the end of the day, it was the opinion of Windsow – and one shared by Barrett, as it happened – that Sundridge had long ago ceased to see 'guilty' or 'innocent', only 'successful' and 'failed.'

Instead of responding to Sundridge thusly, as Barrett expected him to, Windsow suddenly spun upon his heel. His gray-blue eyes had now clearly warmed from ice to frost, and finally, to their ordinary, milky calm.

Windsow nodded toward Barrett and jerked his hands from his coat pockets. "Barrett! Walsh!" cried he. "Call up the cab!"

Without a further word he walked back to his officers. His gait was loose-kneed and calm, with none of the angry stamping and snorting he had heretofore displayed for Sundridge.

A bluff, to be sure, but one that clearly had had the desired effect upon the retired barrister.

This was proven out by the Sundridge's final, arrogant words as Barrett and Walsh began to follow Windsow into the dark, curtained interior of the private cab.

"The peasants say that policemen are dirty!" Sundridge called out. "That you are all little more than common workmen who consider themselves better than their fellows!"

Barrett paused, his ever-present irritation at Sundridge's manner abruptly blossoming into unexpected anger. He paused, most of the way into the cab, and turned to point one gloved finger in the direction of Sundridge.

"A gentleman should watch his tongue," he said, "or find it bitten off . . . accidentally or otherwise."

Sundridge laughed, a sound that was coarse and drenched with contempt. "Pawns you are," he said, loudly. "Nothing but pawns for your Queen!"

"Come along now, Barrett," said Windsow, quietly. "He shall get his in time."

Chapter II

1886
or The Period Before the Beginning of the End

Time continued to pass for Barrett – but perhaps, most unfortunately, not for PC Walsh or for Inspector Felix Windsow.

The Inspector's Case, known variously to the police as "Windsow's Obsession" and to the public as "Windsow's Folly", remained one of those instances that haunts men's memories for years to come. The murder of Doctor Timon Nowak remained unsolved, but not for lack of effort by those who had been involved.

Still, the barrister named Sundridge had dared to mock the Brotherhood. More important still, the police were loath to lose against such a bloated, vile specimen of humanity as Sundridge.

So Windsow continued to watch, and the Brotherhood persisted when it could, and more time passed.

The good inspector kept his gaze firmly upon Sundridge – always watching, always hoping. He pushed himself hard, for too long and for too little reward. Until one day he became ill and was forced to retire. Only later was it discovered to be cancer which bedeviled him, and which sometimes left him bound to his bed, writhing in pain.

His case-book was still in his pocket when Inspectors Lestrade and Gregson came to call and found him slumped in his kitchen chair, dead.

It was not long after that when Barrett's partner, PC Walsh, perished unexpectedly in the line of duty, leaving behind only an angry widow.

Barrett alone remained of those who knew of Sundridge's crime and believed in his guilt as it pertained to the murder of Dr. Nowak.

But Barrett was now a shadow of his former self. He knew this to be true, because the knowledge of his station was unavoidable. Now loosed of the police force, pensioned out and invalided, Barrett sustained himself by selling eel soup from a small wooden street cart.

Not a day went by when Barrett did not think, even just briefly, of the incomplete legacy represented by his life and by the premature deaths of the inspector and his erstwhile partner.

An incomplete legacy it was, Barrett knew. The perfect summarization of several incomplete careers and one very incomplete resolution to a murder.

Nothing pokes and prods and sometimes pricks at man like unfinished business, however. It was, Barrett thought, worse than a missing tooth.

His one comfort, if it could be called that, was his possession of Inspector Windsow's case-book.

Bound in cloth and worn by the passage of time, it had been passed on to him by Lestrade, as it was a policeman's unspoken right when it came to such things.

As he pushed his rickety cart back to the shop-kitchen that he rented for a few shillings a night, Barrett held the old case-book close to his breast, and continued to think of it as he so often did.

Chapter III

1891
or The Present, Without Sherlock Holmes

The sky was as gray and cold and ominous as molten iron, but Inspector Geoffrey Lestrade suspected that the Meteorological Office would have reported the autumn afternoon as being merely "cool and unsettled."

That there were likely to be such ghastly affairs as thunderstorms and harsh westerly winds in the hours and days to come would perhaps cause them to upgrade their assessment to "cold and breezy". But somehow, he doubted that it would.

For a moment, the horrible, shifting clouds deigned to part and a brief sliver of sun shone through. It was just enough to remind Lestrade that a bright, clear world existed beyond the realm of the umbrella and the rubber Mackintosh.

It was a place, Lestrade could not help but remind himself, that seemed a world apart from the one in which he presently found himself.

Just as quickly as it appeared, the rift in the clouds vanished – driven no doubt, by the gust of sudden wind that snatched at Lestrade's umbrella and simultaneously drenched him with standing water from a large, nearby puddle.

"Bloody hell!" Lestrade exclaimed, hopping away from the cobblestone lake like a man whose feet had suddenly burst into flame.

Upon reflection, it seemed to Lestrade to be the perfectly appropriate end to an otherwise pointless day.

It had been months now since Lestrade had been "between jobs" after the Home Office had released him for duties. It had followed the last Trafalgar Square riot, and the reason he had been given at the time was "inefficient leadership".

That was the political translation of the events that had transpired. However, the truth was quite a bit murkier on the whole.

As it happened, two of the PC's under Lestrade's direction had failed to follow his orders concerning hygiene and general behavior with the ladies of East London, and thusly found themselves invalided out of the force.

Dirty, filthy, lazy – the two officers in question had been all of those things – and perhaps, Lestrade had learned later, even worse than he had known.

Still, Lestrade had attempted to set both men upon the straight-and-narrow.

His efforts had been rewarded by his temporary removal from the police force, despite the fact that the Home Office was now publicly and internally hailing all prayers of thanks for the gift from God that had removed those rotten apples from the proverbial barrel.

In the end, the men had not gone quietly. It was, Lestrade had learned, not always quite so easy to remove the rotten apples from the barrel when they have connections with the best apples in the bunch. Sometimes, even the better apples were harmed as part of the pruning away process. Painful as it could be to good men such as Lestrade, appearances must be kept.

Until his reinstatement, he had taken on a few humdrum jobs, and he could rightfully say that the life of a private-pay detective was a less than reliable form of income.

It lacked a retirement pension, for one thing, and the odds of encountering a wealthy and grateful benefactor ready to provide him with a substantial reward that he could put into the bank at three-percent interest were fairly slim, if not non-existent at best.

No, private investigating wasn't to his taste. The chaos writ within it had quite rattled his confidence. Lestrade shook his head.

Perhaps Holmes (God pardon the dead) had held some of those same fears, he thought. *What would he have said? Something that'd cut to the bone, to be sure.*

But that was then, as has been said, and this was now.

The autumn season was now growing to a close, and on the whole, Lestrade recognized that saving face for the Brotherhood could have meant far, far worse than a reduction in wages or an extended and unpaid leave of absence.

In the end it had all worked out. Lestrade was now back on the police force and he was chomping at the bit to return to full service.

As he approached the street and the house where he lodged, however, he found himself one more thinking of Sherlock Holmes – and not for the first time. London was just . . . bigger and emptier without that one man.

Lestrade could no longer walk past Baker Street without seeing that singular window, cold and dark, as if the lamp that had once resided there had also lit London's soul. Now, both were extinguished.

There had been disagreements between Holmes and Lestrade, to be sure, and sometimes even with the detective's faithful friend, Dr. John Watson. But all three men had agreed on one thing: That crimes never solved themselves.

Call him a secular, godless fool, but that was why Lestrade and Dr. Watson had relied so much upon the late Sherlock Holmes: Because he knew, and intimately understood, that it was *man* who created crime, and it was man's duty to repair the nefarious activities of his fellows.

Chapter IV

1891
or The Present, With a Case for Lestrade

As he approached his humble lodgings, Lestrade made a deliberate effort to circle around behind the house so as to enter by the back door. His intent was to put up his dripping coat and shoes and spare the front carpets. Upon entering, he was surprised to see his landlady Mrs. Collins there, waiting to greet him with a dry towel.

"I saw you coming," she said before he could thank her. "You have a guest in the downstairs. No card, but you'll be wanting to see her."

"No card? Is she alone?" Lestrade was nervous about women-callers coming alone.

"She is, and with a bad cough at that! She isn't catching, though."

"Did she say so?"

"No, but I know her. She volunteers with me at the charity hospitals from time to time."

"Who is she?"

"Hmph. She can tell you that herself."

Lestrade paused, his face half-wiped. "Mrs. Collins, is one of your friends in trouble again?"

At her frosty glare, he abandoned that approach and hastily pushed on.

"She came alone and without a card. Doesn't that mean she doesn't want a record of her visit?"

"I wouldn't know, because I'm not your guest. We'll let the two of you figure it out."

Lestrade sighed. "Very well. Anything else I should know?"

"She'll tell the truth," said Mrs. Collins, primly. "I'm not sayin' that because I know her. Dr. Watson knows her, too."

That fact made him pause. The Watsons had buried themselves into everything that could keep them busy after Holmes's death. It didn't surprise him that someone knew the doctor, of course – he seemed to know the half of London that was worth knowing.

"Charity work?" He mumbled around the towel. "Is she one of those writers?"

Everyone wanted to be a Henry Mayhew these days, without so much as volunteering a spoon in a workhouse kitchen.

He shook his head slightly. No, it would be unlike Watson to cultivate that ilk.

Mrs. Collins inhaled through her large nose. "I expect you'll be asking her the questions."

Chapter V

1891
or The Present, and The Return of the Moseley Mystery

The visitor to Lestrade's parlour wore black and sat mostly erect in one of the room's horsehide chairs, a seeming half-yard of veil fallen away from her face and pooled in her lap.

"Oh!" His guest coughed. "You must be Mr. Lestrade!" she said, upon seeing him. "We both know Dr. Watson . . . ."

Lestrade was surprised, instantly recognizing in his visitor the dusky complexion and proud nose the stamp of the Konkani people.

Over the years, a rather large lot of them had sailed over with their Portuguese patrons and the men were a familiar sight on the East docks. He had never before seen one of the women-kind.

As he took a seat in the chair opposite her, Lestrade could not help but note under the crinoline a plump woman full of strength – and yet her soft, black eyes seemed to hold a vaguely puzzled look.

"A friend of Dr. Watson," Lestrade said, "is always welcome here, madam . . . ?"

"John assured me I could see you on short notice," she blurted, clearly avoiding the opportunity to provide her name. "He said that you would understand when I say that I have very little time."

For a moment, Lestrade thought of his former friend, the late Inspector Felix Windsow, who had passed away from what was variously known as 'cancer', 'the sugar', or 'wasting disease'.

"I need you to find someone for me, Mr. Lestrade," she said. "If you are interested, that is. There is a reward attached to the resolution of my problem, and besides that, I am happy to pay you above your usual fees and expenses."

Lestrade gulped, trying to imagine the urgency that would have her discussing vulgar money fewer than five minutes into their first meeting. No card. Alone, too upset to give her name in introduction. And now money? What was he getting into?

"I would be pleased to hear your story, madam . . . ?"

"*Doctor*. Dr. Emmaline De Noon, of the School of Medicine for Women."

He blinked, taken aback by this new information. A woman physician? Truly? Lestrade's brain immediately conjured up images of hungry, shivering female medical students keeping warm with the fires of their zealotry, trying to become the next Elizabeth Garrett Anderson.

"Mrs. De Noon – "

"*Doctor* De Noon, Inspector," she corrected him, sharply.

"Right," said Lestrade. "At any rate, eh, Doctor . . . you should know that I am no longer in private practice. In fact, I recently rejoined the police force and am awaiting my next assignment."

"I understand," she said. "John mentioned those two facts to me, and that is why I am approaching you now, before you accept your new duties."

Lestrade considered her words for a moment. She did, in fact, have a point. Until he was officially assigned, there was absolutely nothing preventing him from taking on one final, private commission. He had to admit that doing a favor for John Watson as well as replenishing his depleted funds were also motivating factors.

"A reasonable thing to do under the circumstances," he said. "Please continue, Dr. De Noon."

She inclined her head slightly in gratitude. "It is my fiancé, sir. I am out of my depth and need help in finding the rest of his remains."

Lestrade had been a member of the police for quite a long time. During those years he had grown adept at reading and remembering the many salient facts of a case . . . particularly the terrible elements that one, despite their best efforts, could scarcely forget.

Still, some cases stood out more than others, and this was no exception.

As Dr. Emmaline De Noon completed her sentence, and then reached out to pick up her teacup, Lestrade felt his heart lurch, each of her words emerging slowly but with sustained force.

"You may know of him as Dr. Timon Nowak, part of what you policemen refer to as the Molesey Mystery."

Chapter VI

1891
or The Present, and Finding George Barrett

The following morning dawned as dark and foul as a murderer's heart. Rain poured down from the sky like the tears of a widow, each drop falling upon a lonely and unmarked grave.

Lestrade found himself once again hurrying through this terrible deluge, his reliable umbrella and his rubber Mackintosh coat managing to stave off the worst of the storm.

He hadn't seen much of George Barrett since his invalidation. A cordial nod on the street and a cup of eels on a damp day with a bit of fresh gossip was the long and short of it. Their friendship was allowed to exist now that rank didn't stand between them. He liked Barrett for being a good man. He respected him for keeping his wits sharp.

When Barrett opened at his knock, Lestrade was astonished at the man's appearance. Thinner and harder now, but that spark of life still glittered in his blue eyes and the pride remained in his spine even if his leg slumped after him.

"Lestrade!" said Barrett, clearly surprised to see the inspector on his doorstep.

"Barrett," Lestrade replied with a nod. "Can I have a word?"

"I was just about to sit down to my supper . . . ." said Barrett, not finishing the sentence.

That was clearly not the case, as the former officer appeared to have not had a proper meal in a very long time. It was readily apparent to Lestrade that eel soup could only carry a man so far in terms of health and vitality.

"Why don't you lock up," said Lestrade, lightly, "and come with me? I'll buy us both something to eat. I have some questions for you about one of Windsow's old cases. D'you still have his note-book?"

"Of course," Barrett said stoutly.

"Bring it along, please, if you would be so kind."

Chapter VII

1891
or The Present, and A Recollection of a Case

Lestrade preferred to make business in his favourite pub – the Malmsey Keg – it rarely shut down and was open now, serving breakfast. They were able to find a table in the back of the place, away from the other customers, and seated themselves there.

Lestrade watched as Barrett lowered himself into a chair. Pain from the moving pinched his face like a piecrust before he forced it to smooth over. Lord help us from pride, he thought, and resolved to pass a quiet word to Barrett's children about his health.

"If you would be so kind," Lestrade said, "I would like to borrow Windsow's case-book."

"Certainly," said Barrett. "May I ask why?"

"In a moment," replied Lestrade. "But first, you knew the finer details of the murder of Dr. Timon Nowak perhaps better than anyone, other than Inspector Windsow."

"And Walsh," said Barrett. "Don't forget him."

"Of course not," said Lestrade, with a shake of his head. "A tragic case."

"Yes," said Barrett, glumly, and then he was silent.

"So, Barrett, feel free to order what you like," said Lestrade. "And while you wait, I would appreciate it greatly if you would be so kind as to recount for me what you recall of the Nowak case."

"We stopped calling it that a long time before I left the police, you know," Barrett said. "Back then, we called it "The Molesey Mystery". Everyone did, actually."

Lestrade nodded for Barrett to continue.

"On August 4th of 1881," Barrett said, as if reciting from a police report, "the corpse of a naked, well-nourished white man was found floating in the eddies downstream the bridge at Hampton Court."

"In a tiny spot called Molesey Park," added Lestrade.

Barrett nodded. "Correct. The outrage from the people was thick, if you don't recall, Inspector. Molesey Park had been named after the original Molesey, and they were debating there about whether to welcome cottage hospitals for those too poor or ill to take treatment in London Proper."

"I remember that, but only vaguely," said Lestrade. "What was the core of the debate about?"

"That it would bring in undesirable elements, such as the poor and ill who could not take treatment in London Proper."

"'Twas you and Walsh discovered the corpse, eh?" asked Lestrade, although he already knew the answer. Still, he wished to hear Barrett's recollections of the events that had taken place in his own words.

"We did," said Barrett, and closed his eyes for a moment as if remembering that horrible day in excruciating detail. "Davy and I were heading to the canteen after an extra patrol. Was the Anniversary of Gibraltar, as I recall, and the parades were frightful! At any rate, Walsh spied some kiddies along the bank poking at something under the water. I shooed the little ones out of there and Davy just jumped in, thinking to save the poor soul if they might've not yet drowned."

"But it was too late . . . ."

"Aye," said Barrett, "and long before we got there. The poor, sad bloke had no head, you see? It had been lopped off, and none-too-gently."

"What happened next?" asked Lestrade.

Before Barrett could answer, the pub keeper came and took their order. After he was gone, Barrett continued his story.

"There was no clothing on the body," he said. "Took us a minute or two to realize that. The skin was bloated and falling off. Walsh figured the fish had been eating the soft parts. When he said that, I'm ashamed to say that I threw up my lunch right there on the bank."

"No shame in that," said Lestrade.

"Later on, we checked up on the case with the Inspector-in-charge, Felix Windsow. Walsh and I had both taken a sort of long-term interest in the whole thing, truth be told. The inspector told us that the corpse been identified as one Dr. Timon Nowak. Seems the body matched the same man who'd gone missing a week or two before. Same height, a similar state of health. Well-respected, too, and wealthy to the edge of disgrace. He was a cottage hospitalier, too."

"And engaged," Lestrade said, absently, "to Miss Emmaline De Noon, niece of Westminster's Consultory Hydrologist, Regnier De Noon."

"Who also happened to be the loudest voice against cottage hospitals," finished Barrett. "Inspector Windsow told us all about him."

"Felix suspected De Noon from the start, did he not?" asked Lestrade.

"Indeed," replied Barrett. "The Inspector barraged the man with days of repetitious questions. Right hammered at him, and justly so. Wasn't long before De Noon showed up at the station and confessed, babbling the whole while."

"So what happened between De Noon and Nowak? Why did De Noon attack him?"

"Over the cottage hospitals, of course. De Noon and Nowak fought like cats and dogs, or so I understand. In his confession, De Noon said he couldn't remember anything after the fight. And he certainly couldn't remember removing the late Dr. Nowak's head, much less doing away with it so thoroughly that no one could find it."

"Which was attributed to an earlier head injury," said Lestrade.

"No head, no worries," said Barrett. "That was the kind of sick joke going 'round at the time. That's what we thought, at first – or at least, that's what everyone wanted, for the whole thing to just . . . be done." Barrett sighed. "As it turned out, with Dr. Nowak's head still missing, the conditions of his will and testament would stay unfulfilled, and so the pressure was still on, at least for a while."

"Which is where Alexander Sundridge came in?"

"Yes and no," said Barrett. "It turned out that Sundridge's involvement started quite a bit earlier, in fact. According to Inspector Windsow, Nowak's will had been penned by Sundridge decades ago, when Nowak was still a lad. It was iron-clad, don't you know, and stated that his equity would not be released to his heirs until he was 'completely buried as a Christian'."

"I suppose," said Lestrade, "that according to Sundridge, this was taken to mean that the corpse must be buried with all of its body parts intact."

"Of course," Barrett acknowledged. "Which obviously included poor Dr. Nowak's missing head." He shook one finger in the air. "Remember, though, Inspector, that it was not as simple as the estate being held hostage, as it were, by a single barrister of questionable motive. Sundridge also held the esteem of the church, and that made all the difference in the world."

"Which means that as long as Dr. Nowak's remains are incomplete," said Lestrade, "then Sundridge can play with his money until time immemorial."

Just then the pub keeper returned to their table, leaving a plate of eggs and potatoes in front of Barrett and a tankard of John Barleycorn for Lestrade.

As Barrett began to eat – rather bravely considering their topic – Lestrade considered all the facts thus far.

"Tell me," he said at last, "did Windsow suspect Sundridge of any involvement in the murder?"

"Aye, of course he did," replied Barrett. "But having proof is a long stretch away from suspicion, as you know all too well."

"Indeed."

"The other thing that wasn't helping Inspector Windsow was De Noon's head injury," continued Barrett. "He was prone to daft spells in his head from time to time, you see." Barrett tapped himself on the temple. "He'd go to sleep sometimes, just like that. When he was awake, though, he'd turn mean as a rabid dog, with no warning at all. Very nasty. Did you go see him?"

"I checked on him with my sources, but he died in Dartmoor last year. I don't know how the papers missed that. They're usually the first with all the torrid gossip."

"Oh, my. Well, he was worthless anyway. Convinced of his own guilt and that was all he could talk about."

When the two men had finished their respective repasts, Lestrade paid the pub keeper and the two men departed onto the street. Standing there, looking at his old mate, Lestrade was struck by a sudden idea.

"Barrett, I have a proposition for you," he said. "I believe I may, with your help, be able to shine some light upon this case and perhaps bring closure to the widow of Dr. Nowak. Would you be interested in a commission to work with me for a time on it all?"

Barrett stuck out his jaw.

"Yes, Inspector Lestrade," said he. "I do believe that I would be quite interested in doing Mr. Windsow proud."

Chapter VIII

1891
or The Present, and An Old Case Becomes New Again

Several days passed in which Lestrade was startled at a payment from Miss De Noon. Either she had money to burn or she really did have confidence in his abilities. As soon as he could make the time he went to follow up with Barrett.

"You look tired, man," said Lestrade, noting the drawn and exhausted Barrett. "When did you last sleep?"

"Lord, I don't know. I've been going over the maps of the area – "

"Maps?" queried Lestrade. "Whatever for? It's Surrey, not Snowdon!"

"His head has to be somewhere! It's been some years since I re-read Inspector Windsow's case-book. So, then I'd forgotten he was certain – perhaps even sure – that Dr. Nowak's head was hid somewhere on his own estate."

Lestrade stopped cold. "Is that in his case-book?"

"That and more. See?"

Both men leaned over the open case-book and Barrett traced Windsow's handwritten script with his index finger.

"'*Anything tossed into any puddle in the park winds up at the lock,*'" he read aloud. "'*What with the fish ladders and men stationed to make sure the public doesn't do anything stupid . . . .*'"

"It's clear," Lestrade interrupted, excitedly, "that Inspector Windsow believed that Dr. Nowak's head – if it were there in the first place – would have rolled down there by now."

"And De Noon would have known that, wouldn't he?" queried Barrett. "He was a hydrologist, after all."

"I . . . that's a good point," Lestrade muttered. "But would that be credible in the courts? De Noon had already said that he couldn't remember a thing, but he was still sure he killed the man! We can't really ask him anything else at this point without bringing in the Witch of Endor!"

"Exactly."

"This is doomed!" Lestrade complained. "You'd need an expert to look at a skull and recognise the face it once wore. That's a rare talent."

Barrett flipped a few pages further into Windsow's case-book, read a few paragraphs, then grinned like a shark that had just discovered a particularly juicy tuna swimming in front of it.

"According to Inspector Windsow, Dr. Nowak's closest friend, Dr. Caspar Goldwater, swore that he could identify the skull if it is found."

Lestrade blinked. "That's lucky . . . did he say why the doctor was so certain?"

"Not to me, but he was damned confident, and he said that to Windsow in private."

"I'll ask him." Lestrade vowed and made a note. "Today, in point of fact."

"After you do that," said Barrett, "then we need to revisit the Nowak estate. We'll need help with that, Inspector."

"What do you suggest?" asked Lestrade.

Barrett's shark-like grin widened, if such a thing were even possible. "We'll bring in the Widow Walsh. She keeps an eye on Molesey Park, same as I."

"Hang about – What did you just say?"

"It was our case, Inspector! Back in the day, when this was all fresh and new and still foul, we would go there at Inspector Windsow's behest and watch. And spy. Then, when Davy was killed, Mrs. Walsh took over. We both just found ways to keep our business over by the Park."

Lestrade found himself grinning, too. "So, this could work, then!"

"Indeed it could, Inspector. I have to go over there anyway, you see, on account of the clean eels. Got to have clean eels for a proper bowl of soup. That's my reputation!"

Lestrade's dark eyes narrowed with skepticism.

"Which justifies you walking your little cart out of the way and into Molesey Park, instead of paying a penny-per-mile for someone to cart them to you?"

"They ain't my eels unless I've personally inspected them."

"Fair enough," said Lestrade smiled slightly, thinking of the late Sherlock Holmes, who would have appreciated Barrett's logic.

"So, given that you've spent so much time on eel-finding in Molesey Park, have you found anything useful up to now? I know you haven't been well and haven't had much time to devote to it."

Barrett shrugged. "I've learned some over these past years. Sundridge barely leaves the property at all, now that he's retired. I know that."

"And Mrs. Walsh? What does she know?"

"She knows to pay attention," replied Barrett. "She still ekes out a living buying and selling scraps of tea, coffee, and tobacco. That carries her about the neighborhood quite a bit, and she sees a whole lot."

Lestrade had heard enough.

"Let's meet. Pass the word, please? Thursday, eight o'clock sharp. My house. I'll have a joint for supper."

"I'll bring something too." Barrett smiled, and Lestrade saw genuine gratitude in the man's eyes. "My goodness, Inspector, it feels good to be able to say that again."

Chapter IX

1891
or The Present, When Lestrade Hosts an Insightful Dinner

"'Course I keep an eye out."

The Widow was small, sturdy, and plain-spoken. After speaking with her for a time, Lestrade arrived at the conclusion that, had she been born a man, the Yard would have been grateful for her application.

That is, if she even wanted such a thing. The Widow Walsh would never forgive the Met for her husband's death in the line of duty, but she condescended to speak to a few of his former brothers.

Lestrade and Barrett were about it, as far as she cared.

It was Lestrade's house, but somehow Mrs. Walsh managed to take over the meeting and reign as Chair.

"The Park's easy to get in to, and easy to leave. I do business with most of the houses. The men think they're bein' genteel by leaving that last bit of their cigars unsmoked. Reselling it's worth the effort to walk there, though, no matter what the weather."

She pushed out an aisle of discarded supper-plates and put up her tiny face-warmer pipe. The smoke had the air of Cuban Rum.

"And the tea-leaves," she continued after a moment. "No one wants . . . well, they're as wasteful with the leaves as they are the tobacco."

"Same with eels." Barrett nodded wisely.

"You buy *used* eels?"

"Shush, woman. You know that I go there to buy eels off the lads. They like to earn their own spending money as much as anyone, rich or poor. Nice, brackish water, don't you see?"

"Second-hand eels, then, not precisely used?"

Lestrade smiled at the bickering.

"Between the two of you," he said, "I daresay you know more about what goes on in Moseley Park than many of the people who live there."

"Maybe so," replied the Widow Walsh, "but my brain's not the bigger for it."

"Nonetheless," said Lestrade, "I suspect that it's going to be of great help to us. What can you tell us of Nowak's estate specifically?"

"It's much the same as the rest," said the Widow Walsh. "'Cept for the old chapel, and for all the roses."

"Which means . . . ?"

"Regency-era countrified nonsense, really. What makes the estate is the pretty stone chapel – no bigger than a hiccup. 'Twas a Catholic baptismal back in the day. Then the family converted to Protestantism, and when they did, the front became a gardener's shed and the baptismal turned into a shallow well."

"So, they needed the gardener's shed and the well for the roses," said Barrett.

"Right so," said the Widow Walsh with a grin. "Them roses were brought over from Rome by his grandfather. They're like a fancy painting, they are, and nearly as valuable as such. Dark red with petals like fine china. Brambles higher than your head, but for the side facing the road – that's all privet because nobody wants to steal privet."

"But some try," said Lestrade.

"Some," acknowledged the Widow Walsh. "But Sundridge, he has geese to guard the territory. Thieves and collectors who come from all over, wanting a rootling. He hates 'em, he does. Refuses to sell any roots or clips. Claims that's because he's the steward of the property until Dr. Nowak's conditions of the will are met and he's properly buried!"

Lestrade pursed his lip. "He doesn't keep dogs?"

"He doesn't keep *nothing* that can't feed itself. You never saw a stingier man in your life."

"So how much do the thieves manage to get from him, then?"

The Widow chuckled. "Sundridge is hit by thieves so much, he can barely leave. They rob him blind the moment he's gone. They steal the geese too. But he never reports it to the police."

Lestrade shook his head. "I wonder why that is," said he, sarcastically, and all three of them laughed shortly.

"The best part of this all," said Barrett, "is that we *know* why he's being robbed . . . and how. Some sly, shifty people have put secret signs down so anyone who knows the language knows everything about his habits."

"Mmm-hmm," said Lestrade. "Tramp signatures, eh? How wonderful that the two of you know how to read them."

"Nothing wonderful about it, lad," said the Widow Walsh. "Beefy Oliver was kind enough to give some lessons."

"Beefy Oliver? Isn't that – " Lestrade shot bolt upright in his chair. "I just ordered our Christmas geese from that man!"

"And I'm sure he'll deliver as promised!" Barrett guffawed and cracked his thigh with a slap of his palm. Mrs. Walsh snickered.

Lestrade buried his head in his hands. "I think I will definitely go over there for a look. If for nothing else, the geese."

"I shouldn't worry about breaking any laws, Inspector," said Barrett. "Remember, he doesn't report the thefts."

Lestrade sat back up. "Because he swore no policeman would ever step foot on his property without his permission. It said that in Windsow's case-book."

"He did write that," said Barrett. "And Sundridge means it."

"So I've got to do this without raising the man's suspicions."

The Widow Walsh considered his words for a moment. "I might have an idea, Inspector, that could put you on the property and get you a guided tour, too, from the man himself!"

Lestrade and Barrett stared at her, their mouths open in astonishment.

"As it happens," continued the Widow, "Sundridge's got a miserable little housekeeper named Roseen. Poor thing lost her throat to infection as a pip. Dr. Nowak saved her life and she's been there ever since. She won't leave, keeps it all up. Sundridge considers her working there to be for her 'room and board', and she won't contest him." She tapped her temple with a brown finger. "I know her from the market.

She's a simple girl, but she's not thick in the mind. If anyone knows about Sundridge and what he's done, it'd be her."

"So, she can get the Inspector inside the estate?" asked Barrett, hopefully.

"Not precisely the idea I had," said the Widow Walsh, mysteriously, and then she told them her plan.

It was, Lestrade thought, really quite brilliant.

Chapter X

1891
or The Present, When Lestrade Becomes a Thief

"That won't work, sur."

Sundridge looked up from the wreckage that remained from a looted clump of roses, the leaves scattered along with the wayward feathers of the gander intended to guard it, but which had been taken instead.

He peered past the privet and to the dirty little tramp standing on the other side, just a little way along the outer fence, not far from the gate.

A gentleman didn't stare, but this shack-a-back was the worst thing he'd ever seen in Molesey Park. His patches were falling off. The suit had been a funeral black, now spotted with blue where rain-drops had rinsed out the cheap black dye. His shoes were laced with different types of twine. His cap was slightly cleaner – stolen, no doubt. It bent and twisted in the stained hands, just under the odd little grin that Sundridge disliked on instinct.

"You are dangerously closer to trespassing," said Sundridge, without preamble. "Have a care in what you say or I'll send my dogs to you."

"Ah, sur. That's the problem. You don't have dogs. The signs say so."

"What nerve! I never posted such signs!"

"The signs of the road, sur. Marks left behind like men such as m'self. We who do wander, looking for a bit of sup for a lap o'work."

Sundridge glowered beneath a fast-forming thundercloud of comprehension. He rose to his feet and staked from his butchered roses, walking-stick high. "Make sense or beggone!"

"Down there, sur." A blackened finger pointed, guileless against the vulgarity.

Sundridge looked down, to a tiny white glyph chalked at the fence just above the tops of the grass blades. It made no sense to him – nor, he felt, would it if he looked at it from any direction.

"That's a sign uv the road. It means 'No dogs here' and '*Geese*' and '*Rich profits, use caution*'. There's more o' that like, all over th' borders."

Sundridge champed. He snarled. He'd heard of the secret code of thieves, but had never put much thought to it, nor did he ever think there was a reason behind the incessant thievings that had been his fate since taking on the duties of the Nowak Fortune.

Missing geese, roses lopped and sold on the streets, apple scrumpings and – Good Lord! – the mistletoe hunters and holly-and-ivy thieves at Christmas! All this time it had been a calculated siege!

"I'm no fool, you scoundrel. Why are you telling me this?"

"Well, it's hardly fair, is it? Them that did this, they give us a bad name! We're peaceful folk, not bullies!"

The puffed-up bragging of the little man nearly made the old barrister smile. He'd seen this sort of show in the courts.

"And I suppose you'll help me out of charity?"

"Educatin' you was the charity, sur. I c'n do something about this for a dinner. That's all."

The soot-smeared face pouted as a pipe emerged from a dirty sleeve. Snap. A plume of smoke was born.

"I'm no slugabed, sur. I've got work waitin' at the docks. A bit of dinner would get me there faster."

Sundridge didn't want to give up any of his property or part with his food, but it would be less painful if he pretended this was legitimate business.

"And how much 'dinner'?"

"Enough for this." A lidded metal pail was hoisted from his rope belt.

Sundridge thought about it. "Give me that. Now, wait here while I give it the housekeeper. Don't change any marks without me to watch."

Chapter XI

1891
or The Present, When Sundridge Makes His First Mistake

Lestrade, in his guise as the tramp, mistrusted the smug look on Sundridge's face when he came back. It looked like the one on a man who is about to play a fine joke on another.

Well, so what if he does, though Lestrade. *I'm just here to look around . . . .*

"So I'm going to open the gate," said Sundridge, arrogantly. "When I do, you'll come in and you'll show me all that you have to show me of these codes of the thieves who have been robbing me! Only when I'm satisfied that you've shown me everything will you get your bucket back, and your dinner."

Lestrade shrugged. "Agreed."

For the next hour, look around he did. Exhaustively.

It was unbelievable how many signs "sly, shifty and completely horrible people" had put on this tiny bit of land – God help whoever earned their grudges! When someone found ripe pickings, they were sure to spread the word.

Lestrade had worked in disguise many a night, and before his marriage he'd slept rough with many of the genuine tramps wandering for work. Sundridge's lack of popularity, as well as the role the late De Noon had in Nowak's death, was probably a powerful motive for this mischief.

With Lestrade's help, Sundridge soon developed an eye for the signs left discreetly over the estate: A circle split with a diagonal line meant *"Theft worth it"* and showed up with alarming frequency. A row of X's and O's under a wavy line bragged of fresh water.

"Those beggars!" Sundridge swore. "They were trying to steal my water?"

Lestrade blinked and looked around, not seeing where any water could be stolen. He was tired enough that he didn't have to pretend to be a little slow. Every new discovery created a fresh roar of the same outrage.

He gently rubbed out another rune, explaining to Sundridge that the symbol meant *"Owner is out of the house at this time"*, next to a clock-face set for nine o'clock, and a crescent.

"That means they know yer'out next Tuesday," he told Sundridge. "Since that's the last-quarter of the moon."

"They're spying on me!" Sundridge hissed. "I'll set them to rights!"

"Eh, easier to fight fire with fire." Lestrade shrugged again. "Put your own signs down."

"My what?"

Lestrade knelt and drew in the mud of the path. "This means '*Beware of dog*', and here's '*Bad food*', and '*You will get arrested*'."

Sundridge's canny little eyes slitted. "All those meanings in simple symbols!"

"Th' language is meant to be put on fast, and sometimes while running!" Lestrade laughed.

"Right. Put those down. Where every mark was placed, you put those three down!"

They were walking around the little garden-shed-chapel when the wooden door kicked open by a small clog. A too-thin woman staggered out with her arms full of wet laundry.

"Oh, beggin' yer pardon!" Lestrade stammered.

She adjusted the heavy laundry-tub in her arms, frowning slightly.

"Roseen!" Sundridge barked. "Hurry up with that! I told you to see to his dinner-pail!"

For a moment, Roseen locked eyes with Lestrade. She inclined her head slightly, which Sundridge missed, as he was still studying some of the hidden runes Lestrade had pointed out to him earlier.

She returned a few minutes later, carrying Lestrade's pail.

He took it and was shocked at the weight of it, something in it was alive . . . and it moved! He yelped and stepped back, holding the pail as far from himself as he could.

"What is this, sur?"

"Oh, Roseen's a half-wit. I told her to 'fill it up with something', and no doubt, she failed to take my meaning."

Sundridge smiled with the evilest joy the Inspector had seen from any man in years.

"Still," he went on, "we had an agreement, and I *did* put something in the dinner-pail."

If anything, the smile grew more satanic.

"Now be off with you, you laggard, or you'll feel my stick."

Chapter XII

1891
or The Present, When a Soup is More Than a Soup

"That man is an abomination!"

Lestrade's announcement was met with nods and sighs. The little detective slumped into the guest-chair and closed his eyes. "A dinner of live, raw eels! The nerve! I haven't eaten all day! I suppose I've really gotten an authentic disguise now!"

"I was about to put out a cold supper." The Widow tutted. "It'll be on-table by the time you've washed up."

"Sounds wonderful." Lestrade mumbled and staggered to his feet, his limbs feeling three yards longer from the pull of gravity. The slop-sink was closer . . . .

"How much for your eels, Inspector?" asked Barrett from behind him.

"You can have them." Lestrade growled. "Pay me back as you see fit."

"Righty-o and watch out . . . ."

Lestrade stepped to the side as Barrett pushed past him and leaned over the slop-sink. He unclipped the lid and tipped. Contents splashed, and hell slipped its leash.

"Good Lord!" Lestrade exclaimed. "They're hideous little creatures, aren't they? Are you certain you want them?"

"Oh, they'll be fine! Very tender, you know! Go have some tea and I'll sort the beasties right out! Mrs. Walsh, mayn't I trouble you for your block of ice? I'll be glad to buy you a fresh one."

Lestrade blanched and took his chair back as Barrett cheerfully conducted a clean act of murder on the counter beside the sink.

Clearly, he was a professional. In an era where most people made eels writher in salt for hours before killing, he was stubborn about the value of neatly beheading and bleeding before icing to remove the slime.

Suddenly, Barrett cried out and stiffened as if in shock. Lestrade leapt to his feet and rush to Barrett's side.

"Breathe, man!" Lestrade grabbed him by the shoulders and shook him a bit. "What is it? What's the matter?"

Gasping, Barret held up one bunched fist, the fingers now white from the strength of his grip.

Then he opened his hand.

A single gold tooth lay gleaming in the center of his palm.

Chapter XIII

1891
or The Present, When a Soup is More Than a Soup

More than an hour had passed since Barrett discovered the gold tooth lying at the bottom of the pail. It was now cleaned and rested in a sauce-dish, precious as a pearl in a clam.

Careful examination had revealed tiny characters engraved upon the inside of the tooth: *AuH$_2$O*. *Gold* and *Water*, in chemical language.

"When I spoke with him, Dr. Goldwater related to me that he signed the tooth he put into Nowak. The gold was in fair trade for Nowak's work on his wooden leg."

The Widow had loaned her magnifying glass (used for examining the worth of tea-leaves) to the cause. Using it, they could all clearly see the not only the engraved characters, but the scores where the tooth had been wired tightly to another healthy tooth.

"Roseen gave you that bucket," said the Widow Walsh. "When I spoke with her at the market, and slipped her the shillings you gave me, Inspector, I told her to send you some kind of sign when you were on the estate."

"It seems she knew what she was doing," said Lestrade.

Barrett frowned. "These are well eels."

"Obviously, yes," said Lestrade.

"Being *well* eels," explained Barrett, patiently, "then that means they need a well in which to keep them."

"Yes, you keep saying that!" Lestrade snapped.

They stared at each other, then almost as one, they spoke in unison: "The chapel!"

Chapter XIV

1891
or The Present, When Some Things End and Others Begin

Sundridge strode across the packed gravel path to the privet, stick up in outrage, as two uniformed policemen opened his gate for what was obviously a supervising Inspector waiting on the other side.

Just behind the Inspector was a very tall gentleman, smiling from ear to ear. Something about the Inspector – a wiry, short little fellow with a rather rat-like face – seemed familiar. However, Sundridge was too angry at a recognised foe to put it to mind.

"Goldwater! What is this new mischief!"

The inspector stepped between them. "Are you Mr. Sundridge, executor of Dr. Timon Nowak's Estate?"

"Yes! And I say be off!"

The Inspector's face broke into a sly smile as he held up an all-too-familiar paper to the barrister. "That we will not do, Mr. Sundridge. My name is Inspector Lestrade, Scotland Yard. I have a search warrant for Dr. Nowak's property."

Sundridge's face darkened red. Not, Lestrade noted absently, entirely unlike Nowak's prized roses.

"What did you say? On what grounds, sir?"

"I was hoping you'd ask that," said Lestrade. "For illegal confiscation of evidence. For willfully withholding information in a murder investigation. For fraud, abuse of legal authority . . . but that's all really just extra detail at the moment, Sundridge. For now, suffice it to say that you are not presently under arrest for murder or for accessory for murder. However, I would advise you to stay where you are and think of who might represent you in a court of law."

"You have no evidence!" The old man's head twisted back and forth as the bobbies made a beeline straight for the chapel and the shallow well.

Roseen ran out of the kitchen entrance, pale and wide-eyed.

Spectators were starting to gather now: Neighbors, delivery-boys, a passing eel-man, and a short little charwoman.

"Oh, but we do have evidence." Mr. Lestrade pulled out a small gold nub. "Dr. Goldwater?"

Goldwater stepped forward, his kindly face now cold with anger. "This is one of the teeth I wired into the mouth of my friend, Dr. Timon Nowak. There were four others, side by side, to repair those missing from an injury in our youth. I will be pleased to testify in court the tooth is my work."

Sundridge was paper-pale in the face of his ruin, but he stood firm. "What would I have to do with that poor man's tooth?"

"After Dr. Nowak was murdered, it was *you* who placed the head in hiding. It was lucky for you at the time that enough of him was found to close the case . . . but *not* to meet the conditions of the will!" Lestrade sneered at Sundridge. "You obstructed the law, sir. What made you think of the baptismal font as a hiding place? A sadly neglected well used to water the Nowak Roses, forgotten by nearly everyone . . . Just a small well of soft water good for roses, laundry . . . and eels in the bottom, to keep the vermin at bay."

The grubby little eel-man stepped forward then, and to Sundridge's surprise, addressed him directly.

"You'll not remember me," said Barrett, "but I remember you all-too-well, Sundridge. You have no one to blame but yourself and your evil deeds for all that is about to happen to you."

He nodded toward Roseen.

"Had you not been so cheap and unwilling to pay for her meals, Roseen might not have resorted to eating eel soup. And she might not have found Dr. Novak's tooth inside of one of them!"

Roseen stopped a few feet away, staring contemptuously at Sundridge. Because she could not speak and say the things writ so clearly in her expression, she did the next best thing . . . and spit directly into Sundridge's face.

He recoiled in horror, even as a shout of triumph erupted from the old chapel.

"It seemsthat we have succeeded," said Lestrade to Barrett.

"Indeed," said Barrett. "Felix Windsow would have been proud."

Lestrade didn't need to see what the uniformed policemen had found in the shallow chapel well, and he watched with no small measure of satisfaction as Sundridge, the once powerful man, shrank in on himself, and then staggered backwards until the privet caught his back.

Dr. Timon Nowak's missing head was, at long last, found.

> *"I think you want a little unofficial help. Three undetected murders in one year won't do, Lestrade. But you handled the Molesey Mystery with less than your usual—that's to say, you handled it fairly well."*
>
> *Sherlock Holmes* – "The Adventure of the Empty House"

Appendix:
The Untold Cases

The following has been assembled from several sources, including lists compiled by Phil Jones and Randall Stock, as well as some internet resources and my own research. I cannot promise that it's complete – some Untold Cases may be missing – after all, there's a great deal of Sherlockian Scholarship that involves interpretation and rationalizing – and there are some listed here that certain readers may believe shouldn't be listed at all.

As a fanatical supporter and collector of pastiches since I was a ten-year-old boy in 1975, reading Nicholas Meyer's *The Seven-Per-Cent Solution* and *The West End Horror* before I'd even read all of The Canon, I can attest that serious and legitimate versions of all of these Untold Cases exist out there – some of them occurring with much greater frequency than others – and I hope to collect, read, and chronologicize them all.

There's so much more to The Adventures of Sherlock Holmes than the pitifully few sixty stories that were fixed up by the First Literary Agent. I highly recommend that you find and read all of the rest of them as well, including those relating these Untold Cases. You won't regret it.

David Marcum

A Study in Scarlet

- Mr. Lestrade . . . got himself in a fog recently over a forgery case
- A young girl called, fashionably dressed
- A gray-headed, seedy visitor, looking like a Jew pedlar who appeared to be very much excited
- A slipshod elderly woman
- An old, white-haired gentleman had an interview
- A railway porter in his velveteen uniform

The Sign of Four

- The consultation last week by Francois le Villard

- The most winning woman Holmes ever knew was hanged for poisoning three little children for their insurance money
- The most repellent man of Holmes's acquaintance was a philanthropist who has spent nearly a quarter of a million upon the London poor
- Holmes once enabled Mrs. Cecil Forrester to unravel a little domestic complication. She was much impressed by his kindness and skill
- Holmes lectured the police on causes and inferences and effects in the Bishopgate jewel case

The Adventures of Sherlock Holmes

"A Scandal in Bohemia"
- The summons to Odessa in the case of the Trepoff murder
- The singular tragedy of the Atkinson brothers at Trincomalee
- The mission which Holmes had accomplished so delicately and successfully for the reigning family of Holland. (He also received a remarkably brilliant ring)
- The Darlington substitution scandal, and . . .
- The Arnsworth castle business. (When a woman thinks that her house is on fire, her instinct is at once to rush to the thing which she values most. It is a perfectly overpowering impulse, and Holmes has more than once taken advantage of it

"The Red-Headed League"
- The previous skirmishes with John Clay

"A Case of Identity"
- The Dundas separation case, where Holmes was engaged in clearing up some small points in connection with it. The husband was a teetotaler, there was no other woman, and the conduct complained of was that he had drifted into the habit of winding up every meal by taking out his false teeth and hurling them at his wife, which is not an action likely to occur to the imagination of the average story-teller.
- The rather intricate matter from Marseilles
- Mrs. Etherege, whose husband Holmes found so easy when the police and everyone had given him up for dead

"The Boscombe Valley Mystery"
NONE LISTED

"The Five Orange Pips"
- The adventure of the Paradol Chamber
- The Amateur Mendicant Society, who held a luxurious club in the lower vault of a furniture warehouse
- The facts connected with the disappearance of the British barque *Sophy Anderson*
- The singular adventures of the Grice-Patersons in the island of Uffa
- The Camberwell poisoning case, in which, as may be remembered, Holmes was able, by winding up the dead man's watch, to prove that it had been wound up two hours before, and that therefore the deceased had gone to bed within that time – a deduction which was of the greatest importance in clearing up the case
- Holmes saved Major Prendergast in the Tankerville Club scandal. He was wrongfully accused of cheating at cards
- Holmes has been beaten four times – three times by men and once by a woman

"The Man with the Twisted Lip"
- The rascally Lascar who runs The Bar of Gold in Upper Swandam Lane has sworn to have vengeance upon Holmes

"The Adventure of the Blue Carbuncle"
NONE LISTED

"The Adventure of the Speckled Band"
- Mrs. Farintosh and an opal tiara. (It was before Watson's time)

"The Adventure of the Engineer's Thumb"
- Colonel Warburton's madness

"The Adventure of the Noble Bachelor"
- The letter from a fishmonger
- The letter a tide-waiter
- The service for Lord Backwater

- The little problem of the Grosvenor Square furniture van
- The service for the King of Scandinavia

"The Adventure of the Beryl Coronet"
NONE LISTED

"The Adventure of the Copper Beeches"
NONE LISTED

The Memoirs of Sherlock Holmes

"Silver Blaze"
NONE LISTED

"The Cardboard Box"
- Aldridge, who helped in the bogus laundry affair

"The Yellow Face"
- The (First) Adventure of the Second Stain was a failure which present[s] the strongest features of interest

'The Stockbroker's Clerk"
NONE LISTED

"The "Gloria Scott"
NONE LISTED

"The Musgrave Ritual"
- The Tarleton murders
- The case of Vamberry, the wine merchant
- The adventure of the old Russian woman
- The singular affair of the aluminum crutch
- A full account of Ricoletti of the club foot and his abominable wife
- The two cases before the Musgrave Ritual from Holmes's fellow students

"The Reigate Squires"
- The whole question of the Netherland-Sumatra Company and of the colossal schemes of Baron Maupertuis

The Crooked Man"
NONE LISTED

The Resident Patient"
- [Catalepsy] is a very easy complaint to imitate. Holmes has done it himself.

"The Greek Interpreter"
- Mycroft expected to see Holmes round last week to consult me over that Manor House case. It was Adams, of course
- Some of Holmes's most interesting cases have come to him through Mycroft

"The Naval Treaty"
- The (Second) adventure of the Second Stain, which dealt with interest of such importance and implicated so many of the first families in the kingdom that for many years it would be impossible to make it public. No case, however, in which Holmes was engaged had ever illustrated the value of his analytical methods so clearly or had impressed those who were associated with him so deeply. Watson still retained an almost verbatim report of the interview in which Holmes demonstrated the true facts of the case to Monsieur Dubugue of the Paris police, and Fritz von Waldbaum, the well-known specialist of Dantzig, both of whom had wasted their energies upon what proved to be side-issues. The new century will have come, however, before the story could be safely told.
- The Adventure of the Tired Captain
- A very commonplace little murder. If it [this paper] turns red, it means a man's life . . . .

"The Final Problem"
- The engagement for the French Government upon a matter of supreme importance
- The assistance to the Royal Family of Scandinavia

The Return of Sherlock Holmes

"The Adventure of the Empty House"

- Holmes traveled for two years in Tibet (as) a Norwegian named Sigerson, amusing himself by visiting Lhassa [*sic*] and spending some days with the head Llama [*sic*]
- Holmes traveled in Persia
- . . . looked in at Mecca . . .
- . . . and paid a short but interesting visit to the Khalifa at Khartoum
- Returning to France, Holmes spent some months in a research into the coal-tar derivatives, which he conducted in a laboratory at Montpelier [*sic*], in the South of France
- Mathews, who knocked out Holmes's left canine in the waiting room at Charing Cross
- The death of Mrs. Stewart, of Lauder, in 1887
- Morgan the poisoner
- Merridew of abominable memory
- The Molesey Mystery (Inspector Lestrade's Case. He handled it fairly well.)

"The Adventure of the Norwood Builder"
- The case of the papers of ex-President Murillo
- The shocking affair of the Dutch steamship, *Friesland*, which so nearly cost both Holmes and Watson their lives
- That terrible murderer, Bert Stevens, who wanted Holmes and Watson to get him off in '87

"The Adventure of the Dancing Men"
NONE LISTED

"The Adventure of the Solitary Cyclist"
- The peculiar persecution of John Vincent Harden, the well-known tobacco millionaire
- It was near Farnham that Holmes and Watson took Archie Stamford, the forger

"The Adventure of the Priory School"
- Holmes was retained in the case of the Ferrers Documents
- The Abergavenny murder, which is coming up for trial

"The Adventure of Black Peter"

- The sudden death of Cardinal Tosca – an inquiry which was carried out by him at the express desire of His Holiness the Pope
- The arrest of Wilson, the notorious canary-trainer, which removed a plague-spot from the East-End of London.

"The Adventure of Charles Augustus Milverton"
NONE LISTED

"The Adventure of the Six Napoleons"
- The dreadful business of the Abernetty family, which was first brought to Holmes's attention by the depth which the parsley had sunk into the butter upon a hot day
- The Conk-Singleton forgery case
- Holmes was consulted upon the case of the disappearance of the black pearl of the Borgias, but was unable to throw any light upon it

"The Adventure of the Three Students"
- Some laborious researches in Early English charters

"The Adventure of the Golden Pince-Nez"
- The repulsive story of the red leech
- . . . and the terrible death of Crosby, the banker
- The Addleton tragedy
- . . . and the singular contents of the ancient British barrow
- The famous Smith-Mortimer succession case
- The tracking and arrest of Huret, the boulevard assassin

"The Adventure of the Missing Three-Quarter"
- Henry Staunton, whom Holmes helped to hang
- Arthur H. Staunton, the rising young forger

"The Adventure of the Abbey Grange"
- Hopkins called Holmes in seven times, and on each occasion his summons was entirely justified

"The Adventure of the Second Stain"
- The woman at Margate. No powder on her nose – that proved to be the correct solution. How can one build on such

a quicksand? A woman's most trivial action may mean volumes, or their most extraordinary conduct may depend upon a hairpin or a curling-tong

The Hound of the Baskervilles

- That little affair of the Vatican cameos, in which Holmes obliged the Pope
- The little case in which Holmes had the good fortune to help Messenger Manager Wilson
- One of the most revered names in England is being besmirched by a blackmailer, and only Holmes can stop a disastrous scandal
- The atrocious conduct of Colonel Upwood in connection with the famous card scandal at the Nonpareil Club
- Holmes defended the unfortunate Mme. Montpensier from the charge of murder that hung over her in connection with the death of her stepdaughter Mlle. Carere, the young lady who, as it will be remembered, was found six months later alive and married in New York

The Valley of Fear

- Twice already Holmes had helped Inspector Macdonald

His Last Bow

"The Adventure of Wisteria Lodge"
- The locking-up Colonel Carruthers

"The Adventure of the Red Circle"
- The affair last year for Mr. Fairdale Hobbs
- The Long Island cave mystery

"The Adventure of the Bruce-Partington Plans"
- Brooks . . .
- . . . or Woodhouse, or any of the fifty men who have good reason for taking Holmes's life

"The Adventure of the Dying Detective"

NONE LISTED

"The Disappearance of Lady Frances Carfax"
- Holmes cannot possibly leave London while old Abrahams is in such mortal terror of his life

"The Adventure of the Devil's Foot"
- Holmes's dramatic introduction to Dr. Moore Agar, of Harley Street

"His Last Bow"
- Holmes started his pilgrimage at Chicago . . .
- . . . graduated in an Irish secret society at Buffalo
- . . . gave serious trouble to the constabulary at Skibbareen
- Holmes saves Count Von und Zu Grafenstein from murder by the Nihilist Klopman

The Case-Book of Sherlock Holmes

"The Adventure of the Illustrious Client"
- Negotiations with Sir George Lewis over the Hammerford Will case

"The Adventure of the Blanched Soldier"
- The Abbey School in which the Duke of Greyminster was so deeply involved
- The commission from the Sultan of Turkey which required immediate action
- The professional service for Sir James Saunders

"The Adventure of the Mazarin Stone"
- Old Baron Dowson said the night before he was hanged that in Holmes's case what the law had gained the stage had lost
- The death of old Mrs. Harold, who left Count Sylvius the Blymer estate
- The compete life history of Miss Minnie Warrender
- The robbery in the train de-luxe to the Riviera on February 13, 1892

"The Adventure of the Three Gables"

- The killing of young Perkins outside the Holborn Bar
- Mortimer Maberly, was one of Holmes's early clients

"The Adventure of the Sussex Vampire"
- *Matilda Briggs*, a ship which is associated with the giant rat of Sumatra, a story for which the world is not yet prepared
- Victor Lynch, the forger
- Venomous lizard, or Gila. Remarkable case, that!
- Vittoria the circus belle
- Vanderbilt and the Yeggman
- Vigor, the Hammersmith wonder

"The Adventure of the Three Garridebs"
- Holmes refused a knighthood for services which may, someday, be described

"The Problem of Thor Bridge"
- Mr. James Phillimore who, stepping back into his own house to get his umbrella, was never more seen in this world
- The cutter *Alicia*, which sailed one spring morning into a patch of mist from where she never again emerged, nor was anything further ever heard of herself and her crew.
- Isadora Persano, the well-known journalist and duelist who was found stark staring mad with a match box in front of him which contained a remarkable worm said to be unknown to science

"The Adventure of the Creeping Man"
NONE LISTED

"The Adventure of the Lion's Mane"
NONE LISTED

"The Adventure of the Veiled Lodger"
- The whole story concerning the politician, the lighthouse, and the trained cormorant

"The Adventure of Shoscombe Old Place"
- Holmes ran down that coiner by the zinc and copper filings in the seam of his cuff

- The St. Pancras case, where a cap was found beside the dead policeman. Merivale of the Yard, asked Holmes to look into it

"The Adventure of the Retired Colourman"
- The case of the two Coptic Patriarchs

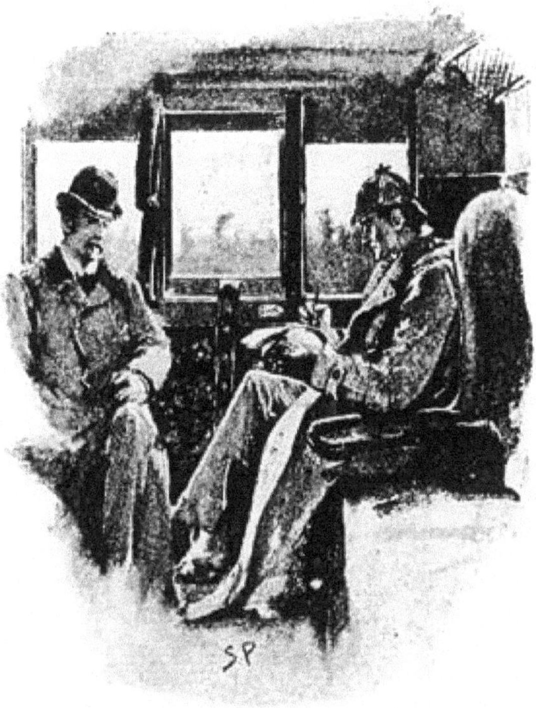
SP

About the Contributors

The following contributions appear in this volume:
**The MX Book of New Sherlock Holmes Stories
Part XI – Some Untold Cases (1880-1891)**

Hugh Ashton was born in the U.K., and moved to Japan in 1988, where he remained until 2016, living with his wife Yoshiko in the historic city of Kamakura, a little to the south of Yokohama. He and Yoshiko have now moved to Lichfield, a small cathedral city in the Midlands of the U.K., the birthplace of Samuel Johnson, and one-time home of Erasmus Darwin. In the past, he has worked in the technology and financial services industries, which have provided him with material for some of his books set in the 21st century. He currently works as a writer: Novelist, freelance editor, and copywriter, (his work for large Japanese corporations has appeared in international business journals), and journalist, as well as producing industry reports on various aspects of the financial services industry. Recently, however, his lifelong interest in Sherlock Holmes has developed into an acclaimed series of adventures featuring the world's most famous detective, written in the style of the originals, and published by Inknbeans Press. In addition to these, he has also published historical and alternate historical novels, short stories, and thrillers. Together with artist Andy Boerger, he has produced the *Sherlock Ferret* series of stories for children, featuring the world's cutest detective.

Deanna Baran lives in a remote part of Texas where cowboys may still be seen in their natural habitat. A librarian and former museum curator, she writes in between cups of tea, playing *Go*, and trading postcards with people around the world. This is her latest venture into the foggy streets of gaslit London.

Brian Belanger is a publisher and editor, but is best known for his freelance illustration and cover design work. His distinctive style can be seen on several MX Publishing covers, including *Silent Meridian* by Elizabeth Crowen, *Sherlock Holmes and the Menacing Melbournian* by Allan Mitchell, *Sherlock Holmes and A Quantity of Debt* by David Marcum, *Welcome to Undershaw* by Luke Benjamin Kuhns, and many more. Brian is the co-founder of Belanger Books LLC, where he illustrates the popular *MacDougall Twins with Sherlock Holmes* young reader series (#1 bestsellers on Amazon.com UK). A prolific creator, he also designs t-shirts, mugs, stickers, and other merchandise on his personal art site: *www.redbubble.com/people/zhahadun*.

Leslie Charteris was born in Singapore on May 12th, 1907. With his mother and brother, he moved to England in 1919 and attended Rossall School in Lancashire before moving on to Cambridge University to study law. His studies there came to a halt when a publisher accepted his first novel. His third one, entitled *Meet the Tiger*, was written when he was twenty years old and published in September 1928. It introduced the world to Simon Templar, *aka* The Saint. He continued to write about The Saint until 1983 when the last book, *Salvage for The Saint*, was published. The books, which have been translated into over thirty languages, number nearly a hundred and have sold over forty-million copies around the world. They've inspired, to date, fifteen feature films, three television series, ten radio series, and a comic strip that was written by Charteris and syndicated around the world for over a decade. He enjoyed travelling, but settled for long periods in Hollywood, Florida, and finally in Surrey, England. He was awarded the

Cartier Diamond Dagger by the *Crime Writers' Association* in 1992, in recognition of a lifetime of achievement. He died the following year.

Ian Dickerson was just nine years old when he discovered The Saint. Shortly after that, he discovered Sherlock Holmes. The Saint won, for a while anyway. He struck up a friendship with The Saint's creator, Leslie Charteris and his family. With their permission, he spent six weeks studying the Leslie Charteris collection at Boston University and went on to write, direct, and produce documentaries on the making of *The Saint* and *Return of The Saint,* which have been released on DVD. He oversaw the recent reprints of almost fifty of the original Saint books in both the US and UK, and was a co-producer on the 2017 TV movie of *The Saint*. When he discovered that Charteris had written Sherlock Holmes stories as well – well, there was the excuse he needed to revisit The Canon. He's consequently written and edited three books on Holmes' radio adventures. For the sake of what little sanity he has, Ian has also written about a wide range of subjects, none of which come with a halo, including talking mashed potatoes, Lord Grade, and satellite links. Ian lives in Hampshire with his wife and two children. And an awful lot of books by Leslie Charteris. Not quite so many by Conan Doyle, though.

Craig Stephen Copland confesses that he discovered Sherlock Holmes when, sometime in the muddled early 1960's, he pinched his older brother's copy of the immortal stories and was forever afterward thoroughly hooked. He is very grateful to his high school English teachers in Toronto who inculcated in him a love of literature and writing, and even inspired him to be an English major at the University of Toronto. There he was blessed to sit at the feet of both Northrup Frye and Marshall McLuhan, and other great literary professors, who led him to believe that he was called to be a high school English teacher. It was his good fortune to come to his pecuniary senses, abandon that goal, and pursue a varied professional career that took him to over one-hundred countries and endless adventures. He considers himself to have been and to continue to be one of the luckiest men on God's good earth. A few years back he took a step in the direction of Sherlockian studies and joined the *Sherlock Holmes Society of Canada* – also known as *The Toronto Bootmakers*. In May of 2014, this esteemed group of scholars announced a contest for the writing of a new Sherlock Holmes mystery. Although he had never tried his hand at fiction before, Craig entered and was pleasantly surprised to be selected as one of the winners. Having enjoyed the experience, he decided to write more of the same, and is now on a mission to write a new Sherlock Holmes mystery that is related to and inspired by each of the sixty stories in the original Canon. He currently lives and writes in Toronto, Buenos Aires, New York, and the Okanagan Valley and looks forward to finally settling down when he turns ninety.

Sir Arthur Conan Doyle (1859-1930) *Holmes Chronicler Emeritus*. If not for him, this anthology would not exist. Author, physician, patriot, sportsman, spiritualist, husband and father, and advocate for the oppressed. He is remembered and honored for the purposes of this collection by being the man who introduced Sherlock Holmes to the world. Through fifty-six Holmes short stories, four novels, and additional Apocryphal entries, Doyle revolutionized mystery stories and also greatly influenced and improved police forensic methods and techniques for the betterment of all. *Steel True Blade Straight.*

Steve Emecz's main field is technology, in which he has been working for about twenty years. Following multiple senior roles at Xerox, where he grew their European eCommerce from $6m to $200m, Steve joined platform provider Venda, and moved across to Powa in 2010. Today, Steve is CCO at collectAI in Hamburg, a German fintech company using Artificial Intelligence to help companies with their debt collection. Steve is a regular trade show speaker on the subject of eCommerce, and his tech career has taken him to more than fifty countries – so he's no stranger to planes and airports. He wrote two novels (one a bestseller) in the 1990's, and a screenplay in 2001. Shortly after, he set up MX Publishing, specialising in NLP books. In 2008, MX published its first Sherlock Holmes book, and MX has gone on to become the largest specialist Holmes publisher in the world. MX is a social enterprise and supports two main causes. The first is Happy Life, a children's rescue project in Nairobi, Kenya, where he and his wife, Sharon, spend every Christmas at the rescue centre in Kasarani. In 2014, they wrote a short book about the project, *The Happy Life Story*. The second is the Stepping Stones School, of which Steve is a patron. Stepping Stones is located at Undershaw, Sir Arthur Conan Doyle's former home.

Lyndsay Faye BSI, ASH is the author of a number of critically acclaimed books, including the Sherlockian volumes *Dust and Shadow*, about Sherlock Holmes's attempt to hunt down Jack the Ripper, and *The Whole Art of Detection*, containing fifteen Holmes adventures. Additionally, she has written *The Gods of Gotham*, which was nominated for the Edgar Award for Best Novel, *Seven for a Secret*, *The Fatal Flame*, *Jane Steele*, and the forthcoming *The Paragon Hotel*. Faye, a true New Yorker in the sense that she was born elsewhere, lives in New York city with her husband, Gabriel.

Mark A. Gagen BSI is co-founder of Wessex Press, sponsor of the popular *From Gillette to Brett* conferences, and publisher of *The Sherlock Holmes Reference Library* and many other fine Sherlockian titles. A life-long Holmes enthusiast, he is a member of *The Baker Street Irregulars* and *The Illustrious Clients of Indianapolis*. A graphic artist by profession, his work is often seen on the covers of *The Baker Street Journal* and various BSI books.

Jayantika Ganguly BSI is the General Secretary and Editor of the *Sherlock Holmes Society of India*, a member of the *Sherlock Holmes Society of London*, and the *Czech Sherlock Holmes Society*. She is the author of *The Holmes Sutra* (MX 2014). She is a corporate lawyer working with one of the Big Six law firms.

Melissa Granger, Executive Head Teacher of Stepping Stones School, is driven by a passion to open the doors to learners with complex and layered special needs that just make society feel two steps too far away. Based on the Surrey/Hampshire border in England, her time is spent between relocating a great school into the prestigious home of Conan Doyle, and her two children, dogs, and horses, so there never a dull moment.

Denis Green was born in London, England in April 1905. He grew up mostly in London's Savoy Theatre where his father, Richard Green, was a principal in many Gilbert and Sullivan productions, A Flying Officer with RAF until 1924, he then spent four years managing a tea estate in North India before making his stage debut in *Hamlet* with Leslie Howard in 1928. He made his first visit to America in 1931 and established a respectable stage career before appearing in films – including minor roles in the first two Rathbone and Bruce Holmes films – and developing a career in front of and behind the microphone during the golden age of radio. Green and Leslie Charteris met in 1938 and struck up a lifelong friendship. Always busy, be it on stage, radio, film or television, Green passed away at the age of fifty in New York.

John Atkinson Grimshaw (1836-1893) was born in Leeds, England. His amazing paintings, usually featuring twilight or night scenes illuminated by gas-lamps or moonlight, are easily recognizable, and are often used on the covers of books about The Great Detective to set the mood, as shadowy figures move in the distance through misty mysterious settings and over rain-slicked streets.

Stephen Herczeg is an IT Geek, writer, actor, and film-maker based in Canberra Australia. He has been writing for over twenty years and has completed a couple of dodgy novels, sixteen feature length screenplays, and numerous short stories and scripts. Stephen was very successful in 2017's International Horror Hotel screenplay competition, with his scripts *TITAN* winning the Sci-Fi category and *Dark are the Woods* placing second in the horror category. His work has featured in *Sproutlings – A Compendium of Little Fictions* from Hunter Anthologies, the *Hells Bells* Christmas horror anthology published by the Australasian Horror Writers Association, and the *Below the Stairs*, *Trickster's Treats*, *Shades of Santa*, *Behind the Mask*, and *Beyond the Infinite* anthologies from OzHorror.Con, *The Body Horror Book*, *Anemone Enemy*, and *Petrified Punks* from Oscillate Wildly Press, and *Sherlock Holmes In the Realms of H.G. Wells* and *Sherlock Holmes: Adventures Beyond the Canon* from Belanger Books.

Mike Hogan (with a story in Part XII as well!) writes mostly historical novels and short stories, many set in Victorian London and featuring Sherlock Holmes and Doctor Watson. He read the Conan Doyle stories at school with great enjoyment, but hadn't thought much about Sherlock Holmes until, having missed the Granada/Jeremy Brett TV series when it was originally shown in the eighties, he came across a box set of videos in a street market and was hooked on Holmes again. He started writing Sherlock Holmes pastiches several years ago, having great fun re-imagining situations for the Conan Doyle characters to act in. The relationship between Holmes and Watson fascinates him as one of the great literary friendships. (He's also a huge admirer of Patrick O'Brian's Aubrey-Maturin novels). Like Captain Aubrey and Doctor Maturin, Holmes and Watson are an odd couple, differing in almost every facet of their characters, but sharing a common sense of decency and a common humanity. Living with Sherlock Holmes can't have been easy, and Mike enjoys adding a stronger vein of "pawky humour" into the Conan Doyle mix, even letting Watson have the second-to-last word on occasions. His books include *Sherlock Holmes and the Scottish Question*, the forthcoming *The Gory Season – Sherlock Holmes, Jack the Ripper and the Thames Torso Murders* and the Sherlock Holmes & Young Winston 1887 Trilogy (*The Deadwood Stage*; *The Jubilee Plot*; and *The Giant Moles*), He has also written the following short story collections: *Sherlock Holmes: Murder at the Savoy and Other Stories*, *Sherlock Holmes: The Skull of Kohada Koheiji and Other Stories*, and *Sherlock Holmes: Murder on the Brighton Line and Other Stories*. www.mikehoganbooks.com

Roger Johnson BSI, ASH is a retired librarian, now working as a volunteer assistant at the Essex Police Museum. In his spare time, he is commissioning editor of *The Sherlock Holmes Journal*, an occasional lecturer, and a frequent contributor to The Writings About the Writings. His sole work of Holmesian pastiche was published in 1997 in Mike Ashley's anthology *The Mammoth Book of New Sherlock Holmes Adventures*, and he has the greatest respect for the many authors who have contributed new tales to the present mighty trilogy. Like his wife, Jean Upton, he is a member of both *The Baker Street Irregulars* and *The Adventuresses of Sherlock Holmes*.

Arlene Mantin Levy RN retired to Colorado in 2015. She practiced as a Critical Care/Trauma Specialist for thirty-eight years in Miami, Florida. During the last four years in Florida, she was a member of the scion *Tropical Deerstalkers*, and since moving to Evergreen, she and husband Mark are members of the scion *Dr. Watson's Neglected Patients*.

Mark Levy BSI is an intellectual property attorney and a member of the *Baker Street Irregulars*. He holds a B.S. degree in Physics from NYU Polytechnic University, a J.D. degree from New York Law School, and an M.A. degree in creative writing from Wilkes University. His passion is writing. He has contributed articles or letters to *The Baker Street Journal, The New York Times, The Mensa Bulletin, The Skeptical Inquirer, The Bulletin of the Atomic Scientists, Videomaker* Magazine, and *The Journal of Irreproducible Results*. His short, humorous essays are broadcast on the public radio show, *Weekend Radio*, and a collection of those polymathic essays, *Trophy Envy*.

David Marcum (who also has a story in Volume III) plays The Game with deadly seriousness. He first discovered Sherlock Holmes in 1975, at the age of ten, when he received an abridged version of *The Adventures* during a trade. Since that time, David has collected literally thousands of traditional Holmes pastiches in the form of novels, short stories, radio and television episodes, movies and scripts, comics, fan-fiction, and unpublished manuscripts. He is the author of *The Papers of Sherlock Holmes Vol.'s I and II* (2011, 2013), *Sherlock Holmes and A Quantity of Debt* (2013, 2016), *Sherlock Holmes – Tangled Skeins* (2015, 2017), and *The Papers of Solar Pons* (2017). Additionally, he is the editor of the three-volume set *Sherlock Holmes in Montague Street* (2014, recasting Arthur Morrison's Martin Hewitt stories as early Holmes adventures,), the two-volume collection of Great Hiatus stories, *Holmes Away From Home* (2016), *Sherlock Holmes: Before Baker Street* (2017), *Imagination Theatre's Sherlock Holmes* (2017), the authorized eight-volume reissues of the Solar Pons stories, the three-volume set of Canonical Sequels *Sherlock Holmes: Adventures Beyond the Canon*, and a number of forthcoming volumes including a Solar Anthology and the complete Dr. Thorndyke adventures. Additionally, he is the creator and editor of the ongoing collection, *The MX Book of New Sherlock Holmes Stories* (2015-), now at twelve volumes, with another in preparation as of this writing. He has contributed stories, essays, and scripts to *The Baker Street Journal, The Strand Magazine, The Watsonian, Beyond Watson, Sherlock Holmes Mystery Magazine, About Sixty, About Being a Sherlockian, The Solar Pons Gazette*, Imagination Theater, *The Proceedings of the Pondicherry Lodge*, and *The Gazette*, the journal of the Nero Wolfe *Wolfe Pack*. He began his adult work life as a Federal Investigator for an obscure U.S. Government agency, before the organization was eliminated. He returned to school for a second degree, and is now a licensed Civil Engineer, living in Tennessee with his wife and son. He is a member of *The Sherlock Holmes Society of London, The Nashville Scholars of the Three Pipe Problem* (The Engineer's Thumb"), *The Occupants of the Full House, The Diogenes Club of Washington, D.C., The Tankerville Club* (all Scions of *The Baker Street Irregulars*), *The Sherlock Holmes Society of India* (as a Patron), *The John H. Watson Society* ("Marker"), *The Praed Street Irregulars* ("The Obrisset Snuff Box"), *The Solar Pons Society of London*, and *The Diogenes Club West (East Tennessee Annex)*, a curious and unofficial Scion of one. Since the age of nineteen, he has worn a deerstalker as his regular-and-only hat from autumn to spring. In 2013, he and his deerstalker were finally able make his first trip-of-a-lifetime Holmes Pilgrimage to England, with return Pilgrimages in 2015 and 2016, where you may have spotted him. If you ever run into him and his deerstalker out and about, feel free to say hello!

Will Murray is the author of over seventy novels, including forty *Destroyer* novels and seven posthumous *Doc Savage* collaborations with Lester Dent, under the name Kenneth Robeson, for Bantam Books in the 1990's. Since 2011, he has written fourteen additional Doc Savage adventures for Altus Press, two of which co-starred The Shadow, as well as a solo Pat Savage novel. His 2015 Tarzan novel, *Return to Pal-Ul-Don*, was followed by *King Kong vs. Tarzan* in 2016. Murray has written short stories featuring such classic characters as Batman, Superman, Wonder Woman, Spider-Man, Ant-Man, the Hulk, Honey West, the Spider, the Avenger, the Green Hornet, the Phantom, and Cthulhu. A previous Murray Sherlock Holmes story appeared in Moonstone's *Sherlock Holmes: The Crossovers Casebook*, and another is forthcoming in *Sherlock Holmes and Doctor Was Not*, involving H. P. Lovecraft's Dr. Herbert West. Additionally, his "The Adventure of the Glassy Ghost" appeared in *The MX Book of New Sherlock Holmes Stories Part VIII – Eliminate the Impossible: 1892-1905*.

Paul W. Nash is a librarian, bibliographer, and printing historian. He has worked at the Royal Institute of British Architect's Library in London and the Bodleian Library in Oxford, and is currently editor of *The Journal of the Printing Historical Society*. He writes fiction and composes music as a relaxation.

Sidney Paget (1860-1908), a few of whose illustrations are used within this anthology, was born in London, and like his two older brothers, became a famed illustrator and painter. He completed over three-hundred-and-fifty drawings for the Sherlock Holmes stories that were first published in *The Strand* magazine, defining Holmes's image forever after in the public mind.

Robert Perret is a writer, librarian, and devout Sherlockian living on the Palouse. His Sherlockian publications include "The Canaries of Clee Hills Mine" in *An Improbable Truth: The Paranormal Adventures of Sherlock Holmes*, "For King and Country" in *The Science of Deduction*, and "How Hope Learned the Trick" in *NonBinary Review*. He considers himself to be a pan-Sherlockian and a one-man Scion out on the lonely moors of Idaho. Robert has recently authored a yet-unpublished scholarly article tentatively entitled "A Study in Scholarship: The Case of the *Baker Street Journal*". More information is available at *www.robertperret.com*

Gayle Lange Puhl has been a Sherlockian since Christmas of 1965. She has had articles published in *The Devon County Chronicle*, *The Baker Street Journal*, and *The Serpentine Muse*, plus her local newspaper. She has created Sherlockian jewelry, a 2006 calendar entitled "If Watson Wrote For TV", and has painted a limited series of Holmes-related nesting dolls. She co-founded the scion *Friends of the Great Grimpen Mire* and the Janesville, Wisconsin-based *The Original Tree Worshipers*. In January 2016, she was awarded the "Outstanding Creative Writer" award by the Janesville Art Alliance for her first book *Sherlock Holmes and the Folk Tale Mysteries*. She is semi-retired and lives in Evansville, Wisconsin. Ms. Puhl has one daughter, Gayla, and four grandchildren.

Tracy J. Revels, a Sherlockian from the age of eleven, is a professor of history at Wofford College in Spartanburg, South Carolina. She is a member of *The Survivors of the Gloria Scott* and *The Studious Scarlets Society*, and is a past recipient of the Beacon Society Award. Almost every semester, she teaches a class that covers The Canon, either to college students or to senior citizens. She is also the author of three supernatural Sherlockian pastiches with MX (*Shadowfall*, *Shadowblood*, and *Shadowwraith*), and a regular contributor to her scion's newsletter. She also has some notoriety as an author of very silly skits: For proof, see "The Adventure of the Adversarial Adventuress" and "Occupy Baker Street" on YouTube. When not studying Sherlock, she can be found researching the history of her native state, and has written books on Florida in the Civil War and on the development of Florida's tourism industry.

Roger Riccard of Los Angeles, California, U.S.A., is a descendant of the Roses of Kilravock in Highland Scotland. He is the author of two previous Sherlock Holmes novels, *The Case of the Poisoned Lilly* and *The Case of the Twain Papers*, a series of short stories in two volumes, *Sherlock Holmes: Adventures for the Twelve Days of Christmas* and *Further Adventures for the Twelve Days of Christmas*, and the new series *A Sherlock Holmes Alphabet of Cases,* all of which are published by Baker Street Studios. He has another novel and a non-fiction Holmes reference work in various stages of completion. He became a Sherlock Holmes enthusiast as a teenager (many, many years ago), and, like all fans of The Great Detective, yearned for more stories after reading The Canon over and over. It was the Granada Television performances of Jeremy Brett and Edward Hardwicke, and the encouragement of his wife, Rosilyn, that at last inspired him to write his own Holmes adventures, using the Granada actor portrayals as his guide. He has been called "The best pastiche writer since Val Andrews" by the *Sherlockian E-Times*.

David Ruffle was born in Northamptonshire in England a long, long time ago. He has lived in the beautiful town of Lyme Regis on the Dorset coast for the last twelve years. His first foray into writing was the 2009 self-published, *Sherlock Holmes and the Lyme Regis Horror*. This was swiftly followed by two more Holmes novellas set in Lyme, and a Holmes children's book, *Sherlock Holmes and the Missing Snowman*. Since then, there has been four further Holmes novellas, including the critically acclaimed *End Peace*, three contemporary comedies, and a slim volume detailing the life of Jack the Ripper. When not writing, he can be found working in a local shop, 'acting' in local productions, and occasionally performing poetry locally. To come next year is *Sherlock Holmes and the Scarborough Affair*, a collaboration with Gill Stammers, in which David is very much the junior partner.

Hailing from Bedford, in the South East of England, **Matthew Simmonds** has been a confirmed devotee of Sir Arthur Conan Doyle's most famous creation since first watching Jeremy Brett's incomparable portrayal of the world's first consulting detective, on a Tuesday evening in April, 1984, while curled up on the sofa with his father. He has written numerous short stories, and his first novel, *Sherlock Holmes: The Adventure of The Pigtail Twist*, was published in 2018. A sequel is nearly complete, which he hopes to publish in the near future. Matthew currently co-owns Harrison & Simmonds, the fifth-generation family business, a renowned County tobacconist, pipe and gift shop on Bedford High Street.

Richard Dean Starr has written or edited more than two-hundred articles, columns, stories, books, comics, screenplays, and graphic novels since the age of seventeen. His original fiction and non-fiction has appeared in magazines and newspapers as varied as *Cemetery Dance*, *Science Fiction Chronicle*, *The Southeast Georgian*, *The Camden County Tribune*, *Suspense Magazine*, and *Starlog*. His licensed media tie-in stories have appeared in anthologies including *Hellboy: Odder Jobs*, *Kolchak: The Night Stalker Casebook*, *Tales of Zorro*, *The Lone Ranger Chronicles*, and *The Green Hornet Casebook*, just to name a few. In addition, Starr co-authored *Unnaturally Normal*, the first *Kolchak: The Night Stalker/Dan Shamble: Zombie P.I.* team up comic book with *New York Times* bestselling author Kevin J. Anderson, and co-edited the *Captain Action* comics line with Matthew Baugh. As a recognized film industry script consultant, Starr has contributed to feature motion pictures starring acclaimed actors including Malcolm McDowell, Tom Sizemore, Amber Tamblyn, Haley Joel Osment, Costas Mandylor, Robert Culp, Richmond Arquette, and Zach Galifianakis, among others.

Kevin P. Thornton has experienced a Taliban rocket attack in Kabul and a terrorist bombing in Johannesburg. He lives in Fort McMurray, Alberta, the town that burnt down in 2016. He has been shortlisted for the *Crime Writers of Canada* Unhanged writing award six times. He's never won. He was also a finalist for best short story in 2014 – the year Margaret Atwood entered. We're not saying he has luck issues, but don't bet on his stock tips. Born in Kenya, Kevin was a child in New Zealand, a student and soldier in Africa, a military contractor in Afghanistan, a forklift driver in Ontario, and an oilfield worker in North Western Canada. He writes poems that start out just fine, but turn ruder and cruder over time. From limerick to doggerel, they earn less than bugger-all, even though they all manage to rhyme. He also likes writing about Sherlock Holmes and dislikes writing about himself in the third person.

Marcia Wilson is a freelance researcher and illustrator who likes to work in a style compatible for the color blind and visually impaired. She is Canon-centric, and her first MX offering, *You Buy Bones*, uses the point-of-view of Scotland Yard to show the unique talents of Dr. Watson. This continued with the publication of *Test of the Professionals: The Adventure of the Flying Blue Pidgeon* and *The Peaceful Night Poisonings*. She can be contacted at: *gravelgirty.deviantart.com*

The following contributions appear in the companion volume:
The MX Book of New Sherlock Holmes Stories Part XII – Some Untold Cases (1894-1902)

"**Anon.**" is a devoted Sherlockian and player of The Game.

Derrick Belanger (who also has a story in Volume III) is an educator and also the author of the #1 bestselling book in its category, *Sherlock Holmes: The Adventure of the Peculiar Provenance*, which was in the top 200 bestselling books on Amazon. He also is the author of *The MacDougall Twins with Sherlock Holmes* books, and he edited the Sir Arthur Conan Doyle horror anthology *A Study in Terror: Sir Arthur Conan Doyle's Revolutionary Stories of Fear and the Supernatural*. Mr. Belanger co-owns the publishing company Belanger Books, which released the Sherlock Holmes anthologies *Beyond Watson*, *Holmes Away From Home: Adventures from the Great Hiatus* Volumes 1 and 2, *Sherlock Holmes: Before Baker Street*, and *Sherlock Holmes: Adventures in the Realms of H.G. Wells* Volumes I and 2. Derrick resides in Colorado and continues compiling unpublished works by Dr. John H. Watson.

Nick Cardillo has loved Sherlock Holmes ever since he was first introduced to the detective in *The Great Illustrated Classics* edition of *The Adventures of Sherlock Holmes* at the age of six. His devotion to the Baker Street detective duo has only increased over the years, and Nick is thrilled to be taking these proper steps into the Sherlock Holmes Community. His first published story, "The Adventure of the Traveling Corpse", appeared in *The MX Book of New Sherlock Holmes Stories – Part VI: 2017 Annual*, and his "The Haunting of Hamilton Gardens" was published in *PART VIII – Eliminate the Impossible: 1892-1905*. A devout fan of The Golden Age of Detective Fiction, Hammer Horror, and *Doctor Who*, Nick co-writes the Sherlockian blog, *Back on Baker Street*, which analyses over seventy years of Sherlock Holmes film and culture. He is a student at Susquehanna University.

C.H. Dye first discovered Sherlock Holmes when she was eleven, in a collection that ended at the Reichenbach Falls. It was another six months before she discovered *The Hound of the Baskervilles*, and two weeks after that before a librarian handed her *The Return*. She has loved the stories ever since. She has written fan-fiction, and her first published pastiche, "The Tale of the Forty Thieves", was included in *The MX Book of New Sherlock Holmes Stories – Part I: 1881-1889*. Her story "A Christmas Goose" was in *The MX Book of New Sherlock Holmes Stories – Part V: Christmas Adventures*, and "The Mysterious Mourner" in *The MX Book of New Sherlock Holmes Stories – Part VIII – Eliminate the Impossible: 1892-1905*

Thomas Fortenberry is an American author, editor, and reviewer. Founder of Mind Fire Press and a Pushcart Prize-nominated writer, he has also judged many literary contests, including the Georgia Author of the Year Awards and the Robert Penn Warren Prize for Fiction. His Sherlock Holmes stories have appeared in *An Improbable Truth*, *The MX Book of New Sherlock Holmes Stories – Part VIII: Eliminate the Impossible (1892-1905)*, and the forthcoming MX collection *Some Untold Cases*.

James R. "Jim" French became a morning Disc Jockey on KIRO (AM) in Seattle in 1959. He later founded *Imagination Theatre*, a syndicated program that broadcast to over one-hundred-and-twenty stations in the U.S. and Canada, and also on the XM Satellite Radio system all over North America. Actors in French's dramas included John Patrick Lowrie, Larry Albert, Patty Duke, Russell Johnson, Tom Smothers, Keenan Wynn, Roddy MacDowall, Ruta Lee, John Astin, Cynthia Lauren Tewes, and Richard Sanders. Mr. French stated, "To me, the characters of Sherlock Holmes and Doctor Watson always seemed to be figures Doyle created as a challenge to lesser writers. He gave us two interesting characters – different from each other in their histories, talents, and experience, but complimentary as a team – who have been applied to a variety of situations and plots far beyond the times and places in The Canon. In the hands of different writers, Holmes and Watson have lent their identities to different times, ages, and even genders. But I wanted to break no new ground. I feel Sir Arthur provided us with enough references to locations, landmarks, and the social conditions of his time, to give a pretty large canvas on which to paint our own images and actions to animate Holmes and Watson." Mr. French passed away at the age of eight-nine on December 20th, 2017, the day that his contribution to this book was being edited. He shall be missed.

Paul D. Gilbert was born in 1954 and has lived in and around Lindon all of his life. He has been married to Jackie for thirty-nine years, and she is a Holmes expert who keeps him on the straight and narrow! He has two sons, one of whom now lives in Spain. His interests include literature, ancient history, all religions, most sports, and movies. He is currently employed full-time as a funeral director. His books so far include *The Lost Files of Sherlock Holmes* (2007), *The Chronicles of Sherlock Holmes* (2008), *Sherlock Holmes and the Giant Rat of Sumatra* (2010), *The Annals of Sherlock Holmes* (2012), and *Sherlock Holmes and the Unholy Trinity* (2015). He has finished *Sherlock Holmes: The Four Handed Game*, to be published 2017, and is now working on his next novel.

John Linwood Grant is a writer and editor who lives in Yorkshire with a pack of lurchers and a beard. He may also have a family. He focuses particularly on dark Victorian and Edwardian fiction, such as his recent novella *A Study in Grey*, which also features Holmes. Current projects include his *Tales of the Last Edwardian* series, about psychic and psychiatric mysteries, and curating a collection of new stories based on the darker side of the British Empire. He has been published in a number of anthologies and magazines, with stories range from madness in early Virginia to questions about the monsters we ourselves might be. He is also co-editor of *Occult Detective Quarterly*. His website *greydogtales.com* explores weird fiction, especially period ones, weird art, and even weirder lurchers.

Arthur Hall was born in Aston, Birmingham, UK, in 1944. He discovered his interest in writing during his schooldays, along with a love of fictional adventure and suspense. His first novel, *Sole Contact*, was an espionage story about an ultra-secret government department known as "Sector Three", and was followed, to date, by three sequels. Other works include four Sherlock Holmes novels, *The Demon of the Dusk*, *The One Hundred Percent Society*, *The Secret Assassin*, and *The Phantom Killer*, as well as a collection of short stories, and a modern detective novel. He lives in the West Midlands, United Kingdom.

In the year 1998 **Craig Janacek** took his degree of Doctor of Medicine at Vanderbilt University, and proceeded to Stanford to go through the training prescribed for pediatricians in practice. Having completed his studies there, he was duly attached to the University of California, San Francisco as Associate Professor. The author of over seventy medical monographs upon a variety of obscure lesions, his travel-worn and battered tin dispatch-box is crammed with papers, nearly all of which are records of his fictional works. To date, these have been published solely in electronic format, including two non-Holmes novels (*The Oxford Deception* and *The Anger of Achilles Peterson*), the trio of holiday adventures collected as *The Midwinter Mysteries of Sherlock Holmes*, the Holmes story collections *The First of* Criminals, *The Assassination of Sherlock Holmes*, *The Treasury of Sherlock Holmes*, and the Watsonian novels *The Isle of Devils* and *The Gate of Gold*. Craig Janacek is a *nom de plume*.

Nik Morton hails from the northeast of England and has lived in Spain with his linguist-musician wife Jennifer for the last fifteen years. He served in the Royal Navy for twenty-three years and has been writing for fifty-three years. He sold his first story in 1971 and has had 120 short stories published – some winning awards – in several genres such as action, adventure, romance, ghost, horror, sci-fi, western and crime. To date, six collections of his short stories have been collected and published, the latest being Leon Cazador, P.I. His Sherlock Holmes pastiche 'The Very First Detective: The Killing Stone' is published in the October 2018 issue of Mystery Weekly Magazine. He has edited periodicals and contributed hundreds of articles, book and film reviews to magazines. He has chaired several writers' circles and run writing and screenplay workshops, and judged competitions. He has edited many books, and for the period 2003-2007 he was sub-editor of the monthly colour magazine, Portsmouth Post, and for 2011-2013 he was Editor-in-Chief of a U.S. publisher but stepped down to spend more time on his various writing projects. Since 2007, he's had thirty books published, among them the psychic spy series: Mission: Prague, Mission: Tehran, and Mission: Khyber, a modern vampire thriller set in Malta, Chill of the Shadow, a Sister Rose thriller, The Bread of Tears, and a romantic thriller set in Tenerife, An Evil Trade. His latest books are a sci-fi time-travel adventure, Continuity Girl, a noir western/homage to Edgar Allan Poe, Coffin for Cash, and the third in a fantasy series (co-written under the pen-name Morton Faulkner), Floreskand: Madurava. His guide Write a Western in 30 Days – with Plenty of Bullet Points is a best-seller and has reviewers recommending it for writers of all genres, not just westerns. To learn more about Nik follow him on twitter https://twitter.com/nik_morton or read his regular blog posts, http://nik-writealot.blogspot.com.

Mark Mower is a member of the *Crime Writers' Association, The Sherlock Holmes Society of London* and *The Solar Pons Society of London*. He writes true crime stories and fictional mysteries. His first two volumes of Holmes pastiches were entitled *A Farewell to Baker Street* and *Sherlock Holmes: The Baker Street Case-Files* (both with MX Publishing) and, to date, he has contributed chapters to six parts of the ongoing *The MX Book of New Sherlock Holmes Stories*. He has also had stories in two anthologies by Belanger Books: *Holmes Away From Home: Adventures from the Great Hiatus – Volume II – 1893-1894* (2016) and *Sherlock Holmes: Before Baker Street* (2017). More are bound to follow. Mark's non-fiction works include *Bloody British History: Norwich* (The History Press, 2014), *Suffolk Murders* (The History Press, 2011) and *Zeppelin Over Suffolk* (Pen & Sword Books, 2008).

Jane Rubino is the author of A Jersey Shore mystery series, featuring a Jane Austen-loving amateur sleuth and a Sherlock Holmes-quoting detective; *Knight Errant, Lady Vernon and Her Daughter*, (a novel-length adaptation of Jane Austen's novella *Lady Susan*, co-authored with her daughter Caitlen Rubino-Bradway, *What Would Austen Do?*, also co-authored with her daughter, a short story in the anthology *Jane Austen Made Me Do It, The Rucastles' Pawn, The Copper Beeches from Violet Turner's POV*, and, of course, there's the Sherlockian novel in the drawer – who doesn't have one? Jane lives on a barrier island at the New Jersey shore.

Robert V. Stapleton was born and brought up in Leeds, Yorkshire, England, and studied at Durham University. After working in various parts of the country as an Anglican parish priest, he is now retired and lives with his wife in North Yorkshire. As a member of his local writing group, he now has time to develop his other life as a writer of adventure stories. He has recently had a number of short stories published, and he is hoping to have a couple of completed novels published at some time in the future.

S. Subramanian is a retired professor of Economics from Chennai, India. Apart from a small book titled *Economic Offences: A Compendium of Crimes in Prose and Verse* (Oxford University Press Delhi, 2012), his Holmes pastiches are the only serious things he has written. His other work runs largely to whimsical stuff on fuzzy logic and social measurement, on which he writes with much precision and little understanding, being an economist. He is otherwise mainly harmless, as his wife and daughter might concede with a little persuasion.

Daniel D. Victor, a Ph.D. in American literature, is a retired high school English teacher who taught in the Los Angeles Unified School District for forty-six years. His doctoral dissertation on little-known American author, David Graham Phillips, led to the creation of Victor's first Sherlock Holmes pastiche, *The Seventh Bullet*, in which Holmes investigates Phillips' actual murder. Victor's second novel, *A Study in Synchronicity*, is a two-stranded murder mystery, which features a Sherlock Holmes-like private eye. He currently writes the ongoing series *Sherlock Holmes and the American Literati*. Each novel introduces Holmes to a different American author who actually passed through

London at the turn of the century. In *The Final Page of Baker Street*, Holmes meets Raymond Chandler; in *The Baron of Brede Place,* Stephen Crane; in *Seventeen Minutes to Baker Street*, Mark Twain; and in *The Outrage at the Diogenes Club*, Jack London. His most recent novel is *Sherlock Holmes and the Shadows of St. Petersburg*. Victor, who is also writing a novel about his early years as a teacher, lives with his wife in Los Angeles, California. They have two adult sons.

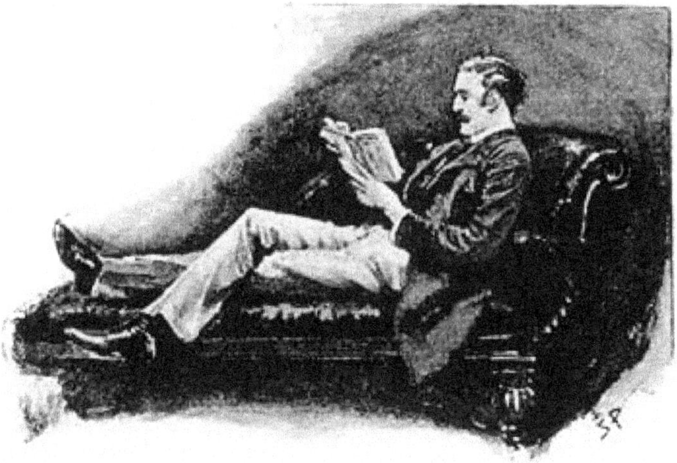

The MX Book of New Sherlock Holmes Stories

"This is the finest volume of Sherlockian fiction I have ever read, and I have read, literally, thousands."
– Philip K. Jones

"Beyond Impressive . . . This is a splendid venture for a great cause!
– Roger Johnson, Editor, *The Sherlock Holmes Journal,*
The Sherlock Holmes Society of London

Part I: 1881-1889
Part II: 1890-1895
Part III: 1896-1929
Part IV: 2016 Annual
Part V: Christmas Adventures
Part VI: 2017 Annual
Part VII: Eliminate the Impossible
Part VIII – 2018 Annual
Part IX – 2018 Annual (1879-1895)
Part X – 2018 Annual (1896-1916)
Part XI – Some Untold Cases (1880-1891)
Part XII – Some Untold Cases (1894-1902)

In Preparation

Part XIII – 2019 Annual

. . . and more to come!

Publishers Weekly says:

Part VI: *The traditional pastiche is alive and well . . . .*

Part VII: *Sherlockians eager for faithful-to-the-canon plots and characters will be delighted.*

Part VIII: *The imagination of the contributors in coming up with variations on the volume's theme is matched by their ingenious resolutions.*

Part IX: *The 18 stories . . . will satisfy fans of Conan Doyle's originals. Sherlockians will rejoice that more volumes are on the way.*

Part X: *. . . new Sherlock Holmes adventures of consistently high quality.*

The MX Book of New Sherlock Holmes Stories
Edited by David Marcum
(MX Publishing, 2015-   )

MX Publishing

MX Publishing is the world's largest specialist Sherlock Holmes publisher, with several hundred titles and over a hundred authors creating the latest in Sherlock Holmes fiction and non-fiction.

From traditional short stories and novels to travel guides and quiz books, MX Publishing caters to all Holmes fans.

The collection includes leading titles such as *Benedict Cumberbatch In Transition* and *The Norwood Author*, which won the 2011 *Tony Howlett Award* (Sherlock Holmes Book of the Year).

MX Publishing also has one of the largest communities of Holmes fans on *Facebook*, with regular contributions from dozens of authors.

www.mxpublishing.co.uk (UK) and *www.mxpublishing.com* (USA)